ALSO BY ANNETTE MCCLEAVE

Bound by Darkness
Drawn into Darkness

SURRENDER TO DARKNESS

A SOUL GATHERER NOVEL

ANNETTE MCCLEAVE

A SIGNET ECLIPSE BOOK

SIGNET ECLIPSE
Published by New American Library, a division of
Penguin Group (USA) Inc., 375 Hudson Street,
New York, New York 10014, USA
Penguin Group (Canada), 90 Eglinton Avenue East, Suite 700, Toronto,
Ontario M4P 2Y3, Canada (a division of Pearson Penguin Canada Inc.)
Penguin Books Ltd., 80 Strand, London WC2R 0RL, England
Penguin Ireland, 25 St. Stephen's Green, Dublin 2,
Ireland (a division of Penguin Books Ltd.)
Penguin Group (Australia), 250 Camberwell Road, Camberwell, Victoria 3124,
Australia (a division of Pearson Australia Group Pty. Ltd.)
Penguin Books India Pvt. Ltd., 11 Community Centre, Panchsheel Park,
New Delhi - 110 017, India
Penguin Group (NZ), 67 Apollo Drive, Rosedale, North Shore 0632,
New Zealand (a division of Pearson New Zealand Ltd.)
Penguin Books (South Africa) (Pty.) Ltd., 24 Sturdee Avenue,
Rosebank, Johannesburg 2196, South Africa

Penguin Books Ltd., Registered Offices:
80 Strand, London WC2R 0RL, England

First published by Signet Eclipse, an imprint of New American Library,
a division of Penguin Group (USA) Inc.

First Printing, January 2011
10 9 8 7 6 5 4 3 2 1

*To Lise, Andree, and Mark, who have supported me in
innumerable ways.*

ACKNOWLEDGMENTS

It takes a village to produce a book, and I'd like to applaud all the wonderful people at NAL who've helped make my dreams reality—editors, copy editors, cover designers, marketing gurus, sales people, production staff, and beyond. Thank you.

To the friends who have offered me words of wisdom, sumptuous picnic lunches, and encouraging smiles during a difficult year—all I can say is you are the best. Really.

1

"**W**e're finally making some headway against the effects of the dark relics. São Paolo just reported their first rise in church attendance in seventeen months, and the survivors of that bus crash in Lima are singing their 'We were saved by an angel' story to the press." Webster removed two red pushpins from his huge map of the world and replaced them with blue ones. "If you hadn't screwed up in Rome, Murdoch, this would have been a positive week."

Jamie Murdoch leaned against the big campaign desk and imagined a target painted on the other Soul Gatherer's back. "I did not screw up. I told you, we were attacked by a pack of flesh-eating gradior demons."

"Did the *cardinale* of the Protectorate end up in the hospital with multiple lacerations and a severe concussion?"

"You know he did."

Webster turned to face him. "Then you screwed up."

Murdoch's hand involuntarily fisted.

"There are still far too many red pins on the map," Stefan Wahlberg said. The plump mage pushed away from the bookcase to study the map in more detail. "Especially in Europe. Even with each city now protected by a principality angel, the number of demon nests continues to grow. We really need to find a better way to beat back the hordes."

"Yes." Lena sat forward on the couch. "We also need to find some way to save the humans who've suffered a havoc bite. Reports keep streaming in. The bastards drain them of energy, then leave them to die."

"There is a way," Stefan said. "But it's a very difficult potion to brew, and it requires an ingredient so rare as to render it impractical. Our best option remains destroying the demon nests."

"I agree." Webster's gaze returned to the map. "Problem is we're outnumbered. The teams we've placed around the world are struggling."

"We're ramping up the training," Murdoch reminded them, ignoring the restless urge that filled his chest every time the talk turned to battle. "MacGregor's putting thirty-two students through their paces this term, and with minor tweaks to the program, he's confident he can double that number on the next round."

"We'll still be behind the eight ball. We need something game changing, like a weapon."

"A weapon?" asked Lena. She tugged the elastic band out of her hair, gathered up the strands that had come loose, and refastened her ponytail. "What kind of weapon?"

"Anything that evens the odds," Webster responded.

"I've read all the grimoires we've acquired, cover to cover," Stefan said. "No such weapon exists."

"Don't be so sure," said Lena.

Murdoch glanced at her. Miracles and churchgoing habits didn't excite him. But weapons did. "Do you know something?"

"Back when I had my amulet, I stumbled across an artifact radiating some serious dark magic. Part of a private collection in Japan."

"What makes you think it was a weapon?" Murdoch asked.

"The owner told me it could single-handedly swamp the forces of evil."

Webster favored his lovely girlfriend with a raised brow. "And you didn't think that was worth mentioning until now?"

She shrugged. "A few months after I sensed it, it stopped giving off vibes. The owner has since died, so I'm not even sure it can be tracked down."

"The owner used those exact words?" Stefan asked, frowning. *"Swamp the forces of evil?"*

"I think so," Lena said. "Why?"

"A century or so ago, there were rumors of a sixth Ignoble. I've seen similar phrasing in the parchments that mention it."

"There's a sixth dark relic?"

Stefan waved his hand dismissively. "The Romany Council investigated the rumors. No truth to any of them."

"I still think it's worth looking into," Webster said. He turned to Lena. "The owner have any family you could contact?"

"A daughter, Kiyoko. But I must warn you, I've known her for years and never once heard her mention the relic."

"Let's send someone over there to check it out. Someone stubborn, someone who won't give up easily." Webster smiled broadly. "That would be you, Murdoch."

"Me?" Murdoch blinked. "I'm headed to Johannesburg, remember? Now that we're going on the offensive, fighting the demons in the trenches, we all agreed there was no better place for me to be than in the thick of battle."

"That was before you put the *cardinale* in intensive care."

"Come on. The team needs a seasoned commander. Who else is qualified?"

"Atheborne."

"No bloody way." Murdoch surged away from the desk, his face hot. Atheborne was a highly skilled warrior, and he'd slain dozens of demons since his fateful landing at Omaha Beach, but he didn't have Murdoch's experience. "I'm the senior Gatherer. It's my assignment."

"Not anymore it's not." The others in the room shuffled uncomfortably. "You guys can go," Webster told them. "Murdoch and I can finish this conversation on our own."

After the library door closed, Murdoch said quietly, "You prick. You're doing this out of spite."

"No, I'm not. If this assignment was limited to kicking some demon ass, maybe I'd decide differently. But it also involves guarding a Protector. Another man just like the *cardinale*. For six long months. And if that Protector goes down, we lose the relic he's entrusted with. There's no way I'm sending a guy who explodes like a bomb at the first sign of danger on a mission this critical. I can't risk it."

Although it was tempting to stomp across the room and take his frustration out on Webster's nose, Murdoch subsided. He was in Webster's house. That called for a little decorum. "I did not explode at the first sign of danger. My berserker took control after we were swamped by gradiors determined to tear us to shreds. And for the record, I succeeded in my mission. I saved the *cardinale*'s life."

Webster's silver eyes held his for a long moment. "Every wound on his body—all seventeen of them—came from *your* sword, not a gradior's claws. So, yes, you saved his life, but you nearly killed him in the process."

"He's alive," Murdoch said.

"He'll be in therapy for months."

True, and the knowledge shamed him. But the past

was in the past. If there was one lesson he'd learned over the years, it was that rehashing his failures ad nauseam wouldn't change the facts. "I'm not pleased with the outcome, but neither do I regret my actions. Any other Gatherer faced with six opponents would have failed."

"Maybe," Webster allowed, closing the wooden panels that hid the map of the world from prying eyes. "But it could easily have gone the other way and you know it. We could be standing at the man's graveside comforting his widow, instead of forking over the dough for his hospital bills. I spent months convincing the Protectorate to trust us enough to guard the Ignobles, and your stunt in Rome nearly cost us everything. I can't let you lead a mission this important, Murdoch. Not when I know your little problem could take the mission south at the drop of a hat."

"MacGregor trusts me," Murdoch reminded the other Gatherer.

"It doesn't really matter what MacGregor thinks," Webster said softly. "He's not in charge anymore. I am."

The muscles in Murdoch's stomach knotted. Mac-Gregor's decision to name Webster as leader still tasted like failure, even after six months.

"I'm not calling your leadership into question," he said. In truth, Webster had done an outstanding job thus far. He had depths Murdoch hadn't suspected, repeatedly displaying not only intelligence but courage and an innate gift for strategy. "I'm giving you my word as a Highlander that I'll lead the South African team to success."

Webster stared out the big picture window. Water dripped from the chairs and umbrellas onto the ruddy-colored cedar deck. The first rainy day in San Jose in over a month.

"I'm sorry, Murdoch," he said. "I can't do it."

An invisible hand clenched Murdoch's throat. His damned berserker was screwing up his life. *Again*.

"Fine," he spit out. In a purposeful display of impressive musculature, he folded his arms over his chest. The soft material of the T-shirt pulled snug over his shoulders and pecs. *Beat* that, *little wharf rat*. "I'll go to Japan. In the midst of global riots and unprecedented numbers of demon attacks, I'll wander off for an unspecified amount of time to check out the slim possibility of an undocumented demon-slaying weapon."

"Excellent."

Murdoch barely resisted a snort. The man was impervious to sarcasm. "But listen up. If I find this bloody thing, you're damned well going to eat crow and give me an assignment worthy of my skills."

The other man smiled. "Sure. Do a good job, don't slice up any innocent people, and you've got a deal."

"Fuck you, Webster."

Genuinely curious, Kiyoko studied the man filling the video screen. Judging by his proximity to the camera lens, he stood well over six feet tall, a notable height in Sapporo. He also had long brown hair swept back off his strong face like a warrior of old. "You're certain he said Lena Sharpe sent him?"

"Yes."

She sat back in her father's executive chair, rubbing her hands over the leather armrests. Even after all this time, the light cinnamon scent of his cologne still clung to everything. "Then he's a fool. Lena and I had a falling-out several months ago. I no longer count her among my trusted colleagues."

The assistant bowed. "Shall I tell him you are unavailable?"

Kiyoko's gaze flickered back to the video screen and the indomitable features of the man overwhelming the front desk of the Ashida Corporation. "Do you think that will discourage him?"

The woman shook her head. "He is very determined."

"Then simply have him wait. His physical stature suggests he is predisposed toward action, and such men are born with little patience. In a few hours, he will grow weary and leave of his own accord."

The assistant bowed again and left the room.

"The real question is not whether he will leave, but why he was sent here," Ryuji Watanabe said, rising from his chair near the huge picture window. His gray wool suit remained unwrinkled despite a long day at the office. "Did you not tell me this Sharpe woman was a thief?"

"Yes." Kiyoko almost added, *But she steals only from known criminals.* Except Lena had proven to be far less honorable than Kiyoko had originally believed, involving her in a nasty deal with the devil. The knowledge still stung.

"And this Murdoch-san does not look like a businessman." Ryuji joined her at the desk. "More like an enforcer."

Or a samurai.

His movements were smooth and effortless. He appeared relaxed, yet his feet were apart, his knees slightly flexed. He did not fidget, he did not wear his thoughts on his face, and his gaze absorbed everything that occurred around him. Kiyoko had no trouble imagining the man with a weapon in his hand, neatly dispatching foe after foe.

"What do you suggest?" she asked Ryuji. Watanabe had been company president for less than three months, but there was nothing tentative about her father's successor. It was hard to watch someone erase her father's stamp with fresh ideas, but Watanabe's natural authority and consistently profitable motives made the changes bearable.

"Allow me to dismiss him. I've dealt with Americans before. I can be, as they put it, quite blunt."

Ryuji had earned his business degree from Harvard. She did not doubt his knowledge of Americans. Still, she was reluctant to press this Murdoch-san into leaving, though she couldn't quite say why. "When pushed, many Americans push back."

"Dealing with them takes a deft touch," Ryuji agreed.

Which her president possessed. Kiyoko sighed. In truth, Murdoch's presence made her slightly uncomfortable. "If you can convince him to leave, I would be most grateful, Watanabe-san."

Ryuji nodded and left the room.

Moments later, he appeared in the camera lens, striding across the white marble lobby to Murdoch's side. The disparity in their physical stature was striking— Murdoch stood a solid foot taller than Ryuji and outweighed him by several kilos.

Kiyoko smiled.

This should be interesting.

Murdoch had declined the seat offered to him by the uniformed woman behind the massive front desk, preferring to stand, even though he'd been warned it might be a lengthy wait. Old habits died hard. On his feet, he had more options. He peered into the glass display cases in the center of the lobby as he waited, noting every person who passed by.

The Japanese businessman in the gray suit piqued his attention the moment he exited the elevator. There was a steely purpose to his step and a confident tilt to his head that instantly separated him from the other men in the lobby. The wretch reeked of importance.

When the fellow smiled at him and extended his hand in a North American–style handshake, Murdoch smiled in return. The wait was over.

"Mr. Murdoch, what a pleasure to meet you," the man said as their hands connected. No limp grip here.

"I'm Ryuji Watanabe, the president of Ashida Corporation."

Murdoch frowned.

Company presidents wearing thousand-dollar suits don't come down to the lobby to greet perfect strangers. They send their secretaries. Or some other lackey. Unless they have no intention of letting said stranger gain entry to the inner sanctum.

"My request was to meet with Kiyoko Ashida," Murdoch said.

Watanabe smiled ruefully. "As I'm sure someone's already informed you, she's extremely busy. I came downstairs to save you several wasted hours. She's not going to see you."

Blunt and to the point. Yet spoken with a friendly air that suggested he was being kind. "Not at all?"

"Your credentials did you in, I'm afraid."

The only credential he'd presented was his association with Lena Sharpe. Which suggested that, contrary to her claim that they were longtime friends, Lena was persona non grata with Miss Ashida. "I see."

"It might be best if you simply left."

Watanabe's smile seemed genuinely rueful. The man was nothing if not pleasant. Yet for some reason, Murdoch felt lacking. Perhaps it was the subtle hint of money that wafted off him—reminding Murdoch all too much of Brian Webster. The clothes, the expensive scent, the perfect presentation. It was difficult not to make comparisons to his own beat-up leather bomber jacket and black twill trousers. The chunky heels and silver buckles of his motorcycle boots seemed large and ostentatious when viewed next to the finely stitched leather of Watanabe's Italian loafers.

He fingered his chin. At least the scruffy beard was gone. After losing half of it to a fiery blast several months ago, he'd shaved it completely. It made him look more presentable. Or so the women he dated assured him.

"It's vital that I speak to Miss Ashida," Murdoch said. "My business has nothing to do with Lena Sharpe. She was merely an introduction. I'm actually looking to purchase an item of rare antiquity with which I believe Miss Ashida may be familiar."

"I understand," said Watanabe, nodding. "And I empathize with your situation. But, unfortunately, Miss Ashida is quite adamant. She will not change her mind about meeting with you. At least, not right away. You could try again in a few months, with better credentials."

A few *months*?

Murdoch grimaced. Imagine Webster's reaction if he returned with that piece of news.

"That won't do," he said softly. "I need to hear Miss Ashida decline in her own words."

"Your need is not my concern." The smile was still friendly, but a glint of something hard had appeared in Watanabe's eyes. He had correctly interpreted the determination in Murdoch's voice as a problem.

"Surely even a busy woman like Miss Ashida can spare me the few moments it would take to say no?"

Watanabe stood taller. He barely reached Murdoch's collarbone. "Do not be difficult, Mr. Murdoch. Insisting will only annoy her further. You will do your cause more good by leaving without a fuss. If you truly want to impress her, come back tomorrow and request another audience."

The advice was genuinely helpful, if not palatable, so Murdoch settled back on his heels. Losing a potential ally like Watanabe would be an error.

"Fine," he said, offering the businessman a slight bow similar to the sort he'd seen many Japanese men present since his arrival six hours ago. "I'll return tomorrow. Please offer Miss Ashida my respects."

Then he spun on his heel and left the building.

* * *

Kiyoko tossed her gold pen onto the desk and stood.

Mr. Murdoch had displayed more restraint than she'd thought him capable of. She'd seen him stiffen at Ryuji's dismissal. Didn't Western men typically use intimidation to gain their desires? The aggressive cant of his shoulders and the jut of his square chin suggested he knew he held the physical advantage and was tempted to use his size to gain his desire. Instead, he'd walked away. *Why?*

A soft knock at the office door lifted her gaze from the video screen. Standing serenely at the door waiting for permission to enter was an elderly man with snow-white hair and long, flowing black robes. Sora Yamashita, her mentor.

"Come in, Sora-sensei," she greeted.

He entered slowly, but with the supple ease of a man many years his junior. "This office looks precisely the same as when your father occupied it. Did Watanabe-san not move in?"

Kiyoko's eyes trailed around the room, lingering briefly on the impressive collection of first-edition paper currencies hanging on the far wall. A significant part of Tatsu Ashida's life was honored here. A part she did not know very well. "He chose the office next door."

"Hmmm." Sora ran a finger through the light layer of dust on a nearby bookshelf. "Your father's assistant tells me there is an American downstairs seeking your attention."

The elder's face was placid, but Kiyoko sensed a great deal of contemplation behind those dark brown eyes. The American interested him.

"A friend of someone I despise," she explained, watching for a reaction. And getting none. "What brings you into the city, sensei?"

"Today was an auspicious day to visit. So here I am."

An appropriate response from a wizened old *onmyōji*

skilled in the calendar arts, but with Sora, nothing was as simple as it seemed on the surface. Nor, for that matter, as simple as the tranquil blue of his auras. Her innate ability to read the colorful life force emanations of human beings offered no advantage with her mentor. "Is this the *forceful man* you foresaw influencing my future, sensei?"

"Possibly," he said. "My divination said he would be a stranger."

"That would be unfortunate. I've sent him away."

The sensei shrugged. "If you were successful in turning him away, then he is not the right man."

Her gaze returned to the TV screen, which now showed an empty lobby. If he was not the man Sora had predicted would arrive, then why did she feel a sense of loss now that he was gone?

Azazel tugged at the constricting knot of his tie as he shut Watanabe's office door and locked it. What a very enlightening handshake that had been. He flicked a switch next to the floor-to-ceiling windows and they instantly became opaque.

Murdoch had no soul.

Very curious. The only soulless beings walking the middle plane were the immortal warriors Death tasked with collecting the souls of the dead. Many things had changed in the two thousand years he had spent trapped in the morass of the between, but not that fact. He'd bet his wing feathers on it. But in his day, Soul Gatherers did not travel the world in search of dark relics.

He murmured a succinct spell and in a blink, without a single telltale spark of red, returned to his private chamber in the shadowy castle his minions had built for him. Travel to and from the between did not have the same restrictions as travel from hell. He wasn't entirely certain why, but logic suggested it was because the between existed within the barrier itself. Not that he cared one way or another. All that mattered was that as his strength returned, he gained the ability to leave his prison and enter the middle plane at will.

"Find me a soul to consume," he said to the nebulous black shape hovering in the shadows near the door.

Once it scurried off, he conjured a bottle of rich red wine. He yanked out the stopper and poured a generous quantity down his throat to wash away the taste of green tea.

One thing was certain: Murdoch was seeking the Temple Veil, just as he was. He'd stake his return to glory on it. Why else would the man have been in Rome when his team of gradiors arrived to collect the Protectorate records of the Veil? Why else would he be here now? While it would be delightful if the fellow had taken the hint and toddled off to wherever he'd come from, the determined glint in his eye said he'd be back. It was just a matter of when.

Time to pick up the pace.

No more gentle wooing of Kiyoko. She had the whereabouts of the Veil stored inside that pretty head of hers, and he intended to pry it out. By force, if necessary. Using arcane magic to unlock her thoughts might alert the archangels to his presence, but it was a risk he had to take. Keeping one step ahead of his new rival was vital.

The door opened and a freshly murdered body—with its soul intact—was tossed inside.

Azazel smiled.

Nothing could be allowed to derail his triumphant return from the dead.

2

Waiting was not Murdoch's strong suit.

Yet here he was, voluntarily twiddling his thumbs until Kiyoko Ashida was done with her very long workday. Because the alternative—waiting until tomorrow— was worse.

He stood across the street from the shiny glass edifice that was the Ashida building and carefully studied every car that left the underground parking garage. Unfortunately, Sapporo was not the bustling metropolis of Tokyo, and his large size drew attention on the quiet treelined avenue. But he maintained his vigilant stance in spite of the curious looks. As the hours passed and night fell around him, however, he grew increasingly impatient. The flight from Los Angeles had been long, and he had yet to eat or imbibe a decent pint of ale.

It was nearing seven p.m. when the wide garage door finally rattled up and a sleek, dark American-made limousine eased into the street, headed north.

Had it not been for his Soul Gatherer enhanced night vision, identifying the occupants through the smoky gray windows would have been impossible. But he was able to spot three people in the back of the car—Watanabe, the young woman he knew was Kiyoko from the photo Lena had given him, and an elderly man with white hair.

His wait was over.

He slid into the tiny rental car he'd acquired at the airport and followed. The cramped interior of the Honda stifled him, but the fear of losing the limo on unfamiliar streets shunted his discomfort to the back of his mind.

After crossing the city and nearly losing his prey several times at traffic lights, he pulled to the curb behind the limousine. It had stopped before a seven-story brown and white building. Murdoch couldn't read a word of Japanese, but the giant 3-D crab hanging over the main entrance marked the place as a seafood restaurant.

The three passengers debarked and entered.

As the limo drove off, Murdoch found himself scrambling for a parking spot, with none in sight. When he returned to the restaurant ten minutes later, he was greeted by soothing koto music and a smiling young woman attired in a navy blue kimono with a bright yellow obi.

"I'm looking for another guest," he told her, speaking slowly in hopes of bridging the language barrier.

"His name, sir?" the hostess asked, glancing down at her reservation list. *English, God love her.* Despite the overwhelming number of Japanese faces he could see, the restaurant clearly entertained tourists as well.

"Watanabe. He's here with Miss Kiyoko Ashida."

Her face remained pleasant, but her voice subtly cooled. "Watanabe-san and his two guests are seated in a private dining room made for three."

In other words, *no way are you expected.*

"Just tell me where they're seated," he said, smiling deeply, leveraging every ounce of his charisma. "I'll stop by, say hello, and maybe Mr. Watanabe will ask you to get him a bigger table."

All hint of friendliness left the hostess's face, leaving only a suggestion of dismissal. Not aggressive, though. The tilt of her head remained remarkably demure.

"That would be irregular, sir. If you give me your name, I will make an inquiry of Watanabe-san. You can enjoy a complimentary glass of sake while you wait."

For such a tiny thing, she was an effective gatekeeper.

If he'd been any less determined, she would have won.

He leaned over her, using his broad-shouldered, six-foot-three frame to emphasize his words. "Here's the truth, lass. I'm going to storm the castle. Either you tell me where Mr. Watanabe and his party are seated and save yourself the embarrassment of having a large Scot peer into every private room, or I go in hard, spilling a lot of green tea. Your choice."

Her gaze dropped. "I will get the manager."

And off she ran.

Murdoch glanced at the intricate electronic seating chart on the console, but it was a blur of incomprehensible Japanese symbols. The only promising clues were the stars marking two rooms—one on the second floor and another on the fourth. Were Watanabe and Kiyoko starred guests? He was about to find out.

Conveniently, with the restaurant only half full because of ongoing protests around the nearby Hokkaido Government Building, he found them on the first try.

As he slid back the rice-paper door of a little room next to an elaborate rock garden, he met Watanabe's gaze over a smoke-stained bamboo table. All three occupants knelt on cushions, sampling sashimi. Raw seafood. *Ugh*.

"Mr. Murdoch," said Watanabe, surging to his feet, his eyes widening with outrage. "This is highly inappropriate. You are interrupting a private dinner."

Murdoch gave the company president only a cursory glance. His attention settled on the woman at the table, a pretty lass in a bright pink sweater set that set off her dark hair and eyes. "Did Mr. Watanabe here happen to mention that I tried a more traditional approach at your office earlier today?"

The woman placed her little teacup on the table. Delicate of feature, but not delicate of nature. No trembles. "He did not need to tell me," she said, only a trace of accent in her perfectly enunciated English. "It was I who asked him to get rid of you."

She rose to her feet in a smooth, seemingly effortless lift of her knees. Her posture was pure serenity. The kind you only get from complete mastery over your physical form.

"Please leave, Mr. Murdoch. I have nothing to say to you."

"I can't do that," he said, strangely unable to take his eyes off her. He'd seen plenty of glossy pink lips and pert little noses. What was it about hers that intrigued him? "I'm on a mission. You may not like the person who sent me, but she assured me you understood the critical nature of my task."

Her brown eyes met his. "I cannot help you."

"I haven't told you what I'm looking for yet."

Watanabe slid the phone he'd just been mumbling into back in his pocket. He said something softly in Japanese to Kiyoko, then addressed Murdoch. "The police are on their way, Mr. Murdoch. If you want to avoid a night in jail, I suggest you leave now."

"I'm not going anywhere until Miss Ashida agrees to give me five minutes. Alone."

"Impossible," Watanabe protested.

The elderly man quietly sipped his tea, seemingly oblivious to the tension in the room. Kiyoko touched his arm, encouraging him to rise, but he ignored her.

Out of the corner of his eye, Murdoch noted the arrival of two robust youths, both wearing black robes similar to those worn by the placid, tea-drinking elder.

Japanese bouncers. A small bubble of heat rose in Murdoch's chest, a mild response to possible danger.

"In any case," Watanabe added, guiding Miss Ashida toward the door with his hand on her elbow, "we won't be continuing the conversation. We're departing."

"Not until I get my five minutes."

Watanabe frowned. "Don't make this more difficult that it needs to be. These men"—he pointed to the two standing just behind Murdoch—"are here to ensure that Ashida-san and I depart without incident."

"If they touch me," Murdoch said softly, "they risk their lives."

The elder finally got to his feet, smiling faintly as he brushed imaginary wrinkles from his robes.

"Threats are unnecessary," Watanabe responded.

"It wasn't a threat. It was a warning." Murdoch didn't have time to explain. He again tried to connect with Kiyoko Ashida, facing her squarely. "Five minutes. That's all I ask."

She didn't respond. She just kept walking.

The two men at Murdoch's back stepped closer, clearly intending to prevent him from interfering with her exit, and the warmth in his chest burst into a small fire. Only two men, so the blaze was containable. For now.

But there was no way Murdoch could allow Kiyoko to leave without a chance to discuss the collection of relics she'd recently inherited from her father. If the weapon he sought was among them, it could save the world a whole lot of grief. As she passed by, he put out a hand, intending to snag her sleeve.

But her reflexes were excellent. She yanked her arm away before he could reach his objective, and in the process, her fingers lightly grazed his.

Murdoch's eyes rolled back in his head.

A wave of hot, liquid pleasure raced up his arm and

splashed into his chest, nearly taking him to his knees. He swam in it—his blood pounding, his breath short, his senses alive. The fiercest desire he'd felt in his entire seven-hundred-year existence licked across every inch of his skin, thrilled every nerve ending, and sent every drop of blood rushing to his groin. The urge to sink into Kiyoko Ashida's warm embrace was so keen and unrelenting that goose bumps sprang to his skin and saliva pooled in his mouth. He wanted her as he had never wanted any woman before. It was both utterly blissful and horribly terrifying.

Terrifying, because his berserker rejoiced at the sudden lack of restraint. It rose up in a red tide of fury, filled every empty thought, and swallowed him whole. At precisely the same moment, the two young warriors tasked with protecting Miss Ashida made the error of grabbing his arms and dragging him backward. Lost in a sea of bloodlust, Murdoch knew only one thing—he could not let Kiyoko leave. A vague memory of his mission lingered in his berserker-controlled thoughts, but the dominant motivation for all that followed was a primitive, almost bestial certainty that the female in the pink top belonged to him and no one could be allowed to take her away.

He yanked his arms forward.

The first guard sailed through the paper door enclosing the room across the hall and landed atop a variety of fine crab dishes. Rice porridge flew everywhere and the couple inside jumped up and flattened themselves against the faux rock wall. The second guard held to Murdoch's arm with an admirable grip, but he was no match for the berserker power that fueled Murdoch's every action. A heavy fist to the face sent him flying, too.

But the bouncers had succeeded in their primary goal—slowing Murdoch down. By the time he freed himself, Kiyoko and her two male escorts had reached the stairs.

As they disappeared from view, he released a bellow of pure rage and dove for the stairwell, pulling his sword free of the invisible scabbard on his back. Panicked diners scrambled to get out of the way. But the two young warriors were not done. Displaying an unwavering, if foolish, dedication, they attacked him again, this time with their weapons in hand. One wielded a gleaming katana, the other a *nunchuck*.

Just short of the door, with a savage growl of frustration, Murdoch was forced to turn and face his opponents.

Kiyoko dove into the limousine, followed closely by Ryuji. Sora took his usual sweet time, refusing to be rushed. Once the sensei was inside, a uniformed employee shut the car door, and they pulled away from the curb, leaving the restaurant behind.

"What a shame we had to leave," her elderly mentor said as he settled into his seat and adjusted his robes. "Watching him fight would have been quite entertaining."

Kiyoko barely heard him.

She was still reeling with the aftereffects of the man's brief touch. Her heart was racing, her face was flushed, and her hands were trembling. Ripples of hot, titillating desire continued to torment her body.

"Are you well?" Ryuji asked, staring at her with obvious concern in his eyes.

What was she to say? That she'd never felt more alive or more aroused in her life? Hardly. Careful not to catch Sora's all-seeing gaze, Kiyoko turned her head and peered out the window. "I'm fine. He barely touched me."

The limousine slowed.

Up ahead, the intersection was blocked by hundreds of protesters. They carried signs blaming the collapse of a local food-processing plant on greed and mismanagement. These were dark days. Companies were folding all over Japan for similar reasons, a very painful trend for a country where many people spent their entire working lives with one employer.

The driver opened the privacy partition and glanced at them through the rearview mirror. "The usual route to the estate is blocked. A detour is required."

Watanabe nodded. "Do what you must."

The glass partition slid up again, and the car made a right turn, avoiding the bulk of the protestors.

"I suspect we'll have difficulty getting reservations at that restaurant again," Sora said, amused. "If those crashing sounds were reflective of the damage he was inflicting, Mr. Murdoch will have a substantial bill to pay when all is done."

"No less than he deserves," Ryuji retorted, settling back against the leather seat. "I hope the police lock the madman away."

"He was quite sane until the end," Sora said thoughtfully. "Impatient, yes. But not a raving animal. It almost seemed as if touching Kiyoko-san set him off."

She glanced at him, and immediately regretted it.

His eyes were steady. *Knowing.*

Her flush deepened. "Surely not. It was a fleeting moment."

Actually, she had no doubt that the trigger had been her touch. The collision of their flesh had been explosive, on both a sensual and an energetic level. The cause was a mystery, though. If he was possessed, it hadn't shown up in his auras. There'd been no tainted mix of gray and black. And the presence of a demon did not explain her reaction. She'd touched other possessed individuals in the course of her endeavors, and none had ever given her a jolt like this.

"Obviously," said Ryuji, "there can be no more contact with Mr. Murdoch. If he returns to the office tomorrow, I shall have security remove him from the premises."

Kiyoko did not respond.

Her eyes remained trained on the passing landscape, a soothing peace stealing over her as the lights of the city gave way to the silhouettes of the hilly countryside.

Dismissing Murdoch was not as easy for her as it was for her company president. The effects of his brief touch still surged through her veins. In addition to the edgy arousal, her heart beat with a firmer rhythm. Her auras were a bright royal blue once more and gentle waves of intuition were lapping at her subconscious. After months of suffering, she could almost believe she was cured. Except that the power was bleeding away, fading quietly into the night like the exquisite waves of lust.

And the blame for her disquiet didn't lie entirely with his touch.

Even before he'd reached for her, her pulse had been racing. Spying on him via the camera had not prepared her for the force of his physical presence. He had dominated the open restaurant space with thoughtless ease, his large size and bristling power epitomizing the term *alpha male*. And she'd fallen helplessly under his spell. Surprising, to say the least. Prior to this evening, had she been pressed to describe her ultimate male companion, she would have listed features more in keeping with Ryuji's sharply elegant face and intelligent brown eyes. Large muscles, an aggressive jaw, and eyes the rusty color of autumn leaves had never appealed to her before.

Yet there was no denying the tug of desire.

Or its raw intensity.

The limousine pulled off the highway and onto the familiar well-tended dirt road leading to the estate.

Then again, she was not a nun. One did not reach the age of twenty-four without experiencing the fluttering heart and damp heat of arousal. But she'd never experienced anything quite like this. Even a solid half hour after leaving the restaurant, even after the unbearable edge of need had worn off, the lingering sensations wracking her body could not be captured with such weak words as *flutter* and *arousal*. *Explode, shudder, devastate, burn.* Those did a better job, and even they did not quite express what she was feeling.

Strange.

And humiliating.

Years of study, long hours of learning to control the inner workings of her mind, all lost in an instant. All scattered like the wind with a single glancing touch. Her reaction to Murdoch had been that of a novice, of an untrained acolyte, not the enlightened response of a master. Yet a master was what she purported to be. As the direct descendant of Abe no Seimei, the most venerable *onmyōji* wizard of all time, she was presumed to be uniquely capable of leading a group of mystical warriors against the current madness in the world.

"Even a master can stumble," Sora said softly.

Her gaze flew up to meet his.

Ryuji huffed. "You're not suggesting Murdoch is any form of master, are you?"

The old man shrugged. "Everything about him whispered *warrior.*"

"Whisper? Ha. Nothing about the man is a whisper."

Sora tilted his head. "Do you agree, Kiyoko-san?"

Recalling her first impressions of the images on the video screen, she shook her head. "The subtleties speak louder than the roars. He moves with the grace and purpose of a highly trained soldier, not a simple antiquities dealer."

Ryuji frowned. "Perhaps you should verify his credentials with your mutual acquaintance."

"No." Calling Lena was out of the question. It would take more than a visit from an intriguing emissary to forgive the woman for involving her in a scheme that went against every principle she held to. Every value Tatsu Ashida had instilled in her.

She blinked rapidly, swamped by a sudden rush of memories.

The hole her father left was still deep. For twenty years, ever since the death of her mother, he'd been her lodestone. Always patient and purposeful, he had schooled her in the *onmyōji* ways—revealed the secrets of their ancestral spells, trained her to the sword, and shared all that he knew of fighting evil. His belief in her destiny had been unwavering, but the light shone less brightly now that he was gone.

The majestic sweep of the compound's stone gate appeared out of the gloom, and the limousine braked to a halt before the torii. Kiyoko smiled at the two large *niou* statues overlooking the entrance. The familiar fierce stone guardians resembled Murdoch.

"The only way to get to the root of why Murdoch-san is in Japan is to ask the man himself," she said, taming the eager surge of her pulse with a studied breath. Would his appeal be just as potent the second time around?

Ryuji expressed his opinion with a silent glare.

"I do think there is more to Mr. Murdoch than meets the eye," Sora said, as they exited the car.

"Perhaps," Ryuji allowed, "but he's dangerous."

He turned to Kiyoko.

"Will you be coming into the city tomorrow? I'll understand if this unfortunate situation discourages you from making the trip, but we made excellent progress with the manufacturing reports today and I should like to continue."

She smiled. "Yes, I'll be there. You've been most generous with your time, Watanabe-san. I greatly appreciate your willingness to allay my fears about the state of the company."

"It is both my pleasure and my duty," he responded.

"You are, after all, our majority shareholder." He offered her a gracious bow, then got back in the car.

As the limousine circled the small parking lot and headed back down the lane to the main road, Sora observed, "He's smitten with you."

Kiyoko frowned. "He knows my commitment to the *onmyōji*."

"Your father married. It's not beyond imagining for you to wed someday, too."

"My father didn't share my destiny, sensei. Or face my current dilemma. How can I marry a man when I know that I will be leaving him soon to join Abe no Seimei in the great fight? Besides, Watanabe-san has said nothing to indicate an interest."

Her mentor accepted the arm she offered him. "Perhaps not, but he has hardly left your side since Tatsusan died. And by wedding him you would guarantee the company a strong future."

Kiyoko resisted a grimace. Her commitment to the survival of her father's company was no secret—she had abandoned the familiarity of the dojo every day for the last week to examine the company accounts. This was Sora's subtle way of questioning the wisdom of her decision. "With the current spread of evil, there are no guarantees."

Passing by the gate to the training compound, they strolled down the path to the house, a low-lying mist clinging to their feet. The sprawling, single-story traditional home sat majestically on a rocky outcrop overlooking the valley, the peak of Mount Tengu in the distance. The view was unrivaled. Kiyoko's father had built the house adjacent to the much older dojo before she had been born. The house was large by Japanese standards, a gift offered to his new bride in 1975. Too large, really, which was why she had begged the sensei to move in with her when her father passed away three months ago.

They were met at the main entrance by Kiyoko's only formal retainer, Umiko. The woman was nearing seventy, but she had served the Ashida family with straight-backed devotion for more than fifty years, and she proudly served Kiyoko. Almost as if she'd caught word of Kiyoko's arrival from the wind itself, the housekeeper held a tray of rice crackers and green tea, steam still rising from the pot. No doubt her prescience was attributable to something much more mundane than the wind—like a quick call from the limo driver as he pulled up—but Kiyoko preferred an air of mystery over the truth.

Umiko slid open the decorated shoji partition, stood, and placed the tray on the low table in the main room. Then she bowed and retreated to the kitchen, her cream-colored kimono softly rustling against her ankles.

Kiyoko knelt on the square cushion before the table and lifted the pot. "Tea, sensei?"

He nodded. "Explain to me, in detail if you will, precisely what occurred when Murdoch-san touched you."

Because she'd been expecting the question, Kiyoko was able to tame the color in her cheeks. But not the tiny flip of her heart. "For a brief moment, I experienced a deep and intimate connection with the man."

Sora's gaze found hers as he accepted the brimming teacup. "Did you share some of your own energy, as I taught you to do when healing?"

"No." She forced a swallow of tea down her tight throat. She had not attempted that maneuver since she'd stumbled upon the crumpled figure of her father in the office garage, severely burned and near death. "I have no energy to spare—you know that."

"Then how do we explain the man's sudden ferocity?"

Kiyoko shook her head. "He already had the power, dormant within each cell of his body. My touch released it, though I know not how." Which was true, but only half the story. Explaining the rush of arousal that had preceded Murdoch's descent into fury was a little awkward. Tiny ripples of sweet desire still washed over her from time to time.

"Dormant power," repeated Sora thoughtfully. "Hmmm. I've seen descriptions of something similar, but I cannot recall where. I will have to consult my journals to investigate."

Having shared her every thought with Sora since agreeing to study under him twelve years ago, Kiyoko felt compelled to add, "A jolt of energy shot from his body into mine. I can feel the remnants even now."

"Yes," Sora said. "I saw it enhance your auras immediately."

"Do you think this meeting is significant?"

"Well, it does explain the forceful description of the man I divined entering your life, doesn't it? As to what impact he will have on your future, that remains to be seen. Perhaps it was a solitary alignment of events, never to be repeated." He sipped his tea.

"Or?"

"Or perhaps it is the answer to your prayers. If Murdoch-san indeed contains a rare power within his body, you may be able to leverage it . . . rekindle your ki and gain the strength to transcend."

"We'll never know the truth if he leaves Japan," Kiyoko said slowly, excitement stirring in her belly. The thought of seeing Murdoch again was very appealing.

"True."

Kiyoko stood and walked over to the open window. Darkness masked the palette of November browns that painted the valley, but gave a surreal glow to the moonlit river below. "Then we should invite Murdoch-san to the dojo. I'll send Yoshio and eight of our best warriors to accompany him."

Sora smiled. "I hope that's enough."

*   *   *

Murdoch closed the door to the shower stall with a crisp snap.

What a bloody awful night. He'd lost track of Kiyoko Ashida, drawn far too much public attention, and racked up a whopping bill at the restaurant that he had no spare funds to pay. It could have been worse, though. Had the two warriors not hobbled away at the first bleat of sirens in the distance, he might have kept fighting until the police showed up.

Killing cops would have brought him to a new low.

Hands braced on either side of the white ceramic sink, he peered at his face in the foggy bathroom mirror. Not a scratch on him. Not a bruise or a strained muscle anywhere on his body.

Unfortunately, his two opponents couldn't say the same. Both had left with a collection of injuries ranging in severity from a gut wound to a broken limb. Exceptionally nimble, they'd lasted longer than most, but judging by the way their feet had begun to drag, their destinies had been about to meet the cold hard ground. Given that their only crime had been protecting a young, defenseless woman, that knowledge didn't sit well.

What the hell had happened?

Sure, his berserker was a tad unruly and taming the beast was a constant battle, but tonight it had beaten him senseless. He'd lost complete control, much as if he'd been thrust into a situation with overwhelmingly poor odds and his berserker had burst free in a last-ditch attempt to survive. But against two puny humans, such a severe reaction didn't make any sense.

He rubbed his bare chest with a rough hand.

The minutes following his descent into full-on berserker rage were a blur of battle moves. But his memory of the moment just before he sank beneath the waves remained clear as spring water: *The accidental touch of Kiyoko Ashida's hand.* The sultry hot brush of skin against skin, the sweet burn of desire in his veins, the sudden and very urgent need to possess her.

In seven hundred years of existence, he'd encountered every type of woman imaginable and enjoyed every delicious facet of physical desire. Hell, he'd long ago lost count of the number of women he'd tupped. But the craving that had risen up inside him tonight could barely be described as desire. It was more like . . . mindless frenzy. He'd wanted Kiyoko so badly that his knees had gone weak and his wits had fried. Tossing her over his shoulder and absconding with her had seemed a perfectly rational notion.

Not that rational thought had prevailed. No. Primitive instinct had taken over.

And that had left the door wide-open for his berserker.

Murdoch spun on his heel and returned to the main living area of the hotel room. The room was comfortably large, with a modern king-sized bed and plenty of space to move around. But the hotel's ample hospitality was diminished by the nine black-robed men who waited outside the bathroom door, swords strapped to their sides.

Any other man dressed in nothing but a towel, with sopping-wet hair hanging to his shoulders and his weapon lying useless on the bed, might have felt intimidated. Murdoch had to squelch a bubble of satisfaction.

Nine was much more of a fair fight than two.

3

Unfortunately, killing nine of her men would not endear him to Kiyoko Ashida. And she was all that mattered right now. Murdoch's gaze roamed the faces of the men, seeking the leader. It took a moment to identify the lad in the sea of stoic expressions, but the firmness of one man's stare gave him away.

"Is this an invitation?" he asked pleasantly.

The warrior nodded. "Ashida-san requests your presence."

"Really? So that grand exit she made a couple of hours ago was just for show?"

The young warrior responded with silence. A clearly disapproving silence.

"And where will this meeting take place?" Murdoch asked.

More silence.

Not the chatty sort, apparently. And too arrogant by half. Good thing for this bunch that going along for the ride served his purpose, else he might have been tempted to pummel a few heads just to soothe his pride.

Murdoch brushed past the lead warrior and strode to the bed. Unzipping his heavy canvas backpack, he dug for some clean clothes. White T-shirt, black jeans. Same as always. He whipped off the towel with a complete lack of modesty and proceeded to dress. With the last buckle on his boots fastened and his shoulders encased in his bomber jacket, he snatched his sword off the bed. Daring his new friends to object, he waved a hand at the door.

"All right, lads. Let's find out what Miss Ashida has in store for me, shall we?"

Although it was only a routine demon roust, Emily followed Brian's instructions to the letter. Trouble could happen in San Francisco as easily as anywhere else. She waited until her watch said 2:15, then entered the deserted warehouse through the side door. Lafleur and Hill were on her heels.

The dark ooze of demons swallowed her almost immediately. Not a literal ooze, of course. A mental one. After a year and a half of battling demons, her senses had become attuned to their creepy essence, and she could find them even with her eyes closed.

But when entering a nest of havoc demons, it was best to keep your eyes open. Avoiding the broken glass and metal bits littering the floor, Emily slid silently along a partition wall and under the sagging pipes of an old duct system, her sword in her hand. The nest was in the furnace room in the basement, but a havoc demon could pop upstairs at any moment and blow the place sky-high.

Forming a nest allowed the demons to pool their energy and remain on the middle plane indefinitely. Using the nest like a staging area, the hellspawn could launch much longer and more vicious attacks. Which was why destroying them was a high priority.

Em reached the door to the basement at the same time Brian arrived from the front of the building. He wore his usual demon-hunting attire—designer jeans, a T-shirt, and a pair of badly scuffed Nike sneakers. His girlfriend, Lena, stood behind him, looking fierce with her tightly bound hair and vigilant stance.

Twelve, Em mouthed to Brian. An even dozen demons.

He nodded, then tugged the door open and skipped down the stairs, two at a time. The rest of them followed.

The rectangular room was dimly lit. Only one sputtering candle stood in the center of the pentagram painted on the floor. Stuffing-challenged cushions and piles of fast-food wrappers rimmed the outer circle, crediting the summoning to juvenile delinquents.

Emily rolled her eyes. *Giving teens everywhere a bad name.*

Empty crates and a collection of old janitorial supplies were stacked against the longest wall. In the far west corner of the room, where the shadows were deeper and darker, a gray knot of writhing limbs obscured the unpainted cement and rickety shelving.

The nest.

Taking the lead, Brian dove at the softly humming dark mass, his blade slicing through the air with ruthless intent. He cut through the shield around the demons, creating a long, thin rift in the protective bubble and exposing them to the open atmosphere. Immediately, the babble escalated into a crescendo of howls and twelve demons swooped out into the room, their agile, winged bodies diving at the Soul Gatherers.

Em ducked.

The trick to defeating a havoc is never to let it grab you.

Which wasn't as easy as it sounded. Havocs were almost invisible. Only a faint outline of their bodies showed up, and even that appeared as a shimmery, transparent flicker. If you weren't quick, they had a nasty habit of digging their claws into your clothing, increasing their hum to a fever pitch, and exploding. All in the space of a few seconds.

Em closed her eyes and let her senses find the demons.

In her mind, she swiftly identified the twelve patches of putrid ooze that represented the demons, separating them from the brilliant white light pulsing at the core of each Gatherer. Then she attacked.

Her sword was short and light, specially designed to suit her teenaged body. She let instinct guide its swing, and with a soft swoosh of air, struck one of the havocs accurately in the throat, killing it instantly. As demon gore slid down the blade, the steel brightened with green luminescence and vibrated with the pent-up energy of a demon blood enhancement spell.

Em dodged an incoming demon, pivoted smoothly, and thrust the blade into the belly of another of the creatures. The move took her a shade too close to the tip of Brian's sword, and she felt the cold steel slice into her arm.

He swore.

She ignored the wound and dove at yet another prey.

With six Gatherers fighting alongside her, each of them a seasoned warrior with immortal strength and dazzling speed, the battle did not last long. In no time at all, twelve bodies were heaped atop the pentagram and sprinkled with holy water from Lena's purse.

"Time to call in the cleanup crew," Em said with a satisfied grin.

Brian lifted his gaze from the demon carcasses. "You take too many risks, Emily. Do you really need to fight with your eyes closed?"

"Sorry. I know it sounds weird, but closing my eyes helps me see them. I didn't mean to spin so close to you." Glancing at the bleeding wound on her arm, she willed it to mend. The flesh instantly knitted, leaving only healthy pink skin. "All better."

"*All* will only be better when I don't have to send a fifteen-year-old into a nest of demons," he said grimly.

"I'm going to be sixteen in a couple of weeks. Practically an adult. I'll be able to get my driver's license."

He grunted. "Don't remind me."

A flash of blue electricity forked through the attic, grounding against a folded metal chair and the blades of a rusty fan. The air dried and the sharp scent of lemons filled Em's nose. A second later there was a pop, and a handsome young man with long brown curls and a loose skater-boy outfit appeared out of nowhere.

"Uriel," Em greeted with a smile.

The archangel smiled faintly in return, then nodded to Brian. "Great job. No one was hurt?"

Brian sent a pointed glare at Em, then said, "No, we're all good. How did the Virginia miracle go?"

"Excellent." The young man raked a hand through his hair and grinned. "The virtue angels are quite impressive. They chose a firefighter who was already admired for his bravery and had a habit of kissing his Saint Christopher medallion before entering a burning building. With their divine help, the fellow guided his team to the exact locations of eight trapped people and pulled all of them out of the structure before it collapsed. It made the late-night news and will be all over the Richmond papers in the morning."

"Gotta love good news," Brian responded, sheathing his sword in the leather baldric at his side. His broad hand reached for Lena's, and he tugged her close. "Speaking of which, we heard from Murdoch. The sixth Ignoble might be more than a rumor after all. He says he's got a solid lead."

Uriel pointed at the stack of demon carcasses. "Let me take care of this, and then you can tell me what he found."

Brian nodded. "Meet you back at the ranch house.

Okay, folks, let's vacate the premises. We don't want to be here when our little band of Satanists returns."

He and Lena led the Gatherer group up the stairs.

Em stayed behind.

She watched Uriel rub his hands together, admiring the fat globs of white sparkles dripping to the floor. A look of intense concentration briefly overwhelmed his glowing beauty, then a flash of brilliance exploded into the room and the havoc bodies dissolved into a pile of pale gray dust. He murmured several indiscernible words and the painted pentagram faded, sinking into the cement.

"Uriel?"

He glanced up at her. "Is something wrong, Emily?"

"Not exactly." She drew in a deep breath and mustered her courage. "There's a plan for me, right? It's pretty obvious the Trinity Soul is expected to fix this whole mess with Satan and the relics. Well, it would be really helpful to know how. And when."

His brown eyes gentled.

"The situation is very fluid, Emily. We can sense the momentum building, but at this point we cannot see what shape the final confrontation will take. A lot depends on our actions over the next few months."

She frowned. "Doesn't God know everything?"

Uriel shook his head. "The future has not been written, only loosely sketched. There are still many possible outcomes."

"But how do I know I'm learning the right stuff? How do I know there's not some special tool I'm supposed to have that I know nothing about?"

"There is no special tool, Emily. *You* are the tool."

"Makes sense," Em grumbled. "I sure *feel* like a tool."

He frowned, confusion in his eyes.

"*Tool* is another word for *moron*." She sighed. "Look. Here's the problem: The Gatherers have a job to do. I don't. I'm not responsible for anything. Since no one knows what I'll be called upon to do in the Apocalypse, they make me study everything. But that just makes me a master of nothing. It would be nice to have a task I can focus on."

"I understand that you're frustrated. But you must be patient, Emily. Everything will become clear in time. Just continue to study, and learn as much as you can."

"I *have* been learning. Lots. Ask Lachlan," she said. "I can pop wherever I want, whenever I want. I can recite forty-plus spells from memory, and I'm getting pretty darned good with a sword. That's not the point. With focus, I could become an expert at something. Maybe I'm supposed to spend some time with you and the angels? See the job from a different perspective?"

"No. The lessons you must learn are here, among your own kind."

"My own kind? As far as I know, I'm the only one of my kind in existence. Unless there's some other Trinity Soul you forgot to mention?"

He cut through her sarcasm with a reproving stare. "You're still a human, Emily."

"Barely."

"The middle plane already offers you a unique perspective, one that neither Our Lord nor Satan possesses. You see things we do not. Use it to your advantage."

"I don't actually see them. More like hear them."

His brow arched. "Them?"

"The creatures from the between. That's what you meant when you said I could see things you guys couldn't, right? Because the barriers God erected between the planes don't work on me?"

"Not exactly," he responded drily. "I only meant that you could see into all three planes. What noises do you hear from the between?"

"Lately? Screams and wails and moans. Like some-one's torturing them. Makes it kinda hard to sleep. Thank goodness it's not every night."

"Can you make out any words?"

She shook her head. "No, but they repeat one sound a lot: *say-sell*. Or something like that."

Uriel's face lost all expression. "Azazel?"

"Yeah," she said slowly, "I guess it could be Azazel. Why? Does that mean something?"

He nodded. "Azazel was the leader of the Watchers, a group of fallen angels generally credited with large-scale corruption of the human race."

"Was?"

"He perished in the Great Flood."

"Oh." Em hadn't actually listened that closely to the moans. In fact, she'd done everything she could to shut them out, including pulling the pillows around her ears. "Maybe I was wrong about the sound."

"Perhaps." Uriel raked his hand through his curls once more. "Or perhaps the reports of Azazel's demise were exaggerated. Perhaps he survived in some lesser form."

"That would be a bad thing, right?"

He nodded. "He was once the most powerful of all the fallen angels. His might exceeded that of Lucifer. Even as a lesser being, he could be a formidable opponent."

"What would he be doing with the creatures of the between?"

Uriel grimaced. "I have no idea. I need you to listen to the sounds again, Emily. Try to verify whether they are indeed naming Azazel. The likelihood that he sur-vived is slim, given that we've not heard from him in all this time, but it pays to be careful."

"And if I'm convinced they're saying his name?"

"Call me immediately."

"Then what?"

He frowned. "Nothing. Just call me. Michael and I will sort it out."

Of course. Teenage immortals who find clues to the coming Apocalypse should immediately hand them over and stop thinking about them. But she'd already said her piece about getting more involved and frankly, this fight was getting old. She had exams to worry about.

"You got it."

Kiyoko rolled out of her futon just before dawn.

There seemed to be no point in remaining in bed when sleep continued to elude her. If she was going to see Murdoch's face every time she closed her eyes, she might as well go down to the training compound and face him in person. As she wrapped her black belt around her white *dōgi,* a knock rattled the partition.

"Yes?"

The door to the main living area slid open, revealing a kneeling Umiko. "Breakfast is ready, Ashida-san."

"Is Yamashita-sensei already up?"

Umiko gave a quick nod. "As always." She stood and backed away.

Sweeping her hair up in a quick ponytail, Kiyoko padded across the tatami mat and joined Sora in the lantern-lit tea room. The table was spread with an assortment of dishes, including rice and broiled salmon, but Kiyoko chose only tea. Her stomach would not handle food right now.

Sora looked up from his miso soup. "Not hungry?"

"I'm anxious to get down to the dojo."

"Eager to train, or to see Mr. Murdoch?"

"Both."

The sensei carefully scooped up the last of his soup with his spoon. "You insult Umiko-san by failing to eat."

She chose not to respond. Eating simply wasn't pos-

sible until she saw Murdoch and confronted the strange
feelings that refused to let her go. Besides, the poor man
had been waiting for hours. She had intended to greet
him when he arrived, but her energy levels were not what
they used to be and she'd fallen asleep around one a.m.

Her teacher sighed. "We will go, then."

After making their apologies to Umiko, they donned
sandals in the entranceway and took the short path
along the cliffs to the back gate of the compound.

Mr. Murdoch stood just inside the door in the main
hall, looking less than thrilled. Judging by the various
cuts and bruises on the nine men who surrounded him,
the wait had been unbearable.

"About bloody time," he grumbled, as she and Sora
entered.

Sora studied the guards with a critical eye. Although
none of them flinched, Kiyoko could sense their shame.
"Did you object to our invitation, Mr. Murdoch?"

"No," the big man said, his voice a dry rumble of
Scottish brogue. "We simply had a miscommunication."

He looked at her while he spoke, his gaze trailing
over her face in leisurely detail before slipping lower to
study her clothing. Considering that he stood five feet
away, it was an amazingly intimate experience. Kiyoko's
heartbeat sped up and goose bumps rose on the back of
her neck. She felt *claimed*.

"Over what?" she asked.

"My boots."

She glanced at his feet, which were bare.

"Aye," Murdoch said drily. "I removed them. But it
would have saved everyone a lot of grief if they had
asked instead of demanding. My collection of possessions is small, but what I own, I keep."

Sora nodded. "We shall endeavor to better explain
our requests. Have you anticipated why we insisted on
your presence here today, Mr. Murdoch?"

"You want to talk about what happened yesterday."

"Yes," Sora agreed. "But I also wish to know more about what you are. You are clearly no ordinary man."

Murdoch shrugged. "I'm a large fellow with an anger-management problem."

The master turned and, with a quick word, dismissed the warriors.

Kiyoko frowned as the *senshi* bowed as a unit and stepped away. Respect for her mentor demanded that she remain quiet about any misgivings, but a ripple of alarm ran down her spine. Murdoch had already proven himself a very dangerous man.

"I wish you to speak freely," Sora said gravely. "Kiyoko-san and I will keep your confidence, Mr. Murdoch, I assure you. But you must be open and honest if we are to truly understand what occurred."

"What can I say? I grew up in a rough neighborhood."

The note of amusement in his voice was faint, but Kiyoko caught it. He was toying with them, assuming them uneducated. "I am aware that Lena Sharpe is a Soul Gatherer, Mr. Murdoch. That she is a disciple of Death tasked with protecting the souls of the dead from demons."

His brown gaze found hers once more. "Lena Sharpe has a big mouth."

Kiyoko shook her head. "I can accuse her of many things, but not of compromising secrets. I tracked a demon to a bridge overpass one night and stumbled upon her battling the creature."

His brow furrowed. "*You* tracked a demon?"

She waved a hand at the loosely knit groups of warriors eating breakfast at the collection of tables behind them. "That's what we do. We are disciples of the great *onmyōji* wizard Abe no Seimei. Since the last days of the Heian Period, we have blended the divination and calendar arts with the way of the warrior, slaying demons by whatever means we can. Our purpose is to right the balance of the world."

Murdoch crossed his arms over his huge chest.

Sora added, "There are small bands of *onmyōji* warriors spread across Asia and disciples around the globe. As the demons surface, so do we. Surely you can see how a group such as ours might be needed, Mr. Murdoch? These are difficult and turbulent times, and the devil must be fought on every level."

"I didn't think Buddhists believed in the devil."

"The philosophy of *onmyōjō* predates the teachings of Buddha," Sora replied, smiling lightly. "While the two philosophies have gained much from each other over the centuries, *onmyōjō* differs from the practices of traditional Buddhism. More mystical. Less formal. Do I believe that darkness can rise up inside of men, influenced by external forces? Yes, I do. Just as I believe that keeping dark and light in proper balance is, and must remain, a constant battle."

"Our beliefs," Kiyoko added, "encourage us to seek our salvation from within, not without. Ultimately, to win, it is mortal man who must resist the spread of evil, not immortal man." She met Murdoch's gaze again. "Are you a Soul Gatherer like Lena-san?"

He returned her stare for a moment. "Aye."

"But she does not fight as you do, like a typhoon of power and anger. There is something unique about you."

"I'm what the Norse call a berserker. At certain times, I am consumed by a warrior rage that knows only battle." He paused. "Most of the time, the rage is tightly leashed, but when my berserker is set free, I am no longer in control. He is."

Sora nodded. *"Onimusha."*

"Sorry. My Japanese is nonexistent."

Kiyoko smiled. "An *onimusha* is a fierce warrior with an internal demon."

Murdoch shrugged. "That's as good a description as any. Is that why you brought me here? To discuss my berserker?"

"Not precisely." Sora inclined his head toward Kiyoko. "We are interested in the reason you lost control of your berserker at the restaurant."

A rueful smile graced the big warrior's lips. "That makes three of us."

"And we wish to know whether it was a unique event."

Murdoch's gaze returned to Kiyoko. Curiosity and a touch of amusement lay in the depths of his eyes. "What did you tell him?"

Struggling to tame a blush, Kiyoko said, "The truth. That in a single brief touch I was able to sense the fierce power lying dormant in your body, and that a burst of that power then flowed into me."

His lips twisted wryly. "I see."

Kiyoko's gaze dropped to her feet. *Oh, my.* Had he felt the same arousal? The same burning need to press hot damp skin against hot damp skin? That was beyond uncomfortable.

Sora's eyes narrowed. "Was your experience different from Kiyoko-san's, Mr. Murdoch?"

"Aye."

Kiyoko closed her eyes. If he admitted having similar feelings, if he went into any kind of detail at all, she would never be able to look Sora in the face again.

"Wasn't the same at all," Murdoch said quietly. "I didn't get a blast of energy. I just fell immediately into my berserker rage. It swallowed me whole, in the blink of an eye."

Kiyoko released the breath she was holding. Lifting her eyes, she met Murdoch's again.

His expression was unreadable.

"Have you experienced a similar reaction in the past?" Sora asked.

"No. This was a first."

"Then, with your cooperation," said Sora, "we would like to test your unique connection with Kiyoko-san. To see if we can duplicate it."

Murdoch glanced at Kiyoko's hands, then back to her face. Something hot now burned in his eyes, and Kiyoko knew without a single doubt that he'd shared her intimate reaction to their touch. And that he was recalling the sensations in vivid detail. Every last one of them.

Murdoch kindly released her gaze and turned back to Sora. "Will I get my five minutes alone with Miss Ashida if I agree?"

Annoyed that he'd made his request of Sora, Kiyoko answered sharply, "Yes."

He smiled faintly. "Fine. I'll play guinea pig. Shall we go outside?"

"We'll adjourn to the dojo," Sora said. "Plenty of open space there." He peered over his shoulder. The nine young warriors were seated at a nearby table, eating breakfast and monitoring the discussion with wary eyes. At his nod, they abandoned their meal and left the building.

Sora, Kiyoko, and Murdoch followed.

The dojo stood across the courtyard from the great hall, a wide-open structure with slatted wood floors worn smooth by thousands of bare feet. The *senshi*, now garbed in traditional armor, bowed as a unit when they entered.

Murdoch frowned at their presence.

"Please forgive our precautions," Sora said to him. "This is a dangerous test, and I cannot allow Kiyoko-san to be injured."

Immediately Murdoch's expression cleared. "Aye."

"Good. Shall we start? Please take off your jacket."

Murdoch did not respond.

Sora smiled. "It is an effort to preserve your limited collection of possessions, Mr. Murdoch."

The Soul Gatherer unzipped his coat, peeled it off, and tossed it on the floor.

"Your weapon as well, please," the sensei requested. "We need no unnecessary injuries."

It was Kiyoko's turn to frown. What weapon? She had not noted any weapon, and even with determined study, she could not see one.

Murdoch put a hand to his side and with a soft slither of honed steel, drew a sword from a scabbard. An invisible scabbard. He handed the blade to one of the *senshi*, then turned to Kiyoko. "If you see my face turn red, it means my berserker is about to make an appearance. Don't argue, don't hesitate. Just get out of my way as quickly as you can."

Sora smiled again. "If Kiyoko-san permits a strike, I will be very surprised, Mr. Murdoch. She has been training with me for many years."

Murdoch did not smile in return. If anything, his expression grew more intense. He tapped his broad chest with his finger and said, "Immortal reflexes, plus berserker strength. Trust me. You can be the fastest human on the planet, and you're going to have trouble escaping me. Put those nine lads between me and you first chance you get. Understand?"

Kiyoko nodded. Raising a magical shield might also be wise.

"Lord, I have a bad feeling about this," Murdoch muttered, striding to the middle of the room.

Kiyoko followed.

When it was just the two of them in the center of the dojo, he glanced at her. In a low, barely audible voice he said, "Look, lass. My berserker is a tad old-fashioned, and it has this crazy notion that you belong to him. I've really no idea what will happen when I touch you again. Modern women like to be tough. I understand that, even admire it. But do me a very big favor and let go of your damned pride, just for today. If you think for one instant that I'm going berserk, please run."

It was a strong speech, driven by a combination of gruff honesty and deep-seated honor. And it made Kiyoko's heart flip-flop in her chest. Especially the words *belong to him.*

He gave her another of those piercing stares. This one dark with worry. Then he stuck out his big hand, sighed heavily, and said, "Bloody hell. Let's give it a go, then."

4

Murdoch tried to shake off a sense of foreboding. Learning why he'd lost control at the restaurant was vital, but this experiment was ten kinds of crazy. Some sort of strange, mystical friction existed between him and this woman. Last time, Kiyoko had rendered him weak-kneed and defenseless in an instant. This time? It could be worse.

He wanted to believe he wouldn't hurt her.

But his faith was shaken. His berserker was incredibly possessive around her. It rumbled in his chest even now. All he had to do was breathe in her soft floral scent and those primitive throw-her-over-your-shoulder thoughts would come racing back, pounding at him with every beat of his heart. The beast didn't have a conscience. It wouldn't cry any tears over her demise.

"Let us put some form to this connection, Kiyoko," Sora said. "Start by touching a clothed part of his body."

"I'm not sure that's wise—" Her palm flattened against his chest for a moment, a firm press of warmth that was swiftly gone. Murdoch held his breath, waiting for the explosion of sensation. But it never came. He relaxed. It was possible the incident in the restaurant had been a fluke.

"Now try flesh to flesh."

Murdoch braced himself again, but felt nothing.

Long moments passed. He opened an eye and peered at Kiyoko.

"Have you changed your mind?"

"No." She stood loose and limber, no sign of stress. Her shiny black hair was pulled back off her face and tied in a ponytail. The practical hairdo underscored her femininity with an uncluttered display of her delicate features. In that loose white outfit, she looked so slender and small that an aching tension rose in his chest again.

He lowered his arm.

"Well, I have. This is a damned foolish idea."

Before his hand had fallen to his side, Kiyoko stepped in smoothly, touched his fingers, and spun away.

The stages of his descent occurred in exactly the same order: first the screaming-hot desire, then the unbearable drive to possess, and finally the headlong pitch into berserker rage. But they happened faster and burned ten times fiercer.

Murdoch actually heard himself snarl the word *"mine"* before he lost all rational thought and grabbed for Kiyoko.

Kiyoko had purposely tried to re-create the unexpected nature of the touch—a glancing, chance encounter. But she was completely unprepared for the dramatic change Murdoch underwent.

One moment he was honorably offering to cancel the experiment, the next he was snarling *"mine"* and reaching for her with blurred speed. Had her reflexes not been honed by real battle with supernatural demons, she might not have evaded his grasp. As his hand whipped out to grab her, she fell back, rolled to the left, and sprang to her feet on the other side of the row of *senshi*. Even as she rolled, she murmured the words of a second-level *onmyōji* shield spell.

Good thing, because speed alone would not have kept her safe.

Murdoch barreled through the line of warriors, knocking two aside with a wide sweep of his huge arm, their flimsy first-level shield spells buckling under his onslaught. Uncaring that their katanas sliced into his white T-shirt, Murdoch remained focused on Kiyoko, and his feet followed his eyes. His face was flushed, his eyes glassy, but his attention was unwavering. He came at her like a dynamo of raw purpose and determination.

Several excellent offensive moves passed through her mind.

But she doubted she could hold the fierce Soul Gatherer off. Especially with her insides still quivering like jelly from the aftereffects of his touch—a part of her actually yearned for him to reach her.

She swiftly scuttled back, keeping clear of Murdoch's grasp and leaving the attacking to the four upright *senshi*, who promptly leapt after the huge warrior. She did not leave the dojo. To do so would encourage Murdoch to follow, and letting him loose in the compound would only result in more damage.

Instead, she snatched up a bamboo practice sword from the rack on the side wall, ready to fend him off in any way necessary, and kept to the outer edge of the room. Relying on her shield spell would be foolish.

Sora, who was still standing precisely where he'd stood from the start, quietly ordered the warriors to put away their weapons. "His berserker will remain in full control as long as there is potential danger. Continue to stand between him and Kiyoko-san, but do not attack him."

To the great credit of the *senshi*, they followed his orders, despite the obvious risk. Almost in unison, their katanas slithered back into their scabbards.

Immediately something changed in Murdoch.

A little less heat in his cheeks, perhaps. Or a little more awareness in his gaze. He remained centered on his objective, however, and shoved one of the unarmed *senshi* in the chest to reach her. The poor man flew four feet before landing on the wood floor with an audible grunt.

Kiyoko's advantage lay in her agility. She dodged Murdoch's lunge and with erratic moves kept several paces ahead of him as he chased her about the room. And every passing minute worked in her favor. Despite his continued interest in claiming her, without a visible threat Murdoch's rage quickly cooled.

Less than five minutes after their touch, he abruptly stopped. He went from hot and raging to pale and trembling in just a few moments. As he glanced at the fallen *senshi*, rigid lines of self-disgust appeared on his face.

"Well, that was a royal fuckup."

"I disagree," Sora said. "No one is dead, Kiyoko is unharmed, and we have our answer."

Murdoch raked the long waves of his brown hair back from his face. "I think your men might express a different opinion."

The uninjured *senshi* were aiding their fallen brothers, two of whom cradled arms that were likely broken and all of whom were limping.

Sora bowed to the men, offering them his respect, then ordered them to the infirmary. "Do not berate yourself, Mr. Murdoch. They are used to battle. No man joins us who is not prepared to give his life. What we do is not for the faint of heart."

"You should seek help as well, Mr. Murdoch," Kiyoko said, pointing to his torso. Traces of blood were visible along the edges of the sliced fabric. Annoyingly, her eyes kept straying to the sweat-dampened material clinging to the steely muscles of his chest. "Stitches may be required."

He shook his head. "Flesh wounds."

His gaze lifted to meet hers and a dart of delicious warmth went right to her belly. *Flesh.* Oh, dear. He was feeling the same keen desire, the same sharp need. It was there in his eyes.

And suddenly the full meaning of Murdoch's earlier warning sank in. *Belong to me.* That was why his berserker came after her. It wasn't to harm her. It was to . . .

She blushed to the roots of her hair.

A wry smile lifted one corner of Murdoch's mouth.

"How much of you is left inside when the berserker takes control?" Sora asked.

"Everything," Murdoch responded. His gaze remained locked with hers, his message clear. The heat was so intense Kiyoko had to break off the stare. "The basic motivations are mine. I remember who my enemies are, but my actions become so focused on winning that collateral damage is very common."

Sora frowned.

"*Collateral damage* is an American euphemism for killing innocents and friendlies," explained Murdoch grimly.

"I see." Sora turned to her. "And you, Kiyoko-san, did you feel the same energy burst as before?"

She nodded, not trusting herself to speak.

He would not be pleased to know how deeply disturbed she was by Murdoch. She was supposed to keep clear thoughts and a peaceful inner calm at all times. A master *onmyōji* did not tremble with need and teeter on the verge of throwing herself into her opponent's arms. If he knew the tumult of her desire, Sora might well change his mind about her future, divination or no divination.

"Fascinating," said her mentor.

"Well, as interesting as the experiment was," Murdoch said, "it's not why I came to Japan." He picked his jacket up off the floor and turned to Kiyoko. "Let's talk."

She glanced at him. "Watanabe-san said you were interested in a relic, something my father might have had in his collection."

"That's correct. Some time ago, when Lena Sharpe paid you a visit, she sensed the item in your home."

"My home? But all of my father's antiquities are on display in the lobby of the Ashida Corporation building."

He nodded. "I saw them."

"And was the relic you seek among the collection?"

"No."

She mentally reviewed all of the pieces of art in her home, which was easy because the house was sparsely decorated. "Describe it, please."

"I can't."

She smiled. "If you can't describe it, how do you know it's not on display at the office?"

"I have a dowser," said Murdoch.

"A what?"

He reached into his jacket pocket and pulled out a multifaceted crystal attached to a thin silver chain. Dangling it between his thumb and forefinger, he held it to the light. "A dowser. It tells me if I'm near the item I'm seeking."

"By rotating clockwise or counterclockwise?" Kiyoko asked with a small laugh. "That doesn't really work, Mr. Murdoch. It's a charlatan's trick."

His brow lifted. "It doesn't swing, it vibrates. And I can assure you, the lad who gave me this little gem is anything but a charlatan. He's a very powerful mage."

Kiyoko was about to say something further, but Sora put a hand on her arm, staying her rebuttal.

"I've seen such things," the old master said. "But how did your mage tell it what to look for when you've already admitted you do not know what it is?"

"The object possesses a dark power. We've handled other relics of a similar nature, so Stefan set this dowser up to hunt for an inner darkness."

"Are you suggesting my father was harboring a tool for the devil?" demanded Kiyoko, aghast at the idea. "He would never do that. He was a dedicated *onmyōji*."

"Perhaps he was keeping it safe," said Murdoch softly. "Each of the other relics has a champion tasked with keeping them out of the wrong hands."

The tide of outrage burning in her chest subsided. Protecting. Yes, that sounded very much like her father. She pointed to the crystal at the end of the silver chain. "Is it vibrating now?"

"No."

"So, it's safe to say the item you seek is not in the dojo compound?"

He nodded. "But you don't live here."

Kiyoko got a sudden image of Murdoch inside her home, his huge frame crowding the space, and it sent a strange little thrill down her spine. "Are you inviting yourself into my home, Mr. Murdoch?"

He smiled. "No. But I was rather hoping you'd see your way to offering me a cup of ale before you put a boot to my ass."

"It's rather early in the day for a beer."

"Aye, some might say that," Murdoch said. He tucked the crystal away. "But I was weaned on the stuff. We'll just blame it on the jet lag, shall we?"

Sora smiled and headed for the dojo entrance. Kiyoko followed, slipping her feet back in her zori at the door. The traditional straw sandals were far more comfortable than shoes. "I trust a Japanese beer will suffice? We have no American ale."

"If it's made from hops and fermented, it'll do," Murdoch said, stuffing his feet into his boots. A veritable bounty of silver buckles. "I'm not fussy."

The winding path to the house followed the edge of the cliff quite closely, offering them a spectacular view of the valley as they walked. Kiyoko knew the proximity to the sharp drop often disturbed first-time visitors, and she instinctively moved to claim the position closest to the cliffs. But Murdoch was too quick for her. He subtly inserted his body between her and the edge—ensuring her safety while also avoiding any skin contact.

She smiled.

An *onimusha* who was also a gentleman.

As always, Umiko met them at the door. With a very formal bow for their guest, she ushered them into the wood-floored entranceway, where she offered Murdoch a warm pair of socks. Once his feet were suitably attired, she led them into the tea room, where an assortment of beer bottles stood alongside the teapot on the table. Most prominently displayed was a bottle of Sapporo beer.

Kiyoko smiled. The woman was fiercely loyal, even to the local beer industry.

No sooner had Murdoch ducked under the lintel separating the entranceway from the tea room than he was digging in his pocket for the crystal. Not entirely comfortable with the process, but extremely curious to see the results, Kiyoko watched him dangle the transparent stone on the chain once more.

Her expectations were low.

But apparently Murdoch's were not. As he held the crystal aloft, he closed his eyes and a frown of intense concentration furrowed his brow. A moment passed. The frown deepened.

"No vibration?" Kiyoko asked gently, as she knelt and poured tea into two cups.

Murdoch lowered his arm and opened his eyes.

"The vibration is weak, almost unnoticeable," he said,

dangerously soft. "But it's there. One of you is hiding the relic, most likely beneath a mystical blanket spell."

"I know nothing of an evil relic," she protested.

Murdoch studied her face, reassured by the genuine confusion and shock he saw there. He swung his gaze to the old man, who appeared as calm as ever.

"But *you* do," Murdoch said firmly, lowering himself to a cushion.

Sora picked up his tea. "Sample the beer, Mr. Murdoch. Take a moment to breathe."

"I didn't fly halfway around the bloody world to *breathe*." Although his words spilled out in a rush of irritation, a spark of satisfaction flickered to life in his chest. Webster had thought to send him on a fruitless mission. Instead, Murdoch would arrive home the victor, carrying a prize of immense value. "I came to find a relic that could be critical in defeating Satan. If you're as dedicated to fighting demons as you say, you'll give it to me."

"Nothing is ever that simple."

Kiyoko frowned at her mentor. "What relic does he speak of, sensei?"

The old man stared at her over his teacup. "The Veil."

She went completely white. So white that Murdoch instinctively put a hand to her sleeve to steady her, prepared for a severe case of the vapors. But she dodged his hand and rose to her feet.

"The Veil is a dark relic?" Her voice was thick with disgust, her hands balled into fists at her sides. From what he'd observed so far, a very unusual display of emotion from the woman.

"Not entirely, no," her mentor replied.

Murdoch glanced at Sora. "Not entirely? What do you mean, *not entirely*? If Satan gets his hands on it, will it add to the misery he's currently wreaking on the world? Yes or no?"

Sora sighed. "Yes."

"Then it's a dark relic."

Kiyoko spun around, her arms now wrapped around her waist. "Why didn't you tell me?" she demanded of Sora, her eyes dark and wide.

The old master did not waver. "Because I knew you would refuse to use it."

Use it? Murdoch's gaze flickered from Kiyoko to Sora and back.

"Of course I would refuse," Kiyoko said hotly. "It's *tainted*."

Murdoch put up a hand. "Hold on. Back up a mite. Use it? Who is using it, and how, exactly? It's a bloody spigot of evil."

"The Veil is not a common relic," explained Sora. "It has two separate halves: one light and one dark. With the evil side contained, it is capable of great good."

His answer did nothing to ease the pain in Kiyoko's eyes. She spun on her heel, shoved aside the shoji with a rough snap, and left the room. Murdoch had to consciously stop himself from going after her. What the hell did he think he was going to do? Give her a damned hug? One touch, and *comfort* would be the last thing he'd be offering.

Picking up the closest bottle of ale, he took a large swig. "Might as well tell me the rest of this ugly tale," he said to Sora. "Don't leave anything out."

"The Veil is a remnant of the large curtain that once hung in the door of the temple of Jerusalem," said the old man. "It was used to keep the masses out of the temple, allowing only the priests to enter. But at the precise moment Jesus died on the cross, the Veil was torn in two and fell to the ground, a reflection of God's grief for the loss of his son and a sign that the temples should no longer remain closed to the masses."

Murdoch frowned. "You don't believe in any of that, though, do you? You're not a Christian."

Sora smiled. "What you and I believe differs. This is true. To me, God and Satan are merely personifications of good and evil—the good and evil that reside inside each and every one of us. I do not worship any relics of the Crucifixion, nor do I seek God's forgiveness for my sins. But I *do* believe in the negative power of fear and anger and hatred, and the positive power of hope and kindness and enlightenment."

"And you believe an object can be a container for those powers."

The old man nodded.

"How the hell did a Christian relic end up in Japan?"

"It was brought here in 996 by a religious knight named Richard of Tournai. It was believed that its dual nature was best guarded by masters of the yin-yang philosophy, so he came to study with us. Unfortunately, he was critically injured in a battle with a demon a year later, and we were unable to heal his injuries. On his passing, the *onmyōji* took the relic under their wing."

Murdoch squinted at the elderly man. "By *we*, you mean the *onmyōji*, not you personally, I take it?"

Sora smiled. "Richard-san died over a thousand years ago. Surely my bones do not creak that badly?"

"What is the Veil being used for now?"

"You were correct in your guess that there is a blanket spell on the relic—but only the dark side is caged. The good side is free to be used as the holder sees fit." The old *onmyōji* took a sip of tea.

Murdoch waited for him to continue, but when a moment passed with nothing more than the trickling sound of a fountain, he said, "That's reassuring, but it doesn't explain what Kiyoko is doing with the relic."

"That part of the tale is not mine to tell."

"Don't be evasive, old man. You gave her the damned thing. Just tell me what she uses it for."

"I must respect Kiyoko's privacy." Sora lifted his gaze

from his tea. "Just because our paths led us to this spot does not mean we have the right to trample every blade of grass in view, Mr. Murdoch."

It was a surprisingly effective analogy.

He had no trouble imagining himself as the thoughtless boot and Kiyoko as the tender grass. His large, unwieldy body and uncouth manners versus her delicate perfection and quiet, traditional femininity. Aye, he could crush her in an instant, without noticing he'd done it. But, damn it, he was here for a reason. And that reason had nothing to do with playing nice.

He rolled to his feet.

"Then I guess I'll go talk to the lady herself."

5

Kiyoko was adjusting her bra when Umiko suddenly delivered a spate of frantic Japanese. The old woman's words were a mix of fury and panic, laced with a deep undertone of martyrdom.

"Stop right there, Mr. Murdoch," Kiyoko called out, glancing over her naked shoulder at the paper-thin door and praying it wouldn't slide open. "She's explaining that she's prepared to die rather than let you enter. I'm in the middle of getting dressed."

"Oh."

"Meet me in the garden," she added. "I'll be out in a moment."

"Fair enough." The low, smoky rumble of his voice drifted over her skin, leaving a scatter of goose bumps on the back of her neck. A strange thing to admire about a man, his voice. "Where's the garden?"

"Umiko-san will show you."

Kiyoko made the request of her housekeeper, then grinned at her retainer's muttered response: *Dim-witted bear*. He did rather resemble a large brown bear.

A few moments later, attired in a black skirt, a crisp white cotton shirt, and a warm sweater coat, Kiyoko stepped onto the pathway that divided the raked gravel. She followed Murdoch's dewy footprints to the arched bridge overlooking the man-made pond. All the leaves had fallen, opening the bare black branches and cold clear water trickling down the artfully arranged rock structure to view.

Murdoch was leaning on the wooden railing, gazing into the water, but he straightened as she approached.

"Beautiful," he said.

She nodded. "My father was an avid gardener. He enjoyed strolling through here even in the winter and chose the position of every plant with exacting care. When a thick frost falls, it's like a miniature ice world made just for fairies."

A corner of his mouth lifted. "Aye, the garden is lovely, too."

Warmth surged through her.

Kiyoko dropped her gaze to the water flowing silently under the bridge. Blue sky and a thin gauze of cloud reflected on the smooth surface. Safer to study the scenery than the rugged angles of his face or the intimate humor in his eyes. The palpable tension between them already caused her enough grief. If he dared to mention the arousal she had felt at his touch, her shame would know no end.

"I'm traveling into the city this morning, Mr. Murdoch," she said. "The car will be here in half an hour. What was it you wished to discuss?"

"The Temple Veil."

Her stomach rolled. Learning of the relic's capacity for evil had sickened her. Yet she was not willing to part with it, even with her newfound knowledge.

"It's not for sale."

He leaned on the railing again, the sleeve of his jacket and his broad, square hand only inches away. "Every moment you hold on to it, you risk the fate of the world. If Satan should discover you have it—"

"No one knows except Yamashita-sensei ... and now you. If word of its presence here were to leak out, it would most likely result from your interest. The safest course would be to forget we had this conversation and return to the United States."

"I can't do that. I'm staying right here until I get what I came for."

The leather of his black jacket was thick and strong, scuffed by regular use and worn at the cuff. No delicate, butter-soft calfskin for Murdoch.

"Because you made a promise to your superiors?"

"Because the battle with Satan is one we could lose, and I really hate to lose."

The voice of experience. A quick glance at his face confirmed the presence of fine lines around his eyes and mouth. He wore the signs of his maturity with pride.

"So, the Veil is a weapon," she said softly. "What exactly does it do?"

"It slays demons."

"How?"

A short gust of air left his lips, fogging the air. Kiyoko risked another glance, uncertain whether it was a chuckle or a snort of disgust. His lips twisted. "I have no bloody idea. This entire trip hinges on Lena Sharpe's gut instinct and the impressions she got six months ago, before she lost the amulet."

"She lost the amulet?" The woman's most prized possession, invested with both sentimental and mystical value. "How?"

"Trapping a demon."

Kiyoko bit her lip, thinking. "She sacrificed it?"

"Aye. To save her niece."

The tight muscles of her shoulders eased a fraction. Lena's initial behavior was still unforgivable, but it was heartening to discover the woman had come around in the end.

"Gut instinct," she repeated. "So, there's no actual

evidence that the Veil is a weapon? No documentation of its powers?"

"No."

"Then why would I give it to you?"

"Because even the old man admits it's a dark relic. The bloody thing is dangerous. Not to insult you, lass, but as immortals, we're better able to protect it than your talented but very vulnerable *human* warriors."

A faint breeze blew Kiyoko's unbound hair into her face, and she tucked an errant lock behind her ear. "You're not going to insist that everyone in your group is immortal, are you?"

Silence.

She smiled. "I'm privy to a great deal of information, Mr. Murdoch. I may be human, but I'm not a fool. Ever since Lena-san betrayed my trust last spring, I've been investigating her and her little band of . . . friends."

"Then you know what we're doing."

"Not precisely," Kiyoko admitted. "It's clear you're no longer simply gathering souls. Judging by the flow of people through the ranch, I'd guess you've undertaken the training of other Gatherers—very understandable given the current state of the world. But your group also does an inordinate amount of travel, to places that make no sense. South Africa, for example."

He grimaced. "My boss's pet project—finding and protecting all of the Ignobles."

"Your boss? Would that be Brian Webster?"

"Aye." His hands gripped the wooden rail, knuckles white.

"You don't like him," she guessed.

"Webster and I have . . . issues," he admitted. "But we're committed to the same cause: stopping Satan in his tracks. The devil is making inroads everywhere, even in Asia."

Kiyoko nodded. The toll here was different, but as corruption spread and people continued to turn away from their beliefs, crime rose and the economy grew ever more unstable.

Murdoch straightened, facing her. His body blocked the breeze and instead of cool fall air, she got a subtle whiff of warm masculinity and spicy soap. "I cannot allow another dark relic to fall into Satan's hands. Leaving the Veil here is an unacceptable risk."

His words were weighted with both confidence and passion. There was no doubt he'd do exactly as he promised—protect the Veil with his very last breath, if necessary. It was a testament to his overwhelming charisma and vivid personality that she almost agreed to his demands. But giving up the Veil was impossible. Even if she wanted to, which was still a very debatable point, Sora would never allow her to part with it. "It's a risk you'll have to take."

He reached for her hand, but abruptly halted just short of touching her. "Am I not explaining the risks well enough? Are you not convinced I'm capable of keeping it safe?"

Kiyoko stared at his hand.

Big and square. Tanned from hours in the outdoors. So close to her own flesh that she swore she could feel tiny electric shocks passing between them.

"I understand that if Satan acquires the Veil, his hold over the darkest parts of mankind will increase." It was an outcome so opposite to her principles it made her belly quiver. "And I believe you to be an unparalleled defender."

"Then why not entrust me with it?"

"Because I draw on the Veil's strength."

He frowned. "To do what? Fight demons?"

"That . . . and other things." *Like keep my heart beating.* Kiyoko surprised herself by omitting that detail. Her years of study at Sora's knee had taught her to eschew feelings of pride and vanity, yet admitting that she was weak to Murdoch—arguably the most healthy and virile man she'd had opportunity to meet—bothered her.

She wanted him to see her as she'd been before the attack on her father—strong, capable, wise. She wanted him to admire her. Was that so terribly wrong?

"Whatever your reason is for holding on to the Veil," Murdoch said, ducking down to peer in her eyes, "I can't believe you would think it more important than keeping the relic safe. People are already dying by the thousands, losing their life savings in corporate scandals, and abandoning their hopes for a brighter future—all because two relics have fallen into Satan's hands. Under no circumstances can I allow another to go the same route."

Kiyoko looked away.

"The Veil is an undocumented relic. No one seeks it."

"Nothing remains hidden forever, lass. *I* came looking for it. That means its existence is known, whether you choose to believe it or not."

His words rang with quiet sincerity, and the queasy feeling returned to Kiyoko's stomach. Risking the lives of others for personal gain did not sit well with her, not when she had pledged herself to serving the greater good. But handing the relic over to Murdoch would mean her death.

"I need to go into the city," she said, turning away.

"I'll come with you."

"No, I—"

A muffled shout, followed by several loud cracks, broke the stillness of the morning air, coming from the direction of the training compound up the cliffs. Murdoch's hand shot out, grabbed her sweater-buffered shoulder and shoved her to the ground. "Keep your head down."

"Why?"

"Gunshots." He didn't elaborate or hang around to explain. He just dashed down the path toward the compound with superhuman speed, his weapon drawn as he ran.

A sword. Against bullets.

Guns were not part of the *onmyōji* training regimen. Her warriors trained in the old ways. They fought only with katanas and other traditional weapons, augmented by a few magic spells—because demons didn't bother with guns either. So why had shots been fired?

Kiyoko glanced down at her pencil-thin skirt, now smudged with dirt from the wooden bridge, and frowned. Why had she picked today of all days to dress like a woman? To impress Murdoch? How foolish. She kicked off her heeled pumps and peeled off her sweater coat, tossing it aside.

Then she sprinted up the path in Murdoch's footsteps.

A lone gunman.

Murdoch caught a glimpse of the fellow in the gap between two buildings as he hopped the ten-foot-tall perimeter fence. It was one of the young warriors from the dojo—standing in the courtyard, pivoting slowly, and shooting at anyone who dared move. He was speaking in Japanese, his voice low, urgent, and angry.

Keeping to the thin morning shadows along the wall of the main hall, Murdoch slipped closer.

Getting shot wasn't a big concern—bullets wouldn't do anything more than piss him off—but it might be smart to assess the situation before engaging the enemy. Not that his berserker rated the fellow as a real threat—his blood was only lightly simmering and most of that was the residual effect of standing close to Kiyoko.

At the corner of the building, he paused.

The gunman's back faced him, although the slow circle he was making would have them eye to eye in a moment. Three bodies lay sprawled in the courtyard, unmoving. Impossible to know if they were dead, unconscious, or just playing it safe.

And it didn't really matter.

The gunman held a 9 mm pistol firmly in one hand and some kind of switch in the other. He had three other holsters stuffed with steely black guns, a belt hung with several replacement clips, and something strapped to his chest that looked remarkably like a . . . bomb. This was no accidental firing or ploy for attention. The man was on a mission to kill and be killed.

Murdoch's hand flexed around the leather-wrapped hilt of his sword. An ordinary blade, nothing special. No heavy two-handed superweapon like the one MacGregor carried. Just a sturdy, double-edged broadsword crafted by an ancient Norse sword master and kept in pristine shape by meticulous daily care.

He called it Bloodseeker.

For good reason. The blade was blessed with an uncanny ability to deal a killing blow, and it had served him well long before it received the mystical augmentations provided by Stefan Wahlberg. Its history was as colorful as his.

But before he resorted to slaying the fellow, he ought to try something more diplomatic. Like a sleep spell. *Or not.* The fellow's thumb might accidentally depress the trigger of his bomb and blow up the compound. A bind spell would work, though.

The gunman continued to pivot, wary eyes vigilant for any sign of movement. One more step and . . .

Murdoch cast the bind spell.

It hit the shooter's shield and bounced harmlessly into the air, only a few blue sparks confirming the accuracy of Murdoch's aim. Now alerted to Murdoch's presence, the gunman fired into the shadows with deadly intent.

Now or never.

Murdoch drew on his Soul Gatherer powers and leapt, springing into the courtyard with an easy flex of his thighs. He landed four feet from his opponent and, using the shield-piercing augmentation on his weapon, promptly knocked the gun from his grasp with a sharp whack of steel on steel.

The younger warrior reacted swiftly to the attack. He fell back in a smooth motion, letting go of the switch and drawing his katana. In a flash, he had settled into a firm guard position, snarling at Murdoch in Japanese, ready to battle.

Murdoch felt a warm burn in his muscles.

His berserker doing a lazy stretch.

"You don't want to do that, lad," he said gently. "Trust me. It'll only end badly. Put the sword down."

The gleam in his opponent's eyes remained bright, and the volume of his Japanese lecture only increased.

"Yamete!"

It was Kiyoko, approaching from behind him, speaking in a crisp, unequivocal voice.

Murdoch tensed, his berserker springing to protective alertness. The man had a bloody bomb strapped to his chest, with the bright red thumb switch dangling visibly from a couple of wires. Why the hell hadn't she stayed where he left her?

"Lass," he said, addressing her as calmly as he was able to under the circumstances. "I have this under control. Get the hell out of here."

"Under control? He says he's going to blow up the whole compound."

"Exactly why you need to back up," he muttered.

She ignored him. Continuing to speak to the young warrior in a soothing manner, she tried to step around Murdoch.

He extended an arm. "Over my dead body."

"He just got word his father killed himself after losing the job he'd held for thirty-four years. He's very bitter, but we can still reason with him."

Murdoch trusted his gut. And his eyes. The bomb spoke volumes. "Wrong. He came here to die. Talking isn't going to change anything. I'd prefer not to help him meet his maker, but I'll do it if I must."

Kiyoko said something to the warrior.

Another burst of Japanese spilled from the young man's lips. The lad's eyes were locked on Kiyoko, his face flushed with resentment, and an unsettled feeling landed in Murdoch's belly.

"You're right," she said. "Takeo says he has lost faith in the *onmyōjō* ways, that he no longer believes we can defeat the demons. He has embraced the dark side of his soul, and he is pleased that he has slain several of his fellow *senshi* because it will save them from the futility of our daily demon hunts. He accepts that he will die today."

"Fine," Murdoch said grimly.

"But he wants *me* to do it."

He bristled. "Not in a million bloody years."

"He is my student. It's a fair request." She waved a hand to a warrior standing just inside the dojo. The young fellow raced to her side, presented her with an intricately engraved scabbard, then scurried back. "I will lose face with his peers if I do not grant him his wish, Mr. Murdoch."

"Lose face?" He shot her a quick, angry stare. "You're going to let pride get you killed? You'll lose a sight more than face if you give in to him. He just wants you close enough to guarantee he takes you with him when he flips that damned switch."

"I'm faster than you think."

"I don't care how bloody fast you are," he said hotly. The berserker was clawing its way up his chest. "You're not going to duel a madman with a bomb. Understand?"

"I've fought demons. I can handle a man."

"For God's sake, woman, you just admitted that you trained him to kill creatures more powerful than himself."

"I'm still the teacher."

Murdoch couldn't keep his eyes off the four blocks of plastic explosive strapped to the young man's chest. If the bloody bomb went off, Murdoch would suffer and suffer badly. It wouldn't kill him, but it would come as close to killing him as it was possible to come, shredding his flesh and pulverizing his bones. Imagining that same impact on Kiyoko was almost enough to make him puke up his meager breakfast.

"He's still the one with the bomb."

"Stop worrying," she said mildly, drawing her sword with a light rasp of steel. She bowed to Takeo, and the young warrior bowed back. Neither of them took their eyes off each other. "I'll survive, and so will you. My shield magic is very strong."

Murdoch snorted. "Lass, you'd have to be a mage to manage a shield spell capable of holding off a bomb at close range."

The young warrior was growing antsy, and he took a step toward Kiyoko, brandishing his weapon and snarling an obvious threat.

Murdoch stepped between them with little thought.

Kiyoko's katana sliced through his jacket and into his side, burning along his ribs. She shoved him away, but not before the blood flowed. A warm, sticky stream ran down his side and pooled at the waistband of his trousers.

"Stop trying to protect me," she said angrily.

"My actions are not entirely my own," he admitted, though not one whit unhappy at where his feet had taken him. "Remember what I told you about my berserker and its primitive claim? It's having a little trouble with this scenario."

"I remember. But didn't you also say the basic motivations while you were in the berserker state were your own?"

Murdoch's breath snagged. *True*.

"I think you're blaming your inner demon for your chauvinistic tendencies, Mr. Murdoch. Step out of the way."

He blinked. *Was he?*

Unfortunately, a blink was enough time for Kiyoko to slip past him. She rushed the young warrior with her sword aloft and attacked with a sharp yell.

Kiyoko recaptured her still-water state of mind the moment she entered into battle with Takeo. Tumultuous thoughts of Murdoch fell away, replaced by cool, lethal purpose. She reached the young warrior in two measured steps and engaged him in a flurry of standard attacks and parries, made possible by the steady flow of energy into her body from the Veil.

Sadly, there was no way to undo what Takeo had done here today. His continued existence would poison those around him, robbing the other warriors of the confidence they needed to win. Faith was the mainstay of the *onmyōji*. Without an unshakable belief in the rightness of what they were doing, they would not win the war against evil.

Her opponent attacked fast, but without originality. Lulled by years of sparring with her, he assumed his familiarity with her style and stance would telegraph her next moves, and she took advantage of his arrogance.

Varying her speed and drawing on the entirety of her attack repertoire, she pressed him hard, forcing him back. A flurry of rapid sword strikes, then a spin to the left, and she sliced through his flimsy first-level shield with a smooth arc of her blade.

The detonation switch dropped to the ground.

Takeo had slain his fellow warriors, turned on his own brothers with unforgivable brutality. Even if she managed to convince the young man to return to the fold, the faith others had in him would never be the same. And that reluctance to rely on him would get the rest of her men killed.

She deflected Takeo's swinging sword with her own.

Worse, he now represented the very evil they fought every day. If she showed him mercy—if she allowed him to live—her men might hesitate when faced with evil in the future, wondering if leniency was the proper course of the day.

She could not permit that.

With a wealth of regret and a steady hand, she thrust her katana between the fourth and fifth ribs.

Takeo's eyes lifted to hers the instant her weapon pierced his heart, an instinctive need to connect in his last moments. She grabbed his arm as his knees gave out, her chest heavy. How many times had they dueled together in the dojo? How many hours had she spent with him on his technique? Lowering him gently to the ground, she watched the dark ferment in his gaze fade. Evil had abandoned him to his fate.

"You're good with a sword," Murdoch said grudgingly. He tugged Takeo's sleeve free of her chilled fingers.

"There are times when I wish I were not."

He nodded. "The day you take a life without regret is the day you should lay down your sword and walk away."

Kiyoko looked at him. "Have you killed a man?"

"Worse. I've killed boys." His face was grim. "Lads who never got a chance to bed the girl of their dreams or dance at their own weddings."

His admission surprised her. Such an act did not mesh with the obvious honor that held him upright. "Why?"

He shrugged. "In war, you do what you must."

As the other warriors poured from the surrounding buildings, tending to their fallen comrades, Kiyoko glanced down at Takeo's lifeless face. "You yourself have died."

"Aye."

"What was it like?"

"Unpleasant."

Such a minimalist word. Kiyoko smiled faintly. "Was it a swift passing?"

"No," Murdoch said. "I'm an ornery sort. I didn't go quickly or quietly. I bled out on a battlefield, cursing the seven maggots who felled me with every breath, even my last."

"Did your comrades not try to save you?"

"I was buried deep in the enemy line and there were scores of other wounded men on the field. By the time the healers reached me, it was too late."

"Oh."

He grimaced. "Spare me the pity, lass. I was quite the fool in those days. My death was a blessing."

"I doubt your mother and your wife thought it so."

He said nothing. Just met her stare for a long moment, then turned and surveyed the courtyard. "Three dead. A very unfortunate loss. How do you report this to the authorities?"

"We don't." Kiyoko bent and retrieved Takeo's katana. It would be destroyed, along with his personal possessions. "All who have chosen to follow this path understand that they will not be buried alongside their loved ones."

"They just disappear?"

"Technically, they disappeared the day they entered the compound. For most, that was several years ago. To the outside world we are a martial arts school, and we open a few sessions to the public to keep the authorities from becoming curious."

"And what do you do with the wounded?"

She pointed to the middle-aged woman kneeling in the dirt beside the sole surviving warrior. "We have a full-time doctor on staff and she has a well-equipped infirmary at her disposal. Many of our *senshi* have also received training as field medics."

The phone holstered at Murdoch's waist vibrated. He tugged it free and glanced at the display. "You should hire a mage."

Kiyoko shook her head. "Healing spells are very difficult to perform and the excellent ones demand a gifted practitioner. Unfortunately, there are too few genuine mystic healers in the world. We've not had any luck in finding one."

"You know a great deal about magic," he said with a frown, as he dropped to one knee beside a fallen *senshi*.

Curious, Kiyoko watched him. "Our branch of the *onmyōji* has studied and plied the mystic arts for centuries. Plus, my father was a descendant of Abe no Seimei himself, so we are privy to many of his magical volumes."

Murdoch placed a bare hand on the neck of the dead man, seemingly oblivious to the dark red blood still seeping from the fatal wound. He closed his eyes.

He could have been offering a simple prayer, but Kiyoko knew he was collecting the warrior's soul. Once, back when she and Lena Sharpe had been on speaking terms, they had talked about the gathering process. Lena had described it as a feathery warmth that floated up her arm and wrapped around her heart.

"Kiyoko-san."

She glanced to the left. Sora stood in the entrance to the dojo, his silvery white hair flowing down his back, his hands folded in the long sleeves of his black robes. The very epitome of serenity.

"Yes, sensei?"

"This is a most disturbing event."

She nodded. "Our safeguards were not enough."

"Safeguards?" Murdoch moved to the second body. "What safeguards?"

"The two stone *niou* at the gate," Kiyoko explained, "are tasked with preventing evil from entering the compound. Yet Takeo was able to walk in yesterday without a problem."

"Which means he was either unaffected when he entered, or he found some way to disarm your barrier spell."

She nodded. "And of the two, the second is more likely."

"Can you boost the barrier?"

"That particular spell has served us well for centuries," she said. "I will need to consult my spell books to see if there is anything stronger. I'll inform Watanabe-san that visiting the city today is not possible."

"Nonsense." Sora descended into the courtyard, the trailing hem of his robes soundless as it slid over the wooden steps. "Go. The compound will survive another day in your absence. Ensuring that your father's business remains uncorrupted is as vital as any other task assigned to you. Holding back the darkness takes many forms."

She blinked. Sora was usually the first to remind her of her commitments to the *onmyōji*. "Are you certain?"

"The company car is already at the gate," he said with a faint shrug. "It would be impolite to keep the driver waiting."

"I'll go with you," Murdoch offered, standing.

Kiyoko's pulse accelerated. Forty minutes of close confinement, breathing that warm, masculine scent, feeling the electric tension dance between them the entire time. The journey into Sapporo would be almost unbearable, but deliciously so.

"Surely you would prefer to remain in the country and enjoy the fresh air, Mr. Murdoch?" Sora asked. "Kiyoko-san will be cooped up in an office all day, poring over numbers. Did you travel all the way here from America to see four painted walls?"

Murdoch hesitated.

"Stay," she said to him. "He's right. My day will be quite tiresome for you."

She met his gaze, intending to underscore the message. But what she saw in his eyes surprised her. Her words had failed to discourage him—if anything, they had deepened his chivalry and firmed his resolve. He planned to accompany her. But it was equally clear that Sora did not want him to.

"I will go alone," she said quickly, before he could speak.

She spun around and strode toward the gate, decision made. Why taunt herself? Time spent in Murdoch's company would only make life after his departure more difficult. Yes, he made her feel good, extremely so. But the sheer intensity of her response to him foretold its demise. Such trembling eagerness, such breathless need, and such desperate craving would not endure. *Could* not endure.

As Sora had said, the car was waiting for her at the gate. Umiko stood next to the open door, Kiyoko's shoes, purse, and a fresh shirt in hand. Kiyoko glanced down. Droplets of Takeo's blood stood out starkly on the white material. Her path had been mapped out for years; she already knew her destiny. Still, under the arch of the torii, between the hulking stone statues of the *niou*, she stopped.

And turned.

Murdoch stood exactly where she had left him, a pillar of male presence against the backdrop of the temple, staring at her. Why that meant something, Kiyoko couldn't say. But it did. She nodded to him, accepted her items from Umiko, and slid into the car.

Smiling.

6

Murdoch watched until the car disappeared down the treelined driveway, then faced the old man. "Kiyoko calls you sensei or Yamashita-sensei. What should *I* call you?"

The old man smiled. "Do you desire to join the other men in training today, Mr. Murdoch?"

"No." Searching the house for the Veil would be a much better use of his time.

"Then address me as Sora-san."

"Okay, Sora-san. I'm headed back to the house. I've got a call to make, and then I'm going to relax until Kiyoko returns. Give me a shout if anything untoward happens."

The elder lifted a silver brow. "Untoward?"

"Strange, odd, evil."

"Ah, yes. Faced with such, we would of course require your aid."

Murdoch peered at Sora. Something suggested the old man was enjoying a chuckle at his expense, but the placid expression on the aged face didn't support his theory. "Exactly."

"Thank you, most sincerely." Sora pointed. "The western gate will lead you to the house. No need to leap the fence on your return journey."

Murdoch's hackles rose. Undeniable humor. He met

Sora's even stare. "Where I come from, mockery is an insult requiring a decisive response. Don't test me, old man."

Sora smiled. "Believe me, Mr. Murdoch. No insult is intended. My admiration of you runs deep. If I am amused, it is only by the unabashed way you display your passion."

That didn't soothe Murdoch one whit.

"Holding back has never been my strength," he admitted, his voice soft. "And retreating is only acceptable if it draws the enemy into a trap."

The old man bowed graciously. "Then allow me to be the one who withdraws, Mr. Murdoch. My apologies."

Sora slipped back into the dojo, leaving Murdoch standing in the courtyard. The doctor was busy guiding the transfer of the wounded warrior to the infirmary, and several other men were carefully lifting the dead onto soft cotton litters.

The hairs on the back of Murdoch's neck lifted, and he pivoted. A young man was crouched next to the limp body of Takeo, a man Murdoch didn't recognize. Not personally, at any rate. But the gentle hand to the man's neck—*that* he knew.

The young man stood and faced Murdoch.

Judging by the plump youthfulness of his skin, the lad was no more than twenty. His muscles were well honed, his hair cut short, and his outfit identical to that of any other warrior in the compound. Only a familiar weariness about the fellow's eyes gave him away.

He was a Soul Gatherer.

Since Murdoch could carry only souls destined for the same resting place, and the two warriors he'd claimed were bound for heaven, Death had sent another to pick up Takeo's soul.

Murdoch nodded to his colleague, then took the path to the back gate without a word, allowing the young man to vanish into the shadows, as his role dictated.

Umiko met him at the door to the house.

For a moment, he wasn't sure the old dragon would let him in. Her bearing was stiff, her cream kimono amazingly crisp and unwrinkled. But after glaring at him for a long moment with undisguised annoyance, she stepped back and ushered him inside.

Where she had another beer waiting on the table.

He grinned.

God love her.

He snatched up the beer, took a long swallow, then dialed the main number for the ranch in San Jose. It was early evening in California, so someone ought to be around to answer.

"Hello?" A woman's voice, no Egyptian accent.

"Rachel?"

"Nope, it's Em. Mom's in the studio. That you, Murdoch?"

The quiet, unemotional tone had misled him. The lass hadn't been the same since young Rodriguez left town. "Aye, it's me. How is the training going?"

"Better every day." A short pause. "I miss you."

He frowned. Webster and Emily had been quite close once, but the lad spent a lot less time with the girl now that he was running the show. "I miss you, too, lass. If you need to pop out here for a chat, feel free."

"Thanks," she said. "But between homework and training, I don't really have time. When are you coming back?"

"Soon." Very soon, if all went well. "Is Webster around?"

"Nope. He and a bunch of the others drove off in the Humvee to meet Michael and Uriel. The archangels found another nest of demons in San Francisco."

"Of course they did." Murdoch grimaced. "Why did you stay behind?"

"I have an exam tomorrow," she explained. "English. If I ace this one, I'm back on the honor roll."

"Good for you. Your mum must be happy."

"As happy as she can be with swollen feet and a giant belly. I think she forgot how much fun it is to be eight months pregnant."

"Aye. I'll bet MacGregor is sticking close to home these days."

"Yup. When he's not in the training arena, he's in the office staring at the map, trying to figure out where to send his latest elite Gatherers."

"Is there one assigned to Sapporo, perchance? I could use a little action over here."

She chuckled. "I dunno. I'll check. In the meantime, want me to give Brian a message for you?"

"Aye. I need him to sell my car." Even used, it should bring more than enough to pay for the repairs to the restaurant.

"The Mustang? *Why?*"

"I'd rather not say," he said. An uncomfortable silence hung on the airwaves for a moment, so he added, "But I'd love ya more than life itself if you could convince him to wire me the money in the next day or two, lass."

"Okay. See you when you get back."

Murdoch said his good-byes, then returned the phone to his belt. Despite the gains made in her focus and attitude, he preferred the old Emily to the new. Quiet and obedient didn't suit the girl.

Then again, *girl* didn't suit her anymore, either.

The dreadful goth look had given way to casual western, with her hair returned to its original sandy blond. It made that odd streak of red stand out more, but overall, the natural look was kinder. Minimal makeup, plain jeans, and a simple ponytail snared low on her nape rounded out the new Emily. She would turn sixteen in a few weeks. Definitely a young woman.

Rodriguez would barely recognize her.

Murdoch frowned.

Not that he wanted the lad to resurface. Safer all the way around for him to stay away. Murdoch's berserker had more in common with the Cookie Monster than it did with whatever was crawling under Carlos Rodriguez's skin.

He dug into his pocket for the crystal dowser Stefan Wahlberg had fashioned. The sooner he found the Veil, the sooner he could return to the ranch to give Emily a much-needed hug.

Dangling the chain in the air, he closed his eyes and concentrated. The hum of the Veil had barely been discernible the first time, and he couldn't afford to miss it. One by one, he shut out all the distractions—the trickling sound of the fountain in the garden, the quiet muttering of Umiko in the next room, the wind subtly buffeting the paper doors. Slowly narrowing his focus, he gave his full attention to the crystal.

But the crystal was quiet. Utterly still. No hint of the earlier vibration remained.

His eyes popped open.

Either he'd imagined the hum of the crystal this morning, or the Veil was no longer in the house. Not to be arrogant, but he had a pretty good sense which was the truth. He trusted his gut above everything.

The blasted thing was gone.

But gone where?

He tucked the crystal away. Stupid question. If Kiyoko was using it for something, it made sense that she would have it in her possession.

In his mind's eye, he itemized the clothing and jewelry she'd been wearing when she left. Slim black skirt, white cotton shirt. The shoes and sweater could be discounted—she'd tossed them aside before joining him in the compound and he doubted that she would be that cavalier with the Veil. Unseen, but amazingly easy to imagine draped over her slim form, bra and panties. White, he'd bet, with just a hint of lace.

He grimaced.

Mind on the job, Murdoch.

As far as jewelry went, there were a few possibilities: She wore a silver locket around her neck and a silver bracelet on her wrist, entwined with a shiny black ribbon. If only a strip of the original Temple Veil still existed, one of those pieces could hold it.

There was also a possibility that she carried a pouch of some sort on her body, but he couldn't verify that unless he got close. Sadly, given his inappropriate reaction to her touch, feeling her up would have to be an option of last resort.

But he wouldn't rule it out. Yet.

First, he'd try squeezing the information out of her colleagues.

Kiyoko blinked and the numbers on the page before her swam back into focus. Oh, dear. Had she actually fallen asleep while reading them? For how long? She glanced up to find Ryuji studying her, his handsome face serious. The look in his eyes was warm and admiring, but not overly familiar.

"Your grasp of the intricacies of a balance sheet rivals your father's," he said softly. "In only a few short months, you've mastered the fundamentals of the business. Quite a feat."

She dropped her gaze to the report once more. Apparently, her inadvertent doze had been momentary. "Thank you, Watanabe-san."

"Should I order you an afternoon meal, or would you prefer to stop here?"

Skimming quickly through the remaining pages, she sighed. "There are several hours of study left, and I fear my brain is becoming muddled. I think stopping is the wiser decision."

"But . . . ?"

She smiled. "But there are also matters requiring my attention at the dojo. I am reluctant to make another trip to the city this week."

"Do these matters involve Mr. Murdoch?"

"You know they do."

He leaned across the cherrywood boardroom table and lightly touched her hand. "And you know I disapprove. He's a dangerous man, and I worry about you out there in the countryside with none but an old man to protect you."

"Our students are there as well," she reminded him.

"Still, you are only barely recovered from the illness you suffered after your father's death. I'm the one who found you, remember? For a moment, I thought you were dead, too."

Trying to heal her father's wounds had almost killed her. Spurred by her father's last gasping breaths, she had attempted an ancient and powerful *onmyōji* healing spell. The potent words had eased his pain and stopped the ravage of the demon fireballs, but performing the spell had consumed a massive amount of her core energy. Unable to accept that she'd arrived too late to save him, she ignored the cautionary voice in her head and continued the incantation until her voice was hoarse, mindless of the growing weakness in her limbs.

But he died anyway.

With a shallow heartbeat and clammy skin, she had collapsed on the floor of the parking garage, next to her father's blackened body. That was when Ryuji had stumbled across them both.

Kiyoko squeezed Ryuji's hand in return.

"I do remember. Thank you."

"Those three days after the attack on your father were the most frightening of my life," he confessed. "The intensity of your grief nearly took you from us."

Not grief, a waning life force. She'd have been dead now if Sora hadn't suggested using the Veil as a cure, but Ryuji didn't need to know that.

"But I'm fine now." She gently separated her hand from his and stood. Ryuji was nineteen years her senior, but she hardly noticed the age gap. He was not the least bit stuffy, and they shared a quiet bond of memories of her father. She enjoyed that. "Could you call the car for me? I'd like to return home."

He nodded. Picking up the phone, he placed a quick call to his assistant, arranging for the limousine to take her back to the house. When he ended the call, he shot her a thoughtful look.

"Do not think I am being too forward, Kiyoko-san, but I have a suggestion that might ease both our concerns."

Curious, Kiyoko said, "Go on."

"Technology makes our lives very simple these days. With little effort, I can temporarily move my office to the dojo compound and run the company as if I were here in the office. You would be able to complete the review of the company reports without leaving the countryside, and I would rest more thoroughly knowing exactly where Mr. Murdoch was at any given moment."

Kiyoko hid a smile.

Murdoch wasn't quite as easily boxed as Ryuji might have believed. But it was an intriguing idea just the same.

"I would, of course, sleep in the compound with the students, not up at the house."

"That won't be necessary," she said, gathering up her sweater and slipping her arms in the sleeves. "Yamashita-sensei's cabin stands empty since he moved into the main house. You may stay there."

He bowed. "Thank you. I'll call home and have my housekeeper pack up my necessities. If you don't mind a short detour to pick them up, I'll accompany you on the return trip."

"I don't mind at all."

As she belted her sweater, he asked, "Dare I ask where Mr. Murdoch will be sleeping?"

An excellent question—one to which she'd given absolutely no thought. Murdoch had said he would stay at the compound until he got what he came for. How long he would hold out was anyone's guess, but it was safe to assume several days at least.

"He prefers to bunk with the students," she said. Inviting Murdoch into her house was impossible for many reasons, and Ryuji wouldn't welcome sharing the sensei's cabin. Not with the Scotsman. "Sleeping arrangements are a low priority for him."

And if they weren't . . . ?

Well, she'd deal with that later.

Murdoch used the day as effectively as possible. An angel came for the souls of the two fallen *senshi* a little after ten in the morning. After that, he questioned each of the senior *onmyōji* warriors about Kiyoko and her attire, careful not to give away his motive. Judging by the smirks he received, most thought he was completely besotted with the lass. No matter.

He was casually interrogating the warrior known as Yoshio when he heard the limousine pull up in front of the main gate. He ignored the sudden acceleration of his pulse and did his best to quash a vision of Kiyoko elegantly stepping out of the car into the late-afternoon sunshine.

Attractive, aye.

Off-limits? Most definitely.

As the car door clicked open and the low notes of her voice filtered into the air, it grew increasingly more difficult to keep his gaze locked on the black-belted warrior, who was offering to show him several specialized sword moves. But somehow he managed.

His rigid self-discipline did him proud ... until he heard Kiyoko laugh. A light bubble of genuine amusement. Then his focus shattered. Despite his determination to ignore her, his head swiveled of its own accord. His eyes honed in on her oval face and curved lips with pinpoint accuracy.

But his pleasure was swiftly dashed.

Standing next to Kiyoko, with a proprietary hand on her arm, was Ryuji Watanabe. He was whispering into her ear, and it was clear that the attractive, well-dressed company president had coaxed the delightful laugh from Kiyoko. A low growl formed in Murdoch's throat, and he found his fist wrapped around the hilt of his sword in a single, thoughtless moment.

Fortunately, his loss of control was brief.

Sanity—and the realization that Watanabe would soon climb back into the car and return to the city—prevailed. Murdoch tamed his inner beast with a mental cuff to the head. He forced his fingers to release the sword and drop to his side. Kiyoko Ashida was not, nor ever would be, his. As Sora-san would no doubt say, they were on two different paths. Why couldn't his berserker accept that? Why was it suddenly so bloody attuned to a woman? To *this* woman?

He stood calmly, shoulders sloped with feigned nonchalance, as the limousine driver walked around to the boot of the car, opened the lid, and began lifting boxes to the gravel driveway. The significance didn't register until a futuristic black box with a telescoped chrome handle and wheels was plunked down next to the others.

Not a computer box. Not a briefcase. A suitcase.

He lifted his eyes to Kiyoko's face once more.

She was looking at him.

"I trust the *senshi* found you a bunk to call your own, Mr. Murdoch?" she asked.

"Aye."

"Good. Because we picked up your bag at the hotel and settled your account. We'll see you in the morning." She nodded politely, took Watanabe's arm, and led the Japanese man past the gate and down the stone path toward the house.

Murdoch's gut knotted so tight he could barely breathe. Apparently, while he bedded down in the drafty bunkhouse surrounded by snoring young men, Watanabe would be sleeping under Kiyoko's roof. Even with the dragon lady keeping watch, that notion didn't sit well.

Not one little bit.

"Are you annoyed with Mr. Murdoch?" Sora asked, as he sipped his tea. The lantern lights were low and the midnight air cloaked the house in a peaceful hush. "You refused his every request to meet this evening."

"No." She had avoided him, but not because she was annoyed. Kiyoko bent and touched her nose to her knees, enjoying the stretch of her tight leg muscles. Wearing high heels all day had cramped her calves. "But I do find him rather forceful. I needed time to think, and he barely gives me room to breathe."

"Indeed."

Palms flat on the tatami, she slid smoothly into the plank position. "Does the divination my father did at my birth give any clue to *how* I will transcend?"

"It only identified you as the one who will join Abe no Seimei in the endless fight. You know this already."

"It foretold my unique ability to manipulate the Veil's power," she pointed out.

"That was part of the prophecy. Proof, if you will, that you are indeed the descendant with the right skills."

She sighed. "Does that not suggest that as my ability to leverage the Veil decreases, my right to transcend wanes, too?"

"No. It is not your skill that is waning, but rather the blanket spell cast over Veil's dark side. As with anything in nature, the two halves are in a constant struggle for balance, and for a time, the dark side is winning. It is consuming the positive energy flow."

Kiyoko walked her feet back to her hands, then slowly rose to full height. "Which would not be a problem if I didn't depend on that energy for survival."

Glancing up from his tea, Sora nodded. "If we can find some way to tap into Mr. Murdoch's dormant power, are you prepared to transcend immediately? Abe no Seimei did not transcend until he had lived a full life as a mortal. But your choices are different."

She gave her mentor a rueful smile. "Choices? In a month or two the positive energy from the Veil will be completely gone."

"You have at least one option. If you walk away from your current role and cease to use magic, you could live another decade or longer."

Kiyoko stared at him. Abandon the fight against evil? Let others take up swords against the demons while she sat back and watched? Not possible. "I can't do that."

"Then we must move swiftly. While you are still healthy and the chances of success are excellent."

"Shall I explain my destiny to Murdoch then? Ask him to aid me?"

"To do so will doom your efforts," Sora said. "To successfully transcend, you must hide your soul from the goddess of Death. Since she is Mr. Murdoch's master, sharing the details of your destiny with him is the same as sharing them with her."

"Oh." Did he share *everything* with Death? How disconcerting. "Leveraging Murdoch's power won't be easy. The energy that surges through me when we touch is too vigorous to contain."

"Now, perhaps. But with practice, you will learn the exact nature of its ebb and flow."

"So long as Murdoch's berserker doesn't kill me in the process," she responded drily.

"I don't believe he wants to kill you."

Kiyoko barely held back a flush. She didn't believe he wanted to kill her, either. "I meant in the maelstrom of his rage, by accident."

Sora was silent for a moment. "Perhaps we can reduce that risk. If you were to teach him the art of *zazen*, he might gain a stronger rein over his berserker."

"I'm not certain allowing him to join the meditation sessions would be wise. There's a possibility that he'll lose control of his berserker as he struggles with the concept of inner release. He may end up disrupting the sessions."

"I agree. Individual tutoring would be best."

The skin between Kiyoko's breasts suffered a sudden wave of damp heat. "You wish me to spend time *alone* with him?"

"I do. But I can see the notion concerns you." Sora's eyes narrowed. "Does your reluctance have anything to do with the invitation you extended to Watanabe-san?"

"No," she protested. "Watanabe-san offered to set up a temporary office in your old cottage to save me further trips into the city. Once we complete the review of the company reports, he will return to Sapporo."

"Then it is fear that motivates you."

Fear of falling victim to her own desires, perhaps. "Although fear sometimes halts us when we should move forward, it is also a reminder of the possible consequences. More time spent with Mr. Murdoch will increase the chance of an accidental touch."

He nodded again. "But if you replace chance with purpose, and slowly accustom him to your touch, his response may lose its fury."

Kiyoko stuffed her feet into a pair of sandals, then joined him at the table. Kneeling on a dark blue cushion, she reached for the stoneware teapot. "So, the plan is twofold: teach him better control and train him to my touch?"

A low chuckle escaped Sora's lips. "Mr. Murdoch must, of course, be a willing pupil. Fortunately, I believe he aspires to greater self-discipline, so he should be amenable to your teachings."

She refilled the sensei's cup, then poured tea for herself. "I'm not so sure. If he thinks it will endanger me, he's likely to refuse."

Sora smiled. "Then your first task is to convince him that you will remain safe."

Kiyoko grimaced. "No. First, I must convince myself."

7

Frustrated didn't even begin to describe Murdoch's mood.

As if Kiyoko's refusal to see him last night weren't galling enough, she'd managed to elude him this morning, too. He'd stalked up the pathway to her home first thing, determined to gain entry. Even the dragon lady hadn't been able to hold him off. Hounded by a furious spate of Japanese he had no hope of understanding, he had searched every room. But the house was empty. No Kiyoko. It was only when he consulted with his new friends in the dojo compound that he discovered her whereabouts. She and a team of warriors had departed on a demon hunt in the middle of the night.

A demon hunt.

Without telling him.

Shrugging off his leather jacket and tossing it over a nearby bush, he swore. The woman had a bloody death wish. He rolled his shoulders to warm the muscles, then drew Bloodseeker from its sheath, rendering it visible. In an almost unconscious routine, he stepped through the four primary guard positions and simulated several opening attacks. The leather wrap of his hilt fit snugly against the calluses formed centuries ago on his right palm and thumb, and the familiar moves settled his thoughts.

"I see you were a student of Johannes Liechtenauer, Mr. Murdoch," Kiyoko said from behind him.

He spun about.

Her loose white gi and ponytail lent her such a slim and feminine appearance that he instinctively lowered his weapon, despite the glistening steel katana she held. Dark circles under her eyes spoke to her eventful night, but she was otherwise hale and hearty. Which was the only reason he didn't paddle her ass.

"And others, including Agrippa," he acknowledged.

"What? No Japanese masters?" she teased, smiling.

"I'm always willing to expand my repertoire." The silver necklace and bracelet were both present. No earrings, though. And if she was carrying a pouch, it wasn't anywhere obvious.

"Good," she said. "I was rather counting on that."

He frowned. "For what?"

She gestured to one of the smaller buildings on the other side of the compound, next to a well-tended herb garden. "I'm about to begin my training routine. Will you join me?"

The structure was tiny, unlike any training facility Murdoch had ever seen before. But having just said he was open to new ideas, he could hardly refuse. He nodded and led the way inside.

Inside was a single narrow room decorated with tatami mats, cushions, and a sunken hearth. At one end of the room a painted scroll hung on the wall. He turned to find her standing immediately behind him, close enough that he could easily drink in her jasmine perfume. His pulse leapt and he made no effort to tame it.

"What do you do in here?"

"Meditate."

Murdoch raked a hand through his hair. "Don't take this the wrong way, lass, but I'm going to pass on the meditation. I'm all for mental discipline, but sitting on my ass contemplating my navel is not my cup of tea. I'd much rather have joined you on the demon raid you and your foolish friends embarked on last night."

"We have a set routine. You would have disrupted it."

Like her closeness was disrupting the normal flow of blood through his body? "You should have at least told me you were going."

"Why? So you could order me to remain at home?"

"Aye. You do not heal the way a Soul Gatherer does. Nor are you blessed with the enhanced sight, smell, speed, and strength we have. Taking on demons by yourself is sheer lunacy. This talk of becoming a master of meditation is only proof that you've no idea what you're up against. *Demons* don't bloody well meditate, I can tell you that."

"You see meditation as a form of inaction."

"Aye. Because it *is*," he bluntly pointed out.

She shook her head, the tip of her ponytail peeking briefly over her shoulder. "That assumes action is only physical. What does your brain do while you are fighting, Mr. Murdoch?"

A memory of his last battle resurfaced—fending off the six gradiors trashing the Protectorate offices in Rome. "Notes the position of the enemy, gathers clues about what my opponent is going to do next, chooses the moves I must make to reach my objective."

She hung her katana on a wall mount. "So, you would agree that situational awareness is as important as the physical actions you take?"

"Aye."

"Well, meditation is about expanding your awareness. The objective is not, as you stated, to withdraw from the world. It's actually the opposite. To experience reality and understand your place in it." Crossing to a cushion, she sat. "Understanding your relationship with the world around you will give you greater control over yourself." She looked up. "You are interested in achieving greater control, are you not? Sit."

Actually, at that precise moment, he was interested only in the expanse of pale skin her gaping gi revealed. His motivation for taking a seat opposite her was merely to get a better view of it. But sit he did.

"What now? Do I close my eyes?" he grumbled.

"No, *zazen* requires open eyes. But first we need to assume a proper meditation posture."

"Don't expect me to bend like a pretzel. I'm seven hundred years old."

She chuckled. "You look remarkably good for a man of your age. Proper posture requires your knees to be flush with the cushion. Can you do a half lotus, like this?"

She tucked her left heel against her buttocks and lifted her right heel into her lap. It made his knees ache just to watch her.

"No," he said.

"Then kneel." Rolling back, she grabbed a short, tilted stool from the corner of the room. "And sit on this."

Carefully avoiding her fingers, he accepted the seat. "This is a lot of effort to go to just to think."

"We will be doing this several times a day, so get used to it," she replied. "Once you have mastered *zazen*, we will attempt to touch again."

He grinned. "Is that your way of confessing you can't get enough of me?"

Her expression remained neutral. No smile.

"Come on. Admit it," he continued, egged on. "You felt exactly what I felt when we touched, and you'll do anything to feel it again."

She blinked.

"The hot rush of blood through your veins, the heavy pound of your heart against your chest, the edgy, almost unbearable need. You remember what it was like, don't you?"

"Not really."

"Liar."

"My goal is to reach the point where touching you engenders no reaction whatsoever," she responded flatly.

"No reaction whatsoever?"

"None." Her gaze dropped. "Are you ready to begin?"

"No." He knelt and leaned back on the stool. It was remarkably comfortable, even for his war-torn knees. "Why do you care what happens when we touch? Once you give me the Veil, we've no need to see each other again."

Her lips tightened briefly. "The emotions that besiege me when we touch run contrary to my desire for inner tranquillity and enlightenment, so I seek to tame them."

He studied her for a moment. "I rather like the way you make me feel. If it weren't for that small problem with my berserker, I'd pounce on you this very moment. I'd offer you no reprieve until you screamed your pleasure to the heavens and finished with a huge smile on your face. There's more than one way to find tranquillity."

Her eyes lifted to meet his, and she flushed crimson. "Do you always say what's on your mind?"

"Aye. It saves time."

Any lingering coolness in the November air melted away under the heat of their shared gaze. It was a moment of unabashed honesty, a complete lack of artifice or cloaking. They both wanted each other.

And they both knew it was impossible.

"That small problem with your berserker is why we are here," she said, lowering her eyes and grasping for her composure. "The discipline inherent in *zazen* may help to avoid the loss of control you experienced. We're going to start by focusing on your breathing."

"Just so you know," he said drily, "it was empty

thoughts and a complete focus on the physical that led to my berserker gaining control in the first place."

"Do not empty your thoughts. *Zazen* is about being fully engaged with the world, not about being empty-headed. The focus on breathing is only to rid you of distraction."

"Fine."

"Eyes open," she admonished him. "Half-lidded is best. Pick a spot on the floor three feet in front of you and stare at it."

"Lass? Your *lap* is three feet in front of me. How am I supposed to focus on my breathing when I'm staring at the very thing that's driving me to distraction?"

"Concentrate. You do know how to concentrate, don't you?"

Murdoch straightened his shoulders. "Sarcasm does not become you."

"Focus, Murdoch. Cup your weaker hand with your dominant hand, then put your thumbs together to form an oval. Hold your head high and align your spine perpendicular to the floor. Now breathe deep. From your gut."

Such a simple thing, the dropping of the salutation in front of his name. Hardly worth the contented sigh he suppressed. But the implied intimacy pleased him immensely. Eyes on the white cotton gi in front of him, he pulled in a deep breath.

"Release the breath slowly, feel it leaving your lungs, leaving every muscle, leaving your body. Draw in another. Feel the coolness in your throat, the expansion of your lungs, the stretch of your diaphragm."

Having committed to the exercise, he followed her directions with diligence and centered his attention on the steady rhythm of his chest. The delicate sound of her voice never faded from his consciousness, but it *did* settle in some soothing spot outside his body. By the fourth breath, his Soul Gatherer senses had come fully alive. Not only could he track the flow of every indrawn molecule of air, but he could feel the gentle pressure the air placed on each inch of his skin. He knew which slow swirls had entered from the chilly outdoors and which had slid along Kiyoko's heated body before wrapping around him.

She continued to speak, but her words lost meaning.

With every slow, deep draw of air, he got a taste of Kiyoko. The floral scent of her shampoo, the fresh cleanliness of her soap-washed skin, even the faint trace of green tea on her breath. He experienced it all.

And his berserker took notice.

There was a rumble under his breastbone, a stirring of the beast that he likened to hunger. The first preludes of change assailed him—a heightened temperature, the slight swelling of his muscle tissues, the swift distribution of oxygen to the farthest reaches of his body—and he was forced to quash them. He wanted nothing to interfere with the heady enjoyment of her presence, because this was as close to touching her as he was likely to get. And it was strangely satisfying. Or it was until he caught the spicier note wafting off her left shoulder. A more masculine scent. Citrusy. Complicated. Expensive.

Watanabe's cologne.

He kicked the stool away and surged to his feet.

"I'm done." Taming his berserker took a great deal of effort, and his words came out stilted. Bloody hell. She'd recently spent time with the wretch, somewhere confined, somewhere his scent could pool around her and cling. Watanabe had *touched* her.

She frowned. "You barely began."

"My senses are more acute than a human's," he said, "and are more easily overwhelmed. Believe me, stopping now is wise."

Before someone got hurt.

He drew in a deep, shuddering breath.

Damn it. This was so unlike him. He wasn't normally a jealous person. Not about women. Holding on to them—allowing their lives to become entangled with his—never ended well, so he dated a lass once or twice and then moved on. Jealousy didn't suit his lifestyle. But this crazy attachment his berserker had for Kiyoko didn't follow any rules.

It was all about want and *need*.

"Your self-control is very rigid," Kiyoko said. She got to her feet and crossed the mat to his side. "But that works against you in meditation. You must interact with your environment, not hold yourself aloof from it."

He glanced down at her. The top of her head came only to his shoulder. "You're not actually suggesting I let go, are you? Allow the berserker to surface?"

"Something must give. You carry a wall everywhere you go."

He snorted. "What happened the other day in the dojo is only a sampling of what my berserker can do. If I gave it full rein, we'd all regret it. Believe me."

Her fingers grazed the loose material of his T-shirt over his abs, sending an acute thrill of awareness rippling through his body. "I'm not advocating a complete loss of control, just a managed flow in and out of your body. Believe it or not, there is strength to be gained from the world around you. Even the mightiest tree must sink roots into the ground and blend with the earth or fear the next powerful wind."

Murdoch forced himself to breathe. How easy it was to imagine those slim fingers dancing along his bare flesh, driving him to distraction. How easy to envision hauling her against his chest and kissing her until she sighed with delight. But such thoughts were madness.

Although his thigh muscles quivered in protest at the unfamiliar movement, he retreated. Her hand dropped away, falling to her side. "Lass, I'm not a tree. I'm not even a man. Don't make the mistake of trusting me to act like one."

He met her eyes—and allowed her to see the turmoil of his efforts to control his berserker. Purposely trying to frighten her. Because the beast was raging inside, demanding to be set free, just as she encouraged. And it wanted *her*. With a tight, hot burn that begged to be satisfied.

Mine, it howled. *Mine, mine, mine.*

When her gaze dropped under the sheer intensity of his stare, as he knew it would, he turned and left the room.

Kiyoko's heart beat like that of a terrified lamb. He had tried to frighten her, and he had succeeded.

I'm not even a man.

Those words said it all. *Honest* and *brutal*, the words defined both Murdoch and his actions. No self-pity, no sorrow, and no compromise. It was difficult not to admire him for his fierce resolve and his pledge to do no harm.

But those very qualities might be her downfall.

During meditation, the potent hum of his immortal strength had stood the hairs on her body on end, but she'd been unable to tap into it. The berserker power she so desperately needed lay on the other side of a rigid wall of self-control.

Of course, Murdoch's self-control wasn't the only barrier.

Guilt also entered the mix.

She despised the necessity of tapping into his power without his explicit permission. But according to Sora, sharing her plans would force her to walk away from her role as an *onmyōji*. And while she found such a purposeless future horribly distressing, it was the knowledge that she would be slamming the door on her father's dreams for her that stung the worst. From the moment he'd read the stars at her birth, he had dedicated his life to seeing her fulfill her destiny.

Kiyoko put her hand to the silver locket around her neck.

Her father had been so certain of her future. So sure. But to fulfill her father's vision, she had to convince Murdoch to loosen the constraints on his berserker.

Kiyoko grimaced.

What sort of miracle would it take to do *that*?

Today's meditation had failed, but the sessions might still have merit in the long run, so she would continue them. And her touch to his clothed body—while not as potent as touching his skin—had definitely produced a reaction. Continued touches might eventually accustom her to his presence . . . as long as her own responses didn't get the best of her. She'd barely resisted the urge to slide her hand up his chest to the warm skin of his throat.

A dangerous desire if ever there was one.

The beast inside him was immensely powerful. Twice she'd touched his flesh, and twice a sluice of radiant energy had swept through her. It had been enough to light up every cell in her body and stir her to unprecedented life. It passed through her in a blink, followed quickly by a wave of passion almost equal in strength.

The point being, *it passed through her*.

To transcend, she would need to cultivate that power—gather it, internalize it, and build on it. No easy task.

"How did you fare?"

Kiyoko glanced at the doorway.

Sora stood there in his black robes, his arms folded into the long sleeves. *He* was confident she could do it, but then again, the old *onmyōji* was confident about everything.

"His restraint is exceptional," she said. "I could not enter his auras—let alone reach the berserker under his skin."

The elder frowned. "Did he not make a sincere attempt to become one with his world?"

"He did. But his Soul Gatherer senses are heightened, and it took only a few moments before they were overwhelmed. He was forced to stop."

"Ah. A complicated man, our Mr. Murdoch."

"Too complicated." Kiyoko sighed. "Perhaps there is some other way for me to claim my destiny, sensei."

"Perhaps," Sora allowed. "But it cannot be coincidence that your paths have crossed, not when he possesses the very power you need. Nor can it be coincidence that the Veil now binds you to a common course."

"We are not on a common course," she protested. "He seeks to take the Veil away, while I seek to keep it."

"Your larger goal is the same. You both seek to destroy evil."

Kiyoko tightened the knot of her belt. "Murdoch has no respect for the work we do. He thinks we are fools for taking on the demons."

The old man shrugged his narrow shoulders. "He knows nothing of the powers you will inherit when you transcend. Your ability to wield magic will grow tenfold, your body will heal itself when injured, and your divinations will become more precise. Perhaps even more important, you will breathe new life into the *onmyōji* warriors you lead. You will add a new layer to the legend of Abe no Seimei."

Crossing the room, Kiyoko slipped her feet into her straw thongs. "How can you be certain that my destiny is still to transcend, sensei? Is it not possible that my fate has changed since my father's death?"

"The stars are the stars, Kiyoko-san," he said, waving

her out of the meditation room ahead of him. "They say what they say. You are needed in the battle ahead."

She stepped out into the midday sun. His words were easier to believe after last night's demon raid. Despite Murdoch's fervent belief that she and her *senshi* were incompetent, they had routed a hellish beast who'd taken up residence in a Sapporo bathhouse, tainting the hot mineral waters with disease.

"Then I'd best stride forward and meet my destiny."

"You are absolutely the luckiest chick in the world," Sheila said with a heavy sigh.

Em hefted her textbooks into her other arm and dug into her pocket for her cell phone. "Why? I'm pretty sure I just flunked my English exam." She glanced down at the screen. A text from her mom. "My mom won't be here for another half hour. Want to hang in the cafeteria?"

"Um, I think you're already busy. Isn't that one of your stepdad's sword students?"

Em glanced up. Her best friend was nodding toward the front doors of the school . . . where the lean body of a young archangel slouched against the white brick wall. Uriel. "No, but you've probably seen him at the ranch. He visits us from time to time."

"Is every guy in your life the hottest thing ever?"

"I'm not sure *hot* is the right word to describe Uriel," Em said drily. Tucking her phone away, she veered left down the hall toward him, Sheila in step.

"Are you kidding? Look at him."

Em looked. And made a serious effort to see the angel from Sheila's point of view. Lanky, muscular build. Long, loose curls that hung past his shoulders. A perfect face, a faint glow of intensity, and a casual confidence most men would never attain.

Okay, yeah. Maybe he was hot. But . . .

"He's too old for you."

"So says the girl who dated a twenty-two-year-old when she was fourteen."

"I was—" *under the influence of a lure demon.* But that wasn't an explanation Sheila was ready to hear. "Infatuated. It was stupid, I admit it."

"And what about Carlos? He was seventeen."

Em swallowed tightly. Thinking about Carlos still hurt. She sensed him sometimes, vaguely, on the edge of her consciousness. A familiar, soothing presence that made her ache with loss and wonder how he was doing. But the mental walls she'd learned to put up had helped. She no longer thought about him every five seconds or cried at the drop of a dime.

"Let's not talk about Carlos."

"Sorry," Sheila said, with a sympathetic grimace. "Are you dating this Uriel?"

"No." Em snorted. "Definitely not."

"So, you could set me up, right?"

"Trust me, Sheila. You don't want a date with Uriel." The implications of that scenario were downright ugly. "He's majorly unavailable."

"Married?" Sheila asked in a whisper as they drew closer.

"To God," Em answered with a nod.

"Oh."

"Hi, Uriel," Em said in greeting to the archangel.

He straightened and smiled at Sheila.

Em made the introductions, shaking her head at the way Sheila melted when Uriel took her hand. Her friend was already half in love.

"Did you need something, Uriel?" she asked.

He nodded. "Could I have a private word?"

"Sure." Em nudged Sheila with her elbow. "I'll hook up with you in the caf."

" 'Kay." The other girl wandered off, glancing back several times, clearly reluctant.

Em wrinkled her nose at Uriel. "If you're going to drop by my school, could you be a little less glowy? And wear some different clothes?"

He glanced down at his jeans and T-shirt. "What's wrong with my clothes?"

"Nothing. That's the problem. You don't look anything like an angel. You look like a hot guy, but you're not. Cut it out."

His brow lifted. "How is an angel supposed to look?"

"Cherubic. Harmless. *Sexless*."

"I see." Amusement softened his eyes.

"Oh, never mind." Em grabbed his arm and tugged him outside to the wide cement steps. There was a cold, damp wind blowing in from the coast and most students were taking refuge indoors. "What's up? Got news on Azazel?"

"I was rather hoping *you* had news."

"Things have been pretty quiet the past couple of days. I haven't heard anything. If I had, I'd've called you. Honest." She eyed his neutral expression. "Did you talk to Michael?"

"Yes."

"And?"

"He says there's no evidence to suggest Azazel survived the flood. The horrific crimes for which he was renowned ceased at that time, and nothing of consequence has since been attributed to his name."

"Nothing of consequence?" Em pulled the hood of her red Aéropostale sweatshirt over her head, blocking out the worst of the wind. "Does that mean some things *were* attributed to him?"

"A few. But they were minor and not unique to Azazel. Seduction of innocents, excessive greed, that sort of thing."

Em tilted her head. "So, if Michael doesn't think Azazel is alive, why do you look so worried?"

He smiled faintly. "Very astute, Emily. I *am* worried. I've been thinking about the creatures of the between. There was a time—before the Great Flood—when there were only a few such creatures. That they now exist in such quantity that you can hear them is bothersome. That they fear something is even more bothersome."

"Even if it's not Azazel."

He nodded. "Even if it's not Azazel."

"What do you need me to do?" she asked, hopeful.

"Nothing yet. Just listen and report back to me as we discussed before. I'm going to investigate further."

"Are you sure you don't want me to try popping into the between to see what's going on?"

"Definitely not," he retorted. "Until we have a better sense of what's going on, I insist you remain on the middle plane. Even an immortal can suffer greatly at the hands of bone-sappers and gradiors."

Bone-sappers did exactly what it sounded like— they sapped the bone out of you. Not fun. And gradiors were zombies with a fancier name. Undead flesh eaters. Again, not fun.

"Okay." Em glanced at the glass doors of the school. "I should get back. I've got a history exam to prep for. Need anything else?"

"No, thank you." As she turned to leave, he put a hand on her sleeve. "Are you all right? You're very agreeable these days."

She tossed him a weak smile. "I'm fine. Just growing up, like everyone wants me to."

The look in his eyes said he didn't buy her explanation, but he didn't press, either. Which was a relief, because lying to an archangel would probably be a sin.

8

Delicate fingers trailed across his back and down his spine, sending a host of tiny shivers rippling to his toes. Murdoch rolled, caught her teasing hand in his, and drew it to his lips. Despite the blunt-cut nails and sword-callused palm, it was a feminine hand, half the size of his and incredibly, intriguingly soft.

Their gazes met, hers a little uncertain.

He placed her hand upon his chest, giving her the means to reject him but hoping she would not. Then he leaned in, seeking her mouth with his. She did not resist. Rather, she entered the game with enthusiasm, folding her other arm about his neck and tugging him closer.

She tasted just as he had imagined she would—a potent combination of sweet and spicy, light and firm, bold and submissive. As anticipated as that kiss was, when she opened her mouth and invited him deeper, his head swam. His blood sang and his skin grew tight and eager.

With a low groan of pleasure, he pressed her back into the pillows and took all that she offered.

His hand slipped over her hip, raked up the hem of her nightgown, and discovered a smooth expanse of tender flesh. Breathing became a challenge as he kneaded the soft satin of her skin with a desperation born of long, unbearable waiting. The damp heat between her legs and the heady scent of her arousal teased him, taunted him, spurred him. Undeniable need poured through his veins to his groin and, shuddering, he slipped his hand around the globe of her buttock to the warmth that welcomed him.

"Murdoch-san."

He tensed, resisting the cool politeness in that voice.

"Murdoch-san."

Murdoch opened his eyes. And blinked. Twice. He was alone in the bunk, surrounded by dozens of other beds, all of them empty and tidily made. He blinked again. Yoshio, the senior *onmyōji* warrior, stood over him, frowning.

Sweet Jesu, he'd been dreaming.

Possibly moaning in his sleep.

"Murdoch-san, my apologies for waking you, but the sensei has requested to meet with you," Yoshio said, glancing at the sheet over Murdoch's body, then quickly looking away.

No need to guess why.

Murdoch casually moved his hand and adjusted the sheet so his erection wasn't quite so obvious. The morning woody didn't embarrass him—hell, most men got them. The self-pleasuring didn't bother him either, even though it had been a very long time since he'd been that invested in a dream. But he was a tad concerned about what he might have mistakenly uttered while lost in his erotic fantasy. Her name, for example. That could potentially cause grief.

"Which sensei would that be?" he asked. "Yamashita-sensei or Ashida-sensei?"

The young man's gaze returned to his face. Calm, clear, and unflustered. "Yamashita-sensei."

Excellent. It didn't appear that he'd gasped Kiyoko's name in the midst of a pleasurable stroke. "Please inform him I'll be but a moment."

Murdoch rolled out of bed and snatched his duffel

bag off the floor. Remnants of the dream clung to him, leaving an ache in his chest and disappointment slurring through his body. Damn it, he could still taste her on his lips, still close his eyes and recall the fragrance of her skin in perfect detail.

It wasn't bloody fair.

Not only did he suffer the most unimaginable lust when he touched her and battle a ridiculous urge to snarl a warning to all other males whenever he saw her, but he was haunted by her in his sleep. And there wasn't any way to rid himself of the itch—acting on his desire was impossible.

Unless he was willing to risk her life.

Damn it. Hadn't he been punished enough for his decision to drink that blasted Norse potion? If he could take that moment back, he would. A thousand times.

He jerked his white T-shirt over his head.

But the moment for regret was long past. The berserker was a tightly ingrained part of him—had been for seven hundred and twenty-seven years—and he was as responsible for its actions as he was for his own. In truth, the only days he could control were the ones in front of him. If he wanted to avoid further regrets, he'd best retrieve the Veil from Kiyoko and return to California. The sooner the better.

He carefully zipped his jeans.

Yoshio led him across the courtyard to a building that Murdoch had not yet visited—a small single-level pagoda next to the main hall with a large gold, black, and red painted cabinet as its centerpiece. The doors of the cabinet were open and Sora sat cross-legged on a cushion before them, perusing a scroll spread across a low podium.

As Murdoch crossed the room, barefoot, the old man glanced up. "Sit, please." He waved a thin hand at a second cushion, then returned his gaze to his studies.

"I prefer to remain standing."

Sora lifted his eyes again. "That would be most impolite, Mr. Murdoch. *I* am sitting. Would it truly trouble you to sit for a moment while I finish what I'm doing?"

No, sitting wouldn't trouble him. But having the old man take him to task for being impolite most definitely did. He dropped to his knees on the cushion, smoothly but reluctantly. "You need to convince Kiyoko to give me the Veil."

"You are concerned for its safety."

"Aye." And for Kiyoko's safety. But explaining why was not a conversation he wanted to start.

"I understand."

But Sora didn't volunteer to do anything about it. Just ran his finger over a series of intricate drawings painted on his scroll, then glanced at a calendar and frowned. Murdoch held back a pained sigh. "I've already been here longer than I'd planned. I need to get back to the United States. She listens to you. I'm certain she'd give me the Veil if you pointed out the wisdom of doing so."

"That may be true."

Again, no offer to help. "Will you tell her to give it to me?"

"The issue of the Veil will sort itself out in good time." Sora slid two pieces of wood off the scroll and allowed it to roll back up. "I'm curious about your role as a Soul Gatherer, Mr. Murdoch. Will you indulge me by answering a few questions?"

"No."

The elder glanced up. "I beg your pardon?"

"I said no. I'm not interested in answering a bunch of damned questions. Not without some assurance that you'll help me obtain my goal."

Buried in the depths of Sora's calm gaze was a glint of something hard. "And I'm not interested in helping you obtain your goal without knowing more about you and your motivations."

Hell and damnation.

It was a reasonable request. *He* wouldn't hand over a valuable relic to someone he knew nothing about, either. It would be a lot easier to capitulate if the old man weren't so bloody annoying, though.

"Fine," he said. "I'll answer a few questions. But first, I've got one of my own."

Sora spread his hands wide. "Ask."

"If I satisfy you that my credentials are genuine, will you help me convince Kiyoko to give up the Veil?"

He shook his head. "I would recommend she keep it."

"Even when you know that every moment she holds on to it endangers her? Why?"

"Why are you so certain she in danger?"

"Because I've seen the lengths Satan is willing to go to acquire these relics and increase his power. He's not sending callow, inexperienced demons to seek them out. He's sending his most formidable warriors. None of whom have been easy to defeat, by the way, even by immortal standards. Even with an army of ninjas at her back, Kiyoko doesn't have the strength to withstand such an assault."

"Kiyoko-san is unique."

Murdoch nodded. "Sure, she's a gifted swordsman. I admit that. But those skills won't be enough. Defeating a couple of pith demons who steal souls is not the same as defeating a martial demon capable of demolishing buildings. Or a lure demon capable of twisting your very thoughts."

The old man set aside the scroll and moved the podium, then rose to his feet in a dignified flow of limbs. His robes never once revealed more than a socked toe. "She is the only one in a millennium to display equal mastery of the martial arts, the mystic arts, and divination. The only one born with the true promise of her ancestors."

Murdoch sighed. "Look, I'd be the first to acknowledge that the woman is bloody marvelous. But she's human, damn it. She can die. Far too easily, as far as I'm concerned."

"Which brings us full circle," the old man said. "I know you are Death's servant, that you owe her your allegiance and your obeisance. I presume that means you are here to collect a soul. Whose?"

A ripple of displeasure ran down Murdoch's spine at the word *servant*. "I am no one's servant. I gather souls, as is my duty, but I do not blindly follow orders."

Sora frowned. "Does that mean you can refuse to collect a soul marked by Death?"

"No. If she places her helix upon someone's cheek, then the fate of that soul has been decided—a fate I can neither change nor deny. But I do not answer only to Death. I also answer to my conscience. And that leads me to further my own tasks, such as keeping dark relics out of Satan's hands." Murdoch pushed to his feet, now towering over the old sensei. "I am not here on a mission for Death."

"Does she know that you are here?"

Murdoch grimaced. "Without a doubt."

"Then she supports the protection of these relics?"

"*Supports* is too strong a word," Murdoch said drily. "*Condones* would be closer to the truth."

"Until such time as it interferes with her own ambitions."

Murdoch skewed a glance at the old man. "Aye, that's probably accurate."

Sora turned and shut the doors on the painted cabinet. "Thank you for your honest and helpful responses, Mr. Murdoch. I'll offer this in return: Help Kiyoko-san understand your berserker and you'll make it easier for her to give up the Veil."

Murdoch frowned. "I'll tell her what I know, but I do not fully understand the beast myself. The potion I drank was the instrument of a Norse god."

Sora nodded. "Odin, the god of war. I've read several accounts of his soldiers having such skills. Fear not—Kiyoko's interest lies less in the origins of the berserker than in how it manifests inside you."

"Why does she need that information?"

"She's on a personal journey."

"A journey? What does that mean? Can you never just answer a question with a simple truth?" Murdoch demanded, exasperated. "Does everything need to be a bloody riddle?"

"Calm is a virtue, Mr. Murdoch," Sora admonished.

"So is being direct. Answer the question. Why does Kiyoko need to know anything about my berserker?"

"I should think that is obvious." Sora tucked his hands into his long sleeves. "Based on the way she's able to instantly call your berserker to the surface, it's clear that she and it have a common destiny."

She and *it*? "That's ridiculous."

Sora shrugged. "I believe that Kiyoko-san is the lake of tranquillity needed to balance your berserker's existence."

Tranquillity? Was the man mad? When the two of them touched, anything resembling tranquillity flew right out the window. For both of them. Kiyoko felt exactly the same sensations he did. He'd stake his very existence on it. But she'd clearly never mentioned her hot, sweaty, and totally stirred-up feelings to her revered mentor.

Maybe he should set the record straight.

*   *   *

Kiyoko knew the instant Murdoch entered the meditation hall. Not because he made any noise. Just the opposite—the silence in the room deepened. Perhaps his body blocked the wind at the door, or perhaps his weight upon the floor silenced the faint creaks of the building. Whatever the cause, the quiet grew.

"Come in, Murdoch," she encouraged, without lifting her eyes. "I hope you dressed comfortably. After meditation, I thought we'd take a run outside the compound."

He crossed the room and without a word dropped to the cushion in front of her. As usual, his legs were encased in black jeans and when he knelt, the material pulled snug over the heavy sinews of his thighs. Kiyoko tried not to notice.

But the dreams that had tormented her all night did not make it easy.

He cupped his hands together and made a perfect oval with his thumbs. "I just had a little heart-to-heart with Sora-san."

The gentle rumble of his accent sent a thrill over her skin. The deep roll of his *r*'s evoked a rush of vivid memory. In her dream, he had groaned when she clutched at the long locks of his hair and opened her mouth to his kiss. Deep and guttural, a perfect reflection of satisfaction.

"Oh?" she responded, more breathless than she'd planned.

A brief pause. "Are you all right?"

"I'm fine."

Nothing a peaceful meditation and a run through the forest wouldn't cure. She let go of the memory, settled her breathing, and sought the serenity of blending her being with the world around her.

"He has no clue about the raging-hot desire, does he?"

Her eyes flew up to meet his. And a furious blush rose

in her cheeks as a myriad of dreamy details escaped the tethers of her mind. The rough texture of his callused hands on her buttocks, the hungry demand of his lips on hers, the unbearable tension in her belly. "What?"

He stared at her. His brows furrowed.

She licked her lips, which were suddenly dry, and his gaze dropped to them briefly before returning to her eyes.

"Why are you blushing?"

"I'm not used to talking about *raging-hot desire* with a man I barely know," she said. The blush deepened with her lie. If he only knew where her imagination had taken her this morning . . .

He leaned closer. "It's more than that."

She lowered her eyes to avoid the perceptive intensity of his. "I hope you didn't take it upon yourself to educate Sora-sensei."

"You can barely look at me. Why?"

"I've already explained why. We should focus on our meditation. Lower your gaze, Murdoch."

For a moment she thought she had succeeded in diverting him. But then he murmured, "I don't know about you, but I didn't sleep very well last night. Crazy dreams. I was in the middle of a truly wicked one when Yoshio woke me."

Kiyoko's breath snagged in her throat. *No.* Surely not.

"This will be a good test of your concentration, then," she said, resisting the urge to look up. "See if you can put your difficult night behind you and bring peace to your thoughts."

"Did I imply my night was difficult? My apologies. Nothing could be further from the truth. The dreams were very enjoyable. So enjoyable that I resented being woken."

Kiyoko swallowed.

The same was true for her. She still felt cheated. The dream had seemed so blissfully real that when she woke alone, she had actually shed a tear. Just one. "You are not giving this exercise your full attention, Murdoch. Pay attention to your breathing."

"I'd rather pay attention to yours."

This time she did not succeed in taming her gaze. Her eyes lifted. And the smoldering heat in his eyes nearly bowled her over. "You are creating complications that will not serve either of us well. Inner peace comes from stemming your desires and embracing simplicity."

He continued to speak as if he had not heard her. "You know what's strange? I'd swear that everything in my dream was real. Not a single detail was wrong." Closing his eyes, he leaned toward her hair and breathed deep. "Not one."

Kiyoko relaxed a little.

Perhaps he hadn't had the same dream as she, after all. Because hers had gone far beyond the superficial. She had discovered several things about Murdoch that were currently hidden beneath a layer of demure clothing. There was no way to know if the muscles on his back were truly as toned as they had appeared, or whether there was actually a thick white scar on his left shoulder blade.

"That's not the proper breathing technique," she coached. "Pull each breath into your belly."

"Every nuance of your scent, every glisten of light in your hair, every shadowy curve of your flesh is accurate."

Her heart tripped and stumbled. *Flesh?* How much flesh?

"You dreamed of me?" she asked, aiming for an appropriately scandalized note. In truth, a bead of warm pleasure burst in her chest. His description of her was almost poetic.

"Aye."

He didn't sit back, just opened his eyes. And explored her face in slow, steamy detail. As if there were some secret hidden in her features that he must puzzle out.

"As I said, it was a very enjoyable dream."

He was close enough that Kiyoko could have touched him. Rubbed her thumb over his bottom lip, as she had done in the dream. If only she dared to bridge the four-inch gap between them, she could confirm whether the taste of his lips ran as true to her fantasy as his enticing scent—soapy freshness blended with hints of male musk and leather.

But, of course, that was impossible. One moment of contact and the fantasy would come to an abrupt end. There would be no kiss, no groan, no caress. Just a quick descent into berserker rage and a dash for the door.

Kiyoko grimaced.

Murdoch was a test of her commitment.

"I'm happy that I was able to please you. Now sit back and relax, Murdoch."

He smiled, a slow bloom of wry amusement. "More tease than please, I'm afraid. The dream didn't last nearly long enough."

She favored him with her best imitation of a cool stare. "If this is the extent of your self-discipline, I admit to being disappointed. For some reason, I assumed a man of your sword skills would have more willpower."

The insult rolled off him without denting his smile. "I've decided self-discipline is overrated. Stamina is a better quality in a warrior. I pride myself on having the strength and endurance to last the full stretch of battle and not fall short of victory."

Kiyoko nearly choked.

Even though English was her second language, it was impossible to miss his underlying meaning. *Arrogant* didn't even begin to describe the man.

"Did you come here to talk or to train, Murdoch? If

talk is your goal, I suggest you return to the main hall and seek out one of the other *senshi*. If improving your skills is your aim, you must apply yourself."

He sat back. "Talk is merely a diversion, and I can train anywhere, at any time. I came here to be with you."

It was difficult to find fault with such blunt honesty.

"Then please adhere to my conditions for remaining," she said. "Put your all into the training, or find some other way to while away the hours."

"As you wish."

Without further quarrel, he lowered his eyes and resumed the proper physical alignment.

Kiyoko studied him for a moment, admiring the width of his brow and the strong angle of his chin. Then she, too, settled into a peaceful pose.

Sifting through Kiyoko's thoughts was not as easy as Azazel had hoped.

This was her second visit to the cottage, and he still didn't have the information he wanted. He pushed away from the table and studied his handiwork. The will-sap spell wasn't the problem. Her eyes were blank, the corporate reports forgotten. She responded eagerly to his every command. She would offer up the balance of her bank account if he were to ask. But her responses to his questions about the Veil were decidedly vague and unhelpful.

Someone, perhaps even Kiyoko herself, had put a memory charm on her.

And thus far, no amount of mystical pushing, pulling, or shaking had broken it.

He snatched her pen from her nerveless fingers, closing his fist tightly around the cylinder. Tighter, until he felt the soft metal give. Then tighter still. He crushed the engraved writing implement into a mangled metal ball, then threw it across the room. If he didn't need Kiyoko's skills as a yin-yang master to unlock the dark side of the Veil, he'd kill her right now.

Bitch.

Apparently, locating the Veil would require a more creative solution. A back door, if you will. She had information inside that pretty little head that would aid him. No doubt of that. It was simply a matter of asking the right questions and using the right amount of force.

Murdoch's patience was near its end.

Since querying the *senshi* had not turned up any clues to the whereabouts of the Veil, and Sora had refused to order Kiyoko to hand it over, inspecting her jewelry was the obvious next step. But he preferred to borrow the items without her knowledge, and that required excellent timing and a very careful touch.

Unfortunately, he was a little short on steadiness. Thanks to a second straight night of heated dreams, the tension in his body had reached a fever pitch. He could barely lift a bottle of ale to his lips without spilling half the contents.

Working up a sweat in the outdoor exercise yard helped to dissipate some of the harrowing frustration, so he spent a good portion of his spare time there. Umiko had miraculously procured loose navy track pants and a pair of canvas trainers, both in his size. She had delivered them to him yesterday with a case of Sapporo ale, thereby becoming one of his favorite people in the world, her dragonlike protection of her mistress notwithstanding.

"Mr. Murdoch?"

He lowered his sword and pivoted.

There before him, resplendent in a sharply tailored dark gray suit, white shirt, and blue-striped tie, was Ryuji Watanabe. Smiling. Friendly. Even faintly admiring.

"Aye?"

"Pardon my interruption, but I wondered if you might have seen Kiyoko-san this morning? She and I were to review the fixed-assets report at nine, but she did not meet me as planned."

"Perhaps she recalled that it was Sunday and decided to take a break," Murdoch suggested nicely. One of the primary assults on his patience was the endless time she spent with Watanabe, poring over corporate financial data.

"Perhaps," Watanabe said with a rueful smile. "But it was her idea to work today, not mine. The incident with Takeo has heightened her fears that the company might fall prey to betrayal from within. I take it you haven't seen her?"

"No."

"Since I appear to have some free time," Watanabe said, "would you care to join me for a coffee? I acquired a taste for Starbucks when I lived in Boston, and I've brewed a pot in my cottage."

Murdoch glanced down at his damp and wrinkled T-shirt. "Regrettably, I'm in sore need of a shower before I contemplate socializing."

"I understand. Would it offend your sensibilities if I remain here to watch you practice? Your sword and cutting techniques are different from those of the others. Very elegant and, judging by the hum of the air as your blade passes, deceptively powerful."

It was damned hard to hate a man who plied you with compliments.

"Have you studied the sword yourself?" Murdoch asked, as he moved smoothly from ox guard to cross strike and back to ox guard.

"No," said Watanabe with a short laugh. "A few obligatory lessons in kendo are all I can claim. I'm much more formidable with a pen."

Or a man who feels no shame in admitting his limits.

Damn him.

"Yoshio mentioned that Kiyoko went for a run a half hour ago," Murdoch offered grudgingly. "She should return shortly."

"Excellent. I'll be able to reschedule our meeting." Watanabe pointed to Murdoch's weapon. "Is this a Scottish blade? The design on the hilt appears to be some sort of knot work."

Murdoch held the blade out so the other man could view it better. "No, it's Norse. A Viking blade forged in the thirteenth century."

Watanabe's eyebrows lifted. "And it's still usable? I would have thought such an old blade would be severely worn."

"It's been treated well," Murdoch said. "Regularly cleaned and oiled, and never permitted to rust. It's still in excellent shape."

"But not as strong as a blade made from today's modern steel composites, I should imagine."

Murdoch nodded. "You know your metals."

Watanabe shrugged. "In addition to the food products for which we are most renowned, Ashida Corporation manufactures home appliances. One of our more profitable divisions."

"Have you worked for the company long?"

"Only a year." The Japanese man's gaze slid left, to the figure of Yoshio, who had stopped his own training to watch Murdoch. When the young warrior realized he'd been noticed, he bowed to Watanabe and resumed his sparring with another *senshi*. "Kiyoko's father hired me away from a major competitor with the specific goal of having me replace him one day. Little did we know that *one day* would arrive so soon."

Murdoch gave Watanabe's unlined face a second look. Japanese executives tended to be older, more seasoned. "How old are you?"

"Forty-three. It was an honor for the board to name me as president. Were it not for my relevant experience and the wishes of Tatsu Ashida, I'm certain the position would have gone to another."

While Watanabe excused his embarrassing youth, Murdoch mulled over the man's maturity. Forty-three would make him at least fifteen years older than Kiyoko, a rather large age gap. Perhaps his jealousy of the man was unwarranted.

"Kiyoko's father took me under his wing and treated me as the son he never had. He had hoped that Kiyoko and I would wed, so that the company could remain in the family."

Or not.

Murdoch did a lunge thrust into open air. It was only partially successful in distracting his grumpy berserker. "Did he express that wish to Kiyoko?"

"Yes," Watanabe said. "But his desire may not be hers, and I'm not interested in a loveless marriage. I have not mentioned it since her father died."

Watanabe was a better man than he. Were it not for the disastrous effects of their touch, Murdoch would have long since coaxed Kiyoko into some quiet place in the wood to convince her of his interest.

He straightened.

Not that he had marriage on his mind. The whole *I'm not aging but you are* issue was guaranteed to sever even the most heartfelt bond.

His peripheral vision caught the inward swing of the east gate. Kiyoko entered the compound dressed in her typical white gi, hair queued at her nape, a sheen of sweat upon her brow.

"I have no right to ask it of you, Murdoch-san, but I would appreciate if you kept the last part of our discussion to yourself," Watanabe murmured, as Kiyoko approached at a jog.

Mention that his competitor for her attentions was offering the permanence and stability of marriage when he could not? Not bloody likely. "She'll not hear it from my lips. You have my word."

"Thank you."

Kiyoko jogged over to them, her gaze on Watanabe's face. Clearly remorseful, she placed a hand on his sleeve, pale against the dark material. "Ryuji-san, my sincere apologies. I am most embarrassed to have forgotten our meeting this morning."

It was a completely innocent touch. Nothing sexual about it at all. But that didn't stop Murdoch's blood from heating with his berserker's jealous fury. His fingers tightened on the leather grip of his sword. There was nothing he desired more than to remove Kiyoko's hand from Watanabe's sleeve, but instead, drawing deeply on his warrior discipline, he ever so gently slid his sword back into the scabbard belted at his waist.

His mission was the relic, not the woman.

9

The dreams were taking their toll. Kiyoko had never forgotten a meeting before, especially one she set up herself. But she'd tossed and turned all night, woken up in an agitated state, and desperately sought a run through the woods. Anything to cool the racy thoughts of Murdoch that continued to provoke her.

And it had worked. Only moments after she exited the compound and began her run, her years of training reasserted themselves and she slipped into a state of supreme awareness and inner tranquillity. The whisper of the wind through the branches, the scent of pine in the air, and the firm press of her feet against the give of the earth became her world for a time.

One glimpse of the damp T-shirt clinging to Murdoch's chest and arms, and her serenity was lost, though.

"I hope you can forgive my lapse," she said to Ryuji.

"Think nothing of it," he responded. "We can easily reschedule. And it *is* Sunday. Perhaps you should take a break."

"Great idea," Murdoch said quietly.

"Actually, it's not," she rebutted. She needed to find a way to defuse the sexual tension between them. And she needed to do it swiftly. "Meditation with Murdoch is a much better idea. Ryuji-san, I would be most grateful if we could postpone our review session until later this afternoon. Perhaps four or four thirty?"

A flicker of irritation passed over Watanabe's face, then was gone. "Of course. I've got some telephone calls to make anyway." He bowed to them both and then departed, circling the bell tower pagoda to reach the west gate.

Gathering her courage, Kiyoko faced Murdoch. "We could both use a wash and a fresh set of clothes before we start."

He crooked a smile at her. "Shall we do it together?"

"No," she said, taking a step back. That smile was altogether too charming. "Definitely not. Meet me in front of the meditation hall in fifteen minutes."

"Fifteen minutes," he agreed.

Kiyoko was actually ready in twelve. Rather than return to the house, she used the communal basin behind the main hall to wash and swapped her running attire for a clean jacket and wide-legged *hakama* pants in the dojo. Despite her speed, Murdoch was already waiting for her when she arrived at the meditation hall. He wore his standard jeans and T-shirt, his leather jacket abandoned. His brown hair hung in wet waves, as if he'd miraculously found the time to wash it.

"Are you certain you want to try this again?" he asked. "We haven't had much success so far."

"Only because you allow yourself to be distracted."

"Aye," he agreed. "I find it infinitely appealing to consider the many things I could be doing alone with you in a small room other than breathing."

She shook her head. "Which is why we will not be going inside. We will be practicing walking meditation today. Same upright posture, same cupping of hands, but instead of sitting, we will walk clockwise around the courtyard. You will go first, I will follow."

Murdoch folded his arms over his chest. "And to think I put cologne on for this."

"You did?"

"I did." He tipped his head up and leaned in, presenting his tanned throat to her nose. "Smell."

She *did* smell the scent. A deep, warm draft of citrus and spice. He was so close, it was impossible not to. "Why?"

"To attract females. Or to be more blunt, one female."

She blinked. "Me?"

"Aye, you."

"Then you made a miscalculation. Turn south, please."

He frowned. "What miscalculation?"

She pointed. "Face the main gate, Murdoch."

After studying her resolute expression for a narrow-eyed moment, he turned. "What miscalculation?"

"I prefer the way you smell *without* the cologne. Walk."

"I'll remember that." Pulling himself to the full measure of his six-foot-five frame, he stepped forward. An unhurried pace, with nice even footfalls. "Where is everyone?"

Kiyoko followed him, admiring the surprising grace of his large body.

"In the dojo, performing *kenjutsu* kata—formal practice moves done with wooden swords." His shoulders were very broad. She could see nothing past him. "Enough chatter, Murdoch. This is meditation, not conversation. Pay attention to your breathing and to your steps. Feel your heel, sole, and toes connect with the ground and then lift off. Be aware of the courtyard. The grass, the gravel, the air. Experience the walk with your full body and mind—the beauty and simplicity of each step. Your mind should not wander, but if it does, bring it back to your steps and your breathing."

For once, he behaved.

In less than half a turn of the courtyard, they had both settled into a calm, easy awareness. Kiyoko waited until the color of Murdoch's auras shifted from orangey-red to a gentle violet before making another attempt to breach his wall of self-control and reach his berserker. Since none of her previous attempts had met with success, she altered her approach.

Instead of trying to blend the broad edges of their auras, she narrowed her focus to the bluest spot she could find. Surely the most peaceful place would also be the most open place?

But it was as firmly locked as the rest of his auras.

She could sense the coil of his berserker beneath, but could not access more than the first few inches of his auras before colliding with his wall of self-control.

Frustration bubbled, but she forced it to fall away.

Murdoch had good reason to build such a formidable wall, and he'd had several hundred years to perfect it. Hardly any wonder that she was unable to breach it after only a few days. Time and effort would eventually reveal a way in, but the thought of subjecting herself to weeks of this intense sexual teasing was unbearable.

They walked quietly around the courtyard for twenty minutes before Kiyoko gave up. With a sigh, she halted next to the fish pond and its softly trickling water structure. The courtyard was still empty.

"Enough, Murdoch."

He stopped and turned. "That sounded almost final."

A silvery white koi swam leisurely around the edge of the pool, its long, flowing fins and tail sweeping through the water. "You never quite give your all to the meditation. You continue to hold a piece back. I'm not sure how much value the practice is giving you."

"You know why I can't let go completely."

She nodded. "I do. But I also know that until you can

embrace the whole of who you are, until you and your berserker are one, you will never find real peace."

"You don't understand the horrors it's capable of."

It. The word hung there, cool and empty, a perfect opening. She took a deep breath and dove in. "You mean the horrors *you* are capable of."

His face darkened. "I am not it, and it is not me."

"You're wrong. We are all a balance of dark and light, Murdoch, even you. You prefer to box up your dark side, shunt it aside as if it's some strange, untamed creature trapped inside you, but in reality, it is half of who you are."

"Bollocks." Hands fisted, he took a step across the gravel toward her, then halted. "I was a whole man before I drank the potion. A weak, sickly man with the blurry vision of a cow, perhaps, but a whole one. After I drank the potion, I could feel the berserker inside me, writhing like a snake, threatening to choke out my honor and my pride. It. Is. Not. Me."

Kiyoko chewed her lip. His auras were pulsing now, dark red coiling around the blue like the snake he just described, smothering. Should she push him further? Or play it safe and stop?

"And where is that weak, sickly man now, Murdoch?" she asked softly.

The muscles of his jaw hardened until they resembled bone. "Don't. Don't begin to suggest that the man I was is gone. He is the only thing keeping the beast inside me in check."

"I'm not suggesting he's gone. I'm suggesting that you cannot separate the two beings as easily as you like to believe. You are strong, healthy, and gifted with better eyesight, all courtesy of that *beast* within you. How can you deny that the two sides united form a better whole? Let go. Embrace both sides of your personality."

The gap between Murdoch and her disappeared in

a single stride. He grabbed her shoulders with rough hands, shoved her back until she collided with the wall of the ceremonial hall, and ground out, "Are you certain you want me to open the cage, Kiyoko? Because the beast wants out. And he wants something you're not prepared to give him."

She met his gaze, fearful but ready. "It's not your berserker who wants me with that terrifying intensity. It's you, Murdoch. There is no separate entity. If you want to kiss me, then kiss me."

It was a huge risk to challenge him. Even if Murdoch accepted that his berserker was truly him, it would take a tremendous amount of self-knowledge and self-discipline to balance such a fierce duality. He might not be able to stop. Judging from the play of furious emotions on his face, he was already very close to losing control.

"Honor and courage and intelligence are as much a part of you as the strength and health of the berserker," she added. "You have the ability to walk away, if you so choose. It *is* a choice, Murdoch. Your choice."

His gaze drilled into hers.

Kiyoko returned his stare, left breathless by the cocoon of his body heat and the sheer force of his masculinity.

A pause settled on the world. The sounds from the dojo faded into obscurity and the air grew still with anticipation. The searing heat of his clenched hands seeped through her jacket as he continued to pin her against the building. There was a long moment when Kiyoko wasn't sure which route he would take.

But she knew the instant he decided.

Her heart felt like it would burst from her chest.

He was going to kiss her.

Murdoch ignored the voice in his head. The one that reminded him of his long and brutal history with the berserker, the one that kept insisting that history repeated itself because of stupid decisions like the one he was about to make.

He let his eyelids drop.

His focus narrowed to Kiyoko's mouth. Currently unadorned by lipstick, her lips were parted slightly. As her breath passed raggedly between them, the full lower lip trembled faintly. It wasn't fear, he was certain of that. She had goaded him to this point on purpose, pushed him to the brink of sanity for a reason.

She wanted this kiss as badly as he did.

And just like that, he surrendered. Because as much as his conscience told him there was no hope, he wanted her words to be true. He wanted to own the beast inside him, to have the power to tame it. He wanted to end the senseless destruction and the careless acts of violence.

He wanted *her*.

He wanted every dream he'd enjoyed over the past few days to be possible, to be real.

The grip of his hands on her slim shoulders eased and he bent his head to hers. Slowly, savoring every delicious sensation. The soft heat of her breath on his skin, the subtle feminine scent that was just her, the minute adjustment she made to the tilt of her head to give him better access. He memorized it all.

Because there was no telling how much he'd remember once he actually touched her.

He hovered a millimeter from her lips.

Lord, she was lovely. Since his arrival at the dojo, he'd become quite adept at turning a blind eye to the details of her appearance. A form of self-preservation, perhaps. He'd made a concerted effort to see only the competent martial artist, the serene monklike *onmyōji*, the intelligent young businesswoman.

But this close, her beauty overwhelmed him.

The delicate oval of her face. The bright, clear eyes. The lustrous shine of her smooth black hair.

Damn. He wanted her so badly, his balls ached.

But kissing her was a horrible risk. Maybe he could control his berserker. Maybe it would all turn out okay. But if he went solely on experience, on the very real mistakes he'd made in the past, more likely he couldn't.

He dropped his hands from her shoulders, but did not step away. He couldn't. His damned feet refused to budge.

Fearing a loss of his resolve, he closed his eyes to her beautiful face. There was something thoroughly unjust in knowing the one person he wanted most would forever be off-limits, forever outside his grasp.

He sighed . . .

. . . and she captured his breath with her mouth. She pressed her velvet-soft lips to his and gave him a gift he had no right to claim—an eager, inviting kiss.

Every nerve ending in his body exploded with pleasure, overwhelmed and at the same time begging for more. A wave of heat rolled over him, leaving beads of sweat in its wake, and the walls of his self-control came crashing down. His hands snatched her to his chest, crushing her soft body against his hardness in response to some primitive need he could not name.

But hot on the heels of pleasure came the beast. Murdoch felt it claw up his chest, choking him, cloaking him, and he made every effort to rein it in.

No. Not *it. Him.*

Kiyoko flung her arms about his neck, fueling the bonfire of his need and inviting his berserker to take the lead. The familiar red mist clouded his vision, and his muscles expanded until the material of his T-shirt stretched taut and the waistband of his jeans dug into his flesh.

Murdoch sucked in a shuddering breath.

Hurting Kiyoko was the last thing he desired. If his berserker was truly a facet of his self and not some foreign creature, he should be able to step away. All he had to do was own the beast. Claim it. Assert his dominance over it and . . .

Let Kiyoko go. Release her.

His hold on her gentled, and a swell of pride rose in Murdoch's chest. He was in control.

Unfortunately, the moment was short-lived.

Kiyoko's hips ground against his in needy abandon, and his head swam. A low growl rumbled in his chest and his big hands yanked her body off the ground. He deepened the kiss to bruising force. The berserker wanted more, so much more. It howled inside him, spinning like a tornado in his gut, demanding the last constraints be dropped. Kiyoko whimpered faintly under his assault and a rumble of feral satisfaction rose in his throat.

Murdoch held on, desperately struggling to keep his head above a rising tide of beastly desire.

Open your hands and let her go. You can do it, Murdoch. Just—

His berserker froze in taut awareness, sensing danger. A missile sang through the air, breached his shield, and burrowed deep in his right shoulder. Dull pain accompanied it—barely enough to make him flinch, but more than enough to prod the beast into unmitigated rage.

Instinct took over.

In a blink, any pretense of containing the power coursing through him fell away. Murdoch was yanked below the surface in one sharp tug of a mighty dark fist.

Kiyoko felt Murdoch jerk and then shudder.

His lips left hers, and a snarl of undisguised fury seared her face before he released her and spun around. Breathless and weak-kneed from his kisses—and her own equally powerful desires—she fell back against the wooden wall. She couldn't see around his body, but she had a very good idea what faced him. A small army of *onmyōji* warriors.

The dojo was silent.

Indeed, the entire compound had an air of quiet purpose.

And there was an arrow protruding from Murdoch's right shoulder. An arrow fletched with the black wing feathers of a golden eagle—feathers Sora had painstakingly collected from a nest at the summit of a mountain aerie.

Murdoch drew his sword with a silky rasp of steel. Lost to his ancient and primal berserker, he presented his back to her with no regard for her ability to deal him damage. Rather, his stance was protective, his body forming a sizable barrier, ready to stop any and all intruders.

Kiyoko was not insulted.

There was something oddly sweet about his determination to keep her from harm. But she couldn't dwell on it. His impenetrable wall of self-control was gone, and the savage pulse of his berserker lay right on the surface, unrestrained. It would require a large outlay of energy, but this was an opportunity that might not soon come again. There was no better time to steal into his auras.

She cupped her hands in meditative repose, stared at the twin rows of silver rivets on Murdoch's black leather belt, and ruthlessly tamed her ragged breaths into an even flow. Spurred by the tentative nature of the opportunity, she quickly settled into deep meditation—intensely aware of the brewing battle in the courtyard, yet neither frightened nor roused to anger by it.

His auras were a sight to behold.

A moil of red so dark it was almost black, surrounded by a thin shell of glowing gold.

Even though she'd been blessed with an ability to see auras from birth, Kiyoko had never seen the like of these. Most people's auras were a blend of colors, with the most dominant hue suggesting an overall state of being. Murdoch's were uniquely focused. They brought to mind a red and black dragon spitting golden fire. A fanciful thought, perhaps, but a surprisingly effective description.

And the image caused her to hesitate.

But only for a moment.

She extended her auras slowly toward Murdoch, the throb of power emanating from his body so intense it lifted the hairs on her arms. That feeling was familiar. But the stinging burn she experienced as she drew closer was not. Unfettered, his energy radiated outward with the strength of a thousand bonfires, frying the fringes of her auras. As the berserker gained more control, the wall around Murdoch's inner thoughts weakened and then crumbled. She caught flashes of memories—glimpses of battles he'd fought, lives he'd saved, and promises he'd upheld. Even as he scorched her, he won her admiration.

Flatten yourself upon the ground, Kiyoko-san.

The silent message from Sora entered her mind at the precise moment the thirty-two warriors in the courtyard shifted their stances. From readiness to attack.

Alarm tore through her.

And Murdoch reacted to her fear as if he could feel it. He released a savage roar that shook the wall at her back and reverberated in her chest like a clap of thunder. His sword arm swung, the blade whistled, and Sora bled.

"No!"

Panicked, Kiyoko tried to dive under Murdoch's arm and rush to her mentor's side. But the berserker-possessed Soul Gatherer would have none of it. His elbow plowed into her gut, sending her flying back against the ceremonial hall. She hit hard, slumping to her knees, dazed and bruised.

Another threatening roar rattled the buildings in the compound, this one aimed as much at her as at the warriors surrounding him, an underscoring of his primitive claim. What was it Murdoch had once said? *What I own, I keep.*

"You don't own me, you dim-witted bear," she muttered, rising to her feet. "And you're about to learn that you shouldn't turn your back on me."

She tugged her katana free of its scabbard.

But she never got a chance to wield it. Murdoch took a large lurching step back and slammed her against the wall again, knocking the weapon from her grasp. At first she thought it was a strategic if somewhat frustrating move on his part, but as the weight of his body settled upon her with increasing force, doubt formed. The crush of his rock-hard body on her chest prevented her from breathing. And when he stumbled and fell on her, she knew for certain it was unintentional. Even as a berserker, he would never purposely hurt her.

Awareness of her predicament came too late for her to raise a protective shield. The sudden collapse of his full weight atop her and the subsequent three-foot drop to the ground broke ribs. She heard them snap. *Felt* them snap.

Biting her lip against the sharp pain, she pushed at his huge body, trying to free herself. But he was completely limp, and she, crammed awkwardly against the building, was unable to shift him. His muscles were larger as a berserker. Was his weight increased, too? It certainly seemed so.

One small miracle—they hadn't landed on her katana. The sword had rolled to the left when it hit the ground, but she couldn't see it. She couldn't see much of anything, truth be told. Except Murdoch's hair, his bloodstained T-shirt, and increasing numbers of black spots.

It would be rather unfortunate to die suffocated beneath Murdoch's body. Not quite the illustrious future Sora had hoped she would enjoy.

Sora. Was he alive?

Kiyoko's chest burned, her lungs demanding air. She opened her mouth and sucked hard, but got nothing. The black spots threatened to overwhelm her vision. Using her last tendrils of consciousness, she extended her auras, searching for the old sensei. She found Murdoch, his auras slowly returning to a calmer violet. Reaching farther, she found Yoshio and several other warriors, all pale blue. But no Sora.

She withdrew, drained and dizzy.

If he was gone, the blame would lie with her. She had taunted Murdoch to the brink of his self-control, blatantly encouraging his berserker to surface.

The black was a swirling sea now.

Kiyoko fought to stay conscious, hoping that at any moment Yoshio and the others would pull Murdoch off and save her. But the battle proved difficult. Her limbs grew cold and heavy. Weariness filled every muscle, and her eyes drifted shut.

If she didn't do something swiftly, she would die.

A pointless, pathetic death.

She weakly extended her auras once again, not far this time. Just to the edges of Murdoch's gently pulsing energy. With her last conscious thought, she sent a silent whisper into his being.

Roll over. Please.

Then the sea picked her up and swept her into the darkness.

10

Murdoch woke up with his face mashed into the grass, a mouthful of dirt coating his tongue. The most excruciating headache he'd ever had the misfortune to endure throbbed inside his skull, and spitting out the dirt only made the pain worse.

He actually felt queasy.

Sitting up, he rubbed his shoulder, which also throbbed.

His shirt was hard and crusty beneath his fingers, and a thick scab had formed on the skin below it. Narrowing his eyes to filter out the annoyingly bright sunlight, he spied an arrow on the ground.

Someone had shot him.

Who, he couldn't recall.

He picked up the arrow and studied it. Had to be a mystically enhanced arrow—nothing else could have pierced his skin, not while he was in berserker mode. And he *had* been in berserker mode, that much he knew. Because he remembered every one of those last moments before the beast swallowed him up—the incredible feel of Kiyoko in his arms and the sweet press of her lips against his.

He glanced at the wall of the ceremonial hall.

She was gone. In fact, the courtyard was completely

empty . . . except for her discarded katana, lying a few feet away on the gravel.

He frowned.

Kiyoko, like anyone who bet her life on the quality of her blade, usually took great care of her weapons. Leaving her prized blade exposed to the elements was out of character. Such carelessness implied distraction. But what sort of distraction? If she had drawn her weapon to fend him off, which seemed logical, what would make her toss it aside? The quantity of scuff marks in the gravel around him suggested the confrontation had expanded to include at least a dozen of her young *onmyōjō* warriors. Had he . . . ?

A heavy lump settled in Murdoch's belly as he peered at his hands. Yes, there were dark red speckles on the back and fingers of his right hand. Dried blood. He'd injured someone. Perhaps slain someone.

Memories stirred, and the hairs on his neck lifted.

Dear Lord, had he injured *Kiyoko*?

No. He shot to his feet, the pain in his head a mere inconvenience now. He would not have hurt her. Not on purpose, at any rate. But by accident? It had happened before. It could certainly have happened again.

He spun in a circle. Anyone injured would have been taken to the doctor. But where the hell was the bloody infirmary? Most of the buildings in the compound were familiar, but there were a few he had yet to enter. The one at the far northeast corner was the forge, and the four smaller huts near the main gate were housing for the senior warriors like Yoshio.

But there was a slightly larger pagoda near the entrance as well. And the doctor had taken the wounded warrior in that direction.

He ran down the gravel path.

His guess about the infirmary proved correct. Inside the building he found a small treatment room, a two-bed ward, a lab, and a large closet filled with medical supplies. But no doctor, and no Kiyoko.

Which only increased his sense of dread.

If they were at the house, then it was almost certainly Kiyoko who was injured. And if they were off to the hospital, the injuries were grave. Steeling himself for the worst, Murdoch exited the compound between the two frowning *niou* and made his way to Kiyoko's front door, where he politely knocked.

Umiko slid the partition open.

The scathing look on the old woman's face when she spied him soured his mouth. So, it was true. He was officially scum of the earth. He had injured Kiyoko.

"May I come in?"

Umiko glared and refused to step aside.

"I need to see her," he said quietly.

She responded with a few terse words of Japanese that he didn't understand. Not that he needed an interpreter—her meaning was very clear. *Over my dead body*.

Murdoch was debating how hard he should push when an authoritative male voice spoke from the shadowed interior of the house. More Japanese. More words he didn't understand. But the rancor left Umiko's eyes and she nodded. She shuffled back a few feet and bowed, inviting Murdoch inside.

He swiftly unbuckled his boots, kicked them off, and stepped into the house.

Sora stood in the center of the main room, looking decidedly his age. He had droplets of dried blood on his pale chin, and white cotton bandages peeked from the neckline of his black robes.

When he saw Murdoch's gaze linger on the bandages, he said ruefully, "You are exceptionally fast. I leapt, but the tip of your blade caught me nonetheless."

Murdoch raked his hair back from his face. "My

apologies, Sora-san. Demons open a portal the moment they think they're losing, and they often try to make an escape. My berserker has become quite adept at making a last-minute bid for the killing slice."

Sora's eyebrows lifted. "I'm grateful that, in this case at least, you failed."

"I, too. I'm hoping that everyone survived?"

"Only Kiyoko and I were injured."

Murdoch's gaze drifted over the sensei's shoulder to the partitioned room where Kiyoko had previously dressed. The sliding door was shut, but he could see the shadow of a person moving inside. "How is she?"

"Not well."

"Did I—" Murdoch's throat tightened to such a degree that he couldn't get the word out. Not on the first try. "Did I cut her?"

"No." The old man shook his head. "The blame for her injury lies with me, not you. I did not fully anticipate what might happen after I shot you."

"The arrow in my shoulder? That was you?"

He nodded. "I prepared the arrow with a great deal of care. Not only did I place a very powerful shield pierce spell upon it, I added a sleep spell."

Murdoch snorted. "You knocked me out."

"Quite effectively."

"But . . . ?"

Sora smiled faintly. "You are correct. There is a *but*. You went down as I predicted, but you fell upon Kiyoko and crushed her. Broke two ribs, the doctor says. Yoshio attempted to pull you off, but in your last moments of consciousness, you created a repel shield that prevented him from reaching you. The weight of your body nearly killed her."

The chill of narrowly averted disaster claimed him.

"Indeed," Sora added. "Were it not for your spontaneous roll to one side, I think the outcome would have been summarily grim."

"May I see her? I must make my apologies."

"Not just yet," the old man said. "She still needs a great deal of rest."

Murdoch frowned. "For broken ribs?"

"Her injury is more complicated than a few broken bones. She overextended herself while she was trapped, and her efforts exacerbated a previous injury."

Umiko appeared with a tea service, which she laid out on the table next to the inset hearth. No ale today. Only green tea and spiced rice balls.

Murdoch waited for her to leave, then asked, "What previous injury?"

"Three months ago, Kiyoko interrupted the fatal demon attack on her father and took a significant blow to the chest."

"She's shown no sign of weakness during training."

Sora lowered himself stiffly to one of the cushions around the table. "The physical healing was swift. Like many young people, she was back on her feet in a matter of days. It was her ki that suffered the critical damage." He reached for the teapot, and winced.

Murdoch strode to the table, picked up the ceramic pot, and poured the old man a cup of tea. As he replaced the pot on the table, he slid the bowl of rice balls a few inches closer.

"Her ki?" he prompted.

The old man cupped his tea in two thin hands and brought the steaming liquid to his lips for a slow sip. "Her spiritual energy. Kiyoko is a gifted mystic, and she draws on her ki to perform her spells. As one might expect with a beloved parent, she went to extraordinary lengths in her attempts to heal her father that day. Unfortunately, in so doing, she drained her ki to such a low level, it was unable to regenerate. Were it not for the Veil, she would have died."

Of course. The goddamned Veil.

Murdoch dropped to the cushion opposite the old man. "The Veil gave her some kind of energy infusion?"

"Not precisely." Sora sipped his tea again, taking obvious comfort from the warm drink. "Think of it more as a pilot light. As long as it is lit, she can use it to create her own energy. But if the pilot light goes out . . ."

Murdoch stared at the parchmentlike texture of the old man's closed eyelids. "You're suggesting that if I take the Veil away, I'll kill her."

"Yes."

"I don't believe it. Kiyoko's face is quite expressive. She's been tempted to give it to me on more than one occasion. If she depended on it to keep her alive, I doubt giving it up would even cross her mind."

Sora opened his eyes. "Thinking about giving it up and actually doing so are two different things, Mr. Murdoch. Her desire to do the honorable thing constantly battles her selfish need to hold on to the Veil. That's only natural for a person of Kiyoko's character. But she knows the consequences."

He set his cup down.

"I fear it is your well-motivated demand for the Veil and the nag of her conscience that are causing the current crisis."

"You mean her weariness?"

Sora rose to his feet, already looking more hale and hearty. There was some color in his cheeks now. "It's more than weariness. She has again drained her ki to a dangerous level, and this time her recovery rate is concerning. The Veil's power remains strong, but Kiyoko is not responding to it as she once did."

"But she *will* recover."

"I believe so, yes. The doctor assures me she is steadily improving."

Murdoch regained his feet with one forceful push. He had to see her. Mostly to reassure himself that he hadn't slain her in his berserker rage, but also to see firsthand the effect of her diminished ki. Otherwise, he wasn't sure he could accept Sora's bizarre tale. "I want to see her."

Sora waved a hand toward the back of the house. "A quick look will do no harm. But if you wake her, I will be most displeased."

At Murdoch's gentle knock, the partition slid open. The doctor nodded politely to him, then stepped aside to give him a proper view of the futon and the woman who lay under the sheets, still and fragile.

Murdoch was shocked. Kiyoko's chest slowly rose and fell with regular, life-sustaining breaths, but her face had a hollow look he knew only too well—the look of a soul ready to depart. Her shoulders were bare and thin, her black hair stark against the pillow. Reconciling this image with the vibrant, purposeful woman he'd kissed in the courtyard only a few short hours ago was a struggle.

He had done this to her.

With his uncontrollable berserker rage and his ridiculous urge to possess her.

"As hard as it may be to believe," Sora said quietly from behind him, "she should be back to normal by the evening meal, except for the broken ribs. Her vital signs are all strong, and her ki is improving minute by minute."

"Was that intended to ease my guilt?" Murdoch asked. "If so, it was ineffective."

"Pointing fingers to lay blame is rarely productive," Sora replied. "Looking for the lesson is a better use of your time. I wonder, for example, why Kiyoko did not cast a shield spell upon herself. The broken bones could have been averted."

Murdoch glanced over his shoulder. "The same could be said for you, old man."

The sensei smiled. "My error was not in failing to raise a shield, but in failing to raise a strong enough one. Your sword has a superior shield-piercing capability."

"Thank Stefan Wahlberg for that."

Sora lifted a brow.

"The Romany mage who supports our efforts," Murdoch explained. He backed out of Kiyoko's room and invited the doctor to slide the partition shut once more. "A very talented fellow."

"Indeed. Is he also the one who placed the dimensional shift upon the scabbard to make your sword disappear when sheathed?"

"Aye."

Sora rubbed his chin. "I hope I have the opportunity to meet the man one day. He's blessed with skills of which I have rarely seen the equal."

Murdoch nodded. "I've only known one other mystic of his caliber in the many years I've existed. A Scottish druid back in the thirteenth century."

"Someone you sought to help free you of your berserker potion?"

"Yes." But that was water long passed under the bridge. He would never be free of the berserker. Murdoch brushed past the old sensei and headed for the front door. "Excuse me. I have a pressing need to walk."

"I understand. A westerly direction will eventually take you to the village. A southerly direction will take you to the sea. Take your pick. I'll call your phone if Kiyoko's condition changes."

He nodded and tossed Sora a half smile. "Don't wait up."

Opportunity was knocking.

Azazel watched Murdoch stride across the grass and

head down the mountain slope toward the village. By the sound of things, the Soul Gatherer intended to be gone for several hours, which should be just enough time to execute a raid. Nothing too elaborate. Just a quick search and snatch.

But first he needed a diversion.

A demon attack on the house, for instance. Unfortunately, he couldn't simply call in a strike. Satan was unaware that he had survived. For good reason. If he revealed himself before he returned to full strength, his rivals for the Great Lord's attention, Lucifer and Beelzebub, would use their considerable might to crush him. Orchestrating a demon attack under the circumstances would be difficult.

But not impossible.

Satan's legions of drones constantly tested the barrier between hell and the middle plane, seeking entrance. They would instantly punch through a weakened area. If he softened this one little spot, right in front of the house, the demons would take care of the rest. It wouldn't matter how many succeeded in punching through, or what type of demon appeared.

Kiyoko was weak as a kitten, so she wouldn't put up much of a fight. And as for the others . . . Well, none of them were real threats.

If all went well, he might get lucky and come away with the Veil. Save the day, and all that. But he'd be happy with the oracle scrolls Kiyoko had told him about in their last session. And the attack alone would earn him a shiny black feather. Perhaps more than one, if a number of *onmyōji* died in the process.

He rolled his shoulders to release the strain of containing his wings inside his slender body.

Really, it was all win.

He had nothing to lose.

*   *   *

Sweat beaded on Murdoch's chest and trickled down his belly as he ran through the trees and leapt down rocky precipices. This part of the island was largely unpopulated, dotted with mountain peaks, crystal clear lakes, and meandering streams. Steering clear of the odd farmhouse, he managed to stay out of sight as he tore along at a blurring pace, heading toward the village. His berserker was quiet, so it was just him and his immortal body burning up the calories.

Or it was until he ran smack into two gray-faced ghouls.

Still traveling at full tilt, he sent the pair flying into the brush like an emaciated set of bowling pins. Momentum carried him forward another ten feet, despite his efforts to stop. He tripped over a bony leg and almost crashed into the elegant white-haired woman standing in the shade of a huge fir tree. He found his balance just before his head plowed into her gut.

"Bloody hell."

"I wouldn't know. I've never been there."

Murdoch glared at her. "What in God's name are you doing standing here in the middle of nowhere? Do you take some perverse glee out of surprising people?"

"Not *people*," she said. "Just you."

"Lucky me. What do you want?"

"Your tone is inappropriate, Gatherer." Attired in a black-and-white silk kimono and traditional geisha makeup, Death flicked her fan. Her twin ghouls regained their feet and took up protective positions behind her, their gray shrouds billowing in the breeze.

He snorted. "You should be used to it by now. We've been keeping company for how long?"

"Seven hundred and twelve years."

He shrugged. "If you say so. I've stopped counting."

A flash of annoyance crossed her face, quickly replaced by a smile that only made her look more coldly beautiful. "I require you to perform a special task for me."

"Sorry. I'm busy."

"I have crushed bugs more respectful than you." Her pale blue eyes narrowed. "You owe me, Gatherer. Your debt is not even close to being paid."

"I've served my original five-hundred-year term and half of another. I'm fulfilling my debt. I owe you nothing more than to gather souls. Check the contract."

Her crimson lips tightened. "One hundred and seventy-three."

Murdoch rubbed his hand over his chest, soaking up the sweat with his T-shirt and easing the ache that blossomed under his sternum at her words. "I need no memory prod."

"You've clearly forgotten the size of the favor I granted you, Murdoch. One hundred and seventy-three lives in exchange for a second five-hundred-year term. I released all those souls. For you."

"You had not marked them yet."

"Of course not. Had they been marked, no deal would have been possible. Still, they were on the list. Had they not been, you'd never have come to me begging for their lives. They were scheduled to die in a horrible clan feud, as I recall. Murdered in their beds by that ugly fellow MacDonald."

Arguing against the truth was a pointless endeavor.

"What do you want?" he asked wearily.

"I made a bargain with Webster and he appears to be reneging on his end."

He lifted a brow. "So? I doubt you made the deal without arranging a penalty. Why involve me? Just call in your marker."

"My, my. Have you no care for the man's future, Murdoch? You don't even know what the penalty is, yet here you are, heartlessly eager to make him pay."

"I'm not his nursemaid."

Reaching out, she caressed his jaw with an icy finger, her lips pouting. "I miss the beard. Were you horribly upset when you had to shave it off?"

"Cease your chicanery." He grabbed her wrist and pulled her hand away. "I'm not so easily duped. Clearly, you want him to fulfill his obligation far more than you want him to pay the penalty. What was he supposed to do for you?"

"Nothing onerous. Merely fetch me a trinket."

She had demanded one of the relics? Surely not. "What trinket?"

"That's none of your concern. I don't need you to collect the item—that's Webster's job. I need you to convince him to part with it."

"If it's one of the dark relics," he said, lowering his chin, "you're asking the wrong man."

"Bah." She waved a cavalier hand. "Your collection of relics is of no interest to me. I only approved the hunt for them to keep Satan on a short leash. The item I seek is one of more consequence."

"The Shattered Halo," he guessed.

She said nothing, just smiled coolly.

"How do you expect me to sway him? He and I are hardly the best of friends."

She shrugged. "You respect him, he respects you. There must be some room for influence within that relationship."

"I'm in Japan. He's in California," he pointed out.

"Which is why I'm here," she responded. "Wrap up this dreary business quickly and return to San Jose. I'm growing tired of the delay."

"It's not that simple."

"Of course it is. Just take the Veil and leave."

He sighed. "To a woman with no conscience, I suppose everything is simple. For me, the decision is harder."

She wrinkled her nose. "Does this have anything to do with that old man, the teacher?"

"Sora? No. Why?"

"I've never liked him. He's a sneak and a thief."

"Really?" The sensei was annoying, true enough. Always talking in riddles. But a *thief*? "What did he steal?"

"I'm through with talking. You know what I want, now deliver." Death whipped out her fan again. "And you might wish to turn around and head back to the compound. The village is not worth your time."

Murdoch cut his liege a short bow and detoured around the tree and her entourage, striding through the grass. "Thank you for the advice, but I'll keep going. I need to think."

"I do like my Gatherers to spend an appropriate amount of time reflecting upon their sins," she called after him. "But if you don't turn around, you'll lose the Veil."

He stopped and spun to face her.

"What do you know?"

"Everything, of course." Death smiled. "Your new friends are being attacked by a horde of nasty pith demons even as we speak. If I were you, I'd run."

Then she was gone.

"Kiyoko-san."

Kiyoko opened her eyes.

"Kiyoko-san," repeated the female voice, low and urgent. "Wake up."

Groggy and confused, Kiyoko turned her head to view the frowning face of Umiko. It was hard to see in the darkened room, but the fierce grip the old woman had on her arm told her plenty. "What's wrong?"

"We are under attack."

Kiyoko sat up. Or tried to. A sudden and severe stab of pain in her chest brought tears to her eyes, and she fell back against the pillow. Ah, yes. Broken ribs. How could she have forgotten her failed experiment in the courtyard? "By whom?"

"Demons."

Gritting her teeth, Kiyoko finally succeeded in sitting up. "Are you certain?"

"I've seen them. Fireballs shoot from their fingertips."

Kiyoko grimaced. That certainly sounded like demons. "Fetch me my sword."

"No, you are too weak to fight. For the moment, your warriors are keeping the demons at bay, fulfilling their vow to protect you. But they will not last long against such might. Do not waste their gift. We must use the passage through the rocks to escape."

Her father had been a very practical man. Once he decided to wed and have a family—a great risk for an *onmyōji*—he made arrangements for every conceivable scenario, including the need for escape. When he built the house, he created a passage below the floorboards of the kitchen. But it had never been intended for him. Only for his wife and daughter.

"You go," Kiyoko said firmly. "I must stay."

"To die?" Umiko asked, anxiety eroding the usual respect from her words. "Why? If you engage the enemy in your current state, you will not survive. If you escape now, you can live to fight another day."

"I cannot abandon Sora and the others." She rolled out of bed, using a spell to dull the protests of her battered body. Crossing to the east shoji, she slid the translucent panel back a few inches so she could peer out. "Don't worry. I'm not a fool. I won't pitch myself into the heat of the battle. I'll remain in the house. But I'm not leaving."

Umiko glared at her. "You are as stubborn as your father."

Kiyoko smiled. It was the highest compliment the old

housekeeper could have paid her, and they both knew it. "Honor us both, then. Take my parents' wedding photo with you when you leave."

Umiko stared at her for a moment, then nodded and scurried from the room.

Kiyoko turned her attention to the events outside. A wall of *onmyōji* warriors stood halfway between the house and the compound, wielding their swords with practiced ease, deflecting fireballs, and holding off the twenty or so demons bent on burning down the house. Yoshio was front and center, as always, aggressively battling demons in the two-sword style. He showed no sign of tiring, but the same could not be said for the warrior to the right of him. Even as Kiyoko watched, the young man fell under a hail of fireballs.

Under other circumstances, she would have rushed to his side. Or at the very least sent a flurry of protective spells in the young man's direction. But her ki was still a low flicker in her chest, not the intense thrum of power she could normally harness, and with the significant distance between her and the men, her options were limited.

All she could manage was a blind spell.

She tossed it anyway, hoping the simple defense would give the fallen warrior the moment he needed to regain his feet. But it was a vain hope. Her men were not prepared for such a large-scale battle. Typically, they fought two or three demons at a time.

Almost as proof of her point, she saw Yoshio break from the line of warriors and dash up the path toward the house. An instant later, the middle section of the line crumpled and a horde of demons rushed forward.

Kiyoko stepped back from the window, eyeing the mulberry bark that covered the shoji. The house would not provide much protection against fire.

"Kiyoko."

She glanced up. Sora stood in the main living space with protective armor over his black robes. Like Yoshio, he held two swords, one short and one long.

"Can you fight?"

"Not well," she answered.

He strode toward her, frowning. "Where is the Veil?"

The Veil. Of course. She wore it so close to her skin that she tended to forget it was there. Before she could reassure Sora that it was safe, Yoshio burst into the room, gripping the neckline of Ryuji's expensive suit in one hand and his long sword in the other. "I found him hovering outside the door. The demons are almost upon us."

Ryuji was wide-eyed and pale, clearly flummoxed by the attack. But there was no time to explain.

Sora tossed Kiyoko his prized katana. "I'll find another. Protect the Veil, no matter what the cost. Take the passageway."

Then he turned to Yoshio. "You and I will defend the door as long as we can, and hopefully give Kiyoko-san time to get away."

"No," Kiyoko said. "We leave together. All of us."

Handing Sora back his weapon, she looked him firmly in the eye, then spun about and headed for the kitchen. As she ran, she murmured the incantation that would summon her *shikigami*. Only a handful of *onmyōji* over the centuries had been blessed with the talent to control the little spirit imps, and those that could usually required focused effort to bring forth one. Kiyoko could summon multiple *shikigami* with ease, and when they awakened, they fell over themselves in their eagerness to do her bidding. As they did now. A dozen invisible spirits suddenly swarmed about her head, batting her softly, gently rubbing along her skin, then darting away, behaving much like the feline familiars they were often compared to.

Kiyoko gave them an order, and they were off.

"A small body of determined spirits fired by an unquenchable faith in their mission can alter the course of history," murmured Sora as she lifted the wooden floor panel that hid the metal door to the passage.

She glanced at him. "Confucius?"

"No, Gandhi."

She smiled. "Wise man."

"Indeed."

The house shook violently on its posts, ceramic bowls and pots crashing to the floor around them. Kiyoko hastily slid the lower door aside, exposing the tunnel carved into the rock.

"Kiyoko-san, you go first," Sora said.

She nodded and quickly slipped into the cool, damp tunnel. Just as she was about to duck her head and disappear down the dark passage, she heard a fierce guttural roar vibrate through the air. It was followed by a swell of supportive yells from the *onmyōji* warriors.

She glanced up at Sora, who shrugged.

"It would seem Mr. Murdoch returned earlier than expected. I'm not certain even his berserker can triumph over twenty demons, but I would say that our odds of survival just improved dramatically. Go, Kiyoko-san."

"But—"

"Your duty is to protect the Veil."

"But—"

"And *our* duty is to protect you. Go, Kiyoko-san." The pleasant tone had disappeared, replaced by firm command. "Now."

Kiyoko entered the tunnel.

Ryuji followed her in, then Sora, and finally Yoshio. When all four of them were in the passage, Yoshio pulled the wooden panel over the opening and slid the metal door shut, leaving them in total darkness.

It took a moment for their eyes to adjust, then the

glow of luminescent meter marks on the walls appeared out of the gloom, subtly lighting the curve ahead. Amazing how reassuring a series of small green dots could feel. Especially when the rough walls on either side pressed against their outstretched palms and the roof nearly grazed their heads.

She moved swiftly down the tunnel.

Murdoch was strong, smart, and a seasoned demon fighter. He would survive. No other outcome was worthy of consideration. When the conflict was over, he would greet her with that arrogant, lopsided grin and applaud her for keeping the Veil safe. He would.

"The door opens to a narrow ledge on the cliff," Sora reminded her, as they rounded the third and final bend in the tunnel. "After that, we must climb."

"I remember."

When she was younger, her father had insisted on random practice escapes. The worst had been a drill enacted in the pitch-black of midnight. Scrambling up the cliff face in the dark, unable to see the small steps carved in the rock and occasionally losing her footing, had given her nightmares for weeks afterward. Fortunately, today's climb would be made in broad daylight.

Just as they reached the final curve in the tunnel, Kiyoko's big toe connected with something thin and hard. The item skittered across the rock floor, hit the wall, and shattered.

"What was that?" Ryuji asked.

"I'm not certain," said Kiyoko, sliding her feet cautiously in the direction of the broken item.

Sora glanced over his shoulder. "You'll only injure yourself. We must keep going."

"It could be something important."

"Nothing is more important than getting you and the Veil to safety," he said firmly. His hands felt along the rock face for the recessed door latch.

Kiyoko bent and picked up the item, shaking it loose from broken glass. The outer edge was a wooden rectangle, carved with an intricate design that stopped her heart. She didn't need to see the rendering to recognize the many bumps and sharp points. She'd run her fingers over this wood too many times not to know what it was. The lovely maple-leaf picture frame that held her parents' wedding photo.

Umiko would never have left it here.

Not willingly.

"Wait! Don't—"

The tunnel door slid open with the smooth rumble of well-oiled gears.

11

The house was a total loss.

As the berserker rage slowly retreated from his veins and his sense of self returned, Murdoch sighed over the damage. Walls gone, floors smashed, and ceilings collapsed. What hadn't been already destroyed would soon be consumed by the flames licking up numerous posts and beams. Kiyoko would be devastated.

On the positive side, the demons were dead.

Between his raving berserker, several very useful Romany spells, and the skill of the young *onmyōji* warriors, they'd managed to take down all twenty of the wretched hellspawn. It hadn't hurt that the demons had been oddly distracted. Swatting at the air about their heads, pitching random fireballs into the night, roaring with rage for no obvious reason. Whatever the cause, he and the others had benefited. They had suffered only one casualty—a young man who fell to a barrage of fireballs before Murdoch arrived.

He frowned.

One casualty, assuming Kiyoko had gotten out before the demons reached the house. He hadn't found any sign of her in the wreckage, so it was a fair assumption.

Just not a sure bet.

Call him a Nervous Nellie, but Death's warning was still ringing in his ears. *If you don't turn around, you might lose the Veil.* If Kiyoko had made an easy escape before all this started, why would there be any risk to the Veil?

There wouldn't.

Murdoch pointed his sword at the young *onmyōji* who had rallied the others to fight at his side. The warrior had taken a fireball to the left shoulder during the battle, yet he stood tall and straight. "You. How would the others have escaped the house? Is there a planned escape route?"

The blank stare he got in return had him biting his tongue. The lad clearly didn't speak English.

"Kiyoko? Sora-san? Umiko?" He spun around, pointing at various places around the demolished house. "Where did they go?"

The young man's eyes lit up, and a rush of syllables poured from his lips. He leapt over a burning post and headed for the back of the house. Kicking aside pieces of broken pottery and splintered ceiling panels, he cleared the floor in what used to be the kitchen. He pushed a carved wooden square near the wall and the floor panel popped up on one side. The young man lifted the panel and pointed to the metal door beneath.

Murdoch slid the metal door to one side and peered into the dark cavity. A tunnel.

He rubbed his chest.

Two obvious options, then. Drop into the tunnel and follow, or determine where the exit was and head overland. With his enhanced Gatherer speed and ability to see in the dark, the direct route through the tunnel was the obvious choice. Claustrophobia shouldn't enter into his decision at all. The air in the tunnel wouldn't actually disappear the moment he stepped inside, nor would the walls actually close in on him. The fear was all in his head.

He jumped into the tunnel.

Being a coward wouldn't save the lass. He glanced up at the young *onmyōji* and with no hope of being understood said, "Go around. Meet me at the other side."

Then he took a deep breath, bent forward so the roof wouldn't touch his head, and jogged into the gloom.

Kiyoko's warning came a moment too late. The tunnel door slid open to reveal a huge red *oni* demon pitching fireballs. Reacting swifter than she thought possible, Sora threw himself against the rock wall and miraculously dodged the first hellish orb. Kiyoko yanked Ryuji behind her, stepped back, and muttered the incantation required to raise a shield around them both.

A ripple of fear ran through her. There were four additional hulking outlines posed against the bright sky, and they were challenging opponents. The heavily muscled, seven-foot-tall beasts oozed a deadly poison from their thick red hides and wielded massive clubs capable of crushing rock—clubs they were currently using to expand the opening of the tunnel with ground-trembling force.

"What *are* those things?" asked Ryuji, his voice hoarse in her ear.

Kiyoko didn't answer. Pulling him down, she avoided the swift slice of Yoshio's blade as he leapt past them to enter the fight. Without a weapon, all she had to offer was magic. But she could do better than a simple blind spell now. Her ki had gained more strength during the trek through the tunnel.

Still, she had to choose wisely.

There was little hope that Umiko had survived an ambush, but if she had, and if she lay wounded outside the mouth of the tunnel, a spell like rock shower would finish her. Recalling her *shikigami* was also out of the question, because they might still be aiding Murdoch and the others. No, a two-pronged attack made the most sense: a culling spell to siphon off the battle fervor of their opponents and feed it to the team at the house, and a dragon conjure.

The winged snake dragon would be best.

From experience, she knew that if she blended her mystic abilities with Sora's, the resulting dragon would be almost undefeatable. But the sensei was engaged in a desperate fight for his life against one of the *oni* and disturbing him—even briefly—would be a mistake.

She would have to conjure this dragon on her own.

The ground shook, the walls trembled, and a hail of rock and dust pelted his upper body. Murdoch flattened himself against one wall and sucked in a sharp breath, his heart ricocheting in his chest. *That* sure as bloody hell wasn't in his head. The walls *were* closing in on him.

His mouth dried.

What a horrific finish that would be—lying trapped under a ton of rock, pressed tightly on all sides, unable to breathe for the rest of his immortal term with Death. Two hundred and fifty-six years of his worst nightmare come true.

Ah, Christ. He needed to see light.

And he needed to see it *now*.

Hands chilled with a cold sweat, he put everything he had into a dash for the end of the tunnel.

Kiyoko smiled through her exhaustion.

The dragon was a sight to behold.

A sixty-foot wingspan kept it aloft, a long, powerful tail whipped from side to side, and shimmering blue-green scales covered its huge body from head to tail tip. It not only breathed great gusts of fire at the *oni* demons on the ledge but it swallowed every fireball they tossed at it with a gleam of satisfaction in its black eyes.

Three of the five demons turned to face it, leaving

two *oni* to combat Yoshio and Sora. Improved odds, to be sure, but Sora was injured. Although summoning the dragon had drained Kiyoko's ki to the point where her limbs felt numb, withdrawing from the battle was not an option. Not until it was won. Drawing deep on her remaining power, she strengthened the shields around the two men and tossed small irritation spells at the demons.

The dragon's tail swept one of the *oni* off the ledge. But the acidic poison leeching from the *oni*'s skin drew a pained roar from the mighty beast, and it sank several feet beneath the ledge before regaining its altitude. Its tail was now safely tucked away.

Kiyoko bit her lip.

It would have been far better if the dragon had lashed out in fury, knocking the others off the cliff as well. They had five minutes—ten if they were really lucky—before the poison clawed its way through the dragon's body to its heart. Given the desperate edge to Sora's and Yoshio's battles, that wasn't promising.

Kiyoko tossed an ease-pain spell at the dragon.

Her own ribs were beginning to throb, but the spell was better spent elsewhere. A truth proven moments later when the dragon used the forceful beat of its wings to blow another of the *oni* off the ledge. She shared a triumphant smile with Ryuji, who was plastered against the wall, pale-faced.

But her satisfaction didn't last long.

The third demon howled in rage and threw its powerful club at the winged beast's snout. In a regrettably accurate shot, the dragon took a blow to the head, briefly dazing it. It managed only one more blast of fire before the poison reached its heart and it collapsed, plummeting out of view and down the cliff to the rocky terrain below. The now clubless *oni* was badly burned, but alive.

The odds were still three to two in favor of the demons.

Worse, both Sora and Yoshio displayed obvious signs of tiring—shorter leaps to escape the pounding of the clubs, near misses with fireballs, white lips, and ragged breathing. If Kiyoko didn't act, and act quickly, they would all be dead and the Veil would be lost.

But what could she do?

Fresh air. Blessed, sweet-tasting air from the outside world.

Murdoch closed his eyes as the cool wash of damp fall air hit the back of his throat. Then he frowned. Not so sweet tasting as it ought to be, though. This air was marked with the sharply bitter scent of brimstone.

His berserker hummed beneath his skin.

Brimstone could mean only one thing. He rounded the last corner of the tunnel to the bright light of day and a small but fiercely fought battle. His fingers tightened around the leather-wrapped hilt of his sword. More demons.

His gaze quickly found Kiyoko and Watanabe a few feet back from the fighting. Watanabe hugged the stone wall, trying to stay as small as possible, but Kiyoko stood pale and proud, her hands spread wide, using whatever strength she had to wield magic. Sora and Yoshio were valiantly holding back the demons—three great red brutes, two of them armed with stone-pulverizing clubs.

His blood hummed and his muscles thickened.

Let me loose, his berserker howled.

Murdoch beat his inner beast back with gritted teeth. He couldn't let go. Not here. Even though the demons had widened the mouth, the space available for battle was severely limited. If he let his berserker free, he wouldn't be able to guarantee Sora's or Yoshio's survival.

Suddenly the air around him whooshed, and he felt the feathery touch of numerous wings graze his cheeks.

Bats? If so, even his extraordinary Soul Gatherer vision couldn't spot them. Ghost bats, perhaps.

Under the repeated pounding of a demon club, Yoshio's shield finally crumpled. The club arced toward him yet again, and he dove left. But the uneven floor proved his undoing—before he could launch himself into the air, he lost his footing and stumbled. Fanciful thoughts of invisible bats fell victim to harsh reality, and Murdoch surged through the tunnel to the young warrior's defense.

"Poison skin," Kiyoko gasped at him as he passed.

Trying not to notice how utterly spent she appeared, Murdoch shored up the front of his shield with a Romany ward. Combined with his berserker's natural repel charm, it should be enough to keep him safe. He loosed the bonds on the ancient beast inside him just enough to take advantage of its strength, then entered the battle with a blistering swing of Bloodseeker.

The mighty sword skimmed the top of Yoshio's shield and sliced through the bubble of protection around the demon, driving unswervingly into the bulging biceps of its arm. The creature roared with rage, displaying an impressive set of saliva-dripping fangs, and redirected its hell-forged weapon at Murdoch. But the arm no longer functioned properly. After a wobbly, ineffectual attempt, it dropped the club to its side. Yoshio moved in for the kill.

The third demon lowered its head and charged into the tunnel like a bull. Murdoch ducked around Yoshio, braced his legs for impact, and met the charge full on. His feet slid back a good ten feet before they both ground to a halt.

Then the battle began in earnest.

The demon's strength was impressive. No match for a fully loosed berserker, but a significant challenge for Murdoch in his half-roused state. The pith demons he'd faced outside the house had more in common with pesky gnats than they did with this fellow. The creature slammed him into the rock wall with an easy sweep of its arm, cracking his skull. Damned thing was faster than it looked.

Still, a demon was a demon.

And as such, it belonged in hell.

Murdoch ignored the lump forming on the back of his head, and ducked to avoid a follow-up swing. Best to stay away from those claws. They might well be able to pierce his shield if the demon got a good hold.

"Land true, land hard, land quick," he murmured to Bloodseeker, which now hummed eagerly with the additional potency of a demon blood enhancement spell. Then he gave his berserker an inch more leash and attacked in a flurry of precise thrusts and slices. He became a killing machine. His attack fell into the easy rhythm of a battle-seasoned warrior, his blade struck fast and hard, and victory was his within minutes.

Not entirely due to his talent.

Again, he benefited from decidedly odd behavior on the part of the demon. Wild swings that seemed not to be aimed at him at all. Loss of focus. Strange snarls at the air around its head. Almost as if those invisible bats were pecking at it.

His sword pierced the creature's thick hide with uninhibited enthusiasm.

As the demon shuddered at the end of his blade and slipped to the ground, Murdoch took a deep breath to calm his berserker. He pulled his sword free of the carcass and spun around. To his immense relief, Yoshio had already defeated his wounded demon and had gone to the aid of Sora. Both men smiled triumphantly as the third and last demon crashed to the rock floor, a patchwork of cuts decorating its skin.

Out of the corner of his eye, Murdoch saw Kiyoko slump to the floor.

Watanabe reached her first, dropping to his knees at her side and cradling her head in his lap. He brushed her hair back and stared at her wan face with obvious concern. "We need the doctor."

Murdoch had trouble breathing.

Kiyoko was injured.

The sight of Watanabe's arms wrapped around her tore several of the mental restraints he had on his berserker, which was already dangerously close to the surface. *Christ.* The man's hand was caressing her cheek. Murdoch jammed his eyes shut, struggling to maintain control and avoid ripping Watanabe's head off.

"Did the doctor survive?" Sora asked.

"Aye," answered Murdoch. The one-word response was all he could manage.

"Then let us get Kiyoko-san to the compound as quickly as possible. I assume we can return through the tunnel, Mr. Murdoch?"

"Aye."

"Will you lead the way?"

Murdoch opened his eyes. Watanabe now stood with Kiyoko in his arms, apparently prepared to carry her all the way. He carefully averted his gaze. Puny little Watanabe would be forced to hand her off to Yoshio at some point, guaranteed. He'd love to be there to witness the man's failure, but ... One trip through that blasted tunnel was quite enough.

"No, I'll go overland and meet you at the other end."

Sora skewed him a knowing glance. "It's quite a climb up the cliff face."

"I've no problem with heights." Which was true. A childhood spent scrambling through the Highlands, leaping from crag to crag in pursuit of hare and deer, had given him an excellent tolerance for high places. It was only the caves he'd had trouble with.

"We'll see you at the compound, then."

The little party headed back through the tunnel, led by Yoshio.

As they disappeared from view, Murdoch tried not to worry. She was strong. Her breaths were shallow, but even. And she had Sora with her. She'd be fine.

Ah, hell, maybe he'd better run.

Kiyoko woke up in the infirmary, lying on a very firm, very thin cot. The stark overhead lighting gave her location away. That and the pungent smell of antiseptic.

She tried to sit up.

"Don't even think about it, lass," came a dry voice from the corner of the small room. "You're to stay there until the doctor gives you permission to move."

Kiyoko fell back against the pillow and tilted her head so she could see Murdoch. There were no chairs in the room, and he leaned against the wall looking uncomfortable but resolute.

"How bad is it?" she asked, bracing for devastating news.

"The house is gone, and you lost a young warrior."

"One?"

He nodded. "Just one."

Kiyoko felt a huge weight lift from her chest. Until she recalled her discovery in the tunnel. "Plus Umiko-san."

"Sorry," Murdoch said with a snort. "You weren't that lucky."

"What? Are you saying Umiko-san is alive?"

"Aye, the dragon lady survived," he confirmed.

"How?"

"I found her on the ledge outside the tunnel, clinging to a chunk of rock with more strength than I thought her capable of," he said. "She wouldn't let go until I pried her bloody fingers loose. Considering she had a broken arm and a dislocated jaw, it was an impressive feat."

"Umiko-san is alive." She couldn't hold back a smile.

He responded with one of his lopsided grins, and her heart beat a little faster. "And still giving me hell."

"For what?"

"Pretty much everything," he said. "Your injuries, the demon attack, the loss of the house."

Kiyoko bit her lip to keep from laughing. It sounded so much like Umiko. She could almost picture the little woman shaking her fist at Murdoch. "She has a point. You *did* break my ribs."

He pulled away from the wall, his eyes dark with regret. "About that . . ."

"Oh, stop it. I deserved everything I got. I wanted the berserker to surface, and it did." She sighed. "Besides, it wasn't as if you meant to hurt me."

He was silent for a long moment, staring at the floor.

"The kiss was worth it," she said softly.

His gaze met hers. Dark and steamy. "It was a good kiss," he acknowledged.

Kiyoko lowered her gaze to the white cotton bedclothes. Murdoch must have kissed many women in his lengthy existence. Women far more alluring than she. The moment in the courtyard likely would not make his list of top one hundred kisses.

"Then you shouldn't regret it," she grumbled.

"I said a good kiss, not a smart kiss," he said, advancing to the bed. He dropped to the cot with a jingle of silver buckles. "I've done a number of things I'm not proud of and kissing you in the courtyard is one of them."

"Technically, *I* kissed *you*."

He pinned her gaze. "Technically, I almost killed you."

"Not with the kiss."

He snorted. "That's a debatable point."

Kiyoko felt her first twinge of annoyance. The man behaved as if he was the center of the universe. "Why must you insist on taking all the blame? You know I taunted you, you know I kissed you, and you must know

I had ample opportunity to skewer you had I wanted to."

"Why didn't you?"

She glared at him. "Because I didn't *want* to. Truly, why would I stab you? I like you."

"For the same reason you stabbed Takeo. Because you had no choice. Because sometimes, hurting someone you like is the right thing to do."

Kiyoko smoothed the wrinkles in her sheets. "Had I run you through as you suggest, you wouldn't have been at full strength when the demons attacked. We might all be dead."

"Or you and Sora, without your berserker-inflicted injuries, might have saved the day," he responded.

She sighed. "Why are we debating this? We cannot go back and change what happened. We survived a very difficult day with minimal losses. I find myself more grateful than upset."

"You're right. We can't change the past." He raked a hand through his hair. The strands knotted, then separated under his assault. "But we can sure as hell change the future."

Kiyoko wanted to touch his hair again. The brief moment during the kiss when she'd buried her fingers in those springy waves had not been nearly long enough. "What do you mean?"

He sliced her a rueful look. "Up until yesterday, I was planning to grab the Veil and run."

She frowned. "You don't know where it is."

"That's not exactly true. I know you keep it on your body. I also know it's not in your locket or your bracelet."

She glanced at her bare wrist. "You took them?"

"While you were sleeping," he admitted

Her heart skipped a beat. "What else did you do while I was *sleeping*?"

"Nothing. The plan has changed anyway. You need the Veil to survive."

Her jaw dropped. "How do you know that?"

"Sora-san told me."

"He had no right—"

"Bollocks," Murdoch interrupted. "He had every right. When I first arrived, he knew my goal was to take the Veil, and he had good reason for staying silent. But now? Whatever I did to you in the courtyard yesterday has stolen what little hope you have. Why in bloody hell *wouldn't* he tell me?"

"Because you are not responsible," she answered quietly. "Not for the initial damage, not for your need to take the Veil, not even for what happened to me in the courtyard. Any mistakes were mine, not yours."

"Lass, did you crush yourself?"

"No, but—"

He held up a hand to silence her. "Then let's agree to share the burden, shall we? You baited the bear, and I crushed the life out of you. We'll call it even."

"It's not that simple."

"It never is," he said with a sigh.

He shifted, raising one knee onto the bed to face her squarely. He clearly had something to say, but Kiyoko wasn't listening. The firm heat of his thigh seeped through the sheets to her leg, bringing to mind the numerous heated dreams she'd had about the man. None of which came close to matching the sweet shiver of the real kiss.

Kiyoko sat up, her gaze locked on Murdoch's face.

An odd eagerness raced through her veins. Hot, tense, and full of promise. Another kiss would be exquisite. Risky, yes, but the press of his lips on hers had sent ripples clear to her toes and made every nerve in her body sing—to a tune only he could hear. She wanted another taste.

Now.

His eyes darkened as they continued to stare at each other. He was thinking the same thought, she'd bet her father's katana on it.

He leaned toward her. "Kiyoko . . ."

"Needs rest, Mr. Murdoch," Sora said firmly from the doorway.

Murdoch abruptly sat back. "Aye, she does."

A pang of disappointment filled Kiyoko's chest. But she also recognized that the pull between her and Murdoch wasn't entirely of her own choosing. Something deep and undeniable drew them together, and it tended to override common sense.

"How are you feeling, sensei?" she asked her mentor.

"Fully recovered, thanks to the doctor. You, on the other hand, have not fared so well," he responded. His gaze remained on Murdoch, his expression vaguely disapproving.

Not so vague that Murdoch didn't get the message, though. He rose from the bed with lanky grace and leaned against the small supply counter with his arms folded over his chest. "Which is why I'm here," he said. "I'm taking her back to the United States. With me."

"Absolutely not," Sora said sharply.

"It's not safe for her to remain."

"You are exaggerating the danger."

Kiyoko's gaze bounced between the old man's frowning face and Murdoch's resolute expression. The polite air that had marked their previous conversations was gone. But why?

"What happened?" she demanded.

They ignored her.

"You're standing in the way of her health. Stefan Wahlberg is one of the most powerful mages in the world," Murdoch said. "There's an excellent chance he can heal Kiyoko. He knows of a cure for depleted energy."

"We've consulted with many gifted mystics. None had a solution. Asking Kiyoko-san to travel across the world on a whim is unacceptable."

"Staying here isn't acceptable, either," Murdoch responded.

"What happened?" Kiyoko repeated, louder this time.

Murdoch glanced at her. "While the house was being attacked, someone broke into the dojo and stole all his divination papers. Obviously, whatever barrier spell your friend here put on the compound was a shoddy excuse for magic."

Her gaze slipped to Sora. "Is this true?"

He nodded.

Kiyoko tossed the bedcovers aside and swung her feet to the floor. "I helped prepare that spell," she said. "It allows only named individuals to pass through. One of the *onmyōji* is more than he seems."

"Or perhaps the culprit is one of our guests," Sora said, looking pointedly at Murdoch.

But Murdoch missed the slight. He was glaring at Kiyoko. "The doctor did *not* give you permission to get up."

She smiled and stood. "Report me."

Her ribs hurt, but not as badly as they had yesterday, and her energy level was on the rise. The bead of power in her core strengthened with every breath. The Veil might not be as effective as it once was, but it still worked.

"Kiyoko . . . ," he said, scowling.

"Stop being such a mother hen. Were I a man, you'd applaud my eagerness to be up and about." She snatched her folded clothing from a nearby chair and sidled toward the bathroom, holding the back of her hospital gown together. "I think better on my feet."

She tucked those feet into a pair of bathroom slippers, then slid the door shut. Which gave her privacy, but not peace. She grimaced at the men's conversation as she dressed.

"Why didn't you tell her to stay in bed?" demanded Murdoch.

"Her spiritual energy renews much faster once she's conscious. I trust her to know her limits."

"She was awake when you walked in," Murdoch reminded Sora. "You said she needed rest."

"Perhaps I read too much into her pallor."

"Or perhaps your ability to assess her health is as dismal as your magic skill."

Kiyoko knotted the black belt around her *dōgi* with a sharp tug and slid the door open. "Enough, both of you. I'm not going back to bed, so let the conversation move on." She glanced at Sora as she removed the slippers. "Was the entire oracle lost?"

"Yes."

Her heart sank. "It contained details of the ritual. That could be disastrous."

"The oracle can only be read by a master diviner. The risk is minimal."

"What ritual?" Murdoch asked.

"A coming-of-age ritual," she said, her thoughts already leaping ahead. "I turn twenty-five on January eleventh. Do you truly believe your mage can heal me?"

"Aye."

"Then I'll go with you to California."

"Kiyoko-san," admonished Sora, "that is a rash decision."

She nodded. "Precisely why it is also the best decision. If they expect us to turn left, we must turn right. The ritual will be no less effective done in the United States than here."

"You intend to fly all of the *onmyōji* to California?" he asked, brows raised.

"No, just you and me." She caught Sora's disapproving frown. "We do not know who our traitor is, and I do not have time to ferret out the weasel."

"You are not at full strength. You need greater protection than I alone can provide."

She flicked a glance at Murdoch and smiled. "We are hardly going alone, sensei. Murdoch will be there. Did he not prove his worth in the battle against the demons?"

"His concern is for the Veil," her mentor said. "Not you."

"Sora-sensei." Kiyoko flashed an apologetic look at Murdoch, expecting him to be livid at the accusation. But the Soul Gatherer was staring at the floor again, perfectly calm. "Murdoch is not so callous as you suggest."

Her mentor was not swayed. His mouth remained tight.

Kiyoko sighed. "Fine. We'll bring Yoshio-san along as well. Of all the *onmyōji*, I trust him the most."

The elder nodded. "He was your father's favorite disciple."

"Good," she said. "We leave for the United States in the morning."

12

By the time they landed at Mineta San Jose International, Murdoch's head was pounding. It had been the flight from hell. Seven hours of nonstop torture, courtesy of his very pleasant and affable seatmate—Ryuji Watanabe. He wasn't sure how the man had inserted himself into their travel plans, or how he'd ended up in the seat next to him, and frankly, the reasons were irrelevant.

The fellow was obnoxiously likable. He didn't browbeat Murdoch with conversation. He didn't insist on the aisle seat. He didn't even snore in his bloody sleep. The man was as good a seatmate as you could get.

No, better than good.

He used his travel points to upgrade them all to first class, shared his newspaper, and explained the work he was doing on his laptop in simple and entertaining language. He was amusing and easy to talk to.

Murdoch hated him.

Because if he had had to choose a husband for Kiyoko—other than himself, of course—Watanabe would have topped the list. Hell, as he discovered during the flight, the man was not only a savvy businessman, he was an avid cyclist and a skydiver. Smart, fit, and courageous. Under other circumstances, Murdoch could have imagined them as friends.

How bloody annoying was *that*?

"I took the liberty of hiring us a limousine," Watanabe said, as they both tugged their carry-ons out of the overhead bin. "Less stressful for Kiyoko-san."

"Great."

What else could he say? It was a good idea. Just not one that fit within Murdoch's budget.

"How long is the drive to your ranch?" Kiyoko asked, slipping a pale green trench coat over her floral dress. She stood in the aisle two rows behind him, her hand on Sora's shoulder, and Murdoch found it impossible not to smile at her, despite his headache.

Incredibly beautiful. Even in this sea of travel-weary humanity.

"Once we clear customs it'll take us about twenty-five minutes. We'll get there just before dinner." It wasn't *his* ranch, but correcting her would only draw attention to his penury. "It's in the hills above the city."

Clearing customs took an endless amount of time, but eventually they made it to the waiting limo. The limo company had gone out of its way to please Watanabe and the driver was Japanese. Murdoch had to endure a few minutes of bowing and polite greeting before the conversation returned to English.

The driver grinned at him as he hefted Murdoch's knapsack into the trunk. "The Sharks bit the Blackhawks' asses last night, five-zip."

"Go, Sharks," Murdoch said drily.

Watching sports on television, instead of actively participating, had never held much appeal for him. But many of the Gatherers were enthusiastic supporters of the local hockey team, and he actually felt comforted by the familiar conversation. San Jose had become home.

He clambered into the stretch limo and took a seat next to the robe-clad Sora. Unfortunately, that gave him an uninhibited view of Watanabe curled around Kiyoko as they both looked out a side window at the passing sights, pointing and smiling.

He rolled his shoulders to relieve the tightness.

Damn it. If he could survive a bomb blast courtesy of young Carlos Rodriguez, then he could surely survive this. He'd lost his beard in that big battle last spring, but not his life or his sanity. Jealousy was not going to take him down now.

Why had Kiyoko invited the man to accompany her? It was true that she had yet to complete the review of the company financials. But why drag her company president to California to do what could have been done by phone or e-mail?

The car pulled up at the wrought-iron gate that limited access to the estate. Murdoch rolled down his window and greeted the man on guard duty in a small booth.

"Hill," he said, "we should be expected."

The lanky blond Gatherer smiled. "Yeah, Stefan already took care of things. Go ahead."

"Anything exciting happen while I was gone?"

"The house is still in one piece, we haven't seen any weird purple clouds lately, and MacGregor is still whipping our butts. So, I guess that would be no."

Murdoch smiled as he sat back. The gate opened and the car surged up the long driveway toward the two-story ranch house surrounded by an oasis of green vegetation.

"Who is this MacGregor?" Sora asked. "Is he truly more powerful than all of you?"

"No," said Murdoch, "not more powerful. More skilled with a sword and more cunning. The man fights as much with his head as he does with his blade. I've never met his equal."

Kiyoko met his gaze. "Isn't he human?"

"Aye."

"So, you admit that a human can beat back demons with equal success as an immortal."

Murdoch shook his head as the car came to stop in front of the two story house with its wraparound porch. "MacGregor no longer goes out on demon raids. He remains at the ranch to train other Soul Gatherers."

Kiyoko frowned. "He willingly chose that fate?"

Murdoch grinned. "He's married, with a baby on the way. The decision was made for him."

A young woman with long blond hair descended the front steps and reached the car door before the driver had a chance to get out. She tugged it open, then stood back to let Murdoch exit. "Yay, you're back."

There was a time when Emily would have launched herself into his lap with a huge grin on her face. Now, all he got was a light smile. The original version was better. He crawled out. No car was made with the comfort of a six-foot-five man in mind, so it was a relief to unfold his length. He gathered Emily in his arms for a hug.

"Aye, I'm back." Then he turned. Sora, Kiyoko, and Watanabe had filed from the car. "And I've brought a few friends."

"Yeah, Mom's been trying to figure where to put them all," Emily said, extending her hand toward Sora. "Hi, I'm Emily."

He stared at her slim appendage for a moment, then shook it. "A pleasure to meet you, Emily-san. I am Sora Yamashita." He bowed.

The full round of introductions were made, and Emily adapted quickly, bowing instead of offering her hand to the others. Then she ushered them toward the front door. "Please, come inside."

As the four Japanese climbed the steps, Murdoch whispered to Emily, "Great job."

"Thanks." As Murdoch made to follow Yoshio, Emily snagged his arm. "Uh, one thing, though."

He halted. With Emily, *one thing* could be big.

"I'm getting a strange vibe from the old guy." The young woman wrinkled her nose. "His core energy is gold."

Murdoch blinked. "Aren't your mom and Lachlan gold, too?"

"Yes," Emily said. "But that's what I mean by strange. His is gold, but a different gold. Paler and more sparkly."

"That's not very helpful," he said.

She shrugged. "I'm just telling you what I see."

"Maybe it's because he's older?"

"Don't think so. Mrs. Carlyle, my history teacher, is old and her core is the regular gold."

Murdoch was about to suggest that her definition of *old* might be colored by her youth, but decided the point was moot. Emily was getting strange vibes from Sora. That was all he needed to know.

"Thanks," he said.

Female voices, angry and getting louder by the moment, erupted from the house. One was Kiyoko and the other was . . . Lena Sharpe. Damn. He leapt up the steps and burst through the door.

"You know full well why I withdrew my support," Kiyoko said, standing toe to toe with Brian Webster's half-Egyptian girlfriend.

"And you of all people should know how far someone is willing to go to save family," Lena returned hotly. "You stepped over the line yourself."

Kiyoko's lips tightened. "Do not dare compare my actions to yours."

"Why not?" Lena responded, using her extra height to lean over the other woman. "They were both acts of desperation, both done for love."

"My father would never have condoned my sacrifice of a dark relic to save him."

"He wouldn't have condoned you breaking the *on-myōji* code, either," Lena sneered. "Yet you did."

To Murdoch's utter amazement, Kiyoko lost her cool. She shoved Lena with both hands. The taller woman flew back onto the leather sofa, which slid a few feet on the hardwood floor and knocked Rachel Lewis, Emily's mom, off balance.

Balance for an eight-month-pregnant woman is a tenuous thing. Rachel's hands windmilled, one foot shot out, and she went down. Several Gatherers dove for her, frantically trying to interrupt her descent to the hardwood floor, but it was a collision of body parts, and in the end, Rachel met the floor with an audible *thump*.

For a stunned moment, both Kiyoko and Lena fell silent, horrified. Then they leapt to assist. Emily reached her mother first, sliding across the floor and falling to her knees.

"Mom, are you okay?"

Rachel grimaced. "No. I think my water just broke."

Murdoch's gaze found that of Brian Webster, who had just entered the room from the office. "I'll go get MacGregor," Murdoch said, straightening his shoulders.

The other Gatherer nodded.

The next few minutes were some of the longest in Murdoch's lengthy existence. Telling MacGregor about his wife's fall, watching the man cradle his sobbing wife in his lap, and seeing the family off in the Audi, were all painful. Emily and Tyrone Bale, their resident medic, went with them.

"The baby is fine," Sora murmured quietly as they watched the car speed down the drive. "And the woman is only bruised."

"I hope to God you're right," Murdoch said. He intercepted a sharp gesture from Webster. *Inside,* the thumb said. "Though I have a suspicion nothing will save my ass from a thorough tanning."

He followed Webster into the house and down the hall to the library. Anticipating a dressing-down, he closed the door behind him.

"Why the hell didn't you tell me they hated each other?" Webster demanded, rounding on him the moment the door clicked shut. "I could have had them meet in the arena."

"I forgot."

"You *forgot*?"

As excuses went, forgetfulness had no legs. Murdoch knew that. But it was the truth, and he never shrank from the truth, no matter how ugly it was. "A lot has happened since Kiyoko mentioned she and Lena didn't get along."

"I seem to recall you saying the Japanese were reserved and dignified. But your girl obviously attacked Lena. Why?"

Excellent question. "Lena hit a nerve."

"What nerve?"

"I don't know," Murdoch admitted. "I've never seen Kiyoko this angry."

"Not even when you took the Veil away from her?"

Murdoch resisted the urge to fidget. Real men don't shy from criticism. "I haven't got the Veil."

"Why not?"

"I don't know exactly where it is."

"You—" Webster swallowed whatever he was going to say, then turned and strode to his big campaign desk by the window. "So . . . you spent two whole weeks with her and learned nothing. Congratulations."

"She wears it somewhere on her body."

Webster's brows lifted. "And you, the king of the one-night stand, failed to find it? Oh, my God. Tell me it's not so."

The sarcasm stirred his berserker. Just a bit.

"My relationship with Kiyoko is complicated."

"Of course it is." Webster sighed heavily and shook his head. "You know, I don't really care what your damned excuse is, Murdoch. No doubt you did your usual bull-in-a-china-shop thing and pissed her off. Doesn't matter. Just get the Veil and send her on her way. I don't need any more hassles right now."

"I brought her here to meet with Stefan."

"Yeah, well, good luck with that. He's been acting weird ever since I told him the Temple Veil was real. Barely comes out of his trailer."

"So, you're okay if I introduce them?"

"Yeah. Just make it quick."

Webster turned his back and stared out the window into the night, effectively ending the meeting. But as Murdoch reached the door, he added a few quiet words. "If something happens to Rachel or the baby . . ."

Murdoch hung his head. What could he say to that?

Then he left.

After an understandably subdued meal with her hosts, Kiyoko retreated to the room assigned to her. Sinking onto the king-sized bed, she hugged a pillow to her chest and let the tears fall. She had injured another person. An innocent person who had done nothing more sinister than be in the same room. And all because she'd lost control of her emotions, swamped by guilt. That was her greatest flaw, going too far. If she could take back that thoughtless second, she would.

Her father would have been severely disappointed.

The baby's auras had been healthy, and the mother's auras only slightly distressed, but that did not lessen her crime. She hadn't expected Lena to know about the *onmyōji* code, and the reminder of her breach had sliced deeper than she expected. But giving in to the urge to strike Lena had been a monumental failure of self-discipline, an obvious sign that she was not ready to transcend, no matter what Sora said.

A knock sounded at the door.

Kiyoko hurriedly wiped her tears away.

"Come in."

The door opened. Murdoch. Looking more handsome than any man had the right to.

"I'll be staying in the bunkhouse for the duration of your visit, so I've come to collect a few things," he said, pointing at the closet door. His gaze trailed over her face, then studied her hold on the pillow. "Are you well?"

So this was *his* bedroom. "No."

He frowned. "Your ribs are bothering you?"

"No, my conscience."

"You couldn't have known what would happen."

She grimaced. Actually, had she done a divination, she could have known. But that opportunity had passed. "Have you heard anything from the hospital?"

"The bairn is fine. Rachel is in the throes of bringing him into the world as we speak."

"It's a boy?"

Murdoch frowned. "Of course. Why wouldn't it be?"

She snorted. According to the baby's auras, it was a girl. "You haven't learned as much as you'd like to think in seven hundred years, Murdoch. You still possess a medieval mind-set—boys are a greater prize than girls."

He stiffened. "I—"

"Don't bother to deny it. I see similar attitudes among many elder Japanese. Thankfully, my father and Sora did not view my sex as a limitation."

He smiled wryly. "I've nothing against girls. The world would be a sorry place without them. Had you let me finish, I would have explained that MacGregor already has a fine daughter in Emily, and a son would give him a matched set."

"Excellent recovery."

His smile broadened. "Thank you."

"You're still a chauvinist."

"But I'm trying very hard not to be," he said softly.

Kiyoko shook her head. The man was as charming as he was outdated. But she wasn't in the mood to be swayed. "Please collect your belongings. I wish to be alone to meditate."

"Are you truly set on that notion?" He crossed to the closet. Tugging open a built-in drawer, he scooped up several pairs of socks and boxer shorts. Another drawer held T-shirts, and yet another jeans. "I thought we'd pay a visit to Stefan this evening."

"The mage?"

Logic said Murdoch's mage was unlikely to present a solution that other esteemed mystics had not considered, but logic couldn't tame the swell of hope in her chest. She wanted to be well.

"Aye," Murdoch said. "I'll just drop my belongings at the bunkhouse and then we'll knock on his door."

He stuffed his clothing in a small canvas bag with a drawstring and grabbed a rectangular wooden box off the table under the window.

"You play chess?" she asked, nodding at the box.

His eyes lit with interest. "Aye. Do you?"

"Yes."

He replaced the box. "Excellent. Perhaps we'll play a game later. Come on."

Kiyoko followed Murdoch down the lovely wooden stairway to the front door. None of the wood was painted, only stained, and she enjoyed the natural feel of the home. "Is this your house?'

"No, Webster's."

He didn't add to that. Just waved to the group of Gatherers seated around the stone fireplace in the main room and escorted her out the door.

"Wasn't that rude? Not greeting them?"

"No, we're a rather informal bunch. People come and go and they please." He left the paved driveway and headed across the grass toward two buildings, one very large and brightly lit, the other a single-story cedar-roofed structure with more windows.

Kiyoko could not see a perimeter fence. Of course, her ability to note anything was hampered by the slow heat building in her veins. There was something strangely thrilling about walking side by side with Murdoch in the dark, under a silvery half-moon, their bodies close but not touching.

"This is a very large compound."

"Over thirty acres," Murdoch agreed. "But the main buildings are grouped close together. That's the training arena." He pointed to the largest structure. "Was originally for horses, but MacGregor now tutors the Gatherers there."

She frowned. "That does not seem nearly enough. How many Gatherers are there?"

"Thousands." The stone path took them to the multi-windowed building. "This is the bunkhouse." He opened the door and entered the large living space. Dozens of chairs were grouped around low tables and brightly colored rugs. People—mostly men and a few women—sat, stood, or leaned on every available surface. Drinking, playing cards, watching television. The room was loud with chatter when they walked in but fell silent when Murdoch closed the door.

"Kiyoko Ashida, meet the current group of trainees, affectionately nicknamed Batch Four."

The room erupted into a noisy protest, from which one prominent voice bellowed, "Batch Four, my arse. We're called the Wrath of Conn, ya bloody bugger."

Murdoch grinned. "Touchy bunch."

"The Wrath of Conn?" she asked.

He raised his brows. "What? You're not a *Star Trek* fan? It's a twist on the name of a very old movie"—another chorus of protest—"that attempts to accommodate the ego of the loudest man among them."

"Not the loudest," disputed a short, stocky man with drab brown hair and a crooked smile, as he stepped forward and offered Kiyoko his hand. "The firmest on his feet after a long night in the pub. Conn Quinn."

"Don't believe a word he says. He's Irish," Murdoch said. "Soul Gatherers can't get drunk."

Quinn laughed, unoffended.

Kiyoko shook his hand. "A pleasure, Mr. Quinn."

"Stay here while I put my belongings away," Murdoch said to her. Then he eyed Quinn. "Afford her every courtesy. Annoy her and I'll cut off your drinking hand." Then he abandoned her in a room of unfamiliar faces.

"Can I get ya a pint?" Quinn asked, holding up a long-necked brown bottle.

"No, thank you." Kiyoko let her gaze drift around the room. "How long does each of you train with Mac-Gregor?"

"Three months."

"Thirty new warriors every three months?" She shook her head. Developing fine skills was not something you could rush, and three months was not a great deal of time. But . . . "He'll barely make a dent in the numbers at that rate."

Quinn sipped his beer. "It's a hopeless goal, true enough. But not as dismal as you imagine. MacGregor promotes the best warriors in each group to the rank of lieutenant. A lieutenant is qualified to train others, and each group sends at least a dozen out into the world. We're slowly building an army."

Kiyoko stared down the hallway Murdoch had vanished into. "Is Murdoch a lieutenant?"

"The best." Quinn grinned. "Except for me, of course."

She smiled. "Of course."

"What's a lovely lady like yerself doing with an old dog like him anyway? Stamina decreases with age, you know."

"But skill improves."

The Irishman grinned. Tossing an arm over her shoulders, he leaned in to whisper, "Well, then, my girl, you should know that I've spent the last seventy-nine years perfecting my—"

"Quinn." Murdoch reappeared at her side. "Be careful, lad. You're in danger of losing that hand. If not from me, then from her. Did I neglect to mention that she owns a katana and knows how to use it?"

The warning didn't dent Quinn's smile. But it did encourage him to step away. "Good to know."

Murdoch lightly touched the small of Kiyoko's back. "Let's go."

The layers of her clothing seemed to melt away under the heat of his hand. Although subtle, his touch was intimate, and she knew its purpose—to warn Quinn off. Such an obvious territorial statement would normally have annoyed her, but not today. Today, she wished the claim were true.

Murdoch dropped his hand the moment they left the bunkhouse.

Kiyoko sighed. There were times when she wished she were an ordinary woman with an ordinary life. Times when she wished she could act on the impulses that made her heart beat faster and her palms go damp. Murdoch was everything she wanted in a man—confident, competent, and honorable. But he was outside her grasp. In more ways than one.

They did not take the path back to the main house as

Kiyoko expected. Instead, he led her through the small copse of trees behind the bunkhouse.

"Does the mage not live with you?"

"No, Stefan and his wife live over by the fishpond. Nice enough couple, but rather private."

"So, his wife is not a Gatherer?"

Murdoch held a tree branch up so Kiyoko could pass easily. "No, Dika is a human woman much like any other. I believe they're both from Romania."

They circled an outbuilding with a wide, barnlike door and trod a flower-lined pathway to the metal door of a trailer. At least Kiyoko thought it was a trailer. No wheels were visible.

Murdoch rapped sharply on the door.

A slim, dark-eyed, dark-haired woman answered, wiping her hands on a towel. She glanced at Kiyoko, then smiled at Murdoch. "Sorry, Jamie. He's not seeing visitors today," she said.

Jamie? Kiyoko tilted her head. Was that his given name?

Murdoch sniffed the air. "Are you making cabbage rolls? My favorite dish in the whole world?"

"You know I am."

"Without inviting me in for a sample? Dika, you're a heartless lass." Murdoch smiled deeply at the mage's wife, and Kiyoko's heart thudded. Near impossible to deny a man anything when he smiled with such genuine warmth.

Dika was a stronger woman than she. She shrugged. "Any other day and you'd be welcome. Today, you go without."

"Tell him it's an emergency," Murdoch said.

The smile faded from the other woman's face. "He knows why you're here."

"Then he knows there's a life at stake." Murdoch tugged the door out of Dika's hands, opening it wide.

"I understand he's upset about the Veil, but I refuse to stand out here—"

A plump man with inky black locks falling over his eyes pushed past Dika, blocking Murdoch's entrance. "Upset? You think I'm just throwing a tantrum? You have no idea what you're dealing with. Bringing her here was a huge mistake."

Murdoch sighed. "Of all the people I know, you're the only one who might be able to save her, Stefan. Where else would I go?"

"Send her back to Japan. Bury her under the fish-pond. I don't care what you do with her, just get her out of here." With that, he yanked the door free and slammed it shut.

Stunned silence ensued.

A silence that quickly turned awkward.

"Perhaps I offended him somehow," Kiyoko said.

"Don't be ridiculous," Murdoch said slowly. He stared at the door with a frown. "He must be ill or something. The man's always been a bit strange, but he's basically a good soul. Quick to offer his help, creative in his solutions, willing to risk his life."

"Until now."

Murdoch turned the frown on Kiyoko. "Aye, until now."

"A shame we didn't call him before making this rather long journey," Kiyoko said, trying to disguise her fierce disappointment with a lighthearted smile. "I was hoping to see a bit of California before returning home."

Murdoch didn't answer immediately. His gaze remained steady, holding hers.

Finally he said, "I can't let you go."

The words should have been thrilling. Instead, they were chilling. Her heartbeat slowed to match the painful throb in her chest. She knew precisely what he meant, and it wasn't that he couldn't bear to live without her.

"Unless I leave without the Veil," she said.

His expression tightened. "You'll stay until I say you can leave, and that won't be until you can *safely* leave without it."

Her fingers trembled. Kiyoko tucked her hands into the folds of her skirt and focused on her breathing, ruthlessly settling her thoughts. He had been honest about his goal from the start. Succumbing to the lure of his crooked smile had been her mistake, not his. "Until you say I can leave? Would you rather see me die here, far away from my home, far from all I know and love, than give me the freedom to choose my own fate?"

A riot of emotions played over his face, but for once the berserker did not surface. It was Murdoch alone who answered, his auras a steady pulse of periwinkle blue.

"I will *not* let you die."

Azazel extended his left wing toward the wall of his castle chamber, twisting it slightly to catch the candlelight. He smiled. From his marginal coverts, across his downy alulars, and clear down to the tips of his long sweeping primaries, all was a glossy sea of black. The only gray feathers remaining on his left side were two scapulars up near his shoulder.

He peered in the smoky glass of the mirror.

Barely noticeable.

Of course, had he acquired the Veil, the picture would be even prettier. Murdoch's untimely return had dashed his hopes in a most annoying way. But there would be other opportunities. It was only a matter of time before Kiyoko shared the whereabouts of the Veil, and while he cooled his heels, his army grew in strength. The Scottish Soul Gatherer would not be a problem in the end. Not for a legion of bone-sappers.

The real concern was that girl.

The one known as the Trinity Soul.

Her sensing skills were incredibly powerful. The moment the car had driven onto the estate, he'd felt her testing the edges of his glamour. Only by drawing on the full range of the skills he'd developed over centuries of seducing human women had he managed to keep his true identity cloaked. But that couldn't last. One tiny slip on his part, one moment of inattentiveness, and she'd see through him.

In a perfect world, he would simply kill her. But two ancient primal spells bestowed upon her by Death and God had granted the young female immortality. And kidnapping or harming her would bring the wrath of the archangels down upon his head. How to effectively neutralize her was a conundrum worthy of some thought.

In the meantime, though, every new black feather was cause for celebration.

"I need food," he bellowed.

The heavy wooden door of his chamber swung open and a strong, virile male with dark curly hair was tossed inside. Still proud, the man rose quickly from the cold stone floor, his chin high and his shoulders stiff. But as his gaze took in Azazel's spiraled goat horns, the multitude of glowing runes etched into his skin by his own fingernails, and the mighty black wings, the fool's air of defiance wavered.

The fallen angel smiled. "What's your name?"

"Carl Roche."

Azazel crossed the room and circled his prize, allowing his primary feathers to brush the man's arms and legs. The accelerated pump of blood sang to him, and he leaned in close to let the waves of heat crest over him. "Not afraid, Carl?"

"You and your creepy crawlies don't have nothin' on me, man."

Azazel laughed. "You're a regular badass, are you?"

"I've killed twenty-seven people," Carl affirmed.

"Punks? Hookers?" guessed Azazel with a faint sneer. Unable to resist, he ran a finger along the man's stubbled chin and down his thick neck.

"Regular joes, too. Even kids, if you count those who OD'd on the drugs I sold. Then the number goes up to almost a hundred."

"Oh?" Azazel lifted his gaze from the throbbing carotid pulse whispering his name. "Tell me, Carl. What's the worst thing you've ever done?"

"Strangled my thirteen-year-old daughter to death. The bitch stole my cigarettes."

Azazel raised his brows. "My, that *is* nasty."

Carl nodded, pleased.

"But not nasty enough to dare compare yourself to me," Azazel said. "You don't make bottom rung demon for less than five hundred deaths or monstrous behavior like butchering innocents just for fun. And to reach the top of the ladder where I stand, you must be a truly gifted dispenser of evil. You, Carl Roche, are nothing more than a garden-variety worm."

And with that, he tipped Carl's head to one side and sank his fangs into the pulpy flesh of his neck.

13

Murdoch yanked Kiyoko to his chest, bent his head to her lips, and kissed her with all the frustrated anger searing his veins. And just as she had in every dream he'd enjoyed in the past two weeks, she kissed him back with equal fervor.

He knew it was a dream. He knew because the berserker never surfaced. Never even flexed a toe. But he didn't care. He let the vision own him, savoring every sweet nuance of Kiyoko's soft skin, every heady rub of her lips against his, every bead of sweat that rose on his brow from resisting the urge to take her hard and fast.

He dug his fingers into her hair and angled her head to deepen the kiss. Wanting more. *Needing* more. Her lips parted under the encouraging sweep of his tongue, and he took full advantage. The whimper she released as their tongues tangled set his blood aflame and tightened his skin to painful intensity.

He peeled off his shirt and tossed it aside.

Then just as quickly, he dispensed of Kiyoko's flowery dress, leaving just the soft cotton lace of her underwear, and pulled her back against him. Skin to skin.

The dance of her delicate hands over the hot muscles of his back sent ripples of pleasure to every nerve ending in his body. And the responding pound of his blood near made his eyes roll back in his head. Dear God. He wanted those hands on other parts of his body, cupping him, squeezing him. In three short steps, he had her backed up against a birch tree, grinding his jeans-encased pelvis against her nearly bare body.

Trying desperately to relieve the pressure.

He'd never wanted a woman so badly.

He had to have her.

Releasing her hair, he attacked his belt buckle. But his fingers wouldn't do his bidding. They bumbled the simplest of tasks, and he moaned his frustration against her lips.

She gently brushed his hands away, taking over. Belt, jeans, boxers. Quicker than he thought possible, he was free. But not satisfied. Not even close. He buried his face in the fragrant hollow of her throat and begged.

"Please," he murmured, needing Kiyoko to touch him.

And she did. Mercy, her cool fingers on his achingly tight skin nearly finished him right then and there. But he gritted his teeth and held on. He wanted this never to end. The sensations were so vivid and cruel and beautiful that he could have expired at that moment and been happy.

Then she moved. With one hand holding him steady, she used the other to pump up and down. From the base of his cock to the very tip, teasing every sensitive spot along the way. Perhaps because it was a dream, or perhaps because she was a goddess, the hand stroking him was lubricated, rocking his world with a perfect blend of friction and glide.

The breath caught in Murdoch's throat.

Sweet Jesus.

He really *was* going to die.

It was almost as if she could read every feverish peak of excitement rippling through his body. She knew just how to touch him. Slow at first—oh, so tortuously slow—then faster as the tension in his body rose. Faster and faster.

His breaths grew raspy and shallow.

Every inch of his skin shivered with expectation.

She didn't let up. She teased and taunted his flesh, making his head spin with every perfectly pressured stroke and every creative swirl over the tip.

And he came.

Lord, how he came. In a glorious explosion of sensation, accompanied by a low moan and a soft, adoring whisper of her name. His ears were ringing. His blood was pounding. And the scent that was uniquely Kiyoko filled his nose. Sheer heaven.

A fist pounded on the door. "Murdoch? You in there?"

Murdoch's eyes flew open. Above him was the wood-paneled ceiling of the bunkhouse. Beside him were the twisted sheets of his bunk bed. No Kiyoko. Trying not to analyze the keen sense of loss swirling in his gut, he quickly covered himself with a sheet and sat up.

Just in time. The door swung open and Brian Webster entered the private bunk room.

"You're supposed to wait until I give you leave to enter." Murdoch said, raking his hair out of his eyes.

"You look like shit. Rough night?"

"Do you have a reason for being here at this ungodly hour of the morning, Webster? Or did Lena kick your sorry ass out of bed?"

The other man grinned boldly, not bothered one bit by the suggestion that his love life was lacking. Because it obviously wasn't. "Gotta say, now that I've met Kiyoko, I'm not surprised it took you so long to return from Japan. She's quite the looker. If you need advice on how to get to date number three, call me."

Murdoch scowled. "Just so we're clear, Webster, we are *not* friends. I don't want or need your advice. Go annoy someone else."

"Stop being a grouch." Webster crossed to the window and yanked open the drapes. Even in jeans and T-shirt, the man looked like he'd just stepped out of a damned fashion magazine. "Rachel had the baby."

Murdoch's annoyance slipped away. "Really?"

His boss nodded. "Girl. Eight pounds three ounces. Mom and baby are doing fine."

"Thank God."

"How cool is that? We're uncles."

Murdoch stood, wrapping the sheet around his hips. "*We* aren't anything. *You* are a pain in the ass, and *I* am late for breakfast. Can I have some bloody privacy, please?"

"I'm going." But the wretch didn't leave. "I confess, I thought you'd be up at the house with Kiyoko, not bunking down here. What's the matter? She sleeping with one of the two guys she arrived with?"

Murdoch closed his eyes. *He is my boss. I will not kill him.* With every shred of restraint he could muster, he pointed at the door. "Get. Out."

The door creaked open. "Come out to the arena after you've eaten, so I can teach you the finer points of being a plebe. You really need to show more respect for your betters."

Murdoch lifted his gaze.

One-on-one duels rarely roused his slumbering berserker, and without its preternatural edge he and Webster were evenly matched. Webster had less formal training, but he had a gift for the sword that few men possessed, and he was lightning fast. A sword fight would be an excellent way to blow off some steam.

"I look forward to it."

*   *   *

Emily drove home with Lachlan, exhausted but content. Bale had taken a cab back to the ranch the previous night, and her mom was resting at the hospital, so the car was quiet. She eyed her stepfather's face as he maneuvered the car along the windy road through the hills above San Jose.

"Are you disappointed?" she asked.

He tossed her a quick glance. "About what?"

"That the baby's a girl."

He smiled. "Absolutely not. Katie's healthy, that's enough for me. And from the look of her, I suspect she'll grow up to be a real beauty, like her sister."

"Stepsister."

"Close enough," he said. He tossed her another look. "I thought you were pleased about the baby."

"I am." Just being stupid. Feeling like second fiddle for no good reason. "You deserve to have a kid of your own."

He pressed a button on the dash. A moment later, he pulled into the estate entrance and squeezed through the slowly opening gate, waving to the Gatherer in the booth as they passed. "Katie was a bonus. Being a parent to you was already satisfying. I enjoy the role I play in your life."

She smiled. "Even when I backtalk?"

Lachlan halted the car in front of the house, then turned to face her. "No' so keen about that part, I'll admit. But it's less of an issue these days."

"Yeah, I'm getting older. Got another birthday next week."

"Sweet sixteen." Another smile. This one more sly. "I know."

"Did you get me something?"

"Would I tell you if I did?" He opened the door and climbed out of the car. "And spoil the surprise?"

"You're cruel."

He grinned. "Aye. That's best part of being an evil stepfather."

Spurred by a happy bubble in her chest, Emily hugged Lachlan. "I'm going over to the arena to check on the trainees. Coming?"

"Give me twenty minutes. I need to take a shower and make sure Katie's room is ready for her arrival tonight, and then I'll be there."

"Pulleez." Emily rolled her eyes. "You can't fool me. I know you're calling the florist. How many dozen roses are you sending to Mom?"

He smiled down at her. "As many as they have."

"You're such a sap."

Planting a kiss on her forehead, he pushed her away. "Go."

She obligingly turned. "I'm going to see the mushy note eventually, you know."

"Aye, well, if you hover over me while I craft it, it won't be genuine. Go."

Emily crossed the grass to the arena with a smile on her face. Lachlan was okay. Really okay. She tugged open the door of the arena.

As big as a hockey rink inside, the arena had a sand floor and two sets of bleachers, one on each side. In the center, several mock battles were going on, but the one that immediately caught her eye was the one involving the two Japanese warriors.

One guy, one girl, both dressed in long, wide-legged black pants and elbow-length shirts, with some sort of armor over top. Both fighting with two swords—one short and one long—and both attacking quick as rattlesnakes. They moved with such grace and flowing ease that they looked more like a dance couple than battling opponents.

Totally smokin'.

Brian was talking to one of the trainees, so she scrambled up the right-side bleachers and took a seat next to the elderly Japanese man she had gotten the strange vibes from earlier. Sora something-or-other.

"That's really cool," she said. "The two-sword thing."

"*Nitōjutsu.*"

She grimaced. "Sorry. I don't speak Japanese."

The old man smiled gently. "The two-sword method is called *nitōjutsu*. It dates back to the time of the great samurai."

"Oh." She eyed him more directly. His narrow face was wrinkled and his long hair was white, but his eyes were clear and bright. "Are you their coach?"

"Yes."

Elbows on her knees, she leaned forward, her attention once again drawn to the sword fight. "Bet it takes a long time to learn moves like that."

"It depends on how willing a pupil you are."

"I'm not a very good student. I find it hard to concentrate these days." Em sighed. "Who am I kidding? Not just lately. I've had trouble for the past couple of years."

"Ever since you started noticing boys?"

She flushed. "Maybe."

"Very normal," Sora said, nodding. "Kiyoko-san and Yoshio-san both had the same problem."

"Those two?" she asked, pointing.

"Yes."

"You sure can't tell." The two danced barefoot, sliding across the sand without a wobble and attacking with absolute precision. They effortlessly deflected slices and resumed their guard positions with an enviable speed.

"Because they've learned the art of stilling the mind. You could learn it as well. It's not difficult."

"Hmmm." It was tempting to ask him to teach her, but that seemed pretty rude, considering she barely knew him. "I usually train with Brian, Murdoch, or my stepdad. I've been learning the techniques of the old European masters."

"An excellent foundation." His gaze lifted to the dark red steak in her hair—the bright lights of the arena no doubt made it hard to ignore—and his expression grew thoughtful. "If you desire to learn the Japanese way of the sword, I would be most pleased to be your sensei."

"That means teacher."

He nodded. "You do wish to learn, do you not?"

Em grinned wryly. "Am I that obvious?"

"Yes," he said with a smile. "But enthusiasm is a virtue."

A virtue. She had virtues. How cool was that? "Yeah, I'd really like to learn, sensei," Em said. "When can we start?"

"How about now?"

She blinked. "Uh, I guess so. Do I need a special sword?"

The old man stood. "Not today. We'll start with words, not weapons. Come, let us find a peaceful place to begin."

Em chewed her lip for a moment. The strange vibes she got from him didn't have any hint of darkness, just an air of quiet mystery. Pale gold was, after all, still gold. She glanced at Brian, who was now demonstrating an ox guard for his companion. Then she looked for Murdoch, but the big Scot wasn't anywhere in sight. Oh, well, they probably wouldn't miss her anyway.

"Okay, let's do it."

She followed Sora out of the arena, wondering how he kept the hem of his black robes so clean when it constantly dragged along the ground. Magic, maybe.

A wave of heat rolled over Kiyoko the moment Murdoch stepped into the arena. Her cheeks flushed, but through some small miracle, she maintained her com-

posure and did not falter in her sparring match with Yoshio. A miracle, because this morning's dream had been
the most intimate yet.

The match ended, and she bowed to her opponent.

Yoshio was the closest thing she had to a sibling. He
had arrived at her father's doorstep at the tender age
of seven and had trained alongside Kiyoko every day
since. Although he lived in the compound and not under
her father's roof, they had spent many an hour together
when their studies were done. Climbing hills and trees,
naming shapes they saw in the clouds, laughing over
their first attempts at divination.

He smiled at her.

They weren't as close now. Not since he found his first
girlfriend and became a little more reserved. But he was
never far from her side.

Kiyoko sheathed her katana, then quickly scanned the
bleachers for Sora, skipping over the all-too-appealing
male body standing next to Brian Webster and Conn
Quinn. She wasn't sure she could ever look Murdoch
in the eye again. Not when she knew they shared those
dreams.

Sora had disappeared.

She raised a brow at Yoshio, but he shrugged.

"He left a few moments ago."

How curious. No kata practice this morning. "Shall
we go get breakfast, then?"

Yoshio wrinkled his nose. "Did you see what they
eat in the morning? Everything is dripping in butter or
grease."

"Murdoch said the cafeteria in the bunkhouse serves
all nationalities. We must be able to get some rice and
tea."

A guttural roar echoed through the arena, followed
quickly by the metallic slither of sword against sword.
Immediately, the mock battles around her ceased and

everyone turned to watch, big smiles on their faces. Kiyoko peered over Yoshio's shoulder to see who was battling whom. She wasn't entirely surprised to see Murdoch and Brian Webster locked in a fierce test of sword skills.

But she *was* surprised by the hummingbird-fast beat of the duel. And by the snarling aggression on their handsome faces. A serious business, this battle. Murdoch's swings sang with power and precision, but Webster appeared to be holding his own, attacking and parrying with breathtaking agility.

Both men scored on each other within seconds. Murdoch took a cut to the left arm and Webster a slice to the shoulder. Neither paid any mind. They continued to draw blood with a cavalier attitude that made Kiyoko wince.

"My money's on Murdoch," said one nearby Soul Gatherer.

"Don't be so sure," responded his colleague, tugging his wallet out of his pants and peeling off two twenties. "He won't let the berserker rise during a practice duel, so I'm betting Webster kicks his ass."

"You're on."

Kiyoko grimaced. Bloodthirsty savages, the lot of them. She grabbed Yoshio's sleeve. "Come on. The cafeteria will be nearly empty with this going on."

"You don't want to wait and see if Murdoch wins?"

"No, watching two men slice themselves to ribbons will make it difficult to swallow my breakfast."

He peered over his shoulder at the fight. "None of the wounds are overly deep. They'll heal within hours."

"That's hardly the point." Kiyoko sighed. Yoshio was as bad as the others. He couldn't look away. "Stay, if you like. I'm going back to the house."

Her partner nodded, clearly distracted.

Men.

As she exited the arena into a dull, cloudy morning, she narrowly avoided bumping into Ryuji, who was on his way inside. "My apologies, Ryuji-san. I wasn't looking where I was going."

He smiled. "Neither was I."

It was a very nice smile, one Kiyoko could not help but return. Vaguely self-deprecating to start, warmly admiring to finish. Hard to resist. He was an attractive man, especially in his pale blue sweater and dark gray pants. More important, he knew everything there was to know about Ashida Corporation and could help her understand some of the odd expenses she'd mulled over in the financial reports.

Cold, dry numbers were just the thing she needed to flush the last of those lingering dreams from her mind. "Have you had breakfast?"

"Tea only."

"Would you like to join me?"

"I would." He glanced at the painted white doors of the arena. "Did you happen to see young Emily Lewis inside? Her father asked me to give her a message if I saw her."

Kiyoko recalled her scan of the bleachers. "I don't believe she's here."

"Then I don't suppose the message will matter. He is delayed in attending her practice." He offered his arm. "Shall we go to the cafeteria? They have a small but freshly made selection of sushi. I was actually hoping to talk you about the audit. A number of art pieces belonging to the company are unaccounted for, and I fear they may have been lost along with your father's house. Would you be willing to go through the list with me?"

Kiyoko took his arm. "I'd be happy to."

Her father had greatly admired Ryuji. Not just for his business sense, which Tatsu Ashida had lauded both publicly and privately, but also for his dedication to his

family. Ryuji supported his widowed mother, his two un-
married sisters, and a host of aunts and uncles.

Her father had never pressured her to look at Ryuji
with an eye toward marriage, but he hadn't made a secret of his hopes, either.

Unfortunately, there was no spark. At least not on
her side. And there was certainly nothing remotely like
the fiery need Murdoch inspired in her.

"Kiyoko."

Her heart did a strange little dance at the rumbled
syllables of her name. Amazing. It was almost as if she
could conjure Murdoch just by thinking of him.

She halted, ignoring Ryuji's stiff arm and obvious reluctance to stop. Turning, she faced Murdoch. And suffered another torrid wave of embarrassment. He was
fully dressed—if you didn't count the numerous slices
left by Brian's sword—but in her mind's eye he was as
naked as he'd been in her dream. The dream where she
had brought him to—

"Yes?" she choked out.

"I need to speak with you."

"Surely it can wait until after breakfast, Mr. Murdoch?" Ryuji said nicely. "A half hour would give you
time to patch up those wounds and avoid bleeding all
over Kiyoko-san."

Murdoch favored Ryuji with a cool look. "No, it can't
wait."

Kiyoko assessed the cuts on his flesh. None were serious, thankfully. "Who won the duel?"

"Webster."

Not a hint of shame or disappointment colored his
voice. Not an ounce of concern that he'd been beaten.
How many men could claim such an unshakable ego?

"Did you forfeit?" she asked, curious.

"No."

"But you allowed it to end," she guessed.

Murdoch didn't respond. He just stared at her, his eyes steady and intense. The man had an amazing ability to lay claim to her without saying a single word.

"I'm having breakfast with Watanabe-san," she said firmly. "Afterward, I'll be practicing *zazen* in my room. If you wish to speak with me, visit then."

The muscles in his jaw flexed.

Hoping to circumvent a regrettable spill of anger, she turned away.

"Kiyoko."

There was a wealth of steely promise stuffed into that one word, leaving no doubt that Murdoch was about to take action and that the result wouldn't be to her liking.

She spun around.

"Come here," he demanded softly.

Her pride screamed for her to ignore the autocratic command, or even sneer at it. But wisdom prevailed. Murdoch's sure-footed stance hearkened back to his roots as a medieval warrior—wild, untamed, and unpredictable. Every sinew in his body was coiled tight, every inch of skin radiating fierce intensity. She suspected he was not above punching Ryuji in the face and tossing her over his shoulder.

With a faint tremble, she walked toward him.

She halted several feet away, but he closed the gap with a decisive step. The steamy scent of leather and spent energy washed over her, and her heart skipped a beat. He stared into her eyes for a long, searing moment, then bent to her ear. He spoke in a voice so low and intimate that damp heat stirred the hairs at her temple. "If you are truly fond of Watanabe, do *not* touch him again."

Her lips tightened.

How dare he—

"I don't understand the strange bond between us," he said softly. "But I accept it. Make no mistake. After what we shared last night, there is no going back. You are mine."

Kiyoko was left staring at his back as he opened the door to the arena and disappeared inside.

14

Murdoch searched high and low for Sora, and finally found him up on the hill where the tennis courts used to be. Lying in the crater Rodriguez had made last summer, staring up at the clouds with Emily.

"What in the bloody blazes are you doing?" he asked, glaring down at the pair from the edge of the crater.

Emily sat up, grinning.

"The sensei is teaching me about yin and yang. Totally neat stuff. Day and night, hot and cold, male and female. Each one complements and transforms the other. I'm the yin to Carlos's yang. That's why we fit so well together."

Murdoch winced internally.

Ah, Christ. Just when Emily might be turning the corner on her lost relationship with Rodriguez, the old man was stirring things up again.

"And the lesson requires lying in the dirt because . . . ?"

Sora responded, still peacefully reposed, watching a thin cloud drift overhead. "We were exploring contrasts."

"We were also getting a feel for the five elements," added Emily as she scrambled up the crater wall to Murdoch's side. "Wind, water, earth, wood, and fire."

"Fire?"

She shrugged. "We're having a really dry winter this

year, so no actual flames. But Carlos created this crater with fire, so I figured it was the next best thing."

Murdoch sighed. "Emily, Carlos is—"

"Gone. Yeah, I know." She caught the look on his face and added, "Don't worry. I'm not sneaking off to visit him. He asked to be left alone, so I'm leaving him alone."

"Good lass," Murdoch said.

"But I can still feel him."

If Carlos had been within range of his fist at that moment, Murdoch would have given the Soul Gatherer the thrashing of his life. There was hope in Emily's eyes—bright, shining hope that the lad would return one day and pick up where they'd left off. Whatever he'd written in his good-bye note hadn't been enough. He'd left room for her to dream.

Which meant that there was more heartache to come. Because a relationship between Carlos and Emily was even more impossible than one between him and Kiyoko. The berserker wasn't a monster. It was just careless. The thing that lived inside Carlos and urged him toward violence? Definitely a monster. A red-eyed, crater-forming, skin-searing monster. The explosive battle of last spring had made that painfully clear.

Knowing she could sense Carlos anywhere in the world and visit him in the blink of an eye was frightening. But there was nothing to be done about it, except pray that she stayed away.

"I need to have a few private words with the sensei," he said. "Would you mind heading back to the house on your own?"

Some of the sparkle left her eyes. "Guess not."

"Thank you." He caught her arm as she turned to depart. "I'm driving into town later. Want to come along?"

"In what? Brian sold your Mustang, so you've got no wheels." Her eyes widened. "Wait. Unless . . . ? Jeez, are you offering me a ride on the Triumph?"

"Absolutely not. Your mother would slay me if I let you on the bike. I'll borrow a car."

"You're no fun." But she smiled. "Come find me when you're done." Then she trekked down the hill.

"What did you wish to discuss, Mr. Murdoch?"

Murdoch faced the old man, who now stood on the grass a few feet away, brushing dirt off his robes. "The missing scrolls."

"That will be difficult, as I no longer have them."

"So you say."

Sora sent him a thoughtful look. "Are you suggesting I made a pretense of their disappearance? Why would I do that?"

"To manipulate Kiyoko. Despite her very convincing explanation, I don't believe those papers outline an ordinary coming-of-age ritual. More likely, they offer the promise of greater powers."

"They do."

Murdoch frowned. "You don't deny the true nature of the ritual? That it's intended to increase her demon-slaying powers?"

"No," replied Sora. "But I do deny stealing the scrolls."

"I want the truth this time, old man. What does the ritual do? And what are the risks to Kiyoko?"

Sora returned his gaze calmly. "Why do you assume Kiyoko faces any danger in performing the ritual?"

"Because nothing in this world is free," Murdoch said grimly. He ought to know. "Power always comes with a price. Now, cease your dissembling. What does the ritual do?"

"I cannot say."

"Why not?"

"Because once I tell you, you'll be obligated to share the information with your master."

"My *master*? You mean Webster?"

"No, I mean Death."

Murdoch blinked. His last conversation with the lethal goddess came into mind. The one where she'd called Sora a thief. "You know one another."

"Not really. More like passing acquaintances."

"But you stole something from her."

Sora shrugged his thin shoulders. "A debatable point. The item in question was never actually hers."

"What was it?"

"I cannot say."

Murdoch resisted the urge to grab the man and shake him. Sora was definitely hellspawn. He was too annoying not to be. "Blast it, man. Kiyoko's life is at stake. Stop being so damned difficult."

"I am as eager to save Kiyoko as you are, Mr. Murdoch." The sensei tucked his hands into his sleeves.

"Then why not tell me the truth? Why not let me help?"

"Because you would hand Kiyoko over to Death in the blink of an eye."

Murdoch stiffened. "That's a filthy lie."

"Is it?" Silver-white brows knitted over dark eyes. "What happens when Death lays a hand on you, Mr. Murdoch?"

Murdoch's heart hit the wall of his chest at terminal velocity. The instant Death touched him, she gained access to his memories. *All of them.* He could keep nothing secret, even if he wanted to. But— "She's not interested in Kiyoko. She has her eye on a different target."

"Are you willing to gamble Kiyoko's life on that?"

A heavy weight settled on Murdoch's shoulders. The only safe bet was that Death would always be a sly bitch. "No."

"Then put aside your curiosity about the ritual. Focus your efforts on routing the demons."

"You ask too much." Murdoch folded his arms over his chest. "I don't trust you."

"Not surprising. I've yet to give you reason." Sora smiled. The sort of benign, know-it-all smile that never failed to grate on the nerves. "In all honesty, to win the day, there's only one person you need have faith in. Yourself. I would start there."

The old man nodded pleasantly, then traced Emily's grass-flattened footprints down the hill.

Wretch.

"I sold the statue on the black market for three hundred thousand dollars. It would help me out if you would tell the insurance company that it was in the house when it burned, so I can avoid jail."

Kiyoko lifted her gaze from her tea. "What?"

"Just checking to see if you were listening." Ryuji smiled and poured them both more tea. "You're bored."

Her cheeks grew warm. Ryuji had been an excellent breakfast companion. While they ate, he amused her with stories about his childhood in rural Nagano, politely inquired about typical *onmyōji* rituals, and even shared a few memories of her beloved father.

But he was not Murdoch.

"Not bored," she said. "Momentarily distracted. So much has happened in the past few days."

"Then I suggest we resume our business talks. The corporate art list still needs to be reviewed. It's in my room at the bunkhouse."

Ryuji's smile was so engaging, Kiyoko almost said yes. But time had a tendency to run away on her during sessions with him. Minutes turned into hours. "Would you mind terribly if we postponed? I promised Murdoch I would meet with him after breakfast."

The smile disappeared. "I was hoping to get your

sign-off this morning, so I could fax it to the office. It won't take long, I promise. Half an hour at most."

"I hate to inconvenience Murdoch more than I have already. As you no doubt noticed, he was very eager to speak with me."

A crease on Ryuji's brow briefly signaled his displeasure. "Later today, then?"

They agreed on a time and place to get together and then she left him in the cafeteria, eyeing a cinnamon sticky bun smothered in white icing.

She fully expected to bump into Murdoch on the way back—he'd staked his claim, after all. Every rumble of deep male voice made her heart flutter, every heavy footstep in the gravel behind her made her head turn. But none of the Soul Gatherers she met on her return to the ranch house were six foot five and Scottish.

Sighing, she pushed open the door . . .

. . . and nearly took Yoshio's nose off.

"My apologies, Yoshio-san," she said as he leapt back. "I was—" Distracted by thoughts of Murdoch. Again. "Lost in thought."

"No apology necessary, Kiyoko-san. The fault is mine." His face pale, the young man bowed politely, then ducked out the door.

She stared at the closed door, frowning.

What had he—

"I take it you can now fit me into your busy social calendar?" drawled the low voice she'd wanted to hear for the past five minutes.

She spun around.

Murdoch was lounging against the doorjamb leading into the living room, a wry smile on his lips and a giant mug of coffee in his hand. The sight of him sucked the air out of the room. Broad shoulders draped in smooth white cotton, narrow hips encased in low-slung black jeans, and muscular forearms sprinkled with dark hair. Handsome beyond belief.

And he knew it.

Kiyoko licked her dry lips. "I'm about to meditate."

"Good," he said. "Let's go upstairs and get started."

"I don't think it would be appropriate for us to be alone, given the . . . uh, given the . . ."

"Dreams we've been sharing?" he finished for her.

"Yes."

He pushed away from the wall and sauntered toward her. "Lass, we've already hit second base and we're rounding the corner toward third. At this point, modesty is a rather insubstantial barrier."

"Dreams are *not* reality." She backed up a step.

"Are you certain? You have a birthmark just below your right breast. How real is that?" he asked softly.

Her cheeks flamed. "Sora-san told you."

"No, I've seen it. I've kissed it."

Desperate to shut out his all-too-perceptive gaze, she buried her face in her hands. "Stop."

Heavy footsteps skipped down the stairs from the second floor. "Is everything all right?" asked a male voice. A milder version of Murdoch's Scottish brogue, barely noticeable. MacGregor.

"We're fine," Murdoch responded, taking up a protective stance, his back to her. Hiding her embarrassment from prying eyes. "Headed back to the hospital, are you?"

"Aye." A pause. "Are you sure everything is all right?"

Kiyoko took a deep calming breath and stepped out from behind her huge shield. "Yes, everything is fine. Please offer Rachel-san my most sincere apologies. I'm relieved to know she and the baby are healthy."

MacGregor smiled. "It was an accident—think no more of it. I'll be bringing Rachel and Kate home later today."

With that, he almost flew out the door.

"I've never seen the man smile so much," Murdoch said, shaking his head. "Apparently, producing a babe is a joy like no other."

Kiyoko met his gaze. "Even when it's a girl."

"So it would seem. Shall we go upstairs?" Spying her downturned lips, he added, "I'll keep my distance—you have my word. I've no intention of repeating the mistake of touching you. Believe it or not, it's not my habit to crush women."

"Crush? Perhaps not. But you seem quite content to smother me. Threatening my friends at every turn and claiming me as *yours* is hardly a way to give me breathing room."

His gaze remained level. "Lass, let's be blunt. Dream or no dream, you've been naked and willing in my arms. Call me old-fashioned, but to my mind, that means something."

Willing? More like wanton. "Threatening Watanabe-san was unwarranted."

"Aye, well. I'm a simple man with simple notions." Using his coffee mug, he pointed up the stairs.

Kiyoko obeyed the unspoken command and climbed the stairs. *Simple* was the last word she would use to describe Murdoch. "What does that mean, precisely?"

"I expect my women to be true."

She halted and turned to face him, two steps lower than she was. His eyes were level with hers. There was so much wrong with his offhand remark, she didn't know where to begin. "Your *women*? You have more than one?"

"At the moment? No."

"Are you suggesting that *I* am your woman?"

"Yes."

"Did I agree to that?"

He smiled. "Verbally? No."

"Are you also suggesting that *if* I were your woman—a claim which I dispute—having breakfast with Watanabe-san would constitute being *untrue*?"

His eyes narrowed at her icy tone. "Encouraging his attention is unwise."

"And how does one encourage a man's attention, may I ask? Speaking to him? Smiling? Pouring tea for him?"

Murdoch frowned. "I believe I was quite specific."

"No touching."

"Aye."

"So, accepting a proffered arm on a stroll is forbidden. Is that true with any man, or just Watanabe-san?"

Murdoch stared at her, silent.

She sighed. "He's the president of my father's company. I am making a very determined effort to learn the business. That means spending time with him. Lots of time. Get used to it, Murdoch."

"Admit that you're my woman, and I'll do my best."

"This is the twenty-first century. Men don't own women."

A slow smile spread over his face. "If you prefer to claim me as your man, that's an acceptable compromise."

Kiyoko snorted and continued up the stairs. "Why bother? We can never be a couple. We cannot touch without invoking your berserker."

They entered Murdoch's bedroom—now hers—and closed the door. Kiyoko curled up on the cushioned window seat, as far away from the bed and Murdoch as she could get.

"I thought you said I need only acknowledge that the berserker's actions are my own," he said, trailing her across the room, "and I would gain control over it."

"That's a necessary step, but taming the berserker will not be easy. It will take practice." She tilted her head and studied the rugged angles of his face. "And self-knowledge."

He appropriated the armchair with the lithe grace of a large cat, kicked off his boots, and rested his socked feet on the cushion next to her. Effectively trapping her against the window. "Please don't tell me I need to confess all my deep dark sins, confront my past, and accept who I am. I'm not into psychobabble bullshit."

"Do you *have* any deep dark sins?"

Murdoch cupped his mug in both hands. "If I did, I sure as bloody hell wouldn't admit them to the woman I'm trying to impress."

"But you did commit at least one serious sin. Lena told me all Gatherers are serving time in purgatory."

He sipped his coffee. "Are you back on speaking terms with Lena? I'm happy to hear that."

"Don't change the subject. What was your sin?"

"Adultery."

She feigned a gasp. "You? The one who insists his women be true? Surely not." A flush rose on his cheeks. "Is a single adulterous affair enough to send a person to purgatory? Death must have Gatherers to spare."

"There may have been more than one," he admitted.

"Hmmm. Something tells me there's more to this story that you're saying, Murdoch."

"Isn't seducing a bevy of married women bad enough?"

"To send you to purgatory, perhaps. But not to account for your reluctance to discuss the topic. You're embarrassed. Tell me why."

"I'd rather not."

Kiyoko considered letting him off the hook. He looked decidedly uncomfortable. But confession was good for the soul. "An honorable man would share such information. To ensure that his chosen woman entered into a relationship with open eyes."

"Damn, you're ruthless."

She waited. Patiently.

"All right," he said, on a heavy sigh. "I slept with my brother's wife."

She sucked in a breath so sharp it stung. "You did *what*?"

"You heard me."

"*Why*?"

"Why does any man tup a woman?" he asked drily.

"But she was married to your brother. That's like sleeping with your sister."

"No, it bloody well is not." Sitting up, he set his mug on the table next to his chair. "Margaret was a lovely lass, and I had occasion to sleep with her a time or two before she married my brother. Believe me, she wasn't my sister."

"Did she make the first overture?"

"Is a glance an overture?" he asked. Then he shrugged. "I knew she wanted me. I was off to war the next morn, so I took advantage. That's the whole of it."

His stiff shoulders said far more than his words. He was lying. There was something else about the tale that he didn't wish to reveal. But she chose to let it go.

"Tell me about the potion."

He sat back. "When I was fifteen, I was captured by the Norse in a raid on the coast of Mann. They hoped that I would fill out enough to become a rower on one of their Viking ships. Alas, that never happened. For three years, I was held as a slave in the Northern Isles and worked to the bone. I was near death when a very powerful jarl purchased me from my master."

"He saved you."

Murdoch snorted. "In a manner of speaking. To improve his odds of success in a raid on a neighboring island, he offered me as a sacrifice to Odin, the Norse god of war. He'd have cut my heart out had one of Odin's warriors not stayed his hand."

"You mean a temple guard?"

"No, I mean a soldier acting at Odin's behest. The pagan gods are real. Not as powerful as some myths suggest, but far more capable than you might imagine. They have their own society and keep to themselves, only occasionally interacting with humankind."

A fantastical tale, to be sure, but not beyond Kiyoko's imagination. "Please don't be offended, but why would Odin choose to save you? Of all the men he could have approached?"

"Loki, Odin's court jester, thought it would be amusing to change a frail, sickly lad with poor vision into a powerful warrior with uncontrollable fits of rage."

"Oh."

"The war god gave me a choice. Return home, or swallow his mystical potion and take up my sword as his indentured knight. I chose the potion."

"Did he not explain all that would happen to you?"

Murdoch nodded. "He was quite thorough in his explanation. I was just too stupid to say no. I served him for seven years, then returned home."

A very long and arduous seven years, almost guaranteed. But Murdoch provided no detail, asked for no sympathy. "Your family must have been overjoyed to see you again."

"Not exactly."

She smiled. "Did they think you were a ghost?"

"For a time, they refused to believe I was Jamie Murdoch at all. The changes wrought by the potion were so dramatic that even my own mother did not recognize me."

Kiyoko looked for the wounds in Murdoch's eyes. But he was as calm and confident as ever. Not a hint of distress. "Your common memories eventually swayed her?"

"Aye."

"And?" she prompted again. Frustrating man. How

could he be so generous with some explanations and so stingy with others? "Did she embrace you then?"

"She accepted that I was her son."

Not quite the same thing. "Surely your family must have welcomed another hale and hearty man into the fold? Your new talents must have made them proud."

His socked toe played with a silver buckle on his boot. "My presence was felt. The Vikings never again made a successful raid on our shores, and the MacDonalds ceased to steal our cattle."

"You brought peace to the land."

"No, not peace." He lifted his gaze. "Imagine me as a young man of twenty-five, honed to the sword, seasoned by battle, but never having developed a mote of control over the beast inside. Imagine me set free among tender, breakable humans."

Dread tugged her lips down. "Did you slay a family member?"

"More than one. But my kin adapted, learned to keep their distance as we fought." He sighed. "The problem was not with my own kin, but with the MacDonalds. After my return, the hostilities between our two clans faded, and the MacDonald laird offered me his daughter's hand in marriage to cement our new alliance."

Kiyoko blinked. "You married her?"

"No, there was no opportunity for that. I killed her several months before the wedding. Her, and a dozen fine MacDonald warriors."

"By accident." She was sure of that.

He grimaced. "Is it fair to label anything the berserker does as an accident?"

"How did it happen?"

"She was promised to me. I did not love her—barely even knew her, in point of fact—but my berserker accepted her as mine. When I chanced upon the lady in the apple orchard, kissing the captain of MacDonald's guard, the beast rose up and with one miserable swing of my sword started a bitter feud that would last four hundred years."

Kiyoko lowered her gaze to her hands.

"Had I slain only the soldiers," Murdoch added, "all would have been forgotten. Rough justice, they would have said. But MacDonald's daughter was killed in the fray. And that changed everything."

She nodded. "You died in a battle against the Mac-Donalds."

"Much later. After a wealth of poisonous events colored both sides. By then, even my death could not end the feud."

The story was tragic, but Murdoch delivered the tale with an ironic twist of his lips that discouraged pity. Still, Kiyoko rubbed her arms to banish a guilty twinge. His berserker had already given him much to grieve over. Rousing it to tap into its strength for the ritual might well lead to more. Could she live with that?

She gave his comment a brief, respectful silence, then said, "Do you fear that your berserker will do the same with Watanabe-san as it did with the MacDonald captain?"

A faint smile crept onto Murdoch's face. "I've had seven hundred years to teach the beast some manners. It would take a sight more than your hand upon Watanabe's sleeve to provoke an attack."

She narrowed her eyes. "So, your suggestion that the berserker could break loose at any moment and snatch his life is nothing more than jealous manipulation."

The smile deepened. "Perhaps."

"How very dishonorable of you."

"Not dishonorable," he disputed. "Careful. The connection we share has caught me left-footed on several occasions already. I'd prefer not to learn a harsh new lesson."

"Is such a connection part of the berserker lore?"

He shook his head. "Berserkers are bred solely for war."

Outside, a cloud drifted over the sun, dulling the light in the bedroom to a gentle gray.

"Do you have a theory about why we respond to each other the way we do? About what causes the dreams?" she asked. There was nothing remotely warlike about the way he made her feel. Being close to him was like riding a roller coaster of hot, achy need. The sizzle of awareness and the urge to press her skin to his never faded, never waned. She was almost getting used to its incessant, nagging presence.

"I don't believe in soul mates, if that's what you're asking," he said. "Mother Nature is a wise woman. To create only one mate for each woman and one woman for each man would bring a swift end to the human race."

"I agree." And she did. But Murdoch's crisp repudiation of the soul mate theory still stung. "I suspect it's the Veil."

At the mention of the relic, Murdoch's gaze sharpened.

"Which you carry on your person at all times."

She nodded. "Your berserker is probably reacting to the power of the Veil. Resulting in some kind of mystical storm whenever we're near each other."

The sun reappeared on the other side of the cloud, pouring a bucket of vivid color into the room and spotlighting Murdoch in the chair. He rose to his feet and sought shade. "There's a quick way to test that notion," he said. "Remove the Veil."

The invitation in his eyes was a powerful lure.

Remove the Veil and let us kiss again.

But the eager energy coiled in his body countered the thrill of his words. One mention of the Veil and he came alive. She didn't doubt that he was attracted to her, nor did she doubt that his desire to claim her was real. But given a choice between the Veil and her, he would pick the Veil.

She broke free of his stare and looked out the window. The cedar deck and scattered chairs in the backyard didn't truly interest her, but they provided her with a moment to compose herself.

"I think not. The influence of the Veil is a possibility, not a fact." Taking advantage of her inability to see his face, she forged on. "I have no desire to find myself ripped apart by your berserker because we acted without sufficient proof."

They were cruel words. Hurtful words.

But they were the only weapon she had against Murdoch's charm. Even as she spoke them, her heart shuddered at the lost opportunity to trade the Veil for a few blissful moments in his arms.

"You have very little faith in me," he said.

"This has nothing to do—" A slim figure darted from the evergreen hedge to the red front door of a single-story building farther down the path. A second later, that very same figure glanced quickly over his shoulder, then slipped inside.

Frowning, Kiyoko turned to Murdoch.

"What reason would Yoshio-san have to enter Mac-Gregor's house?"

15

It took a moment for Kiyoko's question to make any sense. Murdoch was swamped by wounded pride. Aye, she had good reason to believe he would hurt her. But hearing the accusation fall from her lips tore a hole the size of Gibraltar in his gut.

"Yoshio?" he asked.

She pointed out the window. "There."

Murdoch followed the direction of her finger. "MacGregor's at the hospital and Emily is down at the arena. There's no reason for Yoshio to visit."

"Shall we confront him?"

Murdoch didn't bother to respond. He led the way downstairs and out the back door. The Judas coins were no longer stored in MacGregor's house, but there were plenty of other valuables inside. "How well do you know Yoshio?"

"Extremely well, or so I thought."

Murdoch tossed her a frown. "Something happen?"

"Not really. Small things. During the demon attack on my father's house, he abandoned his position. That's very unlike him. Then just a few minutes ago, I bumped into him leaving the ranch house. He had no better reason to be there than he has to be in MacGregor's house."

"Could he be possessed by a thrall demon?"

"And still maintain normal auras? I don't think so."

They reached the house. Murdoch peered through the narrow strip of glass next to the door, but saw no movement inside. He twisted the knob and slowly opened the door.

"Stay here," he whispered. "I'll check things out."

Kiyoko arched a brow, drew her sword, and stepped over the threshold. Murdoch held back a grin and followed, protecting her back.

They moved quietly toward the faint rumble of a voice—through the hall, past the kitchen, and down to MacGregor's office. The door to the office was ajar. Enough to let them hear what was being said, but not enough to offer a view of the room. Unfortunately, Yoshio was speaking Japanese.

In a one-sided conversation.

Murdoch glanced at Kiyoko.

She was frowning, and as their eyes met, she held up a finger in a silent request for a minute. The longer she listened, the deeper her frown got. Finally, when she'd heard enough, she kicked the door open.

Yoshio was seated behind the desk, talking on the phone. He leapt to his feet, dropping the phone and immediately reaching for his sword. But as soon as he spotted Kiyoko, he relaxed. His hand fell to his side, and he bowed.

"Ashida-san."

A furious exchange of Japanese took place, with Kiyoko very much the aggressor and Yoshio answering with polite but firm, unapologetic responses.

"Could we do this in English?" Murdoch asked, reaching across the desk to hang up the phone. "My Japanese is limited to *domo arigato* and *hai*."

"He was sharing the details of the ranch layout with the other *onmyōji*," Kiyoko accused. "Against my specific orders."

"Their role is to protect you," Yoshio answered. "To do so, they must have the means."

"One of them is a spy. You are revealing critical information to our enemy."

Yoshio stiffened. "The *onmyōji* are honorable."

"Perhaps *you* are the spy."

His gaze flew to meet hers, then quickly fell away. "Surely you do not believe that. I would never do anything to harm you, Ashida-san. Your father entrusted me with your safety the day of my arrival at the dojo, and I have never ceased trying to prove his faith in me."

At the mention of her father, Kiyoko's stance softened. "What were you doing in the ranch house earlier?"

He withdrew a piece of paper from his pocket and offered it to Kiyoko. A series of Kanji characters alongside what looked like telephone numbers.

She accepted it, her gaze trailing over the information.

"Contact information for the North American *onmyōji*. You stole this from my phone."

He nodded.

"Why?"

"Wait," Murdoch interrupted, shaking his head. "There are *onmyōji* here in the United States?"

Kiyoko glanced at him. "As Sora-sensei mentioned your first day at the dojo, there are *onmyōji* sects scattered around the globe. Our philosophy is an ancient one."

"And they all fight demons?"

"In the beginning, we engaged in martial arts merely as a form of exercise and self-discipline. But when the balance between good and evil was disrupted, we felt obliged to use our skills to defend the innocent. Still, only a handful of *onmyōji* outside of Japan patrol the streets." She held up the piece of paper. "And these are them."

"They live to serve you, Ashida-san," Yoshio said. "I sought to give them purpose."

"Live to serve you?" Murdoch smiled at Kiyoko. "Really?"

She shrugged. "I am a descendant of Abe no Seimei. I carry his sword."

"And, of course, your father's divination says—" Yoshio halted, intercepting a glare from Kiyoko. "My apologies. I spoke out of turn."

"Oh, don't stop there," murmured Murdoch. "I'm all ears."

Kiyoko sheathed her sword. "He has nothing to add. He has never actually read my father's divination. Yamashita-sensei was the keeper of the oracle. The rest of us have only been privy to bits and pieces."

Despite Sora's warning, Murdoch couldn't help but believe the information in the scrolls was vital to Kiyoko's survival. Every conversation eventually pointed there. "Bits and pieces will do."

"Perhaps later," she said. "Yoshio-san, I am greatly unsettled by today's events. Whatever your reasons, stealing information and communicating with the other *onmyōji* without my permission was unforgivable. I'm sorely tempted to put you on the next available flight to Sapporo."

"But, I cannot leave you—"

"The decision is mine to make," she said firmly. "I delay only because my anger currently overwhelms my reason. Whatever I decide, consider your reaction well. A wise man would focus on regaining my respect."

Yoshio bowed his head.

"In the meantime," Murdoch said, not entirely convinced by the young man's apparent contrition, "we can put him under house arrest."

Kiyoko glanced at him. "You mean lock him up?"

"No. After we lost track of a visitor to the ranch last

spring, we invested in some technology. Ankle bracelet and GPS. We tell the software where he's allowed to go, and the instant he steps outside the designated safe area, the alarms go off."

The young warrior's head popped up, his eyes a blaze of anger. "I am not a criminal."

"Good," Murdoch said, snaring Yoshio's sleeve. "Because I've got better things to do than chase you around the ranch. But if you *do* step out of line, be forewarned—my tolerance for deceit is very low and I'm a beast when I'm annoyed." He tugged the young man around the desk. "Let's go."

"He must make his apologies to Mr. MacGregor," Kiyoko said as they left the bungalow and walked up the pea gravel path toward the main house.

"No," Murdoch disagreed. "Just this once, we're going to skip the apology. The man and his wife will be bringing their day-old baby home in a few hours. Definitely not the best time to share the tale of Yoshio's home invasion."

He pushed Yoshio through the kitchen door and down the hall to the small, hot room that served as the Gatherer network hub. Buried under coils of extension cords, teetering stacks of old motherboards, and a pile of empty Jolt Cola cans, Brendan Carter tapped at his keyboard.

The redhead glanced up as Murdoch entered.

"Wow. Did hell freeze over?"

"Very funny." Murdoch shook Yoshio. "I need you to put one of those ankle things on my little friend here."

Carter spun his chair around. "No, seriously. Did some cataclysmic event happen? Because I'm pretty sure you told me you'd never come in here, and *never* has a very specific meaning in the current universe."

"Stop being a wiseass and just do your job."

Carter stood up and extended his hand to Kiyoko.

"Hi. Let's ignore the crusty old Scot, shall we? I'm Brendan. We met your first night here, but didn't get a chance to chat, because he hauled you off to play a game of chess."

"Yes, I remember."

Their hands entwined.

And Murdoch's berserker coughed up a hairball.

Carter might wander about in his stocking feet all day and spout endless acronyms like *VPN* and *BIOS*, but he was not your average geek. He was a Gatherer. And that meant he was first and foremost a warrior. He stood well over six feet, was sturdy as a rock, and handled a sword with great finesse. Only the red hair worked against him.

"We haven't got all bloody day," Murdoch said. "Are you able to fit this man with an ankle bracelet or not?"

"Take a Valium, Murdoch. I know being around technology gives you hives, but a bit of polite socializing isn't going to fry your day."

"I'm not averse to technology," Murdoch disputed. "There are times, like this one, where it can be very useful. But a reliance on it can also encourage lazy, inattentive behavior."

Kiyoko released Carter's hand, nodding. "I agree. We have eliminated all but essential technology from our compound. A warrior with excellent senses can never be let down by an imperfect machine."

And just like that, his berserker curled up with a contented sigh and went back to sleep.

"The ankle bracelet," Murdoch reminded Carter.

"Yeah, yeah. Gimme a sec."

They spent the next five minutes setting up the perimeter triggers on Yoshio's ankle tracker. While Carter was bent to the device, tweaking the fit, Murdoch and Kiyoko retreated to the doorway to escape the heat of the five computers humming away on the rack next to Carter's workspace.

Murdoch closed his eyes and savored Kiyoko's proximity. A scant three inches separated his skin from hers, and with his eyes shut he could almost pretend she lay in his arms. He had so few opportunities to quietly explore the keen awareness that gave him goose bumps whenever he was within ten feet of her.

"Aren't you going to ask about the divination?" she asked.

He opened his eyes and studied the top of her head. The silky sheen of her hair whispered sweet nothings to his fingers. "Anytime you're ready, start talking."

"Divination is one of the *onmyōdō* arts."

"I know that."

"It has been practiced for centuries, and the truly gifted *onmyōji* can predict almost anything, given enough time and effort."

Murdoch found that hard to believe. Even the renowned druid he'd sought counsel from in the thirteenth century hadn't had *that* much control over the stars. "So, you're saying Sora could have predicted I'd show up on his doorstep."

"He did."

"Really?" he said, smiling. "If he knew I was coming, why didn't he avoid that untidy scene in the restaurant? He could have saved those two young warriors a world of hurt."

She tucked an errant strand of hair behind her ear. A perfect pink shell of an ear. That begged to be kissed. "Completing a divination is a time-consuming task— depending on the complexity, it can take anywhere from six to fourteen hours—and the result is only as powerful as the question posed to generate it. Asking *Will I succeed?* yields a vastly different answer than *What will my health be like if I succeed?*"

"There you have it," Carter said, sitting back with a satisfied nod at his handiwork. "He's all yours. The ranch house is off-limits, so you've got ten minutes to get him inside his approved wandering range before the alarms start ringing."

"Thank you." Murdoch waved to Yoshio. "Let's go, lad."

"Hey, Murdoch?"

Murdoch glanced at Carter.

"Anytime you need help, come see me."

Murdoch smiled. "Crow if you must, Carter. I'll not stop you. You get so little opportunity for pride in the lists."

They dropped Yoshio off at the bunkhouse, which was as lively as the sold-out stands of a championship football game. The Gatherer trainees had been handed an unscheduled day of rest thanks to the arrival of Mac-Gregor's baby, and they were taking advantage. Pop and beer and potato chips abounded.

Sloths.

Murdoch was tempted to whip their asses into shape and send them on a five-mile run, but he had more important things to do. Like convince Kiyoko to show him the Veil. He waved at the cook behind the cafeteria counter, who ran over and handed him a knapsack.

"Still interested in meditating?" he asked her.

"Yes," she said, surprised.

"I know the perfect spot." He guided her outside with a hand at the small of her back. "If you're up for a short hike."

"I'd enjoy seeing more of the ranch."

California would never replace Scotland in his heart, but it had its own unique beauty. During the winter months, the parched brown hills gave way to green grass, and the low rolls of the landscape softened to a verdant glory. His favorite spot lay on the east slope of the hill overlooking the ranch house. In the lee of the hill, not a single sign of civilization could be seen—no homes, no fences, no roads. As long as he didn't look up and make note of the contrails left by passenger jets, he could almost believe he'd traveled back in time. In the winter a small pool of water filled the crevice between two rocks, drawing birds and other small creature. But despite the recent rainfall, the rocks were dry.

"This is lovely," Kiyoko said, glancing around.

Murdoch unzipped the knapsack and removed a plaid blanket. Ugly red-and-green thing. MacGregor tartan. He should have been more specific in his instructions. Laying the blanket on the grass, he invited Kiyoko to take a seat. "Sorry. No room for cushions. But I do have hot tea."

She accepted the thermos and poured herself a cup. "Did you really bring me here to meditate?"

"No." He dropped to the ground beside her, reclining on his side with his head propped in one hand. The rough rural setting suited her somehow. She was like a creamy pearl cradled in a bed of burlap. "I have an ulterior motive."

"Which is?"

"I want to see the Veil," he said, meeting her gaze with honesty. "I knew you wouldn't show it to me if there was a chance anyone else would see. But out here, there's only me, you, and the coyotes."

She stared at him.

"So, let's see what you've got under that outfit," he said with a slow smile. "I'm very curious."

Kiyoko put her tea down.

The man's smile was lethal.

Combined with the blatant appreciation that never seemed to leave his eyes, the wry curve of those sensual lips almost did her in. The lazy display of his fabulous body didn't help. Broad shoulders, lean hips, and long, powerful legs. He was a man's man and a woman's dream. Her skin responded with eager excitement, sending goose bumps rippling in several directions. It was all too easy to imagine leaping into his arms and losing herself in his easy charm and unwavering strength.

Luckily, her conscience had a say.

She smoothed her fingers over the soft wool of the blanket instead of the firm line of his jaw. Followed the structured pattern of the plaid rather than diving headlong into the wavy lengths of his hair.

"What advantage will seeing it provide?" she asked.

"Let's call it an exercise in trust."

"Can I truly trust you not to steal it?"

He lifted a brow. "You already trust me not to steal it. If you didn't, you'd never have agreed to be alone with me. We both know I could take it from you right now, with little or no difficulty."

Taking the Veil from her would be harder than he anticipated, but essentially he was right. She *did* trust him not to steal it. "Then I'm still unclear what you hope to gain."

"Nothing."

She sighed. "Don't be difficult."

"The gain wouldn't be mine—it would be yours. If you show me the Veil, you'll be sharing more than its location. You'll be sharing the burden of protecting it."

"With a man who lives five thousand miles away. What good will that do?"

He picked up a lock of her hair, rubbing the dark strands between his fingers, apparently fascinated. "I'm not five thousand miles away right now."

Her heartbeat accelerated.

No, he definitely wasn't five thousand miles away. More like five inches. A slight lean on her part and his hand would be pressed against her breast. Her very eager breast.

"I'll confess," he said, the rumble of his brogue smokier than usual, "I've never been more eager to seek my bed as I have since I met you. My dreams are so bloody incredible that waking leaves an ache in my chest."

Kiyoko swallowed tightly.

"In my sleep, I can touch you freely, kiss you just the way I want, pleasure you until you scream and beg for mercy, and there are no consequences. It's enough to have me praying for a coma."

"None of it is real," she said softly.

His lifted his gaze to hers. Hot, dark, and full of smoldering promise. "I'm not so sure of that. My berserker thinks it's real enough."

Disappointment surged through Kiyoko.

He was back to blaming his berserker, rather than accepting the desire as his own. Proof, if she needed it, that entering into any kind of relationship with Murdoch would only end in heartbreak. She tugged her hair free of his hand, and then lifted the hem of her *kendōgi* jacket to reveal the black cloth belt wrapped around her waist.

"This is the Veil."

He held her gaze for a moment, frowning. Then he glanced down. "Your black belt is the Veil? You wear it in plain sight much of the time."

"Yes."

"Rather brazen of you."

She shrugged. "People often overlook the obvious."

The creases on his brow deepened. "Are you angry with me?"

"No. I simply expect too much."

"From me?" He stiffened. "And I disappoint?"

"You are who you are, Murdoch. To expect more than that is not a failing with you. It is a failing with me."

He smiled grimly. "Ah, the old *it's not you, it's me* argument. Do tell. What part of who I am pissed you off?"

"We should probably get back."

As she rose to her knees, he said, "No, we bloody well should not. Sit down."

The cool authority in his voice halted her. It was the sort of voice that could command an army of men into battle. There was no room for argument, no hope of retreat, and no question but that he would back up his demand with strength and competence. And surprisingly, it didn't annoy her.

She sat.

"What expectation did I fail to meet?" he asked.

"You still do not acknowledge that the berserker is *you*."

He was silent for a moment, thoughtful. "You think that I attribute my interest in you to the berserker."

"Don't you?"

"No."

"Murdoch, be honest. In your mind, you are the calm, rational warrior who prides himself on his self-control. It's the berserker who is responsible for all the passionate, unruly things you do and feel and say."

"Not *all*."

"Most, then. It doesn't matter. The point is if it weren't for your berserker, your attention would have long since moved on to some other woman."

"Not true."

"Forgive me if I disagree."

"Lass, you need to give me some credit." A half smile softened the contours of his face. "First, as I lie here, a little dizzy from drinking in your perfume and daydreaming about trailing kisses down your belly, the berserker is nowhere in sight. There's only me. Second, there is no berserker—nor for that matter any other woman—in my dreams. There's only you."

She melted a little.

Was it wrong to be so easily swayed by a few sultry words? And by his total lack of shame in admitting that her presence made him dizzy? Murdoch had a number of issues, but a lack of self-confidence wasn't one of them.

And she liked that.

A lot.

"Have no doubt," he added. "*I* want you. In ways I can't begin to describe. I've said it before, but it begs repeating—were it not for my damned berserker, I'd leap on you this very moment. I'd steal every breath from your lips, discover every intriguing inch of your body, and drive you as wild as I please, with absolutely no mercy. I'd make you see stars. Me. Not my bloody berserker. Got it?"

"Got it," she croaked. Her body was on fire. She had never wanted to crawl inside someone as much as she wanted to be part of Murdoch and his vivid imaginings right this minute. "Maybe we should nap."

He groaned.

"Lord, if I hadn't promised Emily I'd drive her into town, I'd take you up on that. I owe you one."

One. *An orgasm.* Kiyoko blushed. "I guess we should head back to the house."

His hand slid over her hip, stilling her attempt to rise. Warm, strong, reassuring. "Lass, I'm going to figure this out, I swear. The Veil, the berserker, the whole damned mess. I *will* find an answer."

Outdated though it was, his medieval chivalry stole her breath away. But even as her heart fluttered, her stomach roiled with guilt. He'd been nothing but open and honest, and now he was offering to do everything in his power to help her. Yet she had not shown him a similar courtesy.

He deserved to know the truth. He deserved to know how she was planning to use him. Goddess of Death or no goddess of Death.

"Actually," she said, "I already have an answer. But you aren't going to like it."

* * *

Although Kiyoko's insistence on returning to Murdoch's side had infuriated him, Azazel did all his seething beneath the surface. Questioning her further about the information in the oracle was vital. Instead of allowing her to eat breakfast, he should have dragged her off to his room. He slowly consumed the sickeningly sweet cinnamon roll, displaying all the professional demeanor and unshakable calm that Ryuji Watanabe prided himself on.

Or had. Right up to the end.

No, *including* the end. The man had even died calm. Never begged for his life. Never cried. Worked right up until the end to free himself, yes, but never panicked and never whimpered. He'd been no fun at all. No wonder Kiyoko had been bored.

He deposited his empty tray in the rack near the kitchen and left the cafeteria. The time spent here had not been wasted. A loud young Irishman by the name of Quinn had helped him out immensely. He now knew the Gatherers would be absent en masse on Saturday night. MacGregor had planned a large-scale field mission to wrap up the training session and make up for today's lost lesson.

With almost everyone away, absconding with the Temple Veil would be a simple task. All he had to do now was locate the damned thing. With an old-fashioned physical search, since there was some kind of dampening spell over the ranch. Still, how hard could it be? The relic had to be somewhere amid the small set of belongings she had brought with her from Japan.

He stepped out into the midmorning light and, almost on cue, a cloud slithered over the sun.

Of course, his presence on the ranch presented him with a unique secondary opportunity. If he could find a way to seriously weaken the Soul Gatherers, it would only smooth his way back to the Great Lord's right hand.

Azazel let his gaze wander the grounds, mentally noting the purpose of each building. House, garage, arena ... He paused. A simple wooden structure was visible through the trees to his left, gently releasing thin ribbons of woodsmoke into the air from a metal chimney. An old-fashioned forge, if his eyes didn't betray him.

Where the mage crafted the Soul Gatherer weapons.

Azazel smiled.

Swordsmithing was an art he knew well, having been the tarnished soul who introduced mankind to war several millennia ago. All he needed to do was breathe on the coals to coat them in demonic purpose. Then the next time they were stoked into hot flame, fatal flaws would be injected into the process. Flaws that wouldn't be noticeable until the moment the weapon failed.

Crossing the grass to the small copse, he wended through the tree trunks, keeping to the darker shadows, until he could see inside the open doors of the building. It was empty. An impressive array of hammers and tongs hung on the walls, each neatly in its place. The blower was off and the coal tray in the hearth sat untended, slowly cooling. No half-worked item lay across the anvil; no sword stood clamped in the vise.

He glanced at the closed curtains of a nearby tip-out trailer. No sign of activity at all. It would seem to be a perfect time to—

"Stefan?"

Azazel pulled back sharply, hugging the tree trunk.

It was the girl. Emily. Striding up the gravel path from her stepfather's house.

He held his breath.

If she reached out with her senses, she would almost assuredly spot him. Yes, he still wore the glamour of Ryuji Watanabe, but that wouldn't protect him. The Japanese businessman had no cause to be visiting the mage. He'd be forced to mutter some stupid excuse that did not match the man's intelligence. Questions would be raised. Plus, the more he bumped into the Trinity Soul, the more likely it became that she would see past the edges of his identity cloak.

He did his best to become one with the tree.

"Stefan, I know you're in there," Emily said, reaching the trailer. She pounded her fist against the thin metal door. "I need some help with a fire containment spell. Come on. Let me in."

There was no response from the trailer.

"You're being a jerk." Face screwed up with determination, Emily circled around to the big bay window and tapped. "I'm not going to go away until you let me in."

Now out of clear view, Azazel took a careful step back, avoiding twigs and dried leaves. Better to return after dark, when Emily was indoors with her newly expanded family. He retreated another step. And another.

"You know, I could pop in there if I wanted to," Emily said, her voice muffled by the trees. "Don't make me break Brian's privacy rules."

Confident that he'd withdrawn far enough not to catch her attention, he turned and cut through the trees toward the ranch house. With Emily accounted for, now might be a good time to search Kiyoko's room. Assuming she wasn't entertaining Murdoch there.

He frowned.

Human women had once found him irresistible. Was Kiyoko's fascination with Murdoch an oddity, or a sign that he had lost his touch? He *had* lingered in the between for ages before gaining enough strength to rebuild his physical form. Was it possible his allure had been diminished by the wait?

He certainly hoped not.

16

"**Y**ou can't be serious." Murdoch stared at Kiyoko, hoping to spot a glimmer of a smile. But there was nothing but resolve on her pretty face. "You plan to rouse my berserker, leverage its energy, and transcend to a higher plane of existence."

"Yes."

He shot to his feet. "Well, you must have lost your bloody mind, because that's not a plan. That's suicide."

"It's risky," she agreed. "But not impossible."

He glared at her. "Listen to yourself. You sound like a madwoman. Sora has filled your head with absolute nonsense—this transcending thing is bullshit. There's only life and death. There's no middle ground. Believe me, I've seen enough of death to know."

"Then how do you explain the existence of Soul Gatherers?"

"It's like a stay of execution. Temporary."

"But it's also proof that a middle ground exists." She rose, too, and touched his sleeve. "Think, too, about the pagan gods. You say that they exist, yet they do not reside here on the middle plane with us. Nor do I believe they dwell in the places you call heaven and hell."

"Do you seriously equate yourself with a god?"

She shook her head. "No. I'm just disputing your assertion that there are no other planes beyond the three that you know. The transcendence ritual enables me to hide my soul in one of those other planes, thus preventing Death from claiming it."

Murdoch sighed. "Fine. Let's leave the concept of this other plane of existence alone for a moment. You still intend to get there by rousing the berserker. What part of being crushed to death did you miss?"

"That was an accident."

"Accidents are a regular event around the beast," Murdoch said. "He's uncontrollable."

"I don't believe that."

"Did I not just recite the tale of my lamentable past? The one where I killed a lass for no other reason than that she stood between me and the man I meant to kill?"

"Yes. But I am not a helpless damsel. And you are not the same man you once were."

He raked a hand through his hair. "Any control I purport to have is tenuous at best. All it takes is the right level of danger and I'm lost. I won't allow the berserker to surface around you again. I can't."

"Would you rather see me die?"

He rounded on her. "Of course not. But you don't need to do this. The Veil is still keeping you alive."

She nodded. "I believe I have a few months before my ability to draw from it is gone completely. I can live day by day, slowly growing weaker, until I wither away, gasping for my last breath. Or I can fight. Use my current health to good advantage, risk it all, and make a genuine bid to be whole again. Which would you choose, Murdoch?"

That was an easy answer.

But risking *his* life was very different from risking Kiyoko's. "I still believe Stefan can help. He's being difficult at the moment, I acknowledge that, but he'll come around." He snatched the tartan blanket off the ground and stuffed it into the knapsack. "I'll *make* him come around."

"Time is against us," she said softly.

"We have several months."

"No, we don't. I need a minimum core strength to even attempt the transcendence. Every day my body absorbs less and less of the Veil's power, and because the ritual can be performed only on specific dates, we will soon reach a point where the decision will be made for me."

He grimaced. "How much time are we talking?"

"There are six auspicious days between now and the end of December. Beyond that, Sora-sensei says the chances of success are poor."

Six chances to save her life, then game over. No pressure at all. "When is the first one?"

Her head bent. "Monday."

He stared at her. "You were going to try it without telling me, weren't you?"

A pale pink hue stained her cheeks.

As her color rose, so did Murdoch's suspicions. "And the kiss in the courtyard, did that conveniently occur on an auspicious day?"

The flush deepened.

"I am so going to kick your ass," he said softly.

Her gaze lifted. "I had no choice. Sora extracted my promise not to tell you, in case Death discovered our plans. Even if I had told you what I was doing, you would have refused to cooperate."

"You're bloody right I'd have refused," he said, twisting the canvas knapsack in his hands. "With good reason. Look at what happened."

Kiyoko tilted her head. "What *did* happen, Murdoch? To me, it seemed the berserker did not gain control until Sora-sensei shot you with the arrow. Do you remember kissing me?"

"I remember everything the berserker does."

"Then you remember who did the kissing. Who was it? You or the berserker?"

"Does it matter?" His hold on the knapsack gentled. "I thought he and I were one and the same?"

"Stop being difficult. Answer the question."

"Me." Murdoch hooked the knapsack over his shoulder and began the trek up the hill. "*I* kissed you. But I was barely hanging on, and if you think I'm going to put my desire ahead of your safety a second time, think again."

"Are you sure?" Emily asked Murdoch, admiring the teardrop-cut alexandrite-and-diamond pendant hanging from an elegant silver chain. "It's kind of expensive."

He frowned, taking the necklace from her and handing it to the saleswoman. "Let me worry about the price. You only turn sixteen once."

"But I feel bad. You had to sell your car."

"I really wish you wouldn't keep bringing that up."

"I can't help it. I loved your Mustang, and I'll be reminded that it's gone every time we have to drive downtown in Lafleur's crappy old pickup truck."

Murdoch parted with a wad of his hard-earned cash, accepted the small bag in return, and then led Emily out of the jewelry store and onto Santana Row. "Shall we hit Ben and Jerry's next?"

"Sure."

He watched her twist a strand of blond hair into a tight knot, let it go, then do it again. "You seemed a little quiet on drive down here. Anything on your mind?"

"A couple of things," Emily admitted.

"Such as?"

"While you were gone, I had more of those weird dreams."

He arched a brow. "About the between?"

"Yeah. I talked to Uriel about them, like you suggested, but he doesn't know what the deal is, either. He's checking on some stuff for me, though."

"Okay." He pulled the door open and ushered her into the ice cream parlor. "Is that it?"

"No." Her gaze slid to the sign above the cashier. She chewed her lip as she studied the menu. "I'll have a cup of vanilla."

"You must be the only person on the planet who comes here for the vanilla ice cream," he said drily. "Don't you want to try the Half Baked or the Chunky Monkey?"

"Nope. I know what I like."

He ordered her cup and settled on a Pumpkin Cheesecake cone for himself. "So what else is bothering you?"

"The Japanese guy."

"Sora? Did he do something?"

She shook her head. "No, not the sensei. I like him. He's cool. I mean the other guy."

"Yoshio?"

"Is he the one who dresses like Brian? With the nice sweaters and shoes?" she asked between spoonfuls of ice cream.

"No, that's Ryuji Watanabe." Murdoch glanced at her. "I didn't realize you'd spent any time with him."

"I haven't. But when I went to see Stefan this afternoon, he was there, in the woods."

Murdoch halted in midlick. "You talked to Stefan? He came out of his trailer?"

"No. He's still being a jerk. I really don't understand why he's hiding. I could pop into his trailer anytime if I wanted to. Even into Dika's castle, now that I know the entrance is there."

"He's waiting for me to take Kiyoko away."

Emily rolled her eyes. "You'd think he'd know better, being a mage and all. If the Veil exists, it exists. It doesn't really matter *where* it exists. Trust me. The *where* is a minor detail."

"You can sense the Veil?"

"Nope. Brian already asked me to try. There's none of the rotting algae feeling that signals a dark relic anywhere inside the ranch compound."

Murdoch glared at her. "Webster asked you to look for it? When?"

"Last night. After he talked to you."

"That bloody b—" He suddenly remembered who he was speaking to. "Rotter. He should have warned me. Kiyoko might have felt you searching for it."

"Did she?" Emily stopped eating her ice cream.

"Not as far as I know."

"But she has special senses, like me?" the teen asked eagerly.

"Not quite like you," he said. "She reads auras."

Emily nodded. "The electromagnetic energy that people give off. That's pretty neat. I wonder what she sees when she looks at me?"

"You'd have to ask her." Murdoch dumped his half-eaten cone in the garbage. "Would you mind terribly if we headed back to the ranch? I need to chat with Webster."

"Nah, I'm good. This was nice." She scooped up the last of her ice cream, stuffed the spoon in her mouth, then tossed the cup. The spoon remained in her mouth until they reached the truck, where she stuck the now sparkling white utensil in the air vent, propping it wide-open. "Am I going to get in shit for telling you about the Veil search?"

"I'll be very diplomatic," he promised.

"With Brian?" She scrunched up her face. "No offense, Murdoch, but you guys are always *this close* to punching each other's lights out. Do you even know what *diplomatic* means?"

He grinned. "Perhaps not."

"Yeah, well, try not to kill him, okay? I need someone to train with."

Murdoch tossed her a glance as he coaxed the old

pickup to life. "I'm a better sparring partner than Webster."

"Maybe. But so far, you've been kinda busy following Kiyoko around like a lost puppy."

"Excuse me? Did you just call me a puppy?"

With a little effort, Murdoch managed to keep Emily smiling all the way to the ranch. Not quite the effervescent girl she'd been before Carlos but, hopefully, on the road to recovery.

It was only after he'd parked the truck in the garage and she'd disappeared down the path toward her parents' home that he realized she'd never explained exactly what it was about Watanabe that bothered her.

When Kiyoko pushed open the door and entered the air-conditioned arena, Lena glanced up. If she hadn't, Kiyoko would have made a speedy escape. But since she did, an acknowledgment was in order. "My apologies. I was looking for Sora-sensei."

"He's not here."

"I can see that," Kiyoko said, backing up. "I'll keep looking."

"We can't avoid each other forever."

Kiyoko smiled grimly. "I'm not aiming for forever. Just a few weeks." She opened the door.

"Wait, please." Lena sheathed the sword she'd been practicing with and advanced across the sand. "I owe you an apology and I'd like you to hear me out."

Kiyoko halted, but did not shut the door.

Tall and dark, the female Soul Gatherer had an exotic beauty that she played down with a tight ponytail and stark clothing. Kiyoko had rarely seen her flustered. But she wasn't her usual self today.

Lena stretched the fingers of one hand wide, then relaxed. "I should have been more open about my situation. I should have told you the thrall demons were blackmailing me, maybe even asked you for help. But I've never been very good at that. Asking for help."

Kiyoko waited for more.

And it came. Stilted and awkward, but thick with emotion. "I apologize for involving you in my trade of the Judas coins. I was desperate to save Heather, but I knew you would never condone handing off a dark relic to the demons. It was unforgivable to use you and the other *onmyōji* to help me do it. I'm sorry."

It still stung. They'd been friends for eight years. Ever since they bid against each other over an inexpensive set of Victorian archaeological excavation tools at a London auction. But the healing had to start somewhere.

"I accept your apology," Kiyoko said.

Lena released a soft sigh. "Thank you."

In the past, they would have hugged. Now they shook hands.

"How is Heather?" Kiyoko asked.

"Better every day. After she finished her program at the rehab center, she started volunteering there twice a week. It's been good for her. She's still in regular counseling, and still has some pretty rough days, but I'm hopeful."

"It's good that she has you."

Lena nodded. "Brian's been great with her. They've become quite close. He set her up with an apartment in town, helped her find a job, and introduced her to Narcotics Anonymous."

"I like Brian," Kiyoko said. "But I don't understand the bad blood between him and Murdoch."

The other woman grimaced. "I don't either. They constantly bait one another, and when they duel, I cringe. They push the limits every time. Some days, Brian comes back to the house with sword slices on fifty percent of his body. The weird thing is, I know they respect each other."

"Crazy men."

"Exactly." Lena glanced at her. "Speaking of crazy men, what have you told Murdoch about your father?"

"My father wasn't crazy," Kiyoko protested. "He did not injure other men on purpose."

"No, but he lived two very full and separate lives, enjoying incredible success in both. Dynamic businessman during the day, inspiring *onmyōji* leader at night. I always wondered if he had a rare form of schizophrenia."

"That's not funny."

"Your father would have laughed." Lena's long fingers squeezed Kiyoko's arm. "I loved Tatsu-san. You know that. He was a wonderful man, and I'm happy he died the way he would have wanted, defending the world against demons. But I'm sad that he's gone."

Her friend's dark brown eyes brimmed with sympathy. Sympathy that reached deep into Kiyoko's heart and fed the aching loss she'd blanketed for three months.

"Me, too," she whispered.

"Please don't take this the wrong way," Lena said, "but you are not your father. You do not need to fill his shoes as both corporate mogul and *onmyōji* leader. That was never your path."

Kiyoko's stomach tensed in spite of the gentleness of the criticism. "I'm not trying to do both. Ryuji-san runs the company, not I."

"Really? Because you look like you're being pulled in a million different directions at once. The Kiyoko I knew was confident to the point of annoying and never doubted anything." She grimaced. "The woman who broke *onmyōdō* code to save her father? That was the Kiyoko I knew. I've never seen you this tentative, this unsure. I assumed that since you brought Watanabe-san along with you, the company was dividing your attention."

Tentative. Unsure.

The words were accurate, if uncomfortable.

"No," said Kiyoko. "I'm concerned that the wave of corruption sweeping Asia may have affected the company and I'm personally reviewing the numbers, but I'm not getting involved in the minutiae of the business."

"Then what's wrong?"

Kiyoko took a deep breath, and slowly released it. "Since my father died, everything I've touched has turned to shit."

Lena wrinkled her nose. "You've been hanging around Murdoch too long."

"If you believe Sora-sensei's divinations, I'm the most gifted mystic born into my family in centuries. Yet I couldn't save him, Lena. When I arrived in the garage, he was still alive, still fighting to breathe. I borrowed ki from people around me, I used every ounce of my own, and I still couldn't save him."

The other woman stared at her. "*If?* Are you saying you don't believe the divination is true? The one that predicts your transcendence to the right hand of Abe no Seimei? The one that names you as his immortal disciple?"

Kiyoko didn't respond right away. She let the truth settle around them.

"Consider the facts," she said. "I broke *onmyōdō* code by borrowing ki, I failed to heal my father, and I ended up a broken shell of the person I was. Since then, my spells have not been effective in keeping evil at bay, my own warriors have turned on me, and my home was destroyed by demons. I believed the divination because my father believed. But now that he's gone—now that he no longer supports me—the truth is coming to light. I am not worthy to transcend. He made an error."

"Did you talk to Sora-san?"

"Of course. He says the stars do not lie. But do you

really think he would admit to a twenty-five-year-old mistake? One my father built his entire life around?"

Lena dug the toe of her boot into the sand.

"Here's what I know," she said. "Your father was one of the smartest, savviest men I've ever met. His instincts were incredible. Remember my father's excavation tools? Tatsu-san knew they were far more valuable to me than they were to you, just from watching me bid on them."

Kiyoko nodded. "It was his idea to give you the tools after I won the auction."

"I still have them." Lena smiled. "I can't speak to Sora-san's reliability, but I can vouch for your father's. He had far longer to study you than he did me. If he said you were qualified to transcend, then you are."

"But everything changed after my father died."

"Did it?" Lena tossed her a dubious look. "Are you not the same basic person you were before he died? Shaped a bit by the tragedy, no doubt, but fundamentally the same?"

Kiyoko grimaced. "No, I'm much weaker."

"Physically, perhaps. Not mentally." Lena smiled again, this time with a hint of impish humor. "Do you know what Brian would say if he were here?"

Kiyoko shook her head.

"Let me tell you myself," Brian Webster said, crossing the arena from the weight-training room. Sandy hair askew and T-shirt damp from a workout, he flung an arm over Lena's shoulders and offered Kiyoko a faint smile. "Suck it up, princess. Stop whining and get back to work."

Lena glanced from Kiyoko to Brian. "He's kidding. He says that to me all the time." She elbowed him in the ribs. "Only he grins when he does it."

Her attempt to chide him fell flat.

He held Kiyoko's gaze with frank intensity. "I'm only half kidding. Truth is, Satan doesn't dick around, Miss Ashida. If you're as committed to beating back the fires of hell as we are, I need your cooperation. In case you haven't noticed, we're in a battle for the human race here. Do whatever you need to do to get cozy with the idea, but prepare to hand over the Veil."

The man wore lazy charm like a fine Italian suit, but there was nothing lazy about the promise in his eyes: He would take the Veil by force if necessary.

Only willpower stopped Kiyoko from wrapping her arms about her waist in a protective gesture. "Did you have a time frame in mind?"

"Yesterday would be nice." His comment earned him another jab in the ribs. "The sooner, the better. If Big Red discovers the Veil is here, things will get real ugly real fast."

"Will Monday suffice?"

He sighed. "Not really. But if that's the only choice, I'll take it."

Kiyoko bowed politely to the pair and left the arena. The decision was made then. On Monday, she'd put aside her lingering doubts and move forward with the transcendence ritual.

Sora would be pleased.

Murdoch, on the other hand . . .

All through dinner, Murdoch was treated to strange looks from Kiyoko. Some were thoughtful, some were eager, some were worried. The worried ones bothered him.

"Where's Watanabe?" he asked her when she paused in her conversation with Sora, who sat next to her.

"On a conference call with Japan. It's ten o'clock in the morning there."

"On a Saturday."

She nodded. "There was a fire at one of the manufacturing plants overnight, and he's trying to avert production delays."

Of course he was. The man was a bloody saint. He reached for a second helping of green beans and as he replaced the serving bowl, he asked, "Who cooked dinner?"

"I did."

He frowned at Emily. "You?"

"Mom gave me some pointers," she said, nodding. "She told me if I wanted to eat while she was in the hospital, I'd better learn."

Murdoch perused the half-empty platters of roast chicken, baked potatoes, and cooked vegetables. A simple meal, but well prepared. "She suggested the rest of us were bad cooks?"

Emily swallowed the bite in her mouth, then responded. "No, she said Brian and Lena were bad cooks. Like, 'Allow them in the kitchen only if you are willing to risk food poisoning' bad. According to her, Carter can cook but his talents are limited to steak on a barbecue grill, and you cook like a dream but are never around when the meal prep needs to start. Kiyoko, Yoshio, and the sensei are guests, so she never said anything about *their* cooking skills."

Everyone around the table smiled.

"What did she say about MacGregor's culinary talents?" asked Carter, as he carved a slice of meat off the chicken.

Emily rolled her eyes. "She said he had the potential to be a brilliant chef, but his focus is on other things."

Webster planted a kiss on Lena's cheek. "Isn't the view through the rose-colored glasses of love wonderful?"

"I wouldn't know," she murmured. "I don't own a pair."

"Ouch." He grinned. "Good thing my colossal ego

can handle the truth. Doesn't bother me one iota to admit that if there were no take-out joints, I'd starve."

"Since Emily made the meal, I think the rest of us should clean up," Murdoch said, laying his knife between the tines of his fork.

Carter snorted. "That's the usual deal, bro. You'd know that if you joined us for dinner more often."

Kiyoko glanced at Murdoch. "You don't eat?"

"Of course I eat," he said, tossing a hard look at Carter. "I simply spend more time with the trainees than some of the other Gatherers."

"In other words," Webster said drily, "he does his best to avoid me. Ow." He grimaced at Lena. "Sweetheart, kicking me under the table loses its point in a room full of Gatherers. They all heard it."

Murdoch stared up the table at Webster. "I don't avoid you. I merely find other people's company infinitely more enjoyable."

His boss offered up the same lazy smile he wore during their sparring matches in the arena. "Yeah, getting your ass kicked by me can't be nearly as much fun as guzzling beer and playing darts."

A hollow silence filled the room.

Emily pushed back her chair and stood. "Okay," she said breezily. "On that note, I officially declare dinner over. Lena and Bri, you've got kitchen duty."

Reluctantly, Murdoch took his cue from Emily and began to stack plates. He should never have let Webster win the match so easily this morning.

"Uh, Murdoch?"

He glanced at Emily.

She wore a pained look. "I really appreciate the help, honestly. But maybe you could find something else to do." She nodded toward the kitchen, where Webster had begun to load the dishwasher.

"You think I'd start a fight in his home?"

"No," she said. "But listening to the two of you go at it is really uncomfortable, and we have guests."

He sighed. "I'll try to be good."

"Terrific," she said. "But some breathing space might help. Before we gear up for tonight's field mission, why don't you take that package down to Stefan's trailer and see if the dumb jerk will open the door to take it?"

He glanced around. "What package?"

She pointed to the hall table. A flat rectangular box, wrapped in brown paper. "Came by courier this afternoon. All the way from Romania."

Picking the box up, he shook it. Nothing rattled.

"It's a book," she said.

He frowned. "Are you sure?"

"Yup. A really old book."

"A grimoire?"

Emily scraped the leftover mashed potatoes into a Tupperware container. "No idea. Can't see what's on the pages."

"If it's important, maybe he'll trade it for Kiyoko's healing spell," Murdoch said. He could hope.

"I say give him one shot and if he doesn't cooperate, then whack him over the head with it."

He chuckled. "Sounds like an excellent plan."

Tucking the box under his arm, he left the house. The quickest route to the trailer was via the gravel path to MacGregor's bungalow. Beyond the swimming pool there were no lights, but he didn't need them, anyway.

The path curved past Stefan's smithy on its way to the trailer. Most weekends before the arrival of a new batch of trainees, the mage could be found working far into the night to ensure that all the practice weapons were in good shape. Tonight, his place of work stood dark and silent against the trees. And this was the largest group they'd hosted yet. Seventy-two.

Had Stefan completed all the new swords before

locking himself away? He peered in the window as he walked by, hoping to spot a stack of weapons piled neatly on the ready table.

No such luck. The table was empty. If the mage refused to open the door tonight, it might be a wise idea to consider options in the event of a shortage.

Murdoch halted.

Had his eyes betrayed him? Or had something truly been out of place in the smithy? He could have sworn he'd seen a figure bent over the coal tray. In the dark.

Trusting the knot of tension in his gut, he drew Bloodseeker from its invisible sheath. His instincts had saved his ass many times. He propped the courier package against the smithy wall, then slid the door open and stepped inside.

The figure beside the coal tray abruptly straightened and backed away, leaving a flat bed of coals that for the briefest of moments seemed to glow dark purple. But that may or may not have been real. Hard to say, because Murdoch's attention was focused on the man facing him across the room.

Ryuji Watanabe.

"What are you doing in here?" he asked Watanabe.

"Conn Quinn suggested I visit. He said the swords here were made in an old-fashioned coal forge and that the process was fascinating. You already know my interest in metalworking." Watanabe shrugged. "I just finished a rather grueling conference call and decided to take a bit of a break. So, here I am."

A perfectly reasonable explanation. Not too pat, nicely supported by facts. But Murdoch's instincts said it was a lie.

"A curious person with nothing to hide would turn on the lights," he said. Flicking the switch, he flooded the room with glaring wattage.

Watanabe smiled. "Are you accusing me of industrial

espionage, Mr. Murdoch? I can assure you there's nothing of value to my company in here."

Another very appropriate response.

Negated by Watanabe's all-black attire.

"Drop the charade," Murdoch said. Two could play the lying game. "It's pointless. Emily came to see me after she spotted you out here earlier today."

The smile vanished, replaced by a faint frown. "She's been through a lot, that girl. Her parents' divorce, the split with her boyfriend, and now a new baby in the house. Can't be easy to find your way through all that."

Nice deflection. A backhanded slap disguised as sympathy.

"Look," Murdoch said, rolling his shoulders to ease a familiar burn beneath his skin. "We're both smart men. We don't need to play games. Let's skip the blather and get to the meat of the conversation."

Watanabe's eyes narrowed. "Which is?"

"What kind of demon are you?"

The other man laughed. "Is that a serious question?"

Murdoch lifted the tip of his blade. "When it comes to hellspawn, I've no sense of humor."

"I think it's time to call it a night." Watanabe skirted around the ready bench and strode toward the door. "If I offended anyone by looking around, I apologize, but threatening me is uncalled for."

Pale face, stiff shoulders. The man seemed utterly genuine. But the situation was all wrong. No one explored in the dark unless they had something to hide. As the Japanese man brushed past him, Murdoch loosened the binds on his berserker and leveraged the beast's heightened senses.

The reaction was immediate.

Alarms shrieked in every muscle in his body simultaneously, burning, firming, and stretching his skin to painful limits. The red fury seared his chest and throat as it exploded toward his brain. Murdoch jammed his eyes closed, clenched his sword grip, and waited for the first wave to crest.

There was no question now.

Invisible remnants of dark power clung to the Japanese man's clothing, leaving a microscopic trail in his wake. Watanabe was a demon. And no ordinary demon at that. Most had a limited ability to terrorize the middle plane, using energy at an accelerated pace outside of hell. Lure demons were the only creature he knew who could remain here for days and weeks.

But Emily would recognize a lure demon.

Tethering his inner beast, Murdoch pivoted and followed Watanabe into the night. Whatever form of demon he was, he had to be banished. Now.

But the yard in front of Stefan's trailer was empty.

The bloody wretch had made a run for it.

Murdoch scanned the shadows between the trees. In what direction? The house? The arena? The perimeter fence? If he were a demon on the run, where would he go?

Ah, Christ. The hill.

He took off a run. The top of the hill was the only place in five thousand meters where magic could be performed. Stefan had blanketed the ranch in a mystical black hole to keep surprises at a minimum, but the former tennis courts were outside the umbrella of his spell.

On the hill, Watanabe could open a portal to the lower plane and make an escape.

Murdoch picked up the pace.

Over his already-dead body.

17

"**H**ey, Jason," Emily called to the Soul Gatherer in the gatehouse as she opened the small door in the wrought iron gate. "Thanks for calling me."

The young man returned her wave, then glanced down at his console. "No sweat. Your mom and Mac-Gregor ought to be here in about ten minutes. They called when they exited the highway."

A blue arc of electricity crackled in the air, zapping the gate only seconds after Emily let go of the door latch. Another arc followed moments later, accompanied by the scent of freshly squeezed lemons. Emily crossed her arms over her chest as the air grew tight and expectant, then popped.

Uriel appeared before her on the driveway.

"Way to be sneakeramous," she groaned. "What if a car had come around the corner just now?"

The archangel shrugged. "I checked before I descended. There are no cars within a five-mile radius. Besides, this is important."

"I'm *so* not liking the sound of that," she said.

"Have you heard anything more from the between?"

"No, things have been pretty quiet. Why?"

"Michael had one of heaven's administrators comb through the records of the days following the Great

Flood. She found a single, unverified reference to an ashen angel rescued from the floodwaters."

"Ashen?"

"Pale gray."

Emily rolled her eyes. "I know what *ashen* means. Why would an angel be gray? Was he dead?"

"No, he was not dead. And the color of his skin is far less concerning that the mention of extensive scarring on his torso."

"Why?"

Uriel slid a hand through his curls. "Because Azazel had an intricate weaving of malevolent runes etched into his flesh."

Her heart skidded to a halt at the edge of a cliff. "So, Azazel is alive."

"We believe so, yes."

"But he hangs out in hell, right? With Lucifer and Beelzebub and Satan?" She painted on a smile. "And you guys can track him."

"Not exactly."

"What do you mean, *not exactly*?"

"Unlike the other demon lords, Azazel has not appeared at a monthly soul tally in several millennia. Satan makes no official accommodations in hell for him. Nor do we have any accounts of activity attributed to him. It's like he doesn't exist."

Emily blinked. "You're saying you have no idea where he is? That he could be walking around on the middle plane, sucking souls out of people, and nobody has noticed?"

"We thought he was dead," the archangel pointed out. "We're watching for him now. Very closely. And he can't suck *souls* out of the living. Only blood."

"That's not very comforting, Uriel."

The handsome archangel glanced over his shoulder

at the empty road. "Your parents are almost here. You could help us find him, you know."

"Azazel? How? I have no idea what a fallen angel feels like." Lure demon, sure. Having one for a boyfriend had taught her how to spot one of those slimy bastards. Thrall demon, yup. Couldn't mistake those blue smoky guys for anything else. Fallen angel? Pure mystery.

The archangel tilted his head. "What do you see when you look at me?"

"A regular person. Except for a very thin rim of shimmery white stuff at the edge of your gold core."

"Azazel will appear much the same, except he's unlikely to be white. Black or dark purple, perhaps." The gate creaked and slowly began to open. "You can see every soul on the middle plane, Emily. Do some wide sweeps and if you spot him, call me. Do not engage him. Understand?"

"Got it." Skip the attack on a very powerful fallen angel? She could do that. No problem-o. "Should I warn Lachlan and Brian?"

Uriel nodded. "That might be wise."

The black Audi rounded the corner and surged up the road toward the gate.

"I have to go," Uriel said. "Please be careful."

And with a blue flash in the night, he was gone.

The car purred to a halt beside her and the driver's-side window descended. Lachlan frowned at her. "Is Michael harassing you again?"

"Nah, it was Uriel." She tugged open the rear passenger door and slid in next to the car seat. Katie's red wrinkled face peeked from a swath of pink blankets. Her mom sat on the other side, looking tired but very happy. "I'll fill you in later. Right now, I need to kiss my baby sister."

*   *   *

Murdoch caught up to Watanabe as he exited the trees.

The demon was hindered by the physical limits of his human glamour. Murdoch wasn't. A Soul Gatherer was a spiritual entity of the middle plane and had access to a full complement of skills, with or without magic. Exceptional speed, smell, strength, and night vision. All the things that helped him find and recover souls.

Or fugitive demons.

He slashed at Watanabe in midstride.

And missed. The demon dove and rolled, narrowly escaping the razor-sharp edge of Bloodseeker. As he landed and regained his feet, he shed the black sweater and sprouted a set of massive black wings. A pair of horns curled from his brow and the skin of his upper body and arms glowed dark purple as a series of markings rose up on his pale flesh.

Black feathers.

Did that mean—

A bolt of black lightning darted from the night sky and pierced Murdoch's left calf. Agony shot through him and his leg buckled, nearly taking him to the ground. But the instant the bolt struck, his berserker snapped the tethers holding it in restraint and swamped his body with hot, satisfying rage. His muscles expanded, his skin stretched, and his heart beat with heavy, fortifying pumps of blood. The pain fell away, completely forgotten. The beast took control, destruction of the demon its only goal.

Bloodseeker hummed through the air, slicing through everything in its path, even the tip of a glossy black wing. Feathers flew, and the demon roared in outrage. The creature tossed a second bolt, but it failed to land, repelled by the shield that was as much a part of the berserker as its skin.

The berserker swung again, and cut into the demon's thigh.

Hissing angrily, the demon soared into the air with a mighty flap of his huge dark wings. From his superior vantage point, he flung bolt after bolt of lightning, pitting Murdoch's shield, while remaining out of reach.

The berserker was unable to deal damage to the winged demon. No leap, no feint, no sudden change of direction gained him a point. His sword ripped through empty air. A growl of frustration rose from his throat as he tried again and again.

He had to equalize the battle.

The demon had to come down.

But even with all of Murdoch's whispered advice, the berserker could not entice the hellspawn within range of his sword. All he could do was dodge the energy bolts as best he could and swat at empty air.

Unacceptable.

He pivoted and jogged down the hill to the tree line. With a fierce grunt and a sharp jerk, he pulled a small pine tree from the ground, whipped around, and flung it at the demon. The heavy javelin struck true, and the creature crashed to the ground amid clumps of dirt and needles.

The berserker dashed in for the kill.

He shoved aside the tree and drove his sword tip straight toward the demon's rune-emblazoned chest. The demon's shield held up, but quivered under the powerful force of the thrust. Sensing the imminence of victory, the berserker put both hands upon the hilt and shoved even harder.

And the steel sank in.

But as the hallowed Norse blade parted flesh and ground against bone, something odd happened. The air rippled and bent, the temperature plummeted, and the demon's body disappeared. Leaving Murdoch standing on the hill with his sword plunged deep in the soil.

*   *   *

"For a second there, I thought you said *feathers*."

"I did." Murdoch responded to Webster from the depths of the living room sofa, still replaying the battle in his head. Even the four-hour field mission with the trainees hadn't dulled the memory. "Black feathers, big wings, horns, and a mess of strange symbols carved into its flesh."

"You think it was a fallen angel?"

"Aye."

Webster turned to MacGregor. "What do you think?"

The new father sat forward in his armchair, resting his elbows on his knees. "The black wings and basic human form match the descriptions I've heard."

"But the horns? And the runes?"

MacGregor shook his head. "In most references, Lucifer is described as beautiful. Blond hair, blue eyes, no scars. Were it not for the black wings, he'd be labeled angelic."

"This creature had black hair, not blond," Murdoch said. "Admittedly, I didn't get a look at its eyes. It was dark and I was rather busy at the time."

"Safe to say it wasn't Lucifer, then," Webster said. "So, who was it?"

"Azazel."

Murdoch glanced at the door to the hallway. Emily stood there, looking as grim as he'd ever seen her, a dirt smudge from the training session bisecting her pale cheek. "Tell us what you know, lass."

She slowly advanced into the room, a tray of chicken wings in her hand. Placing the tray on the coffee table, she tossed MacGregor a rueful look. "That's why Uriel was here. I've been hearing—or maybe *feeling* is a better word—these sounds from the between. Uriel's the one who told me about Azazel."

"Azazel is a fallen angel," Murdoch said, taking a cue from Webster's frown. "Once the most powerful demon in Satan's realm. He is a known seducer, and is credited with introducing war and artifice to the human race."

Emily nodded. "That's what Uriel said." Between bites of chicken, she relayed everything she and Uriel had discussed, from Azazel's supposed death to the more recent suggestion that he had survived. "He asked me to keep an eye out for him."

"That's no longer necessary," Murdoch said. He'd slain a fallen angel. Bloody hell. He'd finally done something righteous. "Based on Uriel's description, I can confirm that it was Azazel I killed out on the hill."

"Are you sure he's dead?" Webster asked.

"I put a sword right through his heart," Murdoch said, with a shrug. "None of *us* could survive that."

"And he didn't open up a portal to hell?"

"No red sparks," Murdoch confirmed. "The body vanished, but that might have something to do with the runes on his flesh."

Emily smiled at him. "Good job, Murdoch."

"Thanks, lass." His return smile faded. "As for the task you set me to, I wasn't able to twist Stefan's arm with that package. By the time I got back down the hill, it was gone."

"He snuck out of the trailer and picked it up while you were fighting for your life with a demon?" she asked, scandalized.

"So it would seem."

"What the hell's got into the guy?" Webster asked, looking at MacGregor. "He's gone right off the deep end. Can't you talk some sense into him?"

Lena and Kiyoko entered the house, both wearing a gi and sporting sweaty hair. Kiyoko was guzzling bottled water, her head tipped back and her throat working with each swallow. Murdoch couldn't take his eyes off her.

MacGregor stood. "I can try. But right now I've got a date with a wee lass and a diaper."

Lena snorted as she grabbed a chicken wing. "I've never seen a man look quite so pleased about that chore."

"Good men excel at even the most unpleasant deeds." He smiled at her. "I'll bring Katie over to the house for a viewing in the morning."

The female Soul Gatherer's normally crisp expression softened a little. "A baby in a house full of warriors. That should be interesting."

"I'll come home after I clean the kitchen," Emily told her stepfather.

MacGregor nodded and left.

Lena had a wistful look on her face. Webster tugged her away from the chicken wings and against his chest. He didn't say anything, just held her, displaying more empathy than Murdoch would have given him credit for possessing.

"I'm going to retire for the night," Kiyoko said from the doorway. "It's been a long day."

Murdoch scrambled to his feet. "I'll walk you upstairs."

"That's hardly necessary," she said.

"Actually, it is," he said drily. "I've got something I need to tell you about Ryuji Watanabe."

Kiyoko spent most of Sunday on the phone with the board of directors, dealing with Ryuji's disappearance. The "official" story was that he'd gone out for a bike ride and never returned. She'd even called in the police to support the tale.

The police officer had berated them for allowing him to ride off on his own, but had accepted the story.

The company had a succession plan in place, but losing two top executives in a matter of months had hit hard. The choices for an interim president were not stellar. In the end, the board settled on the head of the manufacturing division, a solid man with a good reputation. But no Ryuji Watanabe. The options would have been better if the board had been seeking a permanent replacement. With the recent rash of failed companies, there were a number of excellent prospects to approach. But there was still hope that Ryuji would reappear and the board acted accordingly.

By the time Kiyoko got off the phone, the ranch house front yard was a hive of activity. New trainees mingled with the old, bags and suitcases littered the lawn, and the oily exhaust of bus engines filled the air. Murdoch shook hands with Quinn and the others, then rounded up the new batch of trainees with an authoritative command. A larger group than the last. Sixty-three men and nine women.

"Did you tell him?" Sora asked as they watched Quinn's van depart for the airport. The cocky Irishman waved to Kiyoko from the backseat.

"No."

"Do you intend to?"

She leaned against the porch beam and stared up at the twilight sky. "He will not endorse the idea."

"Perhaps not. But we need his help."

"Yes, we do." The only star visible at this early-evening hour was Polaris. A lone twinkle in the heavens. "Do you think Ryuji Watanabe was a lie from the beginning? That my father was fooled from day one?"

Sora's gaze followed hers. "I cannot imagine a demon having patience enough to play the part for over a year," he said.

She agreed. Which meant a good man had been murdered—probably several months ago—and they had failed to mourn his passing. And it meant she had given her trust to a demon. Perhaps even fed him valuable information. The notion made her stomach heave. "My father was carrying the Veil the day he died. Ryuji-san was the first to arrive in the garage after the attack."

"You suspect it was he who battled your father?"

Kiyoko nodded. "But why not kill us both that night? Why spare me and leave the Veil behind?"

"Perhaps a simple case of exhaustion? The battle with your father would have taxed the demon greatly. Tatsu-san was a formidable warrior. If the real Watanabe-san entered the garage as the battle was ending, it would have been forced to slay him as well."

"That might explain why I survived the initial attack, but not why I am still here. Why did it not kill me the moment it recuperated?"

Sora scratched his chin. "A valid question."

"We're missing something."

The door to the bunkhouse rattled shut, and she looked up. Having settled his brood in their quarters, Murdoch strode across the lawn toward the house, ignoring the path in favor of the shortest route. He wore a gray long-sleeved T-shirt and his typical black jeans, and his hair hung down his back in a riot of dark waves. Except for those few slightly shorter locks that teased the sides of his face. The ones he shoved away with a careless hand but kept returning to torment him.

It was remarkably easy to imagine him in chain mail. Urging a mighty steed into battle. Mowing down the enemy with his blade, delivering swift, sure justice.

"Does anyone have a pair of tweezers?" he said as he bounded up the two steps onto the porch. "I have a sliver."

Kiyoko's lips twitched.

Or not.

She straightened. "I have one in my purse."

He nodded politely to Sora, then followed her into the house and up to the second floor. "Did you get everything straightened out with the board?"

"As best I could," she said. She pointed him to the

chair by the window, then dug into her purse on the dresser.

"How long before they accept that he's gone?"

"I don't know." She tossed him the tweezers. "It's not a common occurrence, misplacing your president."

Head bowed to his task, Murdoch didn't respond right away. He struggled with the tweezers, made an attempt to grab the offending piece of wood embedded in his skin, then lost the tool when it sprang from his fingertips.

"Bloody hell."

Kiyoko retrieved the tweezers from the floor. "The sliver's in your right hand?"

"Aye." He glanced up. "I don't suppose you could take it out?"

Her brows soared. "Without touching you? I doubt it."

His dark gaze firmed on her face, and she knew where his thoughts had gone. To the hot, delicious gropings that filled his dreams. Just like hers had. "Technically, only the tweezers need to touch me."

"It would be too risky. One slip and—"

"I'll make certain we don't touch," he said.

It was an absolutely crazy idea. The very epitome of playing with fire. But her pulse raced at the notion of being so close to him, breathing in his scent, feeling the warmth radiating from his body.

"All right."

She perched on the edge of the window seat and leaned over his hand. A dart of wood had buried itself deep in the pad of his thumb. But no matter how she angled the tweezers or how she twisted her body, she couldn't quite grip the sliver.

He opened his legs and nodded at the floor. "Sit here."

Her breath caught.

There? Between his thighs? Resting against that smooth-worn denim, grazing the inside of those heavy muscles as she worked? Was he determined to drive them both to the brink of sanity? Or was he purposely pushing himself, taunting himself, testing his ability to resist her?

She sank to her knees on the hardwood.

If he developed the strength to turn her away, her plans for tomorrow would fail. To unleash the berserker, she'd have to convince him to kiss her . . . *seduce* him into breaking his vow. What better place to start than right here?

On her knees, her bottom lip caught artfully in her teeth, she advanced into the vee of his thighs. She paused there, her breasts scant inches from his legs, and released the now swollen lip. To her delight, he sucked in a sharp breath.

"Extend your hand," she said.

He did.

She turned around, leaned back against his pelvis, and tucked his arm tight against her body using her elbow. His hand was now perfectly positioned to work on.

Except that it was trembling.

In fact, his whole body was shuddering.

"Hold still," she said with a grin. "I'll be very gentle, I promise."

"I don't give a damn if you're gentle," he said hoarsely. "Just be quick."

She bent over his hand. "Got it." She held up the tweezers for verification, then released his arm. "I'd kiss the wound better, but . . ."

"No kissing," he finished for her, on a ragged sigh.

She scooted back to the window seat and lifted her gaze to meet his. "No kissing," she confirmed.

He scowled and jabbed his thumb in his mouth.

"Are you done for the evening?" she asked. "Or do you have more work with the trainees?"

"I need to track down some extra practice weapons," he mumbled. "Why?"

"I wanted to discuss tomorrow."

A wary look replaced the disgruntled expression on his face. "What about tomorrow?"

"I'm going to attempt the transcendence."

He shot out of the chair, his wounded thumb forgotten. "No, you're not. We discussed this. I am going to work on Stefan, and you're going to be patient. We have a month."

Kiyoko studied her hands. A more ruthless person would have kept silent, seduced the man, and accomplished her goal. But she was done with lying and hiding. She needed Murdoch to understand, and to willingly offer his help.

"Azazel knew about the Veil."

"You *told* him?"

Her head popped up at Murdoch's angry accusation. "No, of course not. Watanabe was there the night my father died, and now that I know he was a demon, I can't believe it was a coincidence."

He paced the room, from the foot of the bed to the fireplace, his hands fisted at his sides. "That's still no reason to go off half-cocked. I killed the filthy bugger."

"You can't really believe that's the end of it."

"As long as you remain on the ranch, everything will be fine," he insisted. "We can keep the Veil hidden."

"Murdoch," she said softly, "I've corrupted you."

He halted and stared at her. "What?"

"When we first met, your commitment to keeping the Veil out of Satan's hands was vocal and passionate. Today you're willing to invite unmitigated disaster to minimize the risk to a single woman. All because I've personified the consequences."

"That's quite a turnabout. From devoted demon

slayer to weak-willed herald of the apocalypse in less than a month," he said drily.

Kiyoko flushed. She hadn't meant to insult him. "You know the only way to ensure the Veil's safety is to hide it away, buried beneath layers of magic and protected for eternity by immortal warriors."

"I don't deny that."

"Then don't deny my opportunity to do what's right, either. Once I transcend, I'll be able to give up the Veil. If you fear harming me, perhaps we can restrain you for the duration of the ritual."

He snorted. "You think I haven't tried crating the beast in the past? I can tell you, a locked door is pointless. Chains won't hold me. Hell, I've even broken out of a jail cell."

Not terribly surprising. She'd witnessed the enhancement of the muscles in his back and felt the post-berserker weight of his body. "Sora-sensei says a binding spell won't work, either. Any magic I cast to hold you in will also serve to keep me out." She sighed. "The best hope still lies with you."

"No," he said, turning his back on the plea in her eyes. "The best hope lies with Stefan Wahlberg. And by God, I'm going to make the man see reason."

He yanked open the bedroom door and stalked out.

Kiyoko listened to his footsteps pound down the stairs and the front door creak open and slam shut. A moment later, his large and very determined body appeared around the corner of the house and strode down the gravel path. Murdoch was a force to be reckoned with. He might yet succeed in browbeating Stefan and ending this painful trial.

But what if he failed?

Could she do what needed to be done?

Could she go ahead with her plan anyway?

*   *   *

Murdoch hammered the trailer door with his fist. "Open the blasted door, Dika, or I swear I'll rip it clear off its hinges."

The door opened.

Dika stood in the entrance, her arms folded over her chest. Feet planted and brow furrowed, she presented a remarkably formidable barrier for someone so small. "How many times must I tell you to go away?"

He wrapped an arm about her waist, lifted her effortlessly into his arms, and stepped into the trailer. "I'm done with talking. And I'm not going away. Where is the little maggot?"

Setting her down in the kitchen, he scanned the living room. Empty. He flung open the etched-glass door leading to the bedroom. "Is he hiding?"

The bedroom was empty, too. As was the bathroom.

Murdoch returned to the kitchen.

Dika still resembled a feather-ruffled hen. A slender, pixielike hen.

"Where is he?" he asked softly.

She said nothing. But a hint of triumph crooked her lips.

His gaze swung to the far end of the trailer, which was draped ceiling to floor with heavy purple velvet. *Ah, shit.* He crossed to the curtain and swept it aside. A wall of massive gray bricks, darkened with mildew stains and spotted with lichen, greeted him. No archway. No door. Just the solid, impassable three-foot-thick stone of Castle Rakimczyk.

"Call him out."

"I can't."

He spun to face her. "Bollocks, Dika. I know you can reach him. It's *your* bloody castle."

"I never disturb him while he's working."

Working? With the new grimoire? "What's he working on?"

"I didn't ask." She shrugged. "It's not my business."

Murdoch shook his head. "You may fool others with that docile, dim-witted charade, Dika, but you don't fool me. I've seen the way he looks at you whenever he's about to make an important decision. He values your opinion, and that tells me all I need to know."

She smiled, but said nothing. Just turned to the stove and stirred a big pot of something that smelled heavenly.

"How long has he been in there?" Murdoch asked.

"Since dawn."

"Well, then," he said, grabbing a leather armchair and pulling it forward. He flopped onto the seat. "He's got to come out to eat eventually. I'll just wait."

"He hasn't been very hungry lately."

Kicking off his boots, Murdoch reclined the La-Z-Boy. "Have no fear. He'll never resist the smell of your spaghetti sauce. No man can."

"Hmmm."

He glanced over his shoulder. "I don't suppose—"

She handed him a bowl of pasta and a fork.

"God love ya, Dika. You're a saint."

18

When the slithering hisses and moaning voices woke her for the second night in a row, Emily knew she had to call Uriel.

She threw back the covers, slid her feet into a pair of leather-soled slippers, and crammed her Horde ball cap on her head. As she tiptoed down the hall past the baby's room, she heard her mom crooning to Katie in sync with the slow, rhythmic rumble of the rocking chair.

Man, that baby could drink.

Every two hours. Nonstop.

Emily hugged the railing to avoid the creaky spot on the seventh stair and silently made her way to the front door. Why worry the folks? She grasped the brass door latch and pulled.

But it didn't open.

She glanced up. A big male hand held it shut. Lachlan. He was pretty damned good at the stealth moves. She should have used her senses.

"Where are you going?" he demanded quietly.

"Up to the tennis courts. I need to talk to Uriel."

He frowned at her, then glanced up the stairs. "Is there a problem?"

"I'm not sure. The creepy voices in the between are back."

"The ones that told you about Azazel?"

She nodded.

"You shouldn't go alone. I'll come with you."

Emily peeled his hand away from the door. "Uh, immortal girl, remember? I think you should stay here with Mom and the baby."

He stiffened.

"Not that there's anything to worry about," she added hastily. She did a quick check of the ranch grounds. "No alarm bells are ringing, honest. I just want to figure out what the noises mean."

"Okay." His eyes met hers in the gloom. "But if you're no' back in a half hour, I'm coming after you."

"Deal." She opened the door, stepped onto the porch, then paused. "Don't tell Mom. She's a worrywart, and she'll wait up instead of getting some sleep."

"Deal." He closed the door behind her.

The night air was quite cold, and Emily wished she'd brought a sweater. Her cotton pajama set didn't really cut it. Jogging up the path as fast as her slippers would allow, she pretended the goose bumps on her arms weren't there. The lights were still on in Stefan's trailer, which made her curious. But not curious enough to stop.

When she reached the crater at the top of the hill, Uriel was waiting for her. As hotly serene as ever.

"Don't you have bad guys to catch?" she asked, huffing. No point in even asking how he knew she wanted to talk. Angels made a habit of eavesdropping.

"Isn't that why I'm here?"

"Yeah," she acknowledged, still breathless. Man, she was out of shape. Time to take up track and field. "But you're very conveniently around whenever I need you."

He smiled. "Michael made you my ward."

"Your *what*?"

"I'm tasked with looking after you."

"Great," she said. "I'm your job. How cozy."

He tossed her an arch glance.

"Yeah, yeah, I know. I'm being too sensitive. Story of my life." She rubbed her bare arms. "Speaking of being sensitive, I'm hearing those voices again. From the between. And I gotta say, they're more freaked-out than ever."

Uriel peeled off his zippered hoodie and handed it to her. "What are they saying?"

Emily wrapped herself in the loose, warm fabric, breathing in the light smell of lemons. "The same. Azazel."

Uriel was silent, so Emily peeked from the depths of the fleecy cotton. His beautiful face was marred by a frown.

"Is that bad?"

"Perhaps."

"Perhaps *how*?"

He glanced at her. "Are the voice still fearful?"

"Yeah. Totally wetting their pants."

"What have they to fear if Murdoch killed Azazel?"

Emily stared at him. "You're saying he's still alive? That he survived a sword through the heart?"

Grimacing, Uriel shoved his hands in his pants pockets. "I would survive. Any archangel would. Azazel is a fallen angel; therefore it's possible he did, too."

"How?"

"I have no true corporeal form. The image I present to you is merely an illusion to make communication more comfortable."

She scrubbed her face. "So, you can't die?"

"Oh, yes, I can die," he said ruefully. "God could smite me. Satan, too. And a demon lord at full strength could take me down."

"But us puny humans? We can't harm you?"

"It would be very difficult."

Emily whipped off the hoodie and flung it at Uriel. "Maybe you should have mentioned that? It would have been nice to know we were facing impossible odds."

The archangel caught the jacket. "I did warn you not to engage him. And frankly, I had hoped Azazel was lessened by the Great Flood. That he wasn't himself."

A memory stirred in Emily's mind. "What about the Shattered Halo? It leveled *you*. Could it defeat Azazel?"

"It would definitely weaken him," Uriel said. "But the spell to leverage the halo is arcane and extremely difficult to wield."

"You've got a piece, though, right? Of Lucifer's halo? I want it."

His eyes narrowed. "Did you hear what I said?"

"I heard. Hand it over."

"Emily—"

She tipped the bill of her cap up so she could look him squarely in the eye. "Here's the way I see things. The guy is obviously after Kiyoko's Veil, which despite the lack of rotting-algae sensation must be capable of crushing mankind into dust. To my way of thinking, if he's alive, there's an awfully good chance he'll take another stab at it. Do you want me to save the world or don't you? Hand it over."

Uriel returned her stare, steady. "Do you really think you're ready to face Azazel?"

"No," she admitted. "But I've got friends."

He pulled his hand out of his pocket and opened his fingers. In the middle of his palm lay the gleaming fragment of shiny disk that Emily recognized from the battle they'd fought in the Egyptian desert seven months ago. It looked so ordinary, so harmless, so man-made. But she knew what it was capable of. And she knew what an act of faith it was that Uriel was offering it to her.

She took the shard from his hand. It was cool to the touch.

"Godspeed," the archangel said quietly.

Then he vanished in a blink of light.

*   *   *

Murdoch lost the last of his patience at seven in the morning. Swearing a blue streak, he gave the castle wall a spirited kick that shook some mortar loose but otherwise did no damage. He declined Dika's very generous offer of fresh-baked bannock bread, but snatched a mug of coffee from her hand with a mutter of thanks as he departed the trailer. It wasn't her fault Stefan was a bloody git.

When and *if* the wretched mage finally put in an appearance, he was going to strangle him.

Avoiding his fellow Gatherers and the inevitable morning small talk, Murdoch instead opted for a few peaceful hours with his Triumph Thunderbird. This early, the four-car garage was as quiet as a pub on Monday.

After filling a bucket with warm, soapy water and locating a soft chamois cloth, he set about clearing three weeks of accumulated dust off the motorbike. Something about sluicing away the grime, wiping down the steel with measured strokes, and revealing the beauty beneath was soothing. An hour later, the black body gleamed and the chrome handlebars, fork legs, and flared exhaust silencers sparkled.

"So, this is where you've been hiding."

He glanced up.

Kiyoko leaned on the hood of MacGregor's Audi. For once, she was not wearing a gi. Instead, she had poured herself into a pair of stovepipe navy jeans and a pink short-sleeved tee bearing the words *Pink This!* in white. The black belt was slung saucily around her hips and her dark hair hung loose down her back.

He swallowed.

She looked positively edible.

"I'm not hiding," he said, dropping his eyes to the bike and struggling with all his might to stop the rush of blood to his groin. "I'm having a caveman moment."

She crossed the cement floor until he could see the toes of her ballet flats. "A caveman moment?"

"I've withdrawn into my cave to pound a few rocks

with my club. It's how men do their most important thinking."

"I see. Should I leave you alone?"

"No, I'm about done with the pounding."

"Good. I've missed you." She crouched and ran a slim hand over the chrome Triumph badge on the tank. "What a beautiful machine."

Murdoch wasn't sure which comment warmed him the most. But she earned a special place in his heart for admiring the bike. "Aye," he said proudly. "Did you want to take a ride?"

A look of alarm flashed on her face. "It's rather large."

"Not alone. With me."

"I'd love to. But we agreed that it would be unwise for me to leave the ranch."

He tossed the chamois into the bucket. "So we did."

"Would you feel silly taking me down to the gate and back?"

"No." Getting all suited up for such a short ride might be tiresome, though. But he'd do it for Kiyoko. "Do you feel the need to don the full leather kit, or can we stick with boots and helmets?"

"I doubt we'll be traveling at a speed that requires leather." She glanced down at her flimsy shoes. "But I'm afraid I don't own any appropriate boots."

"Lena has a pair that ought to fit you."

"You've taken Lena for a ride?"

"Once or twice." There was an edge to her voice that made Murdoch smile. "She makes a point of confronting her fears. Anything that feels fast and mechanical scares the crap out of her. So, she rides."

"Lena is a very beautiful woman."

He nodded. "I've noticed."

"Really?"

"Aye," he responded easily. "Rather hard to miss those long limbs and large breasts."

Kiyoko stiffened.

"But I'll let you in on a secret, lass," he said, opening the locker next to him and pulling out his helmet and a smaller red one. "My berserker takes no interest in her at all. Barely blinked when she undid the top button of her blouse."

"When she *what*?"

"It was last summer," he said hastily, handing her the helmet. "She was trying to distract me so she could escape."

"The woman has no honor."

Murdoch dug in the locker again. "She was willing to risk everything to protect the people she loves. I cannot fault her aim, even if her methods left something to be desired. Here we are." He peered at the sole of the ladies' boots. "Size eight. Will that fit?"

"Yes."

He watched her bend to swap footwear.

The waistband of her jeans dipped, exposing a strip of creamy flesh and, for a moment, the notion of kissing the two dimples there occupied his every working brain cell.

No, Lena had never come close to stirring him the way Kiyoko did. As exotic as the half-Egyptian woman was, she had a cool, withdrawn air that did not encourage a man to get closer. In all honesty, he wasn't sure how Webster had seen past the thorns to the rose.

Kiyoko, on the other hand, made no apologies for her femininity. Nor did she use it to advantage. Some days she wore pink lipstick, pearl earrings, and floral dresses, and on others she wore stark black and white, no makeup, and a ponytail. There was no attempt to disguise or enhance. Being a woman was simply a facet of her physical being.

A physical being that, coincidentally, made his mouth water.

"This helmet is heavy," she said, turning. She was lost inside, only her eyes visible.

"You look lovely," he said, sincerely. Roses were over-rated. He preferred a soft, glorious, unabashed peony.

Her eyes crinkled into half-moons. "Thank you."

Donning his own helmet and a pair of leather gloves, he straddled the bike. Using the strength of his thighs, he lifted the heavy cruiser off the kickstand. "Up you get, then. On the seat behind me."

She swung a leg over the back, then scooted forward until her pelvis was snug against his buttocks. Her arms wrapped around his waist, belting his loose T-shirt to his body. "Ready."

His heart was thudding like a drum in his chest.

To be fair, it wasn't just her breasts pressing against his back that was driving him crazy. Her fingers were tracing every bump and indent in his abs. Slowly. Accompanied by a faint hum of approval.

He covered her wicked hand with his.

"Lass, don't be cruel."

"It's my intention to seduce you," she said.

He chuckled. "Very sporting of you to warn me. But if you keep doing that, I can't be responsible for keeping the bike on the road."

Her fingers ceased their torment.

"I wish things were different," she said, relaxing against him with a sigh.

Not sure what to make of that sentiment, he thumbed the starter and brought the cruiser to deep, rumbling life. Wishing had never proven a productive pastime for him. He was more of a make-it-happen fellow. Lately, though, life hadn't been very cooperative.

Putting the bike in gear, he throttled up the 1600 cc engine and zoomed past the Audi, out of the garage, and down the long drive. Unfortunately, the cruiser ate up the tarmac in a remarkably short time. He'd barely grown accustomed to the visceral vibration of the parallel twin engine when they arrived at the gate.

Pausing briefly to check on Kiyoko, who gave him a thumbs-up, he spurred the bike back toward the house with a satisfying roar.

His bike, his woman, and an open road.

Did life get much better?

As he neared the large pine tree that marked the split of the driveway between the garage and the house, he spotted a group huddled in front of the house. Webster, MacGregor, and Emily. Engaged in a heated discussion.

Veering right, he circled the rock garden and drew to a halt in front of the porch.

"Everything all right?" he asked, as he tugged off his helmet and eyed the group.

"Where the hell have you been all morning?" Webster asked.

Murdoch didn't respond. Instead, he helped Kiyoko off the bike, then dismounted. "Someone want to tell me what's up?"

"Azazel isn't dead."

Murdoch met Webster's gaze. "I ran him through with my own hand," he said softly, daring the other man to dispute his claim.

"Well, you should have decapitated him. According to Uriel, a fallen angel can survive a sword through the heart."

Murdoch glanced at Emily, searching for the truth.

She nodded. "But he never said taking Azazel's head off was the answer. In fact, he kinda suggested no amount of body damage will finish him off."

"So, the solution must be mystical," Kiyoko said.

"Problem is," Webster said, "the blanket spell Stefan put over the ranch prevents us from using magic."

"Then we'll have to get rid of it."

"That will be damned hard without Stefan," Murdoch

said. "And no one's had any luck prying the wretch out of that bloody trailer."

The group was silent for a moment.

Then Emily said, "I bet Sora could do it."

Murdoch arched a brow. "What? Convince Stefan to exit, or disarm the spell?"

"The spell."

He turned to Kiyoko. "What do you think? Could he do it?"

"He's a gifted mystic. It's possible."

"Getting rid of the blanket spell works both ways," MacGregor reminded them. "For us and for the demons. Before we disarm it, we need to know exactly how we're going to take down Azazel."

"I have something that might help," Emily said. She opened to hand to reveal a shard of the Shattered Halo. "He's an angel, right? So this should flatten him, like it flattened Uriel. If we can figure out how to use it."

Webster's gaze lifted from the shard to Murdoch's face, then slid away. "We need that spell book. The one we found on the body of that thrall demon last summer."

"The Book of Judgment." Lena descended the porch steps cradling a swaddled Katie in her arms. She passed the baby to MacGregor, who immediately melted from hardened warrior into beaming father. "Stefan has it."

Murdoch snorted. "Of course."

"Christ. That pretty much ixnays using the Shattered Halo," Webster said grimly. "Too bad. It was a great idea, Em."

"Yeah." She sighed and offered him the shard. "Maybe you should take it, to keep it safe."

Webster raised both hands and backed away. "Hell, no. Don't give the damned thing to me. In fact, I don't think any of the Gatherers should take it. You hold on to it."

Murdoch grimaced. Leaving it with Emily was no

guarantee that Death wouldn't get her hands on it. "Are we confident that Azazel's not on the ranch right now? We just opened the doors to seventy-two strangers."

"I did a quick read of everyone as they arrived," Emily said, pocketing the shard. "No sign of him."

"She's going to check every couple of hours," Webster said. "With any luck, we'll figure out how to torch his ass before he returns. But you can bet on one thing—he'll be back."

"I'll run through my repertoire of shade spells," MacGregor said. "I hate to use them, but I will if I must."

"No." Lena surged forward, her body rigid with indignation. "No shade spells. Trading material objects for magic power does too much damage to the fabric of the plane. And if you succumb to *their* lure, it won't be long before you find justification for using the void spells that sacrifice human souls."

"I agree," Kiyoko said.

"I applaud your fine principles." MacGregor looked down on the sleeping face of his infant daughter. "But with no mage and no spells more powerful than the simple entity spells generated by our own passions, we haven't got a prayer."

"You don't need to be here," Webster said. "Take Rachel and the baby and get the hell out of Dodge."

"I'll keep that option open," MacGregor said, his resolute face a direct contradiction to his words.

"Don't let your pride hold you here, *mo charaid*," Murdoch added quietly. "Were it *my* wife and daughter, I'd bear jokes about my cowardice clear into the next century if it meant keeping them safe."

MacGregor's gaze met his.

"Webster and I can handle the trainees for a few days," Murdoch said. "This is the easy stuff: Basic footwork and guard positions, physical fitness, and a couple of essential defense spells. You don't start the sparring until week two. Besides, someone needs to break the news to the Protectorate that the Veil actually exists. It might as well be you."

The other man nodded, finally convinced. "I'll have to drag Rachel away kicking and screaming. She'll no' be happy about leaving Emily behind."

"I'm not going anywhere," Emily said quickly.

"No," MacGregor agreed with a faint smile. "You'll stay. Convincing your mother about that will take some work, though. It's your sixteenth birthday tomorrow."

Kiyoko followed Murdoch back to the garage, leapt up on the tool bench, and watched him stow the bike and helmets. The play of his muscles beneath his loose T-shirt fascinated her. "What does *mo carriage* mean?"

He opened the locker. "'My friend.'"

"It's Scottish?"

He nodded. "Gaelic. Hardly anyone speaks the language now, but in MacGregor's time it was the tongue of the Highlands."

"MacGregor's time?"

"Did I not mention he was once a Gatherer? He was born in the fifteenth century."

Kiyoko stared at him, confused. "How can anyone *once* be a Gatherer? Aren't you all dead?"

"Aye," he said, tucking his gloves inside his helmet and sliding it onto the top shelf of the locker. "It's a long story. Suffice it to say he earned his soul back and is now a human."

"Can you do that as well? Earn your soul back?"

"Unlikely. His was a special case. The rest of us will be content if our souls escape the fiery ravages of hell." He looked up then, pinning her with his gaze. A rare note of regret hovered in the dark depths. "I'm sorry that I failed you, lass. I thought I'd rid you of a demon stalker, but it seems I've only made the bastard more dangerous by driving him underground."

"How could you have known?" she asked softly. "Are you clairvoyant, as well as handsome and talented?"

"Lord, you've resorted to flattery. That can't bode well." He closed the locker and held up her ballet flats. "Did you want to change your shoes?"

"No. I think I'll keep these boots."

He arched a brow. "Oh?"

"Lena won't need them any longer, as she will not be taking any further rides on your bike."

The corner of his mouth lifted. "I'll let her know."

Jumping down, she crossed the oil-stained cement floor to his side. She flattened her palm on the broad expanse of his chest, reveling in the firm contours under her fingers. "And to make sure you don't offer rides to any *other* women, I've decided to claim you as my man."

"About bloody time."

"For now." ·

He reached for her hand, as if fearing she might pull away, but caught himself before he made skin contact. "What do you mean *for now*?"

"In less than a month, I'll be returning to Japan."

"Unless I can convince you to stay."

Lifting her chin, she gave him a serious look. "I know my path, Murdoch. I do not mean to diminish what we have, but you are merely a detour on my larger journey." His lips thinned, and she added, "As I am but a detour on yours."

"I would never slur a woman by labeling her a *detour*."

"A joyous interlude, then. An oasis in the desert. How we describe this time doesn't matter." The beat of his heart was strong and steady under her hand, like the man himself. Despite his talk of having many women, she had never doubted Murdoch's ability to be true.

"Once I transcend and free myself from the Veil, the bond we share will be severed."

"And good riddance to it."

She stiffened. "What?"

"It's been nothing but a nightmare," he said grimly.

"I thought you said you enjoyed the dreams."

His hands slid over her hips and around the curves of her bottom. With little more than a twitch, he lifted her up his body until her pelvis mashed into his. Hot and hard.

She wrapped her legs around him.

"Dreams, no matter how good they feel, are no substitute for reality," he said. "My bloody balls ache with the need to take you. I want to touch you freely, without the threat of the berserker hanging over my head. I want to test out every sensitive spot on your body that the dreams have shown me and listen to you moan in my ear. I want to taste your breasts in my mouth, enjoy the ragged breaths that escape your lips as I sink into you, and view the flush in your cheeks as I bring you to release."

Kiyoko's breaths were already ragged.

"Although," he added, grinding against her in slow, delicious circles, "I fear the agony of the wait will prove my undoing when the moment arrives."

"Modern English"—the seam of her jeans struck the perfect spot and her eyes closed—"please, Murdoch."

"I won't last."

"Okay," she said breathlessly. "But don't stop."

A growl of frustration tore from his throat. He maneuvered them over to the Audi and yanked open the back door. "Damn it. Bloody baby seat."

His distraction curtailed the thrusts of his hips, and Kiyoko dug her fingers into the sinews of his upper shoulders. "Don't. Stop."

"Fuck." He bent her over the trunk of the car. "Apologies in advance for any bruises, lass."

Then he proceeded to slay her. With a single-minded dedication to eliciting every variety of moan and groan, he coaxed her body to the very pinnacle of ecstasy. Every press of his body brought new shivers of delight, every muttered endearment new thrills. And his hands were willing participants in the siege. One palmed her braless breast through her shirt, the other squeezed her ass.

It was like being a teenager all over again.

Only with a partner who knew precisely what he was doing.

"Oh," she gasped, as his mouth latched onto her breast, hot and damp through the T-shirt. His teeth found her nipple just as his hips pumped against her. The ripples combined to form a perfect storm of sensation and, with a hoarse cry of his name, she flew apart.

As the shudders of pleasure coursed through her body, his movements gentled, but did not completely stop.

The muscles of his back undulated under her hands, and she desperately wanted to reach under the hem of his shirt to feel the hot satin of his flesh. To feel the real Murdoch, not just the dream. But she could not and would not invoke the berserker. Not now. Not today. This moment belonged to her and Murdoch alone, and it had to last a lifetime.

She buried her face in his hair.

"I love you," she whispered.

Murdoch froze.

Had she truly said what he thought she said?

He was awfully tempted to ask, but the incredulity in his voice might give her the wrong impression. How could she love a man who tossed her over the boot of a car and coaxed a release from her without so much as a dinner date? A man who had near crushed her to death in a bed of thyme? A man who admitted to killing his fiancée? Hell, a man who was no longer even a man, just a soulless sinner. Was she crazy?

"Get up, Murdoch," she said, pushing at his shoulders.

He rolled away from the car, suddenly conscious of his weight. "Are you all right?" he asked warily.

She smiled. "I'm great. That was nice. Thank you."

Nice? *Nice?* She blew his world apart and called it *nice*? As if that weren't bad enough, he found himself responding with, "You're welcome." Like some pansy-assed prep school boy.

"I need a shower," she said.

"Aye, so do I."

The conversation was so bloody awkward, Murdoch had trouble recognizing himself. He'd done the same favor for scores of women and never once felt uncomfortable. He'd even had women tell him they loved him. Not since he shaved off his beard, mind you. Could that be the problem? Was he lost without the beard?

"I'll see you later, then." Kiyoko gave a wave and a half smile, then walked to the door.

His hands fisted, then unfisted. "Wait."

She paused, and turned.

"I'm not entirely certain," he said, "but I think I may love you as well."

She didn't laugh. Which, when he thought about it, was quite an accomplishment. As pledges of undying affection went, it would never make the honor roll. But it was all he had.

And she seemed to accept that.

The smile she gave him was deep and genuine. "You are a good man, Murdoch."

Then she left.

19

Azazel strode into the Hall of Shadows, and the murmuring and wailing abruptly ceased. Fear rose from the packed crowd, a dank smell that soaked into the walls and draperies like stale urine and hung in a cloud over the massive room.

It was time to put his army to the test. Not the whole army, of course. Just the bone-sappers. Gradiors were powerful and nearly unstoppable, but not the best option when stealth was required.

He reached out and with a flick of his wrist forced the nearest sapper to its knees. The inky creature shrieked as it fell, which in turn sent a shiver of dread through its comrades.

Azazel smiled.

Once, when he'd first crawled his way—battered and broken—into the between, the creatures had foolishly attempted to feed from him. But he'd quickly discovered their weakness and used it to his advantage.

Pain.

Despite their ever-shifting shapes and wet texture, they could feel pain. A great deal of it. A stab of energy through the nucleus of nerves that served as their brains, and voilà . . . instant obedience.

He dragged his captive forward, shredding its knees on the stone flooring, until it lay in a ragged heap at his feet. "Rise into the middle plane and bring me news of the Veil. I must know where she hides it. You have my leave to hunt any Soul Gatherers you should chance upon, but do not return unless you have the information I seek."

The creature quivered with understanding. A bone-sapper could not survive sunrise.

"Go," Azazel said.

The creature vanished.

If it returned before dawn, then the next stage of his plan could proceed. If it didn't, he'd simply send another. His army of sappers was several thousand strong. Losing a handful to prove his might would only further his mastery over them.

And eventually one of them would succeed.

"Can you sense the presence of the blanket spell?" Kiyoko asked Sora, as she peered into the murky water of the fishpond.

"Yes. Can you?"

She tossed a bread crumb into the water. The water immediately erupted into a flurry of waves and the bread was attacked by several mouths. Catfish. "I feel *some*thing, but it is ill-defined."

"If you walk up the hill to the edge of it, you'll get a better grasp of its composition," he said. Slipping off his sandals, he walked barefoot in the grass, his robes whispering. "It's an excellent hex. Multilayered and self-repairing."

"Can you disarm it?"

"Not easily," he admitted. "But with time and study, I'm sure I can weave a counterhex."

Another crumb produced a splash and a fin. "How much time?"

"Until I work on it, I can't say."

She glanced up at the trailer, which was visible on the

other side of the forge. Time was a commodity they were quickly running out of. "Could you not consult with the mage? He might listen to you, as one mystic to another."

"I doubt that," Sora said, smiling faintly. "He does not wish me to come near the trailer."

Her gaze slid back to his face. "How do you know?"

"He has erected a barrier spell."

"Specific to you?" At his nod, she sighed heavily. "He's being very difficult, eroding our efforts at every turn. Our dependency upon his good nature is very frustrating."

"Yes." Sora scratched his chin. "Of course, the barrier spell does not prevent *you* from knocking on his door."

"I doubt he would agree to speak with me. He slammed that very door in my face the first night I was here."

"Go as my emissary."

She frowned. "How would that help?"

"The barrier spell is not a blast-repel. It is merely a 'do not enter.' More of a defensive spell than an offensive one." Sora shrugged. "That would suggest he might still extend me a professional courtesy."

Kiyoko tossed the remaining handful of crumbs in the water, inciting a frenzy. "And as your emissary, what shall I do?"

"Ask for the book and the disarm phrase for the blanket spell."

She laughed. "Do you expect him to just give them to me?"

"Yes."

"Why?"

Sora plucked a piece of rush fluff off his black sleeve and blew it gently into the air. "Because he doesn't want to see the Veil fall into the wrong hands."

"Really? He hasn't lifted a finger to help us so far."

"He's busy."

She tossed the sensei a hard look. "With what?"

"Judging by the mystical dust flying about the trailer, I'd guess he's trying to destroy the Veil."

Kiyoko's heart skipped a beat. "Are you sure? Why didn't you mention this? If he succeeds before I transcend—"

"A guess is never certain," he said, with a mild note of rebuke. "As for why I did not speak up, I only just concluded his intent this very minute."

She glanced up at the hazy blue sky. Several hours remained in the day—more than enough time to attempt the transcendence. "When is the next auspicious day?"

"Sunday."

Almost a full week away. "You know the relic well. How likely is it that the mage will succeed?"

Hitching up the hem of his robe, he peered at his toes as he wriggled them in the blades of grass. "I have been searching for a way to destroy the Veil since the day we acquired it. To no avail."

The knot in her belly eased. *Years*.

"But the mage has talents I don't possess," Sora added.

Perhaps. But the sensei was a modest man. He had skills beyond the norm, too. "I've decided not to attempt the transcendence without Murdoch's cooperation. I refuse to delve into his auras and borrow his berserker's strength behind his back."

The old *onmyōji* shrugged. "Then wait. The risk of the Veil being destroyed before Sunday is small."

Kiyoko agreed. Holding Brian Webster off for another week would be a challenge, but with Lena on her side, the chances of success were excellent there, too. Decision made, she once again turned her attention to the trailer. "I just knock on the door and ask politely?"

"Indeed."

"All right." She left him standing by the water's edge and crossed the yard to the trailer. At the stone path leading to the front door, she paused to gather her courage.

Before she could take another step, the door flew open.

The mage stood in the entrance, his clothing wrinkled and askew, his already unruly hair a jumble of dull black curls atop his head. His face seemed thinner than she remembered, even with the dark stubble on his chin. In his hands he held a large square tome embossed with gold foil and Egyptian hieroglyphics.

"Here," he said, holding out the book. "Take it."

She darted forward and claimed the leather tome. It was surprisingly light for such a big book.

"Tell him the disarm spell is on a piece of paper stuck in the front. Now go away."

Kiyoko hesitated. Then decided she had nothing to lose. "If you succeed in finding a way to destroy the Veil, I would appreciate some warning before you do it."

His gaze met hers, bleak. "I can't promise that."

"I don't need a promise, just an effort."

He nodded. "I'll do my best.

Then he slammed the door in her face. For a second time.

Emily was in the middle of a spin attack on Murdoch when a cold finger ran down her spine. Since she was in a warm, brightly lit arena at the time, the eerie sensation startled her enough to throw her off balance, and the tip of her sword sliced through his sleeve and into his arm.

"Ow."

"Sorry." She grimaced at the blood that immediately stained the gray cotton. "Should I get a Band-Aid?"

He peered between the crimson edges of the hole in

his shirt. "No, it's nothing serious." Then he looked up. "Are you all right? You haven't had this much trouble concentrating in months."

"I just got a weird feeling, that's all. You know, like when you go down into a dark basement and you get the creepy sense that something's watching you from behind the boxes of Christmas decorations?"

He stared at her, blank-eyed.

"Oh, never mind." She resumed her guard position, feet planted shoulder width apart. "Let's keep going."

Murdoch did not raise his sword. A frown was gaining ground on his face. "Did you do a sweep for Azazel?"

"Yeah, about fifteen minutes ago. Nada."

"Do another one."

She sighed and closed her eyes. Arguing with Murdoch was pointless. The guy was as bullheaded as they came.

Rolling her shoulders to help her relax, she mentally reached out across the dusk-shrouded acres, sweeping over buildings, land, and trees until she met the fence that bordered the entire perimeter of the ranch. Diving deeper into the buildings, she measured and accounted for each and every person, human and inhuman. None had the purple-rimmed core she'd been told would identify Azazel, and none had the shiny, almost too-perfect core she now associated with Ryuji Watanabe.

"Nothing," she confirmed.

Murdoch wasn't satisfied by her answer. "How many people are on the ranch?"

"Including me and you? Ninety-one. It was ninety-four until an hour ago, when my mom and Lachlan left." She wrinkled her nose. "Did they by any chance leave something with you, to give to me? Tomorrow, like?"

"And where's Hill?"

"Behind you, in the weight room."

"Are you sure? I thought I saw him leave with Jensen."

She gave him her best rendition of an evil eye. "Am I *sure*? Are you kidding? Want me to call him out here?"

"No need to get testy. I'm just being careful." He tapped the flat of her blade with his own. "Let's try that spin again."

She waited until he was in position, then repeated the spin, this time from the opposite side and this time with no error. He had to move swiftly to parry her attack.

"So," she said, as she landed softly in the sand. "With my mom gone, who's going to bake my birthday cake? Do *not* tell me it's Lena, because I'll barf."

Kiyoko left the Book of Judgment with Sora.

Although he freely admitted he could not read ancient Egyptian, he was fascinated by the intricate renderings on the pages. Taking great care not to unnecessarily crease the pages, he spread the book open on one of the tables in the bunkhouse lounge.

"Take it to Lena when you're done," she told him. "She knows which one activates the Shattered Halo, and she can translate the text. She'll also know when they want you to disarm the blanket spell."

The ranch house was quiet when she entered, with only a few faint clicking noises coming from the back room where Carter had his communications hub. Everyone was down at the arena, where the new trainees were being outfitted with practice swords and the basics of how to wield them.

Kiyoko climbed the stairs.

As tempting as it was to watch Murdoch put the group of Gatherers through their paces, sleep had more appeal. The day's roller-coaster ride of emotions had taken its toll. And frankly, sleeping through the last hours of the day was preferable to endlessly second-guessing her decision not to transcend.

She opened the door and flicked on the light.

Darkness was banished to a few small corners of the room.

Her eyes were drawn to the shadow between the dresser and wall, which seemed deeper than the others. Spying nothing but a garbage pail in the gloom, she crossed to the window and closed the curtains.

Sharing her feelings with Murdoch had been a mistake.

He had—naturally and incorrectly—assumed that she needed him to reciprocate. Most people who said *I love you* had an expectation, or a hope, that the sentiment would be returned. She had none. She had simply learned the hard way that life did not always give you opportunity to say the things you wanted to say.

Rustling through her suitcase, which she had yet to unpack, she located a fresh pair of pajamas. Black fleece shorts and a tank top. She peeled off her pink tee, then paused. Listening. Not certain what had caught her attention, she slowly pivoted.

The room was empty, and nothing was out of place.

Still, she hastily tugged the black tank top over her bare breasts. Sora said such moments were caused by the random appearance of ancestral spirits. She grimaced. She did not need her grandparents seeing her naked.

Removing the black belt, she folded it neatly and tucked it under her pillow. Then she finished changing, brushed her teeth, and turned off the light. As she laid her head on the pillow and closed her eyes, a soft sigh froze the breath in her chest.

Her right hand closed around the scabbard of her katana, lying on the bed beside her. She listened very carefully for another sound, ready to leap up and face her attacker. But a long minute passed without incident. Then another. When a full five minutes had gone by, she relaxed and looked around.

Nothing.

Must have just been the floorboards.

Settling her thoughts with a few concentrated breaths, Kiyoko closed her eyes again. Moments later, she was asleep.

Murdoch sank onto the brown velvet armchair in his room, leaned back with the heels of his hands pressed against his eyes, and contemplated the mess that was his afterlife.

For seven hundred years, his goals had been simple: be the best warrior he could be, err on the side of honor, and earn his way into heaven one soul at a time. Yes, he was a tad ambitious and sought reasonable recognition from his peers. Yes, he wanted to earn the title of leader. But in the end, he'd be content so long as Saint Peter didn't kick him in the ass when he showed up at the Pearly Gates.

Or so he'd thought.

Until he met Kiyoko.

Now he wanted something more. Happiness.

He had too little experience with love to use it as a label for how he felt. All he knew was that being with her made him happy, and he wanted the warm feeling she created in his chest to go on and on. Frankly, he wasn't sure he deserved to have happiness, but now that it was within his grasp, he found himself very reluctant to let it go. To let Kiyoko go.

And therein lay the other half of the problem.

This transcendence crap.

He was torn over it.

The promise was very seductive. After all, if she transcended, she would become immortal, like him. Or something very similar. With a human life span no longer their curse, they could enjoy several hundred years together instead of ten or twenty. And even if she chose not to spend those years with him, so long as she was healthy and happy, he'd rejoice.

But what price was he willing to pay?

If the ritual went awry and she died, it would rip his bloody heart out. And if his berserker was the cause of her death, misery would define the rest of his existence.

Laughter erupted in the hallway and several booted feet stomped past his door. He checked his watch. Two in the morning. He had warned the new trainees that tomorrow would start early, but most had been too eager and excited to fall into bed. Gathering was a very lonely role, and this would be the first time many of them had exchanged more than five words with a peer.

He remembered the euphoria.

But it wouldn't make him any more sympathetic when they dragged their lazy, late asses into the arena.

Not that Gatherers needed sleep. They didn't. But newbies tended to live by the same rules they'd followed when they were alive. Which meant they often slept until noon, especially if they had a gather during the night.

He unbuckled his boots.

Tomorrow would be fun.

A fist pounded on his door. "Mr. Murdoch. Ah, shit. Mr. Murdoch, you've got to come. We need you."

He yanked open the door.

One of the trainees stood there. A tall blond fellow, ghastly pale and shaking. There was something that looked suspiciously like puke in the corner of his mouth.

"What is it?"

"It's Derek. Derek Kowalski." The words came out fast. Then he gulped. "Or, at least, I think it's Derek. Oh, God, it must be. I just don't know."

Murdoch's right hand felt for and found the hilt of his sword. "Slow down. What's your name?"

"Johann Werner."

"All right, Werner. Take a deep breath, then lead me to Derek. On the way, you can tell me exactly what happened."

Murdoch followed the man to the side door, and out into the yard. A solitary lamp fixed to the bunkhouse wall held back the dark night.

"We came out for a smoke," Werner said as they walked. "Derek had to take a leak, so he went into the woods. Not far, just behind this tree." The young man halted abruptly. "One minute he was laughing and pissing, the next, nothing. Just silence. I got freaked-out, so I checked on him and this is what I found."

He pointed behind the tree.

Murdoch scanned the trees, looking for anything out of the ordinary. But all he saw were trunks and branches and shadows. No demons. He drew his sword, just to be safe; then he stepped around Werner.

"Christ." Murdoch swallowed.

"Yeah."

If it had been a man once, it didn't resemble one now. More like a lumpy pool of skin, hair, and clothing. No blood, no separated limbs, but there was no doubt the poor bugger was dead.

"It happened so quickly. I never had a chance to do anything. What sort of thing can do that?" Werner asked, his voice begging for reassurance.

Which Murdoch couldn't offer.

"I don't know." He glanced up at the ranch house. The windows were dark except for one lonely light in the back. His berserker flexed under his skin, sending a rush of hot blood coursing through his veins. Kiyoko. "Go back to the bunkhouse, wake everyone, and gather in the common room. Hill and Lafleur will know what to do. No one goes outside until I return."

Werner nodded and took off.

Murdoch crossed the yard to the main house in under ten seconds. He entered the kitchen through the back door. The house was silent and still.

Unlike Murdoch's heart.

Emily first, then Kiyoko, then Webster and Lena.

He darted into the hall and promptly slid on something gooey and soft, nearly falling. A glance down confirmed his worst thought. Another body. Equally boneless. Equally dead. With red hair.

He choked back a wave of nausea.

Dear God. It was Carter.

With as much respect as he could manage, he stepped clear of the puddled flesh. And then ran for the stairs. If anything had happened to—

He couldn't even finish the thought.

Throwing open the door at the top of the stairs, he quickly verified that Emily was still in bed and seemingly whole. She sat up, bleary-eyed, and gasped, "What? What's wrong?"

Murdoch didn't hang around to answer. He tore down the hall to Kiyoko's room—his room—and flung open the door. The bed was empty. *Oh, Christ.* His gaze skimmed the hardwood floor, dread a claw in his chest.

The toilet flushed and Kiyoko stepped out of the bathroom, rubbing her eyes. "What's wrong?"

Her face was puffy with sleep and her hair was a knotted mess on one side, but she had never looked more beautiful or more *alive.*

He breathed.

"Go get Sora. Make sure he's okay." He turned and rapped on Webster's bedroom door. "We've got a major problem."

Webster yanked open the door, Lena right behind him. Both were scantily clad. "What kind of problem?"

Everyone upstairs was safe. Murdoch's pulse ratcheted down a notch as his berserker receded. But he still had no idea what the hell they were dealing with. "I've got two dead Gatherers and no sign of any demons."

He explained what he'd found.

"Boneless?" asked Emily, from her bedroom door. "Did you say they were boneless? As in attacked by bone-sappers?"

"Lord, I hope not," muttered Lena. "To be safe, we should turn on all the lights. Right now. Every one of them."

"Hold on," Murdoch said. "Let's not panic. Bone-sappers feed off spirit bones, not real ones."

Lena nodded. "True. But Gatherers are spirits. A rather meaty form of spirit, perhaps, but we're definitely culled from the primal energy field."

"If we assume that it's bone-sappers," Webster said, "how did they get here? Are we dealing with an open portal somewhere?"

"Absolutely. They have to be escaping somehow."

"No." Emily spoke firmly. "I don't think it's an open portal. I think it's Azazel. He's sending them here."

"What do you mean *sending them*?" Lena asked.

"I think he's figured out how to use them on the middle plane. That's why he's been stirring them up."

"But you've been checking for Azazel every hour or so," Webster pointed out. "If it was him, wouldn't you have known?"

"I was checking for *him*, not for bone-sappers," she said, hugging her pillow to her chest. Her skin had a taken on a greenish cast and her eyes were dark. "I'm sorry. I don't even know what a sapper feels like."

Everyone was silent.

Then Kiyoko said, "I felt something in my room, just before I went to sleep. Something eerie. I thought it was just my imagination."

"Eerie?" asked Emily. "Like something was watching you?"

Kiyoko nodded. "From the shadows. But there was nothing there."

Murdoch tried not to think about the possibility that the creature that had turned Carter into mush had been in Kiyoko's room without him being aware. He glanced at Emily. "You felt something similar. Earlier, when we were practicing."

"Yeah. I did."

Webster grabbed his pants off the end of his bed and thrust a leg in. "Let's pull ourselves together here, people. We need to account for everyone, see how much damage these things have done."

"Should we gather in the arena?" Lena asked, as she, too, threw on clothes. "We've got a couple of hours yet before dawn, and the lights in there are pretty bright."

Webster nodded. "Sounds like a plan."

He and Lena dashed for the stairs.

Murdoch studied Emily's face for a moment, thinking. "Once you feel an entity, you can find it, right?"

She looked up. "Yes."

"Do it. Scan the ranch."

Tossing the pillow aside, she shook out her body and closed her eyes. A few moments later, she opened them again, relief shining in her eyes. "It's not here. The creepy feeling is gone."

Murdoch smiled at her. "Great job, lass."

Then the light left her eyes. "One small problem, though."

"What?"

"Gradiors. They live in the between, too."

He felt the earth shift a little under his shoes. Gradiors were reanimated dead bodies, and they attacked living people, not just the dead. "Excellent point. I'll remind the others. Now go get dressed. We might as well join the others in the arena. I doubt anyone will be able to sleep."

"Okay."

He turned to Kiyoko.

There were so many things he wanted to say to her. How bloody ecstatic he was that she was alive, how his heart had practically ripped out of his chest when he let his fear imagine her dead, how utterly bleak his life would be if she were gone. But none of them were appropriate for the moment.

"Bring your katana."

20

She'd worn it right in front of him, brazen as can be. The black belt. Quite ingenious, hiding it in plain sight. It made perfect sense. The Veil was cloth, the belt was cloth. Rather annoying it hadn't occurred to him earlier, though. He could have saved himself a great deal of effort.

But no matter.

His plan could move forward.

Azazel conjured a feast to his tabletop—braised mutton, candied sweet potatoes, fresh rolls, and plenty of red wine. Orchestrating the death of two Gatherers had blackened another wing feather, and his powers continued to grow.

He would wait a few days—until the exhaustion of remaining alert wrung them into limp rags and their vigilance faltered—then he'd slip in and steal the Veil. He wouldn't have much time to get in and get out, but a well-executed plan did not depend on time.

The question was who to masquerade as.

He slathered butter onto a chunk of bread and stuffed it in his mouth. Butter was one of Satan's better creations. Sinful as hell.

The old man? She trusted Sora explicitly and would open her door to him without pause. But his serenity was difficult to mimic, and the likelihood of her noting a lack of knowledge was high. Murdoch? The problem there was the berserker. She would notice immediately if the colors of his auras were off. None of the other Gatherers would get him close enough, so there was really only one option left.

Yoshio.

Loyal, competent, and willing to bend the rules.

Yes, he would do perfectly.

" 'Night, Murdoch."

He glanced up as the last two trainees departed the arena with a good-bye wave. Both men were smiling. "Good night."

Tensions were finally on the wane.

But the jury was out on whether that was a good thing.

For the first three nights, no one had slept a wink, and tales of how Kowalski had died had circulated endlessly among the Gatherers, becoming more lurid with each telling. On Wednesday, Murdoch had to break up a brawl in the weight room that began because one trainee had failed to wipe down the decline bench after taking his turn.

And it got worse at night. Despite the floodlights installed along every major footpath and the watch posted from dusk to dawn, no one voluntarily stepped outside after dark.

Murdoch grimaced as he checked each of the training swords for serious nicks and scratches.

Azazel had turned a group of powerful warriors into lily-livered shirkers. Even the more seasoned warriors like Hill and Lafleur had been unnerved. Carter had been well liked and one of the most highly skilled among them. If he could be taken down . . .

Yet there hadn't been a single incident since the night Carter and Kowalski died. Not even a stubbed toe. And during training today, everyone had been noticeably calmer. Shoulders were less tight, faces less strained, disagreements less heated.

All of which certainly made it easier to round up volunteers for guard duty. But complacency was their enemy, not their friend. Case in point: The blanket spell had been removed yesterday to permit the magic they would ultimately need to defeat Azazel. Most of the Gatherers saw the disarming as a plus, because it provided them with more ammunition in the event of a fight. They acknowledged that it also unlocked the door for their enemy, but as time wore on and the demons failed to materialize, their concern faded. He'd urged everyone to be more vigilant than ever, but he knew it was a futile effort. Maintaining high alert was too wearing on the psyche for most. Only the Gatherers with battle experience understood.

"Murdoch?"

He spun around to face Webster, who stood just inside the door of the arena. "Aye?"

"She's coming unglued. You've got to do something."

He sighed. Emily was the biggest casualty of the past few days. Her sixteenth birthday had come and gone with little fanfare. She barely even acknowledged the gift Lachlan had left for her—a brand-new lime green Ford Fiesta. She refused to sleep more than a few hours at a time, sweeping the ranch for signs of Azazel or the bone-sappers at regular intervals. Despite everyone's assurances to the contrary, she clearly felt responsible for the deaths of the two Gatherers.

"Can we drug her?" he asked.

"Maybe," Webster said slowly. "But it'll be dark in another hour or so."

Valid point. Not a good time to be without their best weapon. "Talk to Sora. He might be able to help her reach a meditative state. Next best thing to sleeping."

"Really?"

Murdoch shrugged. "According to Kiyoko, it is. Frankly, I never had much luck with it myself."

The other man nodded and turned to leave. Then changed his mind. "You and Kiyoko have a fight?"

"No."

"Hmmm. Call me crazy, but not talking to each other usually means someone's pissed off."

Murdoch fastened the padlock that held the swords to the wall and tucked the key into his pocket. "Emily isn't the only one who feels guilty about Carter and Kowalski. Kiyoko thinks she brought Azazel down on us."

"Can't argue with that," Webster said drily. "She has a point."

Murdoch spun around, his chest burning with indignation. "No, she doesn't. If I had taken the Veil from her in Japan, she'd be dead right now and Azazel would still be on our asses. Don't you dare blame her."

Webster folded his arms over his chest. "Okay. That still doesn't explain why you're not talking."

"She has a solution for severing her connection to the Veil and remaining alive. I think the idea is absolutely asinine."

"Ah." A faint smile hovered on Webster's lips.

Smug bastard. Thought he knew everything there was to know about relationships. Based on one experience. "It involves completely unleashing the berserker."

"Oh." The smile vanished.

"Exactly."

"I'll leave you two to work it out, then."

"Good idea."

Webster left, and Murdoch glanced at his watch. He had every intention of making it work. In fact, he'd arranged a date of sorts with Kiyoko in a half hour. In theory, it was just to play chess, but he was planning to break down a few walls. Explain how he felt. Lay everything out and see what happened.

But first he needed a shower and a fresh shirt.

When dusk fell over San Jose, Azazel sent in the troops. A dozen bone-sappers to pick off the low-hanging fruit and a handful of gradiors to deal with the peskier, more seasoned Gatherers. The Gatherers had conveniently removed the blanket spell, so they were able to surface in the woods next to the bunkhouse instead of making their way down the hill.

The guard outside the bunkhouse door was a little more trouble than expected. Not only was he a seasoned warrior, he possessed a stronger than normal shield and the gradior assigned to take care of him was decapitated before it could break through.

Azazel swept the Gatherer's shield away with a wave of his hand, and called up another gradior to take the broken one's place. Learning his lesson, he enhanced the shield pierce charm on all of the gradiors' claws.

While the undead brain-eater engaged the guard, the bone-sappers skirted the brightly lit areas and slipped into the bunkhouse through every shadowy hole, big or small. Azazel used the front door, placing a barrier spell around the bunkhouse as he entered. It was very kind of them to huddle together in one spot. Made their destruction so much easier.

And this way, Yoshio couldn't escape out the side door.

A truncated scream came from the back of the building just as he strode into the common room, wings boldly displayed. While a few of the Gatherers lounging about stared at him with no recognition in their eyes, most immediately understood they were doomed.

Azazel covered the building in a muffle spell and smiled.

He loved the smell of fear in the evening.

* * *

Murdoch shoved the sopping masses of his hair back from his face and turned off the water. As the drips from the showerhead slowed, he caught the tail end of a sound that could have been a strangled scream.

He glanced at the glass brick window.

The sky was dark purple.

Christ. Bloody short days.

Knotting a towel around his hips, he skated out of the shower on wet tiles and snatched up his sword. Then he yanked open the door to his room. The hallway was completely dark, only a few shiny shards glinting from the carpet. Consistent with all the bulbs being smashed.

There was no time to don boots. He stepped into the glass, sword aloft.

His berserker took care of the pain. As adrenaline sped through his veins in response to danger, so did the familiar red rage. His body heat soared, his muscles swelled, and the urge to flay and maim overtook his usual caution.

He sensed them before he saw them.

Like a cool finger running over his hot skin.

Pushing open the door closest to him, he saw one hovered over the body of a trainee, silently sucking. The trainee's eyes were wide-open, but he appeared to be paralyzed with fear. He lay quiet as the sapper hungrily drew his bones from his flesh. Another sapper hung from the ceiling, cloaked in shade, waiting on a victim of its own.

"Die, ya bloody buggers," Murdoch yelled.

Then he charged.

Today was not one of the five remaining most auspicious days. Those were lucky from beginning to end and pretty much guaranteed success. Today was the next best thing, though. Lucky all day except for noon.

Not perfect, but still a good day to ascend.

Sometimes the opportune moment was better than the perfect moment.

Kiyoko carefully washed her arms and her legs, her feet and her hands. She tied her hair back and removed all traces of makeup from her face. Once she was completely clean, she donned a pair of black silk tank-top pajamas and sat in front of the fireplace to wait for Murdoch.

It was the last waiting she intended to do.

Having endured several painful and heated discussions over the last few days, she was ready to admit defeat. Murdoch would never change his mind. He was convinced that he could not control his berserker. So, tonight when he came to play chess, she was going to attempt the transcendence, whether he was willing or not. Two Gatherers had already paid the price of her desire to make him a partner in the process. Enough was enough.

"Kiyoko-san?"

She glanced at the bedroom door and bit back a groan. Yoshio stood politely outside, waiting for an invitation to enter. She still had not entirely forgiven the young *onmyōji* warrior for contacting his North American brethren behind her back. But turning him away would be rude. "Come in, Yoshio-san. What can I do for you?"

He slipped inside the room and closed the door.

She frowned. "I'm expecting Murdoch to arrive at any moment."

Ignoring her, he crossed to the bed and lifted her pillow. "Where is it?" he asked.

Kiyoko gained her feet, her heart thudding. There was only one thing he could be referring to. Yet she had never mentioned the Veil to Yoshio, nor shown him where she put it while she slept. Which suggested this was not Yoshio at all, but . . .

Azazel.

Her hand itched for her sword.

It lay on the bed, much closer to her foe than to her. But Murdoch had enjoyed no success using a sword against the fallen angel, so perhaps the distance didn't matter.

He spun to face her. "Where is it?"

Magic was the key to survival. She raised a shield, summoned her *shikigami*, and leapt for the Veil, which lay on the table behind her.

As she rolled behind the flimsy protection of the arm-chair, she caught a glimpse of the band around Yoshio's ankle and felt a tiny flicker of hope. Azazel had made an error in choosing Yoshio as his mask. The moment he'd left the bunkhouse/arena area, alarms would have begun to ring. Help would come.

The demon growled and swatted at the *shikigami*.

"This is stupid," he said. "You can't hope to win. Give me the Veil now, and you might survive."

She used his distraction to toss a binding spell.

Which he swatted away as easily as he hurled her valiant tiny imps against the wall. "Are you counting on a rescue?" he asked, grunting as one of the *shikigami* plowed into his chest. "Don't. My former brethren from heaven are currently responding to a series of large-scale demon attacks around the globe. Orchestrated by me. Murdoch is at this very moment locked in a building full of bone-sappers, and Webster is battling gradiors in the front yard. You're on your own."

She tossed an exotic variation of the poison cloud hex at him, hoping the mustard yellow mist would seep through his shield.

He was wrong. He had to be. There were plenty of Gatherers on the ranch. Guards placed at strategic spots for defense. And even now, the ankle bracelet was sending a signal to Carter's . . .

Her follow-up blind spell faltered.

How had she forgotten? Carter was dead. Which meant there was a very good chance no one was listening to the alarm. She really *was* on her own.

Emily's eyes popped open, her gaze locked on the unfamiliar stucco ceiling.

Where was she?

Her gaze darted around the room and then she sighed with relief. Her surroundings weren't completely foreign. This was the guest bedroom in Brian's house. Way to panic for nothing.

Stretching, she rolled off the bed.

The meditation thing had worked. Sort of. Sora had encouraged her not to lose awareness of her surroundings, but after only a minute in the lotus position, her forty-pound eyelids had slid closed. She'd fallen asleep. On the plus side, she felt relaxed for the first time in days, ready to tackle anything.

Leaving her room, she skipped down the stairs to the kitchen and dug through the cupboards for the potato chips she knew would be there. If Brian and Lena weren't immortal, they'd be candidates for a heart attack. Swear to God. She poured herself a glass of milk, stuffed a few barbecue-flavored chips in her mouth, then closed her eyes and did a sweep of the ranch.

Chip bits spewed from her mouth.

Holy fucking shit.

They were everywhere. Dark, creeping shadows, hundreds of them. Maybe thousands. Inky black ooze, filling every corner and slowly swallowing up the bright pulses of energy that represented each Gatherer. Snuffing them.

Her gaze darted to the patio doors. The porch light was out. Oh, God. A wave of dizziness hit her.

Okay, don't panic. Think, Emily. What was the best

thing to do? Save the screaming trainees in the bunk-house? Help Brian with the zombies in the front yard? Or tackle Azazel upstairs? Shit, who was she kidding? Could she really help *any* of them?

She swallowed the sour lump in her throat.

Not without help, that was for sure.

Uriel? Squeezing her eyes shut, she prayed with all her might. But there was no flash of blue sparks, no hint that he was on his way. She couldn't wait. Her stomach heaved with every terrified scream echoing in her head. Gatherers were dying. Lots of them.

She had to do something. *Now.*

Sora was upstairs napping. Stefan was in his trailer. It was a toss-up, really. One mystic or another. But experience put the best odds of success with Stefan. She'd seen him kick serious demon ass. And he was younger. That had to count for something.

She slid open the glass door to the porch.

No time to worry about what waited in the dark. Just run. Around the freakin' hedge and down the path to the trailer. *You can do this.* Taking a deep breath, she ran. On an average day it took her three minutes to reach the trailer. Today it took an eternity. Even with her head down and her legs pumping as fast as she could make them go.

She pounded on the trailer door.

"Open up!" She glanced over her shoulder. A shadow moved in the trees. No, more than one shadow. Six, maybe seven. She was going to die out here. Without waiting for the door to open, she popped into the trailer.

And slammed into Stefan, knocking him to the ground.

To give him some credit, he appeared to be heading for the door. To let her in.

"Sappers. And gradiors. And Azazel." She gasped every word. "Every-freakin'-where."

He blanched. "Where is Azazel?"

"In the house. Fighting Kiyoko." She helped him to his feet. "We've got to do something. People are *dying*, Stefan. All over the place."

He nodded. "Where is Murdoch?"

"In the bunkhouse, but he's—"

"Go help him out. I'll go up to the house."

Fear shivered through her. The bunkhouse was through the trees. "But I can't do it on my own."

"Yes, you can." His gaze pinned hers, firm and confident, more like the Stefan she knew. "You have the skills, Emily. Use them."

For the first time, she noticed a funny smell in the trailer, like way-overdone chicken wings. She glanced around. "Where's Dika?"

"She had to leave for a while," Stefan said, grabbing a black drawstring bag off the leather couch. "She'll be back." Then he was gone, out the front door and into the night.

She stared at the trees.

You have the skills. Use them.

Shit. She could've just popped here from the house. She'd run all the way down the path, practically pissing her pants, all for nothing. And she could pop into the bunkhouse just as easily. All she had to do was imagine herself there, fold the fabric of the universe just right, and . . .

Pop.

Her skin burned as she passed through a barrier spell. She landed smack-dab in the chaos that was the common room and took an elbow in the gut from a Soul Gatherer fighting for his life. Grunting, she dodged out of his way. At least a dozen bone-sappers were preying on the trainees, many of whom were already horrible pools of flesh on the floor.

Murdoch was at the far end of the room, in full-out berserker mode, swinging his sword with blistering speed, battling two sappers at once. Red-faced and pumped with supernatural energy, he had them on the defensive, pressed up against the wall. But their fluid forms allowed them to slip out of his way, avoiding serious injury, and they showed no signs of dying anytime soon.

You have the skills. Use them.

What skills did she have to fight shadowy blobs? Swords weren't very effective from what she could see, and she didn't know a freeze spell. *Note to self: learn a freeze spell.*

But she did know how to pop.

And she could pop just about anywhere. If she could pop into hell and rescue Carlos, then she sure as heck could pop into the between. Especially since sappers couldn't hurt her. She was alive.

The *where* of the between was a little fuzzy, but she'd dreamed about the place enough times. Somewhere between hell and the middle plane. As long as she didn't think too hard about it, she should be able to go there. Now all she had to do was grab one of the suckers. Easier said than done. She eyed the black mucus latched onto a downed Gatherer under the table to her right.

Then stepped within leaping range.

"Come to Emily, you butt-ugly blob."

Kiyoko squeezed the Temple Veil tightly in her hand and drew every mote of power from it that she could. Then she murmured one of the ancient spells her father had taught her and tossed a frozen-tongue curse. It would stop him from uttering spells. Temporarily. Perhaps long enough for her to cast an endurance charm upon herself. She needed it. She was already weakening, and Azazel had yet to throw his might at her.

She wasn't sure why.

Perhaps he feared damaging the relic. It couldn't be the *shikigami*—as effective as their dive bombing was, they did nothing to reduce the power of his spells.

Whatever the reason, she was grateful. She couldn't help but hope that given enough time, Murdoch would come to her aid. Despite Azazel's claim that he was locked in a building full of sappers, imagining him defeated was impossible.

Azazel recovered his speech and flung a spell of his own, and a violent shudder ran through her. A will sap spell, archaic but very potent. For the barest of moments, before her counterspell took effect, her body was not her own. Her thigh muscles flexed, pushing her to her feet.

The fallen angel smiled.

He dropped the Yoshio charade, and appeared to her in his true form: Huge black wings, bare chest etched with runes, chin-length black hair. Strangely alluring for someone with thick horns protruding from his forehead.

"You are a talented mystic," he said. "I'm impressed by the spells you've cast. Many of them are unknown to me." He swatted at the air. "But it's time to stop fighting. Bring me the Veil."

The counterspell took effect, and she dropped back behind the chair. "No."

"You are annoying me."

"Good. It's my aim to make this as difficult as possible."

He chuckled. "Foolish girl. You're alive right now only because I need you. I've had many opportunities to slay you over the past few months and took none of them."

As she'd believed, but never understood. "Why?"

"Because it appears that I cannot take possession of the Veil without your assistance. I tried. After I brought your father to his knees, I attempted to pick it up but couldn't—the blasted thing positively glowed with virtuous energy. By then the self-sacrificing fool was too badly injured to work the necessary magic to free the dark side of the Veil. He lay there, bleeding and gasping and flailing like dying fish."

She gagged.

"I thought I was lost, until you conveniently entered the garage and ran to his side. Your attempts to revive him impressed me, but it was your instant ability to wield the Veil's power that gained my total admiration. It was obvious that mystical guardianship of the relic had passed from your father to you. Now, remove the containment spell and hand me the Veil."

"No."

"Don't be difficult. Your magic is no match for mine."

"You won't be facing *my* magic alone. Others are on their way."

"Still counting on Murdoch to help you out, are you?" he said, amused. "That's very naive of you. He won't be coming."

"Don't underestimate him," she said.

"I don't. But even *he* will struggle with a dozen sappers."

"He'll escape."

"Wishful thinking. The barrier spell I put over the bunkhouse will require better magic than his to breach."

Contemplating Murdoch's dismal odds made her shudder. She thrust her worry for him to the back of her mind and concentrated on her own survival. If Murdoch could not reach her, then she needed help from another source.

Sora.

She could send him a mental message, but reaching out with her mind would seriously deplete her ki, especially if Sora was any distance away. At best, she'd manage three or four more spells after such an effort.

Then she would succumb to Azazel's magic and the Veil would be his.

Was it worth the risk?

She grimaced. Was there really any alternative? She would not last much longer anyway. And she couldn't be sure that Azazel's desire to keep her alive would endure. At any moment he could tire of her puny efforts and slay her. It was Sora or nothing.

She closed her eyes and reached out.

She'd only just found Sora sleeping in his bed when she was knocked off her feet by a silent explosion that blew the door off its hinges, pitching it clear across the room. In a swirl of tingles and sparkles, someone shot to her side and yanked the Veil from her nerveless fingers.

She looked up.

The mage.

But a very different mage than the one she'd received the Book of Judgment from days before. This man had jet-black eyes and a body that radiated an eerie fluorescent green light. There was nothing plump or jovial about him now. Grim resolve leached from every pore. He thrust the Veil into a black bag, then stepped back into the farthest corner of the room and began to murmur unintelligible words that sent a chill down Kiyoko's spine.

"No." Azazel blasted the mage with a dozen bolts of purple, seething energy, one after another.

But they did nothing. The mage's shield held true. And he continued to chant.

Azazel turned to her, his face now a mask of dark fury. "Get it back. Get it back or I'll slay you and everyone in a thirty-mile radius in the most painful way possible. Now."

But Kiyoko knew of no way to retrieve the Veil. The shield surrounding the mage was like none she'd ever seen before, and the bag he'd tucked the Veil into had abruptly smothered its power. She felt its loss immediately. Her fingers and toes went numb, and her heartbeat began to slow.

"I can't."

He raised his taloned hand to smite her.

But Sora appeared at the door, the Book of Judgment in hand, and sent the fallen angel reeling with a powerful blight curse. Putrid boils blossomed on the fallen angel's skin, briefly swelling his lips and the taloned fingers of his hands. Sora glanced at the mage, frowned, then scurried to Kiyoko's side, reading from the book as he crossed the room.

"I hope you like snakes," he whispered to her.

No sooner had he spoken than four huge cobras appeared at the foot of the bed, hissing and spitting blue fire at Azazel, who had only just dismissed the boils.

"A temporary measure," Sora said, as he continued to flip pages and scan the contents. "We need something more powerful."

Azazel fought fire with fire. He hit the snakes with lava firebombs that sprang from his fingertips, roaring with rage as several of his glorious wing feathers were engulfed in snake fire.

"I thought you couldn't read Egyptian."

"That was three days ago." Sora quickly incanted another spell, this one producing thousands of tiny scarab beetles that swarmed the fallen angel.

Azazel fried hundreds with a single blast, barely pausing for the effort.

"We can't do this on our own," Kiyoko said, her limbs so heavy she could barely lift them.

"We can, and we must."

Kiyoko focused the *shikigami* on Azazel's hands, directing them to put out the firebombs before he could hurl them.

Azazel, who never took his eyes off the mage,

smashed the *shikigami* against the wall with a mighty beat of his wings. All the imps fell to the floor except for one, which returned in an uneven flight path to Kiyoko's shoulder.

Angry and sad, Kiyoko sent a blind spell at him.

"Save your strength," Sora cautioned.

"For what?"

She need not have spoken. Emily popped into the room at that very instant, with her arms wrapped around a very large, very enraged, and very nearly naked Murdoch. She quickly released him and leapt over the bed.

Clad only in a bath towel, he attacked the fallen angel. All berserker, all raw destructive power.

His sword, which glowed green like the mage's skin, hummed through the air, a smooth and very lethal extension of his reach. The muscles of his arms and chest bunched and rippled with every swift, sure movement. His hewn thighs flexed visibly under the white terry as he advanced, one relentless step at a time. And for the first time, Azazel retreated.

But the fallen angel wasn't done.

From the lower levels of the house came the eerie shrieks of bone-sappers and the hungry moans of gradiors on the prowl.

Azazel seemed to have an unlimited pool of undead drones.

"We need to slow him," Kiyoko said, breathless. Each intake of air was harder to draw than the next. "To give Murdoch a chance."

Sora nodded. "Emily, do you have the shard?"

From the other side of the room came, "Yeah. But you better hurry. There's like a million icky things crawling out of the ground."

He began the spell, stumbled over a word, and then started again. It was two full pages of incantation and Kiyoko prayed he could complete it without faltering.

She needed to know Murdoch would be safe before she attempted anything.

Without pausing in his recital, Sora put a hand on Kiyoko's shoulder. His fingers were hot on her skin, but the sensation that flowed from his fingertips was cool and tingly. Like a drug injected into her veins, the tingle quickly spread through her body, and where it went, energy bloomed.

Her breathing eased.

He had lent her some of his ki, the crazy old fool. In the middle of the most important incantation of his life. She heaved a grateful sigh and crossed her fingers.

Please. Let him succeed.

21

As fascinating as the fight between Murdoch and Azazel was, and as important as Sora's incantation was, Emily's attention kept straying to Stefan. The eyes like black holes and the green glowing skin? Holy crap. Wicked awesome.

Why he was standing in the far corner with that bag clutched to his chest was a mystery. When he said he was headed over here, she assumed it was to help out, not to do ... uh ... whatever the heck he was doing.

"Ow."

She glanced down at her hand.

The shard was suddenly burning hot and rays of black light streamed between her fingers. Apparently the spell was working. But she kept her hand tightly clasped and waited for a signal from the sensei. She could not afford to screw this up.

The tinkle of shattered glass came from the stairs.

Faster would be good, though.

She shoved a sweaty strand of hair away from her face. Carting a dozen bone-sappers back to the between had been easy. Dealing with the horde slithering up the stairs would be much harder. Like trying to stop a tidal wave from pouring through a screen door.

Not cool.

She glanced at Sora. His head was bent to the book

and his lips were still moving. Come *on*. How much longer could that stupid spell take?

A high-pitched shriek pulled her gaze back to the open doorway. The lights in the hallway had gone out. Her hand tightened around the shard, the jagged edge cutting into her skin. Uh-oh. Here they come.

Sure enough, as she watched, a thin black finger reached out of the darkness and crept up the doorframe to the ceiling. Followed quickly by another. And another. The ceiling near the door was now a writhing black knot. The sappers were gathering strength, preparing to leave the shadows and attack Murdoch.

But that wasn't the worst thing.

The worst thing shuffled into the room a moment later. Gray-faced, glassy-eyed, and ruthlessly focused. A gradior. Headed right for Sora and Kiyoko. Shit, shit, shit.

The smell of putrefying flesh was thick and vile. Death in its ugliest, rotting form.

But the sickly sweet odor didn't bother Kiyoko nearly as much as the sight of the creature's blood-soaked claws. This gradior had successfully penetrated someone's shield, possibly Brian's or Lena's. A horrible thought.

She glanced at Sora.

He was still busy with the spell, but judging by where his eyes were trained, he was very close to done. He needed a few more moments, and she had to give them to him. But how was she supposed to stop a zombie?

"Kiyoko," Emily said softly. "Catch."

The teen tossed the katana and Kiyoko caught it.

"Go for the head," Emily said.

Kiyoko slid her weapon from the scabbard. Even with the energy Sora had donated, her muscles trembled. But the bone-sappers were edging across the ceiling, and

Murdoch's survival depended on her conquering the weakness in her limbs.

She took a deep breath, steadied her thoughts, and engaged the gradior. Its shield was formidable. It took three vigorous, full-bore strikes to break through the protection spell and score blood. Yet its claws ripped through her shield in a single swipe. She had to leap back to avoid being gutted.

Once clear, she struck again, aiming for the neck.

The gradior was slow moving but relentless. Although her sword sliced deeper into the creature's neck with every swing, the gradior continued to attack with impressive, seemingly limitless power.

Kiyoko was not so fortunate. She began to tire. The heavy weariness returned to her limbs, and her chest became a block of ice. Every stroke of her blade took as much out of her as it did her opponent. Her grip on the katana faltered, and she stumbled to one knee. Dismissing her as a fallen foe, the gradior stepped by her and took a swipe at Sora.

"Open your hand, Emily," Kiyoko shouted. "Now."

The spell book took the brunt of the blow, the gradior's claws slicing into the leather cover, splitting the gold leaf in two. But Sora still toppled, bringing an abrupt end to his incantation.

Kiyoko's heart seized.

But she was unable to go to the sensei's defense. The last of her energy pulsed weakly in her chest. Her legs gave out, and she slid to the floor. As she fell, she pitched a look at Azazel, hoping the incomplete power of the shard had been enough to flatten him, at least briefly.

No such luck.

He might have lost some momentum, because Murdoch had the fallen angel up against the wall, his sword cutting into Azazel's chest time and again. But the angel continued to fight back with fury.

Murdoch was not unscathed.

Dark burns marred his left arm and a wide gash parted the flesh on his chest. Blood flowed in enough quantity to turn the towel crimson. To make matters worse, the long finger of a sapper had descended from the ceiling to his shoulder, siphoning bone.

They were failing.

It would have been so easy to give up then. To let her fears over being worthy enough take hold. For an instant, she was tempted to close her eyes and let Death take her. But the moment passed swiftly. Her father had not given up. Not even when the odds were dismal. He had struggled to live and to win, right up to the end. She knew that, because she had held him in those last moments and had felt the resistance to his fate in every ragged breath.

If he could fight to his last breath, so could she.

She was an *onmyōji*.

Not just any *onmyōji*—a master. The direct descendant of the great Abe no Seimei. Stabbing the tip of her katana deep into the wooden floor, she dragged herself to her feet. She still had one option left.

Transcend.

Murdoch felt Kiyoko approach him from behind.

He knew immediately what she was about to do, but he was powerless to stop her. His berserker was in control, operating almost entirely on instinct and battle rage. Focused, as *he* should be, on doing everything in his power to defeat Azazel. The bastard was putting up one hell of a fight.

Murdoch cringed. Kiyoko was already weak and limping. If she came too close—if he struck her by accident—it could very well finish her. And yet she continued to advance.

All he managed was a verbal protest.

"No," he growled.

But it was too little, too late. She already had her hand on his back.

The touch did nothing to him—he was already seeing little more than the red mist of his berserker's fury—but Kiyoko jerked violently. Repeatedly. Like she was having some kind of seizure, or had her hand on a transformer capable of lighting a whole city.

Just as he had predicted, he was killing her.

He howled at the injustice of it, fought for control of the beast in his chest, and willed the energy flowing from his body into hers to cease.

And then, miraculously, the jerking paused.

Just for a heartbeat. Just long enough to prove that some measure of control was possible. Just long enough to convince him he could save her. If he owned the beast inside him. If he accepted that his two halves were one whole. If he allowed himself to acknowledge that the berserker never truly retreated, that it was part of him every waking moment, that it was simply the blood that flowed in his veins.

As he continued to slice and parry and thrust his sword, Murdoch located and found that calm, tranquil spot where his thoughts went when he meditated. He became aware of every muscle in his body, every pump of his heart, every firing of his synapses. He felt every inch of his skin, even the parts that were battered and bloodied, and he found the conduit that was blasting his energy into Kiyoko's body. The small spot where her hand touched his back. Then he turned down the tap and slowed the flow to a steady gurgle.

She stopped jerking.

And for the first time in seven hundred and twenty-seven years, Jamie Murdoch felt whole.

*   *   *

Kiyoko blinked back tears.

Murdoch had gated the flow of energy from his body, but left the conduit open. Not only could she access the berserker power that surged through him with every heartbeat, she could share his feelings. But she had no time to dwell on what she discovered.

Azazel was still wreaking havoc.

She recited the words of the ritual she had memorized as a child and felt the energy swirl inside her, building momentum. The small bead of energy in her gut strengthened and grew. Her ki brightened and her heart pumped stronger and steadier. A soft golden warmth suffused her from head to toe, flushing her skin. The bead of energy rose up outside her body and as it ascended, she felt her earthly bonds release. It was an experience like no other. One she would be hard-pressed to describe. But as her bead of energy rose ever higher, into the mists, she became aware of another bead of energy floating at her side. She turned her head and saw Sora. Or rather, Sora's bead of energy. It was similarly golden.

And she knew, almost as if she'd always known, that Sora was in fact Abe no Seimei, her ancient ancestor and the spiritual leader of the *onmyōji*.

"You have transcended," he said, smiling.

She smiled in return. "So it would seem."

"Now we must put you to work," he said. "In this form, you have all your usual spells at your disposal, plus an ever-regenerating energy. You no longer have to worry about draining your ki. You can call upon bigger and more powerful *shikigami*, and you can infuse more power into your offensive spells. Are you ready to fight?"

She nodded.

"Then focus your attention on the battle below and

stay true to your training. The rest will take care of itself."

The tide of the battle turned in an instant. One second Murdoch was fighting Azazel alone, and the next, he felt Kiyoko at his side, strong and healthy and incredibly lethal. The fallen angel sensed the change immediately.

He pitched a collection of energy bolts at them, then ducked under Murdoch's arm and darted toward Stefan, opening a portal as he ran.

Stefan stood exactly where he'd been the entire time, still chanting, still clutching a black silk bag to his chest. But as Azazel leapt at the mage, something unexpected happened. Stefan vanished. No puff of smoke, no flash of electricity. Just empty space where his body used to be.

Azazel halted in midair, hovering with rapid, small beats of his wings. Realizing his quarry had vanished, he screamed with rage and pivoted, flying toward the portal.

Which abruptly disappeared in a wink of red light.

"Ha!" crowed Emily. "I did it."

Azazel opened another portal and Emily snuffed that one, too. The fallen angel was trapped. And Murdoch, Kiyoko, Emily, and Sora all took advantage, blasting him with everything they had.

The battle might have gone differently if the bone-sappers and gradiors hadn't ceased to fight. But with Azazel under siege, they withdrew with a few quiet hisses and grunts, slithering away into the dark.

After that, it was only a matter of time before the accumulated mystical hits weakened the fallen angel beyond recuperation. Sensing victory, Murdoch swung his sword one last time, and took Azazel's head clear off his neck. No point taking any chances.

*　　*　　*

"Is he in his trailer?" Webster asked, as Murdoch entered the ranch house with Kiyoko.

Murdoch shook his head. They had searched Stefan's trailer and the surrounding grounds with diligence. No sign of him. "Dika's not there, either."

"Fuck." The other Soul Gatherer raked his hand through his hair and paced in front of the fireplace. "How are we supposed to explain to the Protectorate—or Uriel, for that matter—that our mage disappeared with a powerful mystical weapon?"

"Where did you get the idea the Veil is a weapon?" Sora asked, from his perch on the edge of the sofa.

"You mean it's not?"

The old man shook his head. "No. But it presents a great threat to the world just the same."

Murdoch tugged Kiyoko against his chest, thrilling to the idea of being able to touch her at will, with no effect other than a racing pulse. "Enough with the riddles, old man. Spit out the truth."

"It's a gateway." When all he got were blank stares, he added, "It effectively neutralizes the barrier between the planes, allowing unfettered travel."

"So, if Azazel had stolen it like he planned, he could've brought a thousand demons up from hell in one go?" asked Emily.

"Yes," Sora said. "And then he could take those same thousand demons to the upper plane, with no one able to stop him."

"Yikes."

The old man nodded. "We were lucky this time. Those gray feathers in Azazel's wings suggest he was not yet at full strength. Had he been Lucifer's equal, we might not have fared so well. As it is, we are still no further in our quest to curtail the miseries Satan is inflicting on the world—the demon infestations continue to spread."

Webster grimaced. "Yeah. We'll have to come up with

another attack plan. In the meantime, I don't want to lose any ground. Keeping the Veil safe is an absolute necessity."

"Which brings us back to Stefan."

"We have to find him," Murdoch said.

"That won't be easy," said MacGregor. The Gatherer trainer had claimed the leather armchair next to the fireplace the moment he and Rachel had returned. "He's the most gifted mage I've ever met."

Murdoch grimaced. And the most stubborn. As he'd already proven with his refusal to heal Kiyoko, the man was near impossible to sway once he set his mind to something.

"Sora's pretty rockin' sockin'," Emily said.

The sensei smiled. "Thank you for the compliment. But I am most assuredly not your mage's equal when it comes to magic. His repertoire far exceeds my own."

"That settles it," said Webster. "I'm with Murdoch. I say we track the little prick down and relieve him of the Veil. He may have taken the damned thing with the best of intentions, but there's no way I'm leaving something that dangerous in the hands of one guy."

"Especially when that one guy is a mage who occasionally reeks of dark magic," Lena murmured.

"Lena," MacGregor said softly.

"What? I'm just saying what everyone else is thinking."

To which no one had a rebuttal.

When the others had wandered off, either to help with the cleanup or to rest, Emily sidled up to Brian.

"Can I ask you a question?"

He nodded. "What's up?"

She struggled to put her feelings into words. "We just won this huge battle, totally trashed the bad guy, and saved the Temple Veil. Sort of. I did good. I know I did. Not perfect, but pretty damned good."

He smiled. "Damn straight."

"So why do I feel so bad?"

Gathering her close, he gave her a hug. "Because we lost good people, sweetheart. Twenty-two of 'em. And that hurts. When we lose people, the win never feels great. At least, not initially. Later, after the pain recedes a bit, we can take pride in what we did. But right now, all we want to do is mourn the ones who didn't make it."

"Like Carter."

"Yeah, like Carter."

She pushed her face against his chest, so he couldn't see the tears in her eyes. Babies cried, not adults. And definitely not Trinity Souls. "I'm going to miss him."

"We all are."

"Oh, dear," said a sharp female voice. "Why do I always arrive in the middle of these horribly maudlin moments?"

Emily felt Brian stiffen.

"Hey, boss," he said. "I'd say *nice to see you*, but I'd be lying."

Emily reluctantly turned around. Death was not her favorite person. Something to do with that whole plot to kill her last fall, most likely. Hard to like a person who sics a lure demon on you in hopes of eating your soul.

The goddess lay on the sofa looking remarkably like Cruella De Vil. Her white hair was fluffed and puffed, her gown was black and slinky, and her nails matched her lipstick—crimson red. Her posture was all blond bombshell, but someone needed to tell her that Death was never sexy.

"Did I hear you correctly?" the goddess asked. "Did you say you lost twenty-two of my Gatherers?"

"Yes."

She rose to her feet and sauntered across the room. "You owe me, Gatherer."

Brian shifted to put himself between Death and Emily. "I don't owe you. You agreed to help us protect the relics, and unfortunately tonight there were some casualties."

Death offered Emily a cold stare, then smiled at Brian. "While I am annoyed at your cavalier dismissal of my losses, I'm not talking about tonight's fiasco. I'm talking about our deal, Webster. I believe you have something you want to give me."

"No, I don't."

She laughed. "Are you reneging? Do you recall what you bargained for? The soul of one Lena Sharpe? Did you want me to take it back?"

Emily was amazed. She could feel the rage inside Brian's body—the stiff, tight muscles, the heavy pound of his heart—but on the outside, he looked relaxed and comfortable.

"I did not make a deal for Lena's soul," he argued. "I made a deal for her whereabouts. And the price of forfeiture is spelled out in our contract. You can claim another five hundred years of service. That's it."

Death grimaced. "Oh, don't be so difficult. Just give me the shard and we're done. You don't need to forfeit."

"I don't have it."

Her gaze returned to Emily. One hundred percent cool nastiness. "But the brat does. Tell her to give it to me."

Emily squeezed Brian's arm to stop him from answering. He could not afford to piss off Death—he worked for her. She, on the other hand, had no such problem.

"Sorry," she said sarcastically. "Not going to happen. This *brat* has a mind of her own, and she's not interested in doing any favors for an egotistical, power-hungry biotch like you. Take a hike."

"Give it to me, or I'll punish Webster for your insolence."

Worry knotted Em's stomach, but she plowed on. "Whatever deal you made with Brian is between you and him. I'm not part of it. The shard is mine, and I'm keeping it. Simple as that."

Death's eyes narrowed. "Nothing is that simple. Believe me. And you're going to regret this decision, Emily Lewis. Count on that."

Something dark burned in the depths of the goddess's eyes—something that made Em shiver. But handing Death a weapon like the Shattered Halo would be a mistake, no doubt about it. She wouldn't hesitate to step on Uriel and Michael to get what she wanted.

Shoving her hand into the pocket of her khakis, Em gripped the shard tight. "Hurt my friends and the regret will be yours, not mine."

Death smiled. Then she lifted her hand, and without fanfare, vanished.

Kiyoko tugged Murdoch into his bedroom and shut the door.

"Is this really the best place to spend the night?" he asked, looking around.

There were scorch marks on the floor, walls, and ceiling. The armchair still lay on its side under the window. A number of unidentifiable globs had landed on the floor and the Southwestern watercolor print over the fireplace. The mattress lay half on and half off the bed frame.

"We can sleep in the bunkhouse."

He sighed. "Perhaps not. Lafleur and Jensen are still tending to the dead."

She wrapped her arms around his waist. Something she'd previously been able to do only in their dreams. The muscles of his back were as warm and firm as she'd imagined. "I liked Brian's suggestion of an honor ceremony to commemorate their sacrifice. Very appropriate."

"Aye, he has the occasional good idea."

Tipping her head back, she looked in his eyes. "Brian seems to be a good leader, and he's clearly an excellent warrior. He killed two gradiors. Why do you hate the man?"

"I don't hate him."

"You constantly challenge and insult him."

He smiled wryly. "It's what the two strongest wolves in every pack do. Challenge each other. He's the leader, and his job is to take care of the pack. My job is to test him at every opportunity, try to take him down, and press him constantly to prove his worth. If he fails, I take the lead. If he succeeds, he eventually tires of my irritating presence and kicks me out."

Her fingers played with the hem of his T-shirt. "And is he winning or losing?"

"He's winning."

Giving in to an urge that had been hounding her for weeks, she slid her hands under his shirt and up the ropy terrain of his back. "Does that mean you'll have to leave?"

His eyes drifted shut. "Aye, someday."

"Where will you go?" She gently traced the scar on his left shoulder blade. She'd spied it there, exactly where she'd known it would be, when he was battling Azazel.

He drew in a short breath, then grabbed her hips and pulled her tight against his groin. "I haven't thought that far ahead."

"Could you envision living in Japan?"

One eye opened and he peered down at her. "Is that an invitation?"

"Do you need one?"

He smiled. "No."

"Good. It would be terribly tiresome if you always waited for me to speak my mind. I don't always say what I'm think—" Her sentence ended on a shriek as he yanked her off her feet, strode to the bed, and dropped her on the mattress.

"I have a good idea what you're thinking," he said gruffly, as he buried his face between her breasts. "Because I'm thinking the same damned thing."

His lips found her throat, and she arched her neck to give him better access. As good as her dreams had been, they couldn't compare to the heavenly feel of his hard body pressed against hers or the sultry warmth of his breath on her skin.

"You'll have to prove that," she said huskily. "I have some very creative thoughts."

"I'll explore every one of them, I promise," he said, nuzzling the tender skin beneath her ear. "But don't expect gymnastics in the beginning, lass. Give me a chance to show you how well I know the basics. I've had four bloody weeks of foreplay, and I'm strung tight as a bow."

"The basics?" His tongue drew a circle on her skin, and she sucked in a ragged breath. The thrill began there, but quickly rippled out over every inch of her body. Goose bumps rose on her arms.

"Aye." He tore off his T-shirt and tossed it aside. His jeans followed, revealing a truly magnificent body. Not an inch of spare flesh to be seen. "Me, worshiping you in the traditional face-to-face way so I can savor every ripple of arousal on your face. Me, driving you delirious with delight and myself absolutely mad with need. Me, taking you hard and fast and so completely that you scream your release to the heavens. Those are the basics."

"I can live with that."

He pressed her back against the bedclothes with a hard kiss, his hand kneading her breast. There was a little of the berserker in the demand of his lips, in the hungry insistence that she open her mouth to him. And she reveled in it. She loved every part of this man, from his courage and honor to his fervent need to dominate and win. She would forever be grateful that he had claimed both sides of his powerful personality.

Not because that claim had saved her life.

But because the Jamie Murdoch she had glimpsed at the moment of her transcendence was finally a contented man. A whole and united man.

She moaned.

A man who was doing his utmost to prove himself capable of taking her to the stars. With his mouth. On her breast. *Oh, my*. She threaded her fingers into his hair and dragged him even closer.

"Jamie," she whispered hoarsely, encouragingly.

He halted and lifted his head. "What did you call me?"

"Jamie. Isn't that your given name?"

He smiled. A slow, intimate smile. "Aye. But no one calls me that."

"Dika does."

"Does she? I never noticed."

"Would you prefer me to call you Murdoch?"

He kissed her chin. Little nibbles that made her belly quiver. "No. I like the sound of my given name on your lips. Particularly when you say it in that sexy, breathless way. Say it again."

Because she was feeling magnanimous, she did.

Then she wrapped an arm around his neck and drew his lips to hers. It was the first kiss she had ever offered to a man that included commitment. With other men, all she could offer was an interlude, a brief stop on the path to her destiny. With Murdoch, she could open the gate to her heart.

"I love you," she said against his lips.

"I love you, too," he answered. This time without hesitation, without a trace of doubt. And her heart fluttered.

"In case you doubt my sincerity, I plan to spend an eternity proving it to you." His hand slipped beneath the waistband of her pajamas and down to the wetness that waited for him. "Starting right here."

She arched into his hand, seeking a deeper thrill, inviting a deeper touch, and he groaned.

Surrender could be sweet.

GLOSSARY

dōgi—Uniform of "the way." This is the plain white training outfit that Kiyoko often wears.

dojo—The area in which a "way" (specific art or skill set) is taught and practiced. The way of the *onmyōji* is taught in Kiyoko Ashida's *dojo*.

futon—Japanese bedding consisting of a padded mattress and covers which can be folded and then stored away. Since the rooms of a traditional Japanese house often serve multiple purposes, the ability to store bedding is useful.

hakama—Traditional Japanese clothing, belted at the waist and pleated.

kata—Choreographed patterns of movements like those used to practice martial arts.

katana—A single-edged, slightly curved steel sword.

kendo—A modern sword-fighting martial art based on the ancient sword art *kenjitsu*.

kendōgi—Uniform worn by the practitioners of kendo.

ki—Spirit, feeling, or flow of energy.

kimono—Formal Japanese wrapped garment worn by both men and women with an *obi* around the waist.

koto—A traditional thirteen-string musical instrument which is the national instrument of Japan.

niou—A pair of stone guardians that stand on either side of a gate.

nitōjutsu—The art of using two blades in combat.

obi—Sash or belt.

oni—A large red demon from Japanese folklore.

onimusha—A warrior with an internal demon.

onmyōdō—An ancient Japanese mystical practice involving divination and other forms of occultism including calendar arts and healing.

onmyōji—An *onmyōdō* specialist, highly skilled in magic and divination.

samurai—A military noble of ancient Japanese highly skilled in combat.

sashimi—Thinly sliced raw seafood, often served with a sauce for dipping.

sensei—A Japanese title of respect, often used for teachers.

senshi—Warrior, or soldier.

shikigami—A spirit summoned by a practitioner of *onmyōdō*.

shoji—A sliding door or room divider consisting of a frame covered with thin translucent material.

tabi—Japanese socks with a split for the large toe to permit wearing with thonged sandals.

tatami—Mats covered with woven straw which serve as flooring in a traditional Japanese home.

torii—A traditional Japanese gate.

yin and yang—The philosophy that equal and opposite forces exist within everything and are interconnected.

zazen—A meditation method that involves sitting in the lotus position with hands cupped.

Don't miss the first book in the
Soul Gatherers series,

DRAWN INTO DARKNESS

Available now from Signet Eclipse.

Early Sunday morning, Lachlan decided he was ready to confront Drusus.

Three a.m. seemed a natural time to find a lure demon intent on perverting weak souls, and a dark, foul-smelling alley behind a graffiti-decorated apartment building seemed the perfect place to perform a locator spell.

He carefully intoned the words of the spell, ensuring his pronunciation was clear, and then scattered the necessary handful of scorched rat bones. A misty circlet formed in the air above the bones, glowing faintly. In the center of the circle, images began to appear, drop by drop, like paint splatters on a canvas. Each image showed a location around the city. Some he recognized; some he did not. As new drops wiped out old, the images came faster and faster, until his eyes could no longer keep up.

Then they suddenly stopped.

But not in a helpful spot. Instead of the usual pinpointed landmark, all he got was a four-block radius in which to search, just west of here.

With a heavy sigh, he waved the damp mist away and crouched beside his latest gathering assignment.

A gut-shot punk in a black silk jacket lay sprawled amid the rubbish, a small bag of white powder floating in the blood next to him. He placed his hand on the dead man's throat. A drug dealer. How apropos.

The familiar feathery tendrils danced up his arm, but this time there was no balmy warmth, no gentle tranquillity—only the slimy ooze of a rancid soul snaking around his heart. As usual, the sensation evoked a low wave of nausea.

No more than an instant after the ooze leached into his blood, the air around him crackled and dried like mud under the desert sun. It was not unexpected, of course. Unlike angels, Satan's henchmen were never late picking up a soul.

Pop.

Still squatted next to the body, Lachlan glanced up . . . just as a ball of brilliant orange fire plowed into his right shoulder. He reacted instinctively, rolling back and drawing his *claidheamh mòr* as he regained his feet. But the severity of a fireball hitting him full on, without the mitigation of a shield spell, brought tears to his eyes and blood to his lip as he bit down to defuse the pain.

"Hello, MacGregor."

A wave of undiluted agony shuddered through Lachlan, and his voice broke. "Dru-sus."

"Those hurt like hell, don't they?" the lean, blond demon said, pointing to the writhing blackened flesh of Lachlan's shoulder and smiling at his own joke. "I don't normally lower myself to collect souls, but I thought since you were looking for me, I'd oblige."

"Nice of you," Lachlan gasped as he wove a belated shield charm. He blinked until his opponent came into focus.

Drusus walked around him in slow, measured steps, his sharply angled face a study of youthful arrogance.

"I see you're sticking with the tried and true. Nothing modern man has created quite surpasses an excellent blade, does it?" A soft whoosh, and then he, too, held a sword in his hands: a gladius, shorter than Lachlan's sword and engraved up the length with his name in Roman script. "I'd forgotten what it feels like to hold one."

Deep in the shadowy gap of the demon's zippered jacket, a thick gold chain shimmered, a chain strong enough to support a heavy glass reliquary. Lachlan's gut twisted.

"Perhaps you've also forgotten how to use it."

Drusus swung the gladius loosely in front of his body. "You could hope for that, *baro*. But if you recall, it was I who taught you everything you know about fine swordsmanship."

"No' everything."

"I can still picture your face the first time I disarmed you. You, a mighty clan chieftain, and I, nothing but a spindling lad. You were galled."

"I'm less vexed now that I know you cheated."

"Cheated?"

"Demon versus human is hardly a fair fight."

The demon's eyes hardened into shiny beads of jade. "Immortal versus immortal would seem to be a battle of equals, though. What do you say? Shall we engage in a contest?"

"Aye, let's duel. The point of my sword is eager to meet your belly."

Drusus snorted. "I admire your confidence, MacGregor. But perhaps we should get our business out of the way first, on the off chance it's you who perishes and not I. Where's the Linen?"

"I destroyed it."

"Nice try. Unfortunately, destroying a relic of such consequence would leave a mystical residue of mushroom cloud proportions." He glanced up at the sky. "I don't see one. Do you?"

That would have been nice to know. Yesterday. "You don't really expect me to tell you where it is, do you?"

"Of course I do. You owe it to me." The demon's eyes

glittered. "We had a bargain. You were to let me in the back gate so I could steal the Linen. Hiding it was never part of the arrangement."

"Any bargain we struck was voided the moment you invited the Campbells into my home. The deal did no' include the slaughter of my family."

"Actually, it did. I just never told you that part."

Lachlan stiffened. Even though he knew Drusus was a demon, he found it was surprisingly hard to accept that the young man who'd once carried an adoring young Cormac on his shoulders had watched dispassionately as Tormad sliced the boy's throat.

"Apparently, there were words left unspoken on both sides," Lachlan said. "Had you bothered to speak to me before running my brother through, you'd possess the Linen today. Despite the promise I made to protect it, I intended to give the cloth to you."

The demon's face darkened. "You lie."

"Nay, I was your puppet, properly enthralled. But watching my wife's throat cut before my very eyes and listening to Tormod Campbell crow about slaying my bairns shook me free of your clutches, hellspawn. I vowed then you'd never touch it, and I happily did the unthinkable simply to see you thwarted."

Drusus grimaced. "Indeed, I never expected you to entrust it to the very clan that wiped out your family. I could have saved myself several hundred years of searching had I considered that possibility."

"There you have it—the Linen eludes you because of your own mistakes."

"Not mistakes. Just the one. My only error was with you."

Silence fell between them as Lachlan absorbed the significance of that. Irrational or not, being the only one in two thousand years to hoodwink Drusus induced a twinge of pride. Perhaps it boded well for this encounter, too.

"And tonight," Drusus added, "I get the chance to redeem myself. We'll battle. You'll put up a good fight, but I'll win. I'll get the whereabouts of the Linen, and you'll finally get a respectable warrior's death. It'll all end well."

"I'm already dead."

Humor softened the harsh lines of the other man's face. "Yes, well, you know what I mean."

And then, without warning, he lunged. The point of his sword drove accurately at Lachlan's heart, his attack swift and sure—only to be deflected by the *claidheamh mòr*.

"Oh, bravo," Drusus said, unfazed. "I would have hated this to be a one-sided affair."

Lachlan had been about to toss a blinding spell, so it would hardly have been a one-sided affair, with or without his excellent reflexes. But he didn't bother to debate that. He was too busy executing a fierce downward slice toward the lure demon's neck.

Drusus parried it. At the same time, he brought his own flavor of magic to the fight. A dustbowl of swirling red miasma rose up from the damp pavement, encircling the two of them as they dueled. Spinning madly, the crimson tornado lifted higher and higher, until it obliterated every star in the night sky. Then white-hot fireballs began to rain down on Lachlan.

His shield charm took a heavy beating. In a disquietingly short time, the hellish fury pitted the protection spell to rice-paper density. But Lachlan had little time to spare for repairs.

He was battling an expert swordsman.

Had he been the same rough soldier Drusus had manipulated all those years ago, his defeat would have been quick and brutal. The demon held nothing back, hitting his blade with powerful, bone-rattling blows, the kind of blows one avoids in practice sessions for fear of irreparably damaging a blade.

Fortunately, though, Lachlan was no longer a backward Scottish knight who only hacked and thrust. With the help of Italian and Spanish masters, at whose feet he had studied for a hundred years after his death, he'd honed his talents to a lethal edge. Talents that now served him well.

He cut and thrust with smooth, almost effortless technique. He broke through the demon's defenses twice, slicing through the leather jacket and biting deep into flesh. His new sword glowed green with the taste of demon blood.

But victory eluded him.

The sword was not enough. Not only did his opponent's wounds heal with incredible speed, allowing Drusus to continue fighting without respite, but moments after Lachlan scored his second successful slice, the beleaguered shield charm collapsed, leaving him dreadfully barren of protection. He swiftly called forth another, but it was whisked away before it was fully formed, with no more exertion than a horse swatting a fly.

The swirling red vapor dissolved, carried away in wisps on the night breeze. Drusus paused, staring curiously at Lachlan's heaving chest and sweat-drenched brow.

"You Gatherers are little better than humans," he observed, sounding disappointed. "This is hardly the challenging duel I'd hoped it would be."

Lachlan responded by whipping a restraining spell at him, roping the demon in thick white cords and pinning his arms to his sides.

Drusus broke the binds with a single indrawn breath. "Very rudimentary stuff, that. There's a much better spell in the *Book of Gnills*. Where's the Linen?"

As the tattered remnants of the binds fell away, the gap in the demon's leather jacket widened, and Lachlan caught a glimpse of a faint golden glow about his neck—the reliquary. A bitter dose of failure poured into his throat, choking him. Drusus could crush him, right here and right now, if that was his desire. Not without a fight, of course, but slowly, inevitably, courtesy of the indefatigable power the bastard had borrowed from Satan. And when he fell, the souls of his family would be cast into hell, never to be recovered.

No. He could not let them down. Not again. He drew deep on his powers and straightened to his full height.

"Fuck you."

His nemesis smiled coldly. "Don't be foolish, MacGregor. Put down the sword, or I'll be forced to wring the location of the Linen from you. Bit by agonizing bit."

"Go ahead. Try."

"That confidence is born of ignorance. You can't begin to imagine the pain I can inflict." He paused, eyeing Lachlan's firm stance and grip. "Tell me where the Linen is."

"No."

"Tell me where it is, or I'll be forced to take my anger out on Emily."

Unease crept into Lachlan's muscles, numbing the pain of his exertions and slowing his breathing to a barely discernible flow. The demon could jump to Emily's room in an instant. "You won't harm her."

"Are you certain? Are you willing to watch her suffer just to spite me?"

"You've spent a lot of time setting up this lure," Lachlan said. "You won't risk the end result by allowing her to see the real you now." Not when the corruption of a pure soul offered Satan twice the power of an ordinary soul.

"Fine. You're right." Drusus shrugged. "But that still leaves me with the lovely Rachel to play with. And don't bother to deny she means something special. I *know* you."

Her name upon the lure demon's lips was an abomination. It ate away at his insides like acid, but Lachlan successfully reined in his bitterness.

"The man you once knew is dead, inside and out," he said. The words rang with quiet honesty—not too surprising, as he'd endured four hundred years of that truth before waking to Rachel's siren call. "I feel nothing."

"Come now, MacGregor. Death is not a fool. She does not lock a Gatherer's feelings away with his soul. She'd end up with an army of passionless drones, were that the case."

"Death didn't rob me," Lachlan agreed. "I believe that honor is yours."

There was a short pause, then a deep rumble of laughter. "By Satan's glory, are you pandering to my ego? Trying to manipulate *me*?"

"Believe what you want."

The flatness of Lachlan's comment tugged the demon's heavy brows together. "Shall I fetch Rachel and see?"

"It won't matter. I still won't tell you where the Linen is."

"She's a fine woman, your Rachel. Beautiful *and* strong. The sort who quickens your pulse the moment you spy her. Admit it, *baro*. You care for her."

And give the demon a reason to harm her? No. Lachlan drained every speck of emotion from his voice and buried his feelings for Rachel in the deepest vaults of his mind. "I will no' admit what I do no' feel."

"Then I take it you won't mind if I cut in? I have a sense she'll be even more enjoyable than Elspeth was. Did I ever tell you your lovely wife gave herself to me in a desperate bid to save your life?"

Lachlan closed his eyes. The image of Elspeth's torn and sullied gown returned to him in painful clarity, along with the tears on her face and the pallor of her cheeks. His inability to save her shuddered through him once more.

"Bastard."

He dove at the demon, sword swinging.